# A CROSS OF CENTURIES

For our friends Randolph and Renner Loney:

He goes to the prisoner, and she through her eye and camera refreshes our vision.

*They do not rejoice in iniquity, but rejoice in the truth.*

*On worlds gone wandering and lost from this*
*Did Wise Men gather in the dawn*
*In cloudy steams of Beast*
*Within a place of straw now quickened to a Shrine*
*To look upon a stranger Child than ours?*

—from "Christus Apollo" by Ray Bradbury

# CONTENTS

# INTRODUCTION
## *An Epistle to the Curious*

A *Cross of Centuries: Twenty-five Imaginative Tales about the Christ* contains stories that place Jesus, or Christlike figures patterned on Jesus, in hypothetical contexts, out of time or out of place, if not both at once, and then extrapolate the narrative and dramatic consequences of these imaginings. Some of these stories, then, will no doubt strike a few readers, devout Christians in particular, as pushing or exceeding the bounds of religious propriety.

Ridiculing faith or denigrating the figure of Christ was never the purpose of this literary project, however, and I make that point here not only to disarm criticism by anticipating it (a tactic rarely successful) but also to state the simple truth. This project has been important to me for several years, at least since the spring or summer of 2002, when I decided to teach an interim-term course at LaGrange College, a Methodist-affiliated institution in LaGrange, Georgia, called "Images of Christ in Contemporary Imaginative Literature."

In that course, inspired in part by religion professor Dr. David Ahearn's earlier Janterm offering centered on films about Christ, we read several of the stories in this anthology—Bradbury's "The Man," Dostoyevsky's "The Grand Inquisitor," Dozois and Dann's

"Slow Dancing with Jesus," Jeffrey Ford's "On the Road to New Egypt," Jack Slay's "Murmur's Laws," John M. Williams's "Passion," and a brief story of my own, "Sequel on Skorpiós"—as well as three novels, namely, Norman Mailer's *The Gospel According to the Son*, Jim Crace's *Quarantine*, and Nobel Prize winner José Saramago's *The Gospel According to Jesus Christ*.

Other novels and other stories certainly existed as options, but we had only a month, and so I had to pass on titles that I would have included without hesitation in a semester-long course: *Ben-Hur* by Lew Wallace, *The Nazarene* by Sholom Asch, *King Jesus* by Robert Graves, *The Last Temptation of Christ* by Nikos Kazantzakis, *Man of Nazareth* by Anthony Burgess, *Jesus Christs* by A. J. Langguth, *The Shadow of the Galilean* by Gerd Theissen, *The Gospel of Corax* by Paul Park, *Testament* by Nino Ricci, *Lamb* by Christopher Moore, and *Only Begotten Daughter* by the exquisitely mordant James Morrow, to name only a few.

These works—whether reverential, revisionist, skeptical, humorous, satirical, or downright transgressive—all testified to the enduring ability of the historical Jesus, or the Christ of faith, to generate narratives of startling power, moving philosophical reflection, delightful silliness, and/or profound existential outrage. From the beginning, then, I wanted to compile an anthology of Christ fictions that showcased this same dizzying array of personal "takes" on this significant figure. After all, for nearly two thousand years, his worship, meditation, neglect, or conscious rejection has informed the corpus of Western Civilization.

I am a self-declared follower of this Christ, albeit often a doubting, shame-faced, and/or unorthodox one. Like the female Sufi mystic Rabi'a 'al-Adawiya (born in Basra c. 717), I reject the theological necessity of hellfire and paradise, and regard the stick of the former and the carrot of the latter as irrelevant to our need to love God purely, and to love God for bestowing on us the poignant, often painful benison of life. Many will find such a formulation of Christian belief deficient, heretical, or self-contradictory, but I do regard Jesus as the Son of Man and his sacrifice on our behalf as a real sacrifice. Also, at sixty-one, I am capable of no other belief but this doubt-, even heresy-, plagued system, and I am weary of apologizing to myself and, hypothetically, to others for my sustaining private credo.*

The story of this crucified first-century Jew fascinates me. Clearly, it also fascinates others, and in putting together this collection of Christ fictions I hoped to manifest in my literary life a genuine devotional act. From the beginning, I understood that this motive would mean little, if anything, to some of the anthology's contributors. Indeed, why should it? One, or two, or more, might have regarded it, had I announced it upfront, as odd, if not stupid and off-putting. I also understood that this motive would have little or no impact on attracting readers, who would gravitate to this collection for their own reasons, some seeking inspiration, some illumination, some mere distraction, some corroboration of views long held, and maybe a few the fulfillment of needs hard to articulate.

Frankly, I chose the stories in *A Cross of Centuries* to entertain and illuminate, but also to stimulate and provoke: hence the subtitle. I did not seek or solicit stories toeing any party line, not even the Christian one I've already professed. And if I can judge by the authors' stories and their comments about these stories (where

---

* Anyone interested in my fiction-mediated spiritual autobiography may read my story "The Procedure" in *Brighten to Incandescence: 17 Stories* (Golden Gryphon, 2004).

such comments exist), they run the gamut from believers to mystics to agnostics to rational atheists—all for good and sufficient reasons of their own. Hallelujah. I refused to censor any take on Christ, so long as the writer embedded it in a compelling story true to his or her own hard-earned accommodation to life's vicissitudes. And I'm proud of the variety and quality of the contents of this volume, which embodies *a round table of views*—views, whether subtle or explicit, that ricochet off one another in disturbing, synergistic ways typical of any substantive colloquy.

In short, I see *A Cross of Centuries* as a tribute to the documentable impact on our species of the figure of Jesus Christ. At once real and mythic, he of course dominates nearly every story in this book. One contributor, a friend and a first-rate thinker, states in the afterword to his story, "We don't know who he was or what he stood for (even the Gospels contradict his message of peace)," a declaration some may applaud and others dispute. But I would direct readers to *The Historical Figure of Jesus* by E. P. Sanders (Allen Lane: Penguin, 1993), whose book demonstrates that although in some areas Jesus must remain an enigmatic will-o'-the-wisp, "patient spadework" has pierced "the layers of Christian devotion . . . to recover the historical core" (280). And Sanders concludes his testament: "We know who he was, what he did, what he taught, and why he died. Perhaps most important, we know how much he inspired his followers, who sometimes themselves did not understand him, but who were so loyal to him that they changed history" (281).

Even if you buy Sanders's argument, *belief* has its own criteria and rubrics. But, as I pray my explanations have made clear, I did not undertake *A Cross of Centuries* to proselytize, evangelize, or convert. After all, some of these narratives ignore or question Jesus' divinity. I include them because, in addition to their being good stories, I wanted to explore Jesus' impact on a cross-section of people, not just on select believers, and because I *do* hope to attract readers who would never touch a book of Christian theology or evangelism. Nor would I mind if some of these stories perturb or discomfit Christians who have failed to scrutinize what they profess to believe—for *I* believe that just as the unexamined life is not worth the candle, an unexamined faith has no lasting claim on our allegiance. In that respect, I admit that the book could be dangerous, and that maybe not everyone should read it. But in an age when fanaticism runs rampant in many religions, and may appear to define them, stressing the point that we must periodically (rationally) challenge our personal credos strikes me as crucial to our development as compassionate beings and to our species' survival.

Others will likely disagree.

"But if you do," as Ray Bradbury might counter, "don't burn this anthology. Put together an anthology of your own."

Look at the contents. Read the stories and their accompanying commentaries (in some of which you may perceive the hurt or joy feeding the process of invention). These Christ fictions, as already hinted, stalk the entire waterfront—from belief to doubt, from dismissal to slapstick and folk humor, from philosophical inquiry to piquant nostalgia, from existential absurdity to the use of Jesus as a template for christs of the authors' own devising. Further, all twenty-five tales unfold under a colorful umbrella of speculation or imagination.

Notice, too, that writers of the international fame and aesthetic accomplishment of Fyodor Dostoyevsky, Oscar Wilde, Isaac Babel, Jorge Luis Borges, and Romulus Linney stand arm in arm with masterful science fiction and fantasy writers like Ray Bradbury, the late Henry Kuttner, Michael Moorcock, and Gene Wolfe, to name only four of our deft remaining contributors. Not only subject matter but also an earnest vitality unites all twenty-six writers (one story sprang from a collaboration) in a way that surely suggests the arbitrary nature of at least *some* genre labels.

In October 2006, Jeffrey Ford, a multiple winner of the World Fantasy Award for his elegant fiction, invited me to post the contents of *A Cross of Centuries* on his personal blog site, along with a bit of comment. I did so, pointing out that the anthology takes its overall title from Kuttner's "A Cross of Centuries" not only because I admire the story but also because the cross has persisted as a recognizable religious symbol for almost two millennia, and because my contributors wrote their stories in three distinct centuries: the nineteenth, the twentieth, and the twenty-first. I also noted that although I don't see this anthology as an evangelical document, readers are free to draw from individual stories, and from the gestalt of all the stories working together, whatever spiritual, historical, or literary lessons they happen to discover. *I* find uplift of several kinds in the contents, but others will have different cogent and discriminating reactions.

A pair of visitors to Jeff's blog site took me to task for including so few female contributors. Believe me, I recognized this shortcoming from the outset. Initially, though, I found no suitable stories by women, for reasons yet opaque to me, and when I importuned women to contribute originals, they declined to respond or protested that they lacked either the time or the inclination. My high regard for Karen Joy Fowler's "Shimabara," one of the most unusual stories on hand, and the fact that the anthology's contents otherwise pretty much reek of testosterone guarantee that if I ever edit a sequel (a doubtful proposition at this point), I'll take pains to offer more gender balance among its authors. Cross my heart.

Finally, I want to acknowledge contributor Barry Malzberg's

insightful objection to any and all theme anthologies: the loss of surprise and so of pleasure attending readers' awareness that at some point, in some way, the tale before them absolutely *must* deal with an aspect of that theme. Barry also notes that a science fiction or fantasy magazine, or a spicy mystery pulp, likewise sacrifices surprise and thus potential reading pleasure by virtue, or vice, of its chosen editorial purview. I can't refute this objection. Barry sees clearly. In fact, his story, "Understanding Entropy," suffers a small, if unfortunate, compromise in this context, but uses such a brilliant narrative conceit that it triumphs over the innate handicap of its context. Still, I felt it important to gather these twenty-five stories into one accessible package, because of the provocative cross talk they would generate and the undeniable cultural importance of the figure linking them.

I salute you, whoever you are, for picking up *A Cross of Centuries: Twenty-Five Imaginative Tales about the Christ*. I salute all who fostered this project: *all* the living contributors; editors John Oakes, Lukas Volger, Adelaide Docx, and Bill Strachan; agent Howard Morhaim and assistant Katie Menick; friend and advisor Ellen Datlow; friend and bibliographer Michael H. Hutchins; friend, writer, and librarian Michael Toman; friend, colleague, and document merger Laine Scott; and friend, lover, and helpmeet Jeri. My apologies to all those who deserve mention whom I have failed to acknowledge.

Peace upon you, the peace that passes understanding, and likewise a revelatory encounter with these "fictional transfigurations of Jesus."

Amen.

—*Michael Bishop*
*Pine Mountain, Georgia*

*For God so loved his worlds . . .*

# THE MAN
## Ray Bradbury

Captain Hart stood in the door of the rocket. "Why don't they come?" he said.

"Who knows?" said Martin, his lieutenant. "Do I know, Captain?"

"What kind of place is this, anyway?" The captain lighted a cigar. He tossed the match out into the glittering meadow. The grass started to burn.

Martin moved to stamp it out with his boot.

"No," ordered Captain Hart, "let it burn. Maybe they'll come see what's happening then, the ignorant fools."

Martin shrugged and withdrew his foot from the spreading fire.

Captain Hart examined his watch. "An hour ago we landed here, and does the welcoming committee rush out with a brass band to shake our hands? No, indeed! Here we ride millions of miles through space and the fine citizens of some silly town on some unknown planet ignore us!" He snorted, tapping his watch. "Well, I'll just give them five more minutes, and then—"

"And then what?" asked Martin, ever so politely, watching the captain's jowls shake.

"We'll fly over their damned city again and scare hell out of them." His voice grew quieter. "Do you think, Martin, maybe they didn't see us land?"

"They saw us. They looked up as we flew over."

"Then why aren't they running across the field? Are they hiding? Are they yellow?"

Martin shook his head. "No. Take these binoculars, sir. See for yourself. Everybody's walking around. They're not frightened. They—well, they just don't seem to care."

Captain Hart placed the binoculars to his tired eyes. Martin looked up and had time to observe the lines and the grooves of irritation, tiredness, nervousness there. Hart looked a million years old; he never slept, he ate little, and drove himself on, on. Now his mouth moved, aged and drear, but sharp, under the held binoculars.

"Really, Martin, I don't know why we bother. We build rockets, we go to all the trouble of crossing space, searching for them, and this is what we get. Neglect. Look at those idiots wandering about in there. Don't they realize how big this is? The first space flight to touch their provincial land. How many times does that happen? Are they that blasé?"

Martin didn't know.

Captain Hart gave him back the binoculars wearily. "Why do we do it, Martin? This space travel, I mean. Always on the go. Always searching. Our insides always tight, never any rest."

"Maybe we're looking for peace and quiet. Certainly there's none on Earth," said Martin.

"No, there's not, is there?" Captain Hart was thoughtful, the fire damped down. "Not since Darwin, eh? Not since everything went by the board, everything we used to believe in, eh? Divine power and all that. And so you think maybe that's why we're going out to the stars, eh, Martin? Looking for our lost souls, is that it? Trying to get away from our evil planet to a good one?"

"Perhaps, sir. Certainly we're looking for something."

Captain Hart cleared his throat and tightened back into sharpness. "Well, right now we're looking for the mayor of that city there. Run in, tell them who we are, the first rocket expedition to Planet Forty-three in Star System Three. Captain Hart sends his salutations and desires to meet the mayor. On the double!"

"Yes, sir." Martin walked slowly across the meadow.

"Hurry!" snapped the captain.

"Yes, sir!" Martin trotted away. Then he walked again, smiling to himself.

† † †

The captain had smoked two cigars before Martin returned.

Martin stopped and looked up into the door of the rocket, swaying, seemingly unable to focus his eyes or think.

"Well?" snapped Hart. "What happened? Are they coming to welcome us?"

"No." Martin had to lean dizzily against the ship.

"Why not?"

"It's not important," said Martin. "Give me a cigarette, please, Captain." His fingers groped blindly at the rising pack, for he was looking at the golden city and blinking. He lighted one and smoked quietly for a long time.

"Say something!" cried the captain. "Aren't they interested in our rocket?"

Martin said, "What? Oh. The rocket?" He inspected his cigarette. "No, they're not interested. Seems we came at an inopportune time."

"Inopportune time!"

Martin was patient. "Captain, listen. Something big happened yesterday in that city. It's so big, so important that we're second-rate—second fiddle. I've got to sit down." He lost his balance and sat heavily, gasping for air.

The captain chewed his cigar angrily. "What happened?"

Martin lifted his head, smoke from the burning cigarette in his fingers, blowing in the wind. "Sir, yesterday, in that city, a remarkable man appeared—good, intelligent, compassionate, and infinitely wise!"

The captain glared at his lieutenant. "What's that to do with us?"

"It's hard to explain. But he was a man for whom they'd waited a long time—a million years maybe. And yesterday he walked into their city. That's why today, sir, our rocket landing means nothing."

The captain sat down violently. "Who was it? Not Ashley? He didn't arrive in his rocket before us and steal my glory, did he?" He seized Martin's arm. His face was pale and dismayed.

"Not Ashley, sir."

"Then it was Burton! I knew it. Burton stole in ahead of us and ruined my landing! You can't trust anyone anymore."

"Not Burton, either, sir," said Martin quietly.

The captain was incredulous. "There were only three rockets. We were in the lead. This man who got here ahead of us? What was his name!"

"He didn't have a name. He doesn't need one. It would be different on every planet, sir."

The captain stared at his lieutenant with hard, cynical eyes.

"Well, what did he do that was so wonderful that nobody even looks at our ship?"

"For one thing," said Martin steadily, "he healed the sick and comforted the poor. He fought hypocrisy and dirty politics and sat among the people, talking, through the day."

"Is that so wonderful?"

"Yes, Captain."

"I don't get this." The captain confronted Martin, peered into his face and eyes. "You been drinking, eh?" He was suspicious. He backed away. "I don't understand."

Martin looked at the city. "Captain, if you don't understand, there's no way of telling you."

The captain followed his gaze. The city was quiet and beautiful and a great peace lay over it. The captain stepped forward, taking his cigar from his lips. He squinted first at Martin, then at the golden spires of the buildings.

"You don't mean—you *can't* mean— That man you're talking about couldn't be—"

Martin nodded. "That's what I mean, sir."

The captain stood silently, not moving. He drew himself up.

"I don't believe it," he said at last.

† † †

At high noon Captain Hart walked briskly into the city, accompanied by Lieutenant Martin and an assistant who was carrying some electrical equipment. Every once in a while the captain laughed loudly, put his hands on his hips and shook his head.

The mayor of the town confronted him. Martin set up a tripod, screwed a box onto it, and switched on the batteries.

"Are you the mayor?" The captain jabbed a finger out.

"I am," said the mayor.

The delicate apparatus stood between them, controlled and adjusted by Martin and the assistant. Instantaneous translations from any language were made by the box. The words sounded crisp on the mild air of the city.

"About this occurrence yesterday," said the captain. "It occurred?"

"It did."

"You have witnesses?"

"We have."

"May we talk to them?"

"Talk to any of us," said the mayor. "We are all witnesses."

In an aside to Martin the captain said, "Mass hallucination." To the mayor, "What did this man—this stranger—look like?"

"That would be hard to say," said the mayor, smiling a little.

"Why would it?"

"Opinions might differ slightly."

"I'd like your opinion, sir, anyway," said the captain. "Record this," he snapped to Martin over his shoulder. The lieutenant pressed the button of a hand recorder.

"Well," said the mayor of the city, "he was a very gentle and kind man. He was of a great and knowing intelligence."

"Yes—yes, I know, I know." The captain waved his fingers. "Generalizations. I want something specific. What did he look like?"

"I don't believe that is important," replied the mayor.

"It's very important," said the captain sternly. "I want a description of the fellow. If I can't get it from you, I'll get it from others." To Martin he said, "I'm sure it must have been Burton, pulling one of his practical jokes."

Martin would not look him in the face. Martin was coldly silent.

The captain snapped his fingers. "There was something or other—a healing?"

"Many healings," said the mayor.

"May I see one?"

"You may," said the mayor. "My son." He nodded at a small boy who stepped forward. "He was afflicted with a withered arm. Now, look upon it."

At this the captain laughed tolerantly. "Yes, yes. This isn't even circumstantial evidence, you know. I didn't see the boy's withered arm. I see only his arm whole and well. That's no proof. What proof have you that the boy's arm was withered yesterday and today is well?"

"My word is my proof," said the mayor.

"My dear man!" cried the captain. "You don't expect me to go on hearsay, do you? Oh, no!"

"I'm sorry," said the mayor, looking upon the captain with what appeared to be curiosity and pity.

"Do you have any pictures of the boy before today?" asked the captain.

After a moment a large oil portrait was carried forth, showing the son with a withered arm.

"My dear fellow!" The captain waved it away. "Anybody can paint a picture. Paintings lie. I want a photograph of the boy."

There was no photograph. Photography was not a known art in their society.

"Well," sighed the captain, face twitching, "let me talk to a few other citizens. We're getting nowhere." He pointed at a woman. "You." She hesitated. "Yes, you, come here," ordered the captain. "Tell me about this *wonderful* man you saw yesterday."

The woman looked steadily at the captain. "He walked among us and was very fine and good."

"What color were his eyes?"

"The color of the sun, the color of the sea, the color of a flower, the color of the mountains, the color of the night."

"That'll do." The captain threw up his hands. "See, Martin? Absolutely nothing. Some charlatan wanders through whispering sweet nothings in their ears and—"

"Please, stop it," said Martin.

The captain stepped back. "What?"

"You heard what I said," said Martin. "I like these people. I believe what they say. You're entitled to your opinion, but keep it to yourself, sir."

"You can't talk to me this way," shouted the captain.

"I've had enough of your highhandedness," replied Martin. "Leave these people alone. They've got something good and decent, and you come and foul up the nest and sneer at it. Well, I've talked to them too. I've gone through the city and seen their faces, and they've got something you'll never have—a little simple faith, and they'll move mountains with it. You, you're boiled because someone stole your act, got here ahead and made you unimportant."

"I'll give you five seconds to finish," remarked the captain. "I understand. You've been under a strain, Martin. Months of traveling in space, nostalgia, loneliness. And now, with this thing happening, I sympathize, Martin. I overlook your petty insubordination."

"I don't overlook your petty tyranny," replied Martin. "I'm stepping out. I'm staying here."

"You can't do that!"

"Can't I? Try and stop me. This is what I came looking for. I didn't know it, but this is it. This is for me. Take your filth somewhere else and foul up other nests with your doubt and your—scientific method!" He looked swiftly about. "These people have had an experience, and you can't seem to get it through your head that it's really happened and we were lucky enough to almost arrive in time to be in on it.

"People on Earth have talked about this man for twenty centuries after he walked through the old world. We've all wanted to see him and hear him, and never had the chance. And now, today, we just missed seeing him by a few hours."

Captain Hart looked at Martin's cheeks. "You're crying like a baby. Stop it."

"I don't care."

"Well, I do. In front of these natives we're to keep up a front. You're overwrought. As I said, I forgive you."

"I don't want your forgiveness."

"You idiot. Can't you see this is one of Burton's tricks, to fool these people, to bilk them, to establish his oil and mineral concerns under a religious guise! You fool, Martin. You absolute fool! You should know Earthmen by now. They'll do anything—blaspheme, lie, cheat, steal, kill—to get their ends. Anything is fine if it works; the true pragmatist, that's Burton. You know him!"

The captain scoffed heavily. "Come off it, Martin, admit it; this is the sort of scaly thing Burton might carry off, polish up these citizens and pluck them when they're ripe."

"No," said Martin, thinking of it.

The captain put his hands up. "That's Burton. That's him. That's his dirt, that's his criminal way. I have to admire the old dragon. Flaming in here in a blaze and a halo and a soft word and a loving touch, with a medicated salve here and a healing ray there. That's Burton all right!"

"No." Martin's voice was dazed. He covered his eyes. "No, I won't believe it."

"You don't want to believe." Captain Hart kept at it. "Admit it now. Admit it. It's just the thing Burton would do. Stop daydreaming, Martin. Wake up! It's morning. This is a real world and we're real, dirty people—Burton the dirtiest of us all!"

Martin turned away.

"There, there, Martin," said Hart, mechanically patting the man's back. "I understand. Quite a shock for you. I know. A rotten shame, and all that. That Burton is a rascal. You go take it easy. Let me handle this."

Martin walked off slowly toward the rocket.

Captain Hart watched him go. Then, taking a deep breath, he turned to the woman he had been questioning. "Well. Tell me some more about this man. As you were saying, madam?"

† † †

Later the officers of the rocket ship ate supper on card tables outside. The captain correlated his data to a silent Martin who sat red-eyed and brooding over his meal.

"Interviewed three dozen people, all of them full of the same milk and hogwash," said the captain. "It's Burton's work all right, I'm positive. He'll be spilling back in here tomorrow or next week to consolidate his miracles and beat us out in our contracts. I think I'll stick on and spoil it for him."

Martin glanced up sullenly. "I'll kill him," he said.

"Now, now, Martin! There, there, boy."

"I'll kill him—so help me, I will."

"We'll put an anchor on his wagon. You have to admit he's clever. Unethical but clever."

"He's dirty."

"You must promise me not to do anything violent." Captain Hart checked his figures. "According to this, there were thirty miracles of healing performed, a blind man restored to vision, a leper cured. Oh, Burton's efficient, give him that."

A gong sounded. A moment later a man ran up. "Captain, sir. A report! Burton's ship is coming down. Also the Ashley ship, sir!"

"See!" Captain Hart beat the table. "Here come the jackals to the harvest! They can't wait to feed. Wait till I confront them. I'll make them cut me in on this feast—I will!"

Martin looked sick. He stared at the captain.

"Business, my dear boy, business," said the captain.

Everybody looked up. Two rockets swung down out of the sky.

When the rockets landed they almost crashed.

"What's wrong with those fools?" cried the captain, jumping up. The men ran across the meadowlands to the steaming ships. The captain arrived. The airlock door popped open on Burton's ship.

A man fell out into their arms.

"What's wrong?" cried Hart.

The man lay on the ground. They bent over him and he was burned, badly burned. His body was covered with wounds and scars and tissue that was inflamed and smoking. He looked up out of puffy eyes and his thick tongue moved in his split lips.

"What happened?" demanded the captain, kneeling down, shaking the man's arm.

"Sir, sir," whispered the dying man. "Forty-eight hours ago, back in Space Sector Seventy-nine DFS, off Planet One in this system, our ship, and Ashley's ship, ran into a cosmic storm, sir." Liquid ran gray from the man's nostrils. Blood trickled from his mouth. "Wiped out. All crew. Burton dead. Ashley died an hour ago. Only three survivals."

"Listen to me!" shouted Hart, bending over the bleeding man. "You didn't come to this planet before this very hour?"

Silence.

"Answer me!" cried Hart.

The dying man said, "No. Storm. Burton dead two days ago. This first landing on any world in six months."

"Are you sure?" shouted Hart, shaking violently, gripping the man in his hands. "Are you sure?"

"Sure, sure," mouthed the dying man.

"Burton died two days ago? You're positive?"

"Yes, yes," whispered the man. His head fell forward. The man was dead.

The captain knelt beside the silent body. The captain's face twitched, the muscles jerking involuntarily. The other members of the crew stood back of him looking down. Martin waited. The captain asked to be helped to his feet, finally, and this was done. They stood looking at the city. "That means—"

"That means?" said Martin.

"We're the only ones who've been here," whispered Captain Hart. "And that man—"

"What about that man, Captain?" asked Martin.

The captain's face twitched senselessly. He looked very old indeed, and gray. His eyes were glazed. He moved forward in the dry grass.

"Come along, Martin. Come along. Hold me up; for my sake, hold me. I'm afraid I'll fall. And hurry. We can't waste time—"

They moved, stumbling, toward the city, in the long dry grass, in the blowing wind.

† † †

Several hours later they were sitting in the mayor's auditorium. A thousand people had come and talked and gone. The captain had remained seated, his face haggard, listening, listening. There was so much light in the faces of those who came and testified and talked he could not bear to see them. And all the while his hands traveled, on his knees, together; on his belt, jerking and quivering.

When it was over, Captain Hart turned to the mayor and with strange eyes said:

"But you must know where he went?"

"He didn't say where he was going," replied the mayor.

"To one of the other nearby worlds?" demanded the captain.

"I don't know."

"You must know."

"Do you see him?" asked the mayor, indicating the crowd.

The captain looked. "No."

"Then he is probably gone," said the mayor.

"Probably, probably!" cried the captain weakly. "I've made a horrible mistake, and I want to see him now. Why, it just came to me, this is a most unusual thing in history. To be in on something like this. Why, the chances are one in billions we'd arrive at one certain planet among millions of planets the day after *he* came! You must know where he's gone!"

"Each finds him in his own way," replied the mayor gently.

"You're hiding him." The captain's face grew slowly ugly. Some of the old hardness returned in stages. He began to stand up.

"No," said the mayor.

"You know where he is, then?" The captain's fingers twitched at the leather holster on his right side.

"I couldn't tell you where he is, exactly," said the mayor.

"I advise you to start talking," and the captain took out a small steel gun.

"There's no way," said the mayor, "to tell you anything."

"Liar!"

An expression of pity came into the mayor's face as he looked at Hart.

"You're very tired," he said. "You've traveled a long way and you belong to a tired people who've been without faith a long time, and you want to believe so much now that you're interfering with yourself. You'll only make it harder if you kill. You'll never find him that way."

"Where'd he go? He told you; you know. Come on, tell me!" The captain waved the gun.

The mayor shook his head.

"Tell me! Tell me!"

The gun cracked once, twice. The mayor fell, his arm wounded.

Martin leaped forward. "Captain!"

The gun flashed at Martin. "Don't interfere!"

On the floor, holding his wounded arm, the mayor looked up. "Put down your gun. You're hurting yourself. You've never believed, and now that you think you believe, you hurt people because of it."

"I don't need you," said Hart, standing over him. "If I missed him by one day here, I'll go on to another world. And another and another. I'll miss him by half a day on the next planet, maybe, and a quarter of a day on the third planet, and two hours on the next, and an hour on the next. But after that, one day I'll catch up with him! Do you hear that?" He was shouting now, leaning wearily over the man on the floor. He staggered with exhaustion. "Come along, Martin." He let the gun hang in his hand.

"No," said Martin. "I'm staying here."

"You're a fool. Stay if you like. But I'm going on, with the others, as far as I can go."

The mayor looked up at Martin. "I'll be all right. Leave me. Others will tend my wounds."

"I'll be back," said Martin. "I'll walk as far as the rocket."

They walked with vicious speed through the city. One could see with what effort the captain struggled to show all the old iron, to keep himself going. When he reached the rocket he slapped its side with a trembling hand. He holstered his gun. He looked at Martin.

"Well, Martin?"

Martin looked at him. "Well, Captain?"

The captain's eyes were on the sky. "Sure you won't—come with—with me?"

"No, sir."

"It'll be a great adventure, by God. I know I'll find him."

"You are set on it now, aren't you, sir?" asked Martin.

The captain's face quivered and his eyes closed. "Yes."

"There's one thing I'd like to know."

"What?"

"Sir, when you find him—*if* you find him," asked Martin, "what will you ask of him?"

"Why—" The Captain faltered, opening his eyes. His hands clenched and unclenched. He puzzled a moment and then broke into a strange smile. "Why, I'll ask him for a little—peace and quiet." He touched the rocket. "It's been a long time, a long, long time since—since I relaxed."

"Did you ever just try, Captain?"

"I don't understand," said Hart.

"Never mind. So long, Captain."

"Good-by, Mr. Martin."

The crew stood by the port. Out of their number only three were going on with Hart. Seven others were remaining behind, they said, with Martin.

Captain Hart surveyed them and uttered his verdict: "Fools!"

He, last of all, climbed into the airlock, gave a brisk salute, laughed sharply. The door slammed.

The rocket lifted into the sky on a pillar of fire.

Martin watched it go far away and vanish.

At the meadow's edge the mayor, supported by several men, beckoned.

"He's gone," said Martin, walking up.

"Yes, poor man, he's gone," said the mayor. "And he'll go on, planet after planet, seeking and seeking, and always and always he will be an hour late, or a half hour late, or ten minutes late, or only a minute late. And finally he will miss out by only a few seconds. And when he has visited three hundred worlds and is seventy or eighty years old he will miss out by only a fraction of a second, and then a smaller fraction of a second. And he will go on and on, thinking to find that very thing which he left behind here, on this planet, in this city—"

Martin looked steadily at the mayor.

The mayor put out his hand. "Was there ever any doubt of it?" He beckoned to the others and turned. "Come along now. We mustn't keep him waiting."

They walked into the city.

† † †

### Author's Commentary

I wrote "The Man" over fifty-five years ago. I never planned to write the story. In fact, I don't plan to write any of my stories; I simply get an impulse, an impulse that shoves me off a cliff. Then I fall and on the way down I write, until I hit. So the impulse for "The Man" sprang, very simply, from the idea that some rocket people from Earth land on an alien planet and discover that a Christ-like character is living there and influencing its inhabitants. Some of them believe, and some don't, and so I just let my characters write the story. I gave over charge of the story to my characters, and at the end I summed up my feelings about people who either believed in this Christ or failed to believe. I offered an emotional response to this Christ, and in three hours I had finished my story. That's the way I work, the way I've always worked—on all my fictions, all my stories, down all the years.

† † †

*The coming of Christ the folk comedian . . .*

# EARLY MARVELS
## Romulus Linney

Jesus, Saint Peter, and the Holy Apostles, *said the Tuscan,* were on the road from Jerusalem to Galilee, when a man came running to meet them. He was shouting, waving his arms and stirring up a cloud of dust.

He fell on his knees before Jesus.

"Lord!" he said. "Help me!"

"Calm down," said Jesus. "What's the matter?"

"My father! He's dying! He's blue in the face. He's vomiting blood. I've given him all my medicines. They don't help!"

"Your medicines?" said Jesus.

"I'm an Apothecary."

"How old is your father?" asked Jesus.

"Eighty-three, Lord," said the Apothecary.

Jesus looked at his Apostles, who looked back at him. He stared thoughtfully at the wretched Apothecary, who couldn't face the death of his eighty-three-year-old father.

"You love your father?" said Jesus.

"More than anything else," said the Apothecary. "He's a great man."

Jesus picked a little stick off the road and swished it about. "Do you have a family?"

"Oh, no," said the Apothecary, quickly. "I live with Father."

Jesus made little circles in the air with his stick.

"Can you answer my questions, do what I tell you, and believe in me?"

"Yes, Lord!"

"Do you have a bread, pie and cake oven in your house?"

"A what, Lord?"

"A bread, pie and cake oven. In the kitchen."

"Why, yes."

"Is it big enough to reach from here to there?" said Jesus. He pointed with the stick to his foot and then about six feet away.

"I think so," said the Apothecary.

Jesus nodded.

"To save your father," he said, "get him on the baking sheet. Face up. Fire the oven. Slide your father in, just like a pie, and bake him."

"What, Lord?"

"For three hours."

"Like a pie?" said the Apothecary.

"That's right," said Jesus.

The Apothecary turned and ran.

The next day they were on the road from Galilee to Jerusalem. A man came running to meet them, shouting, waving his arms, and stirring up a cloud of dust.

It was the Apothecary. "I carried him into the kitchen. I fired the oven. I rolled him onto the baking sheet. Then I slid him in the oven and slammed it shut."

The Apothecary wiped sweat off his face. He took deep breaths.

"I sat in front of that oven for three hours. It was awful. I heard cracking sounds. My father's bones, burning. Then, after three hours, I heard whistling. Then singing."

"What?" said Saint Peter.

"I pulled out the baking sheet. There lay my father, like a man in bed. He was singing a song about love and youth. He said, 'Hello, sonny!' Not one hair burned, on his whole white head."

"Wonderful!" said Saint John.

"Marvelous!" said Saint James.

"Congratulations, Lord," said Saint Stephen.

They all shook hands with Jesus.

"Wait!" said the Apothecary. "I'm not through."

They turned around to listen to him.

"My father jumped off the baking sheet. He dressed himself up. I had to chase him all over town. He said the most horrible things. He got drunk with the blacksmith, insulted the Mayor, and made indecent proposals to five women and a ten-year-old boy. It's impossible!"

Jesus nodded. "I understand," he said.

"Thank you, Lord," said the Apothecary. "But what am I going to do now?"

"Your father will get sick again," said Jesus. "If doctors can't cure him, forget your medicines, and mine, and let him go."

"Go?" said the Apothecary.

Jesus nodded.

"Can I do that?"

Jesus nodded.

"There's nothing wrong with that?"

"No," said Jesus. "You can get married and be a father yourself. There's nothing wrong with that, either."

"Really?" said the Apothecary, stunned. "Just—let—him—"

"Go," said Jesus, very quietly.

The Apothecary thought a minute, then sighed. He seemed much relieved. He walked away, slowly, thinking and nodding his head.

"Hm," said Saint Peter.

The rest of that day and all the next, Saint Peter walked ahead of everyone else. Head down, hands behind his back, he walked along thinking.

On the third day, a man came running to meet Jesus and his Apostles. He was shouting, waving his arms and stirring up a cloud of dust.

"The Lord!" he said. "I have to see the Lord!"

Saint Peter stopped him.

"Calm down," said Saint Peter. "What's the matter?"

"I have to see the Lord!"

"I am the Apostle Peter, beloved of the Lord. You can talk to me. What's wrong?"

"My mother. She's dying! This morning blood came out of her ears. Her eyes crossed horribly. She fell down screaming. Nobody can do anything for her. I want the Lord to save my mother!"

"You love your mother?"

"More than anything! She's the greatest woman who ever lived!"

"What do you do for a living?"

"I'm a butcher."

"Do you have a family?"

"I never married. I take care of my mother."

"How old is your mother?"

"Seventy-nine," said the Butcher. "When do I see the Lord?"

"Jesus is busy," said Saint Peter.

He bent over, and picked up a little stick from the road. He swished it about.

"Answer my questions, do what I tell you and believe in me. Do you have a bread, pie and cake oven in your house?"

"A what?"

"A bread, pie and cake oven. In the kitchen."

"Yes."

Saint Peter pointed his stick at his toes and then about six feet away. "Would the baking sheet reach from here to there?"

"I think so," said the Butcher.

Saint Peter nodded.

"To save your mother," he said, "get her on the baking sheet. Fire the oven. Slide her in there, face up, and bake her. For three hours."

"You're crazy," said the Butcher.

"I am the Apostle Peter, beloved of the Lord," said Saint Peter. "If you want to help your mother, it's up to you."

The Butcher ran away.

Saint Peter nodded. That was to be expected. He put his head down, his hands behind his back, and walked along again, thinking hard.

Later that same day, they were coming back down the same road when Saint Peter saw a man running to meet them. He was shouting, waving his arms and stirring up a cloud of dust.

Saint Peter thought it would be the Butcher and it was. Moreover, the Butcher had something shining in his hand.

Silver? Jewels? Rewards?

Then Saint Peter saw what he had I his hand, and the smile dropped right off his face, because it was a meat cleaver. The Butcher went after Saint Peter swinging that cleaver in wicked loops and chops. He chased Saint Peter back to Jesus and the other Apostles.

There was a ruckus. There was nothing for the Holy Apostles to do but jump on the Butcher. They got him down on the ground and they sat on him. He squirmed and kicked like a maniac, trying to get at Saint Peter with his meat cleaver.

Saint Peter hid behind Jesus.

"Let me at him!"

"Why?" said Jesus.

"He told me I could save my mother by baking her in the oven!"

"Did you?"

"I did!" said the Butcher. "When I got home, I saw the end had come. I made the fire. I pulled out the baking sheet, put her on it, slid her in and slammed the grate! My mother, burning up. For three hours. Then I pulled her out."

"What happened?" said Jesus.

"What do you think happened?" said the Butcher. "She was burned to a crisp! Down to a little black thing like a cinder! My mother!"

"I'm sorry," said Saint Peter.

"Ahhh!" screamed the Butcher. He tried again to get at Saint Peter with his meat cleaver.

Jesus bent down and took the meat cleaver away from the Butcher. "Let him up," Jesus said.

The Holy Apostles did. They helped the Butcher brush the dust off himself, and apologized for being rough.

"Let's see what we can do," said Jesus.

"Do?" said the Butcher. "What can you do for a cinder?"

"Show us where you live," said Jesus.

They all went to the Butcher's house. They went into the kitchen. They stood looking bleakly down on the baking sheet. There was a charred black cinder lying in the middle of it.

"My mother," said the Butcher.

"How old was she?" asked Jesus.

"Seventy-nine," said the Butcher.

Jesus thought for a minute. "Put her back in," he said.

"What?"

"Fire the oven. Put her back in. Bake her another hour and a half."

The Holy Apostles helped the Butcher. They got the fire going. With great care, so as not to lose the cinder, they slid the baking sheet back into the oven again.

They slammed the grate. They waited.

But an hour and a half is a long time. Some of the Apostles took a nap. Others played stone toss in the Butcher's courtyard.

Jesus lay down for a nap.

Only the Butcher and Saint Peter stayed glued to the spot, staring at that oven.

An hour and a half later, they came running out of the kitchen to get Jesus and the Apostles.

"She's alive!" yelled the Butcher.

"She's singing in there!" yelled Saint Peter.

Everybody jumped up and ran into the kitchen. They all heard her voice.

"Mother?" said the Butcher.

"Pull her out," said Jesus.

The Apostles took hold of the grate, opened it, and seized the baking sheet. They pulled. The baking sheet slid out into the kitchen.

Up went a whoof of smoke. The figure of a woman sat up, smoke curling off her naked arms and legs.

*"Mother?"* gasped the Butcher.

The woman jumped off the baking sheet. The smoke blew away.

"Darling!" she cried.

She grabbed the Butcher. She hugged him and kissed him.

"Ow!" said Saint John.

"Look at that!" said Saint James.

"What a woman!" said Saint Stephen.

Most of her clothes were burned right off her, and she wasn't a day over twenty years old. She had golden skin you could see plenty of, long black hair that streamed down her back. This was a woman to give any man a jolt. Jesus, Holy Apostle, or anybody.

Never mind a Butcher, who knew she had to be his mother.

He tried to get his breath.

"Mother! Please!"

"Oh, darling!" said his mother. "My beautiful baby boy!"

"Jesus!" cried the Butcher. "Help!"

He ran out of the kitchen.

"Darling!" cried his mother.

She ran after him.

"This is serious," said Saint Peter.

"If it is, it's your fault," said Saint John.

"What?" said Saint Peter.

"You got everything mixed up," said Saint James.

"The age wrong, the time wrong," said Saint Stephen.

"I didn't do anything the Lord didn't do," said Saint Peter.

"What kind of stick did he use?" said Saint John.

"Different wood?" said Saint James.

"Fir instead of oak," said Saint Stephen.

"Or thorn instead of yew," said Saint John.

"It was just a stick, lying in the road!" said Saint Peter.

"Mixed up the questions," said Saint James.

"Left some out," said Saint Stephen.

"I did not!" said Saint Peter.

The Butcher ran back into the kitchen.

"Help!" he said.

His mother ran back into the kitchen.

"I carried you inside me!" she cried. "Nothing can keep us apart!"

"Grab her," said Jesus.

The Holy Apostles did. They got the Butcher's mother down and sat on her.

"She feels good!" said Saint James.

"Don't think about that," said Saint John.

"Lord, help!" cried the Butcher.

"Will you do what I tell you?" said Jesus.

"Anything!" said the Butcher.

"Fire the oven again," said Jesus.

The Butcher started throwing wood into the oven.

"Hold her *down!*" said Saint John.

"I'm trying," said Saint James.

"Think about clouds!" said Saint Stephen. "Think about snow!"

"Now what?" said the Butcher.

"Get in," said Jesus.

"Me?" said the Butcher.

"You," said Jesus. "Quick."

"Darling!" cried the Butcher's mother. "Angel!"

"I'll do it," said the Butcher. He jumped onto the baking sheet, and lay down.

Jesus slid the baking sheet back into the oven and slammed the grate.

"My baby!" said the Butcher's mother.

"Let her up," said Jesus.

"How long this time?" said Saint Peter.

Jesus was looking at the floor, counting.

"Eight, nine, ten," counted Jesus.

"What have you done to my baby?" said the Butcher's mother.

"Fourteen, fifteen, sixteen," counted Jesus. "Take her over here."

The Holy Apostles led the Butcher's mother away from the oven.

"Twenty-three, twenty-four, twenty-five," counted Jesus. "Now."

Jesus opened the grate. He pulled on the baking sheet.

There was a little puff of smoke.

On the baking sheet sat a little boy, six or seven years old. He rubbed his eyes and looked around.

"Marvelous!" said Saint John.

"Wonderful!" said Saint James.

"Perfect!" said Saint Stephen.

"Darling!" said the Butcher's mother.

"Mommy!" said the Butcher.

They fell into each other's arms.

"The crucial element," said Saint John, "is the heat."

"I think it's the time," said Saint James.

"It's the wood," said Saint Stephen.

Jesus smiled at the Butcher and his mother.

"Bring your boy up easily," he said to her. "Don't be all over him every minute of the day."

She nodded.

"Honor your mother," Jesus said to the Butcher. "But don't overdo it."

The little boy nodded.

Jesus looked at Saint Peter.

"There," he said.

Saint Peter studied the Lord.

"You are something else," he said.

"That's right," said Jesus. "Follow me."

† † †

## Author's Commentary

When I discovered "The Bible of the Folk," I found to my delight wisdom of illiterate peasants making sense of sermons and

scriptures. Virgins having babies? Mary was sixteen when she met
Joseph, who was ninety-five. Joseph not saying much? He drove
his son Jesus crazy telling him he was nothing special. Saint Peter
was beloved of the Lord? Jesus never got tired of Saint Peter trying
to understand him. Jesus had no sense of humor? Of course he did,
since he was a god made human, and human beings cannot live
without laughter. While he was with us, Jesus was also a good man.
As a good man, he loved us with joy.

† † †

*Pope Pius VI said that a woman cannot be a priest "because our Lord was a man."*

# MIRIAM
## Nōni Tyent

O n the night of the blessed infant's coming, things got compli-
cated. Miriam felt her fetus lodged athwart her birth canal:
prelude to a disaster of which the archangel had given no warning.
Don't be afraid, he had told her, for you've found favor with God.
She had no certainty of that favor now.

The baby comes cross-wise, Yosef cried. Despite the awkward-
ness of his hands, he turned it slightly and so brought it forth.
Yeshua, or The Lord Will Save, came forth dead, mocking the name
that Gabriel had told her to bestow upon it. Now Herod would have
no call to massacre all the male babes in this donkey run of a
village.

Yosef placed the blue child on a stone beside the straw on which
Miriam still lay twisted. He beheld it with both resentment and
wonder then put a hand to his chest and opened his mouth like a
suffocating fish. His eyes bulged and he toppled to the cavern's
hard, uneven floor.

*Yosef!* Miriam cried. And: *Yeshua, my Yeshua!*

✝ ✝ ✝

A bald villager named Gideon took pity on her and saw to both the old man's burial and that of the stillborn Son of God. He sold the spavined animal that had carried her to this place and found her a small room in the crowded caravansary—too late, thought Miriam, too late.

Gideon fed her figs and bread, and in three days she tried to join some Galileans who had heeded the Quirinian census on the road back to Nazareth. Men looked askance, women muttered behind their hands. Because she had no protector, she often overheard the name *Jezebel* or the epithet *whore*.

Again, Gideon rescued her. On a tall whey-colored horse he returned Miriam to the hill cave in which Yosef and Yeshua had died. What did he want? Her heart misgave her. However, if Gideon hoped to rape or murder her, she would fight, she would tear at him like a wounded dog.

But in the cave he expanded and glowed—without growing larger or brighter—and Miriam recognized him as Gabriel, the angel who had erroneously announced the advent of her lost son and a mysterious unending kingdom. His voice, when he spoke, twinned or tripled so that he sounded like a small choir:

Rejoice, Miriam, for you among women are most favored and blessed. The Lord stands with you, His might a cloak about your shoulders.

No, said Miriam. Tell him to get somebody else.

Gideon, or rather Gabriel, dimmed a little. Hear me, child. I bring good tidings from the Highest.

No. I gave my all. It didn't work. Why would God wish me to suffer nine more months of foolish hope and another fruitless labor?

Miriam, hush and obey.

God or demon, He has no right. If He wants his Son to wear the suffering flesh of a mortal, let some other suffering mortal do

His work—a woman whose womb will free, not strangle, His beloved get.

You misapprehend the Lord God's new design.

Why did His first design go awry? Did I anger Him somehow?

No, no—Satan pranked your womb. Now the Highest must answer.

By making me His cow again? Why didn't He just undo that heartbreaking prank and let His little Son live?

Gabriel raised his arms, which now bore snow-white and blue-black plumage, and threw her into shadow.

Enough. The Lord God wishes to anoint and transfigure you, Miriam. He no longer wishes you to bear His Son, but to step forth from this cave as His only inspirited Daughter, the Messiah of this age and all the following.

Miriam's breath stopped but eventually began again.

✝ ✝ ✝

And the brief career of Miriam Messiah had no parallel. Biding her young womanhood in Nazareth, apprenticing as a weaver, she made garments of such perfection that teachers and magistrates alike clamored for them. She traded for lessons with the rabbis and for dispensations from public officials for needy neighbors, but showed no more preference for the rich than for shepherds or tax collectors.

At length, having increased in learning, wisdom, and stature, she left her master weaver to proclaim throughout Galilee and Judea the kingdom of heaven. From as many trades, denominations, and peoples as would hear, she called disciples, both women and men, always with a suspicion that she was not only shadowing her stillborn Son but also extending His lost ministry. She provoked resentment among the hidebound and hostility among the powerful by disputing with the learned outside synagogues and, once, in a court welcoming to women near the Temple. She made bad wine sweet, broken bodies whole, and a host of frenzied minds serene.

Hecklers—Jew, Roman, Samaritan—she disarmed with sage and gentle words. Homilies and epigrams she dispensed with the skill of a venerable apothecary. Demons she cast out with the ferocity of a God-fueled warrior. Healings she administered freely to almost anyone. The arrogant, avaricious, and cruel she rebuked with authority but also with tenderness. The pious, smug, and hypocritical she shoved to the walls of their self-delusions and held them there with questions that stripped them naked of the virtues they thought their dress by birthright or seizure. And so of course they accused her of slander, blasphemy, and unnatural acts with her bemused disciples.

I am Daughter of Wisdom, she said, Queen of Nations, Mother of Faith, Sister of Spirit and Peace. Whosoever would know the Most High's heart need only wrap herself in a robe of my weaving and live within it as if within her own skin. We are fearfully and intricately shaped in Sophia's womb and issue from it primed to glorify both Her and Her all-embracing Partner, El Shaddai.

These sayings and others like them enraged Pharisees, Levites, and instructors of the Law. Meanwhile, talk of herself as Israel's Consolation, and of an enigmatic coming kingdom, unsettled the Roman colonizers, and an advisor to the Emperor himself warned the procurator of Judea to help the Jews suppress this untoward female abomination and threat. Then Dorcas betrayed her, and Miriam was arrested, tried, convicted, scourged, and harried along the Via Dolorosa to a fate that flickered in her awareness like that of a Son she had never fully known.

† † †

Dorcas fled with her silver, but the Jewish and Roman leaders agreed that this heretical Miriamist movement demanded a vivid joint response. During its namesake's trial, they arrested and sentenced to death a host of her disciples, even picking out eleven women to die with Miriam on Golgotha, the Mount of Skulls. This seemed just, given the women's defiance of traditional proprieties and religious strictures and their unswerving loyalty to Miriam. No mild insurrection, it wanted a strong rebuttal, and neither the procurator nor the high priest had any qualms about crucifying eleven women with her. After all, the Romans made few gender distinctions when punishing slaves or foreigners, and once at Ashkelon a ruler named Simeon ben Shetah had ordered over seventy sorceresses nailed up for their presumption and apostasy.

And so Miriam staggered out of the city behind the black Cyrenian carrying her cross. Much of her hair had been snatched away, and blood had dried on her innumerable stripes like hollyberry husks. She looked up. On the small dome of Golgotha a forest of crosses thrust up in two tight rings about its apex. From each cross hung a woman who had accompanied Miriam during the nearly three years of her God-sparked evangelical campaign, but she could not easily identify them because the soldiers, at the behest of her own people's priests, had affixed them to their crosses face-first, out of a weird warped notion of executionary decency.

Still, Miriam knew their names: Abigail, Bilhah, Chloe, the twins Dinah and Rachel, Esther the Matriarch, Merab, Naomi, Shunnamite, Zilpah, and Esther the Maid—all dying, all dying for her, all dying for the Sisterhood of Heaven.

The soldiers nailed Miriam to her cross facing front and naked but for a blood-streaked loincloth. They erected her stake at the top of Skull Mount, the highest tree in a glade of such impalings; and they diced not for her garments, a woman's contemptible things, but for the right to break her legs when the time came and to expose her totally once she had died. Meanwhile, a society of Jewish women—none of them Miriam's followers—prowled the uneven slopes offering drugged wine to the sufferers, but Miriam refused this kindness and her crucified disciples were not physically positioned to receive it, so at length, alternately laughing and cursing, the soldiers chased these sad do-gooders down the hill and back into the city.

Father-Mother, rasped Miriam lowly, why have You forsaken us?

††††

But One was resurrected; and Dorcas, in lifelong atonement for her betrayal, traveled and preached and healed and wrote, so that, several generations on, Miriamism overcame the entire world, and much in the world that was stupid, arbitrary, and cruel inevitably, albeit gradually, lost its foothold.

††††

### Editor's Commentary

Late in the day Nōni Tyent submitted a story to *A Cross of Centuries*. When I asked for an afterword to this succinct little piece, the author wrote, "I have nothing to say about 'Miriam' that the story doesn't already say."

††††

*What if Socrates, a Greek, had died for the Nazarene?*

# FRIENDS IN HIGH PLACES

## Jack McDevitt

In the distance, toward the center of town, he could see the torches. The mob was gathering.

The evening was cool, but he was damp with perspiration. He sensed a presence in the trees—a hawk, probably.

He could still get safely away. Leave now, and he'd be all right. It wasn't as if they'd follow him. But what then? After all this, if he ran, what would be left for him?

He fell to his knees. Help me.

The branches moved softly in the wind. A full moon floated in the late evening sky.

Please.

He could hear distant voices. Shouts. A cheer.

If there's another way to do this—

The garden felt like a barricade, a fortress. A place where he might remain, where they would not find him. Only outside, along the road, did danger lie.

Peter had promised to stand by him. "As long as I have breath in my body." Peter meant well, and he believed what he was saying.

But when the money was on the table, his courage would fail. In the end he would run, like the others, and he would live the rest of his days with that memory.

Can't we find another way?

A cloud drifted across the face of the moon. The torches began to move.

It sends the wrong message, Abba. It will be a hard sell, persuading people you love them when you let this happen to me.

In an odd way, he felt sorry for the individuals in the mob, or for some of them. They were only resisting change, trying to hang onto the past. Some of them, too, would forever carry painful memories of this night.

Why? Why must we do it this way? We create a faith whose governing symbol will be an instrument of torture. They will wear it around their necks, put it atop their temples. Is this really what we want?

Somewhere, on the night wind, he heard a child's laughter, and a dog. He hoped no children would witness his ordeal, but he knew they would. Some of these barbarians would bring their little ones out to watch. It was a savage land.

Are you even there? Why do you not speak? Say something. Assure me, at least, it is not all an illusion. Tell me that this night matters.

Something moved in the bushes off to his left.

He thought of Mary. He had left her in the upper room where they'd all eaten, fighting back tears, demanding to come with him. And she had come, trailing Peter and the others, staying out of sight, as if she thought he would not know.

He trembled at the knowledge she would be there all through this night.

They will remember me on the cross. Surely this is not the image You would have represent your concern for them. For us.

Why not something less gruesome . . . a star, perhaps? Like the one thirty years ago? We had it right, then. That was the way to do it. Or, if that seems too extravagant, a scroll would be good.

The wind died away, and the trees were still.

What is the point of Your being there if we know You only in Your silence?

He heard voices nearby. Peter's. And Mary's.

There came a moment when the moon flickered. He looked a second time and everything was as it had been. He ascribed it to the dampness in his eyes. Moments later Peter was at his side.

"They're here," he said.

† † †

How could he have missed that fact? Some were drunk. Others were just loud. They had stumbled to a halt immediately outside the garden, on the road. He walked past Peter and Mary, waved away their protests, and strode out into plain view. There were cries of *"There he is!"* And laughter.

There were about sixty, almost all men. Some carried clubs and swords. A small troop of guards accompanied them, and several priests, led by Silvanus. He saw Judas, hanging nervously off to one side—another whom the events of this night would haunt, for the few days left to him.

There was something odd about the guards. He needed a moment to see what it was: Their armor had changed. It was brighter, a different style altogether from what he had seen that morning.

Even the helmets were of an unfamiliar design. Not that any of it mattered.

He spotted Saul standing back with the priests and their servants. His great days lay ahead but, at this moment, he was still aligned with the savages.

The mob subsided, grew quiet, beneath his gaze. "Hello," he said. "Why do you come to Cedron? For whom are you looking?"

Silvanus was tall, worn, uncomfortable. He didn't like unruly scenes or violence. Would have preferred to be in his rooms reading the Scriptures. His face had the lines of a man who did not know how to enjoy himself. "We are looking for Jesus of Nazareth," he said. "I am told that is you."

No point denying it. "Indeed," he said. "I am he."

Silvanus nodded. Tried to smile, but ineffectually. "Take him," he said to his servants. "And his friends."

Jesus straightened and peered into Silvanus's frightened eyes. "If you want me," he said, "you have no need of these others. Let them go."

The priest hesitated. Wilted. "Of course," he said. "You will suffice."

Peter and Mary had moved near and now stood on either side of him. Silvanus waved them out of the way. When neither moved, one of his servants drew a sword. Peter, too often the impulsive one, went for his own weapon. The crowd reacted, a few cheering, others screeching. Someone yelled, *"Fight!"* They fell back to make room, and Peter's first blow—awkward though it was—glanced off the servant's blade and then off his temple. The servant screamed and his sword went flying.

Jesus grabbed Peter's shoulder. "Put it away," he said. The servant, on his knees, held his head, blood dribbling through his fingers. Jesus tore a piece of his garment, took the hand away, and pressed it against the wound. "Here, Matthias," he said. "Keep this against it until you can get some help."

The servant stared up at him. "How did you know my name?"

But the guards had already closed around Jesus. "Come with us," they said.

Their accents were Greek.

† † †

They tied his wrists behind him and took him back the way they had come. As it moved, the crowd grew in both size and intensity. Some tried to strike him as they passed. They cried, *"Blasphemer!"* and *"Unholy!"*

Eventually they arrived outside the temple. A brief argument erupted as to which entrance they should use. Silvanus had his way, and they went in through a side portico. He led the way through a series of stone passageways until they finally emerged into the presence of Annas, the high priest.

Annas was thin and weary, tired of dealing with the problems of the world and with lesser men who did not recognize his authority and privilege. He sat atop a platform on a throne of sorts, rolling his eyes in exasperation at the human refuse brought before him. Torches burned close at hand, providing only limited warmth. Silvanus whispered something to him, and he nodded. Then he turned toward the prisoner. "Who are you," he demanded, "that you come here and speak against the Almighty?"

Jesus steadied himself as best he could. He was constantly being pushed and shoved. With his arms secured behind him, he struggled to keep his balance. "You know who I am," he said.

"Yes." Annas jabbed an index finger at him. "And what have you been telling the Faithful?"

The place felt closed in, smoky. He would have preferred the cold night air. "Surely," he said, "you know what I have been saying. Otherwise I would not be here."

A servant raised a staff and swung it at him. Jesus turned to take the blow on his shoulder, but in doing so lost his balance. It caught him as he went down, and he landed clumsily on a stone step. "Don't take that tone with the chief priest," his assailant said, lifting the rod to hit him again—but Annas smiled in what he must have thought a kindly manner and directed him to hold. They dragged him back onto his feet.

"Let me ask you again," said Annas. "What is your purpose? Why do you defy the Scriptures?"

"By what right," asked Jesus, "do you question me?"

His response brought a second blow. He fell again, and his captors laughed.

A skirmish broke out behind him. There were shouts, and a commanding voice: *"That's enough."* Guards, led by an officer, pushed forward through the crowd. One of them shoved the servant aside. "Do not hit him again," said the officer.

Annas jumped to his feet. "Your authority ends at the door, sir."

The officer climbed onto the platform. "My authority extends wherever citizens are abused." He signaled his men to help Jesus to his feet. They took him in charge.

Jesus looked around in confusion. The Romans were helping him? This wasn't the way it was supposed to go.

They led him through the crowd, out of the chamber, and out of the temple.

The moon still rode high in the sky. He glanced up at it.

What's going on? But it was all right. He had no inclination to protest.

†††

They released him from his bonds, but warned him against fleeing. Then they marched him through the streets. "Where are you taking me?" he asked.

"Just walk," said the officer.

They turned toward the Roman barracks. That meant Pilate.

The procurator customarily made his headquarters at the palace of Herod at Caesarea, but he usually attended the annual festivities in Jerusalem.

The grounds were deserted. The night had turned cold. Jesus did not even see the sentries who routinely guarded the place.

They took him inside, led him into an outer room, told him to wait, posted a guard, and closed the door. But it was not uncomfortable. A fire took the chill away, and there was a bench for him to get off his feet. It had already been a long night.

He rubbed his shoulder, which ached from the blows of the staff. He had also bruised his ribs when he fell.

Occasionally, he heard footsteps passing back and forth outside. And he waited.

† † †

Eventually, the door opened, and the officer signaled him to follow. "The Proxenos will see you, prisoner. See that you behave."

The Proxenos? He had never heard that rank before.

He was led down a long corridor, past several empty rooms. They turned a corner and passed through a door into the presence of a tall, dark-haired man with sharply etched features and the manner of an aristocrat. It was a sparsely furnished chamber, warmed by a fire. Although austere, by the standards of the barrack building, it felt almost luxurious. Its lone occupant was gazing at a scroll. He nodded at something, put it aside, and turned his attention to the escort. He paid no attention whatever to Jesus.

He sat on a carved wooden chair. The walls were wooden, covered for the most part with thick woven drapes. A statue of Apollo stood on a side table.

"My Lord Dimonides," said the escort, "this is the prisoner."

"Very good, Lohagos. Thank you."

Lohagos was . . . what? Greek for captain? Jesus felt a flicker of hope. Maybe he would get clear of this situation after all.

Two guards entered and positioned themselves on either side of the Proxenos. The captain closed the door against the draft and stood directly behind Jesus.

Clearly, Dimonides was annoyed. The hour was late, and he had better things to do than trifle with another religious fanatic. He had fixed his attention, Jesus saw, on the three women even then descending into his private quarters.

But the Proxenos had a restlessly energetic personality. He could not shut down operations for the day and leave an unpleasant task for the morning, especially when that unpleasant task might include an angry visit from the priests.

"I've already heard from the authorities," he said, still gazing at the women. Jesus understood that he meant Annas. And Caiphas. They would resent the manner in which the soldiers had snatched him away. "They'll arrive in the morning to demand that I impose fitting punishment." Finally, his eyes turned toward his prisoner. "But you look harmless enough," he said. "What did you do to upset all those people so?"

Jesus smiled. He liked Dimonides. "I challenged their religious views."

"Ah, yes. Of course."

"May I ask, where is Pilate?"

"Pilate?" Dimonides exchanged glances with the captain. "Who is Pilate?"

"The man in charge."

"Really? We know of no one by that name."

"Indeed," said Jesus. A wave of exhilaration rose in him. Thank you, Father. "I must have been mistaken."

Dimonides pressed an index finger to his lips. "I suspect," he said, "that what you really did was challenge their authority."

"You could put it that way."

"Yes. I just did." He glanced over at Apollo. The god stood mute—a striking piece of work. "It's always disconcerting," he said, "when one must deal with people who take their religion seriously."

"I suppose it is," said Jesus.

"You've gone about publicly, I understand, telling all sorts of people that Annas and Caiphas don't know what they're talking about."

"That is so," said Jesus. "They are misinformed."

"Of course they are. But that's hardly relevant. The problem lies in your failure to recognize your own fallibility."

"No doubt."

"But that's neither here nor there either. We're not concerned about theological niceties tonight. We're talking about keeping the peace."

Jesus nodded. "May I ask a question, Proxenos?"

"Yes, you may—so long as it's not religious in nature."

"Of course. How long have the Greeks been in Jerusalem?"

"What are we talking about, prisoner?"

"How long have you controlled the area?"

He frowned. How could the prisoner not know? "About sixty years."

"Sixty years."

"More or less."

Jesus could not restrain a broad smile. "Actium," he said.

"I beg your pardon."

"Antony won at Actium, didn't he?"

"Of course." Dimonides looked baffled. "What are we talking about?"

"And the Greeks don't do crucifixions."

"Crucifixions? Of course not. We try not to execute anyone."

"Very good. A humane policy."

The Proxenos laughed. "We are gratified you approve." His gaze tracked inward, and the hint of mockery went away. "We've executed probably fewer than twenty people over the last four hundred years. Unfortunately, one was Socrates."

"I know."

"Which did nothing for our reputation."

They stood quiet for a time. Jesus heard voices in the corridor. Then everything was silent again save for the crackle of the fire.

"Well," said Dimonides, "I can't allow a trouble-maker to simply run loose. I could put you in a prison, I suppose."

Jesus showed no reaction.

"You wouldn't like that. Better might be exile—get you out of here, so you can't stir matters up. The place is already a cauldron." He leaned forward and braced his chin on his hand. "How about the mines in northern Thrace? The weather's quite nice there this time of year. No? Well, let me see what else I have available."

† † †

Mary was waiting for him, holding a lamp. She threw herself into his arms. "I was so frightened," she said. "All those things you said were going to happen. You had us all terrified!" She was giddy.

"Tell me," he said, "are you surprised that Greeks now occupy the area?"

"I hadn't noticed. Is that right?"

"But you remember the Romans?"

"Of course. Why do you say it that way? As if they're gone?"

"They are."

"Are you serious?"

"Am I not always?"

"No, my Lord, you're not."

"It's probably best if we keep it that way." The air was cool and sweet. "He left your memory intact. Good."

She held onto him as if fearful the mob would come again. "Don't misunderstand me," she said. "I'm grateful that things turned out the way they did. I don't know how to react. But how does it happen you were so wrong about this night? You've always been right about everything else."

He smiled. "It pays to have friends in high places."

Her eyes shone in the lamplight. "So what happens now?"

"I've been exiled."

"That's an improvement over what we were expecting. Where?"

"Alexandria."

"Egypt?"

"Yes." Her hand curled into his. "They want me somewhere out of the way. So I can do no damage."

"Egypt's as out of the way as any."

"Mary, they need a librarian."

"You? Working in a library?"

"I might get a chance to do a little writing."

She uncovered a lamp. "Some philosophy?" she asked.

"Maybe that, too."

"That too? What else?"

"I'd like to try my hand at theater."

"I can't imagine your doing a tragedy."

"Nor can I. I was thinking maybe comedy. I like comedy." He took the lamp from her. Held it high to illuminate the path. And thought how much better it was than a cross.

† † †

## Author's Commentary

I've never felt comforted or encouraged by the notion that God would stand by and allow his son to go to the cross. (If that happened to Jesus, what were *my* chances?) Or that he would be willing to watch casually while tidal waves rolled in and killed tens of thousands. Or lethal diseases ravaged whole continents. Or Nazis ran wild and killed millions.

You have to be willing to overlook a lot to accept the idea that a compassionate supernatural force worries about our welfare. But we are capable of doing it. A man misses a plane, the plane goes down, two hundred people die, but the guy left standing in the parking lot starts talking about how God stepped in to save his life. And we buy it. Never mind the crew and passengers on the flight.

It's a scary world. Hawks grab kittens, whales get beached, children are born with deformities. It would be comforting to think that the universe had a Creator, and that He once came to see what he could do for us.

Nobody asked my opinion, but, in a gentler world, the willingness of Jesus to face execution on our behalf might have been enough to satisfy the inscrutable divine purposes. Let's let it go at that. Let the cup pass. And maybe we would even have discovered something else about our Maker: that someone capable of devising bent space, relative time, and massless particles, would necessarily have a sense of humor.

† † †

*And if a man out of time is incarnate as Christ?*

# BEHOLD THE MAN
## Michael Moorcock

He has no material power as the god-emperors had; he has only
a following of desert people and fishermen. They tell him he
is a god; he believes them. The followers of Alexander said: "He is
unconquerable, therefore he is a god." The followers of this man do
not think at all; he was their act of spontaneous creation. Now he
leads them, this madman called Jesus of Nazareth.

And he spoke, saying unto them: Yeah verily I *was* Karl Glogauer and now I am Jesus the Messiah, the Christ.

And it was so.

## I

The time machine was a sphere full of milky fluid in which the
traveler floated, enclosed in a rubber suit, breathing through a
mask attached to a hose leading to the wall of the machine. The
sphere cracked as it landed and the fluid spilled into the dust and
was soaked up. Instinctively, Glogauer curled himself into a ball
as the level of the liquid fell and he sank to the yielding plastic
of the sphere's inner lining. The instruments, cryptographic,

unconventional, were still and silent. The sphere shifted and rolled as the last of the liquid dripped from the great gash in its side.

Momentarily, Glogauer's eyes opened and closed, then his mouth stretched in a kind of yawn and his tongue fluttered and he uttered a groan that turned into a ululation.

He heard himself. The Voice of Tongues, he thought: The language of the unconscious. But he could not guess what he was saying.

His body became numb and he shivered. His passage through time had not been easy and even the thick fluid had not wholly protected him, though it had doubtless saved his life. Some ribs were certainly broken. Painfully, he straightened his arms and legs and began to crawl over the slippery plastic towards the crack in the machine. He could see harsh sunlight, a sky like shimmering steel. He pulled himself halfway through the crack, closing his eyes as the full strength of the sunlight struck them. He lost consciousness.

✝ ✝ ✝

Christmas term, 1949. He was nine years old, born two years after his father had reached England from Austria.

The other children were screaming with laughter in the gravel of the playground. The game had begun earnestly enough and somewhat nervously Karl had joined in, in the same spirit. Now he was crying.

"Let me *down*! Please, Mervyn, stop it!"

They had tied him with his arms spread-eagled against the wire netting of the playground fence. It bulged outwards under his weight, one of its posts threatening to come loose. Mervyn Williams, the boy who had proposed the game, shook the post so that Karl was swung heavily back and forth on the netting.

"Stop it!"

His cries only encouraged them and he clenched his teeth, becoming silent.

He slumped, pretending unconsciousness; the school ties they had used as bonds cut into his wrists. He heard the children's voices drop.

"Is he all right?" Molly Turner whispered.

"He's only kidding," Williams replied uncertainly.

He felt them untying him, their fingers fumbling with the knots. Deliberately, he sagged, then fell to his knees, grazing them on the gravel, and dropped facedown to the ground. Distantly, half-convinced by his own deception, he heard their worried voices.

Williams shook him.

"Wake up, Karl. Stop mucking about."

He stayed where he was, losing his sense of time until he heard Mr. Matson's voice over the general babble.

"What on earth were you doing, Williams?"

"It was a play, sir, about Jesus. Karl was being Jesus. We tied him to the fence. It was his idea, sir. It was only a game, sir."

Karl's body was stiff, but he managed to stay still, breathing shallowly.

"He's not a strong boy like you, Williams. You should have known better."

"I'm sorry, sir. I'm really sorry." Williams sounded as if he were crying.

Karl felt himself lifted; felt the triumph . . .

† † †

He was being carried along, head and side so painful that he felt sick. He had had no chance to discover where exactly the time machine had brought him, but, turning his head now, he could see by the way the man on his right was dressed that he was at least in the Middle East.

He had meant to land in the year 29 A.D. in the wilderness beyond Jerusalem, near Bethlehem. Were they taking him to Jerusalem now?

He was on a stretcher apparently made of animal skins, an indication that he was probably in the past, at any rate. Two men were carrying the stretcher on their shoulders. Others walked on both sides. There was a smell of sweat and animal fat and a musty smell he could not identify. They were walking towards a distant line of hills.

He winced as the stretcher lurched and the pain in his side increased. For the second time he passed out.

He woke briefly, hearing voices speaking what was evidently some form of Aramaic. It was night, perhaps, for it seemed very dark. They were no longer moving. There was straw beneath him. He was relieved. He slept.

✝ ✝ ✝

*In those days came John the Baptist preaching in the wilderness of Judea, And saying, Repent ye: for the kingdom of heaven is at hand. For this is he that was spoken of by the prophet Esaias, saying, The voice of one crying in the wilderness, Prepare ye the way of the Lord, make his paths straight. And the same John had his raiment of camel's hair, and a leathern girdle about his loins; and his meat was locusts and wild honey. Then went out to him Jerusalem, and all Judea, and all the region round about Jordan, And were baptized of him in Jordan, confessing their sins.*

*(Matthew 3:1-6)*

✝ ✝ ✝

They were washing him. Cold water ran over his naked body. They had managed to strip off his protective suit. There were now thick layers of cloth against his ribs on the right, and bands of leather bound them to him.

He felt very weak now, and hot, but there was less pain.

He was in a building—or perhaps a cave; it was too gloomy to tell—lying on a heap of straw saturated by the water. Above him, two men continued to sluice water down on him from earthenware pots. They were stern-faced, heavily bearded men, in cotton robes.

He wondered if he could form a sentence they might understand. His knowledge of written Aramaic was good, but he was not sure of certain pronunciations.

He cleared his throat. "Where—be—this—place?"

They frowned, shaking their heads and lowering their water jars.

"I—seek—a—Nazarene—Jesus . . ."

"Nazarene. Jesus." One of the men repeated the words, but they did not seem to mean anything to him. He shrugged.

The other, however, only repeated the word Nazarene, speaking it slowly as if it had a special significance. He muttered a few words to the other man and went towards the entrance of the room.

Karl Glogauer kept trying to say something the remaining man would understand.

"What—year—doth—the Roman Emperor—sit in Rome?"

It was a confusing question to ask, he realized. He knew Christ had been crucified in the fifteenth year of Tiberius' reign, and that was why he had asked the question. He tried to phrase it better.

"How many—year—doth Tiberius rule?"

"Tiberius?" The man frowned.

Glogauer's ear was adjusting to the accent now and he tried to simulate it better. "Tiberius: the emperor of the Romans. How many years has he ruled?"

"How many?" The man shook his head. "I know not."

At least Glogauer had managed to make himself understood.

"Where is this place?" he asked.

"It is the wilderness beyond Machaerus," the man replied. "Know you not that?"

Machaerus lay to the southeast of Jerusalem, on the other side of the Dead Sea. There was no doubt that he was in the past and that the period was sometime in the reign of Tiberius, for the man had recognized the name easily enough.

His companion was now returning, bringing with him a huge fellow with heavily muscled hairy arms and a barrel chest. He carried a big staff in one hand. He was dressed in animal skins and stood well over six feet tall. His black, curly hair was long and he had a black, bushy beard that covered the upper half of his chest. He moved like an animal and his large, piercing brown eyes looked reflectively at Glogauer.

When he spoke, it was in a deep voice, but too rapidly for Glogauer to follow. It was Glogauer's turn to shake his head.

The big man squatted beside him. "Who art thou?"

Glogauer paused. He had not planned to be found in this way. He had intended to disguise himself as a traveler from Syria, hoping that the local accents would be different enough to explain his own unfamiliarity with the language. He decided that it was best to stick to this story and hope for the best.

"I am from the north," he said.

"Not from Egypt?" the big man asked. It was as if he had expected Glogauer to be from there. Glogauer decided that if this was what the big man thought, he might just as well agree to it.

"I came out of Egypt two years since," he said.

The big man nodded, apparently satisfied. "So you are a magus from Egypt. That is what we thought. And your name is Jesus, and you are the Nazarene."

"I seek Jesus, the Nazarene," Glogauer said.

"Then what is your name?" The man seemed disappointed.

Glogauer could not give his own name. It would sound too strange. On impulse, he gave his father's first name. "Emmanuel," he said.

The man nodded, again satisfied. "Emmanuel."

Glogauer realized belatedly that the choice of name had been an unfortunate one in the circumstances, for Emmanuel meant in Hebrew "God with us" and doubtless had a mystic significance for his questioner.

"And what is your name?" he asked.

The man straightened up, looking broodingly down on Glogauer. "You do not know me? You have not heard of John, called the Baptist?"

Glogauer tried to hide his surprise, but evidently John the Baptist saw that his name was familiar. He nodded his shaggy head. "You do know of me, I see. Well, magus, now I must decide, eh?"

"What must you decide?" Glogauer asked nervously.

"If you be the friend of the prophecies or the false one we have been warned against by Adonai. The Romans would deliver me into the hands of mine enemies, the children of Herod."

"Why is that?"

"You must know why, for I speak against the Romans who enslave Judaea, and I speak against the unlawful things that Herod does, and I prophesy the time when all those who are not righteous shall be destroyed and Adonai's kingdom will be restored on Earth as the old prophets said it would be. I say to the people, 'Be ready for that day when ye shall take up the sword to do Adonai's will.' The unrighteous know that they will perish on this day, and they would destroy me."

Despite the intensity of his words, John's tone was matter of fact. There was no hint of insanity or fanaticism in his face or bearing. He sounded most of all like an Anglican vicar reading a sermon whose meaning for him had lost its edge.

The essence of what he said, Karl Glogauer realized, was that he was arousing the people to throw out the Romans and their puppet Herod and establish a more "righteous" regime. The attributing of this plan to "Adonai" (a spoken name of Yahweh meaning The Lord) seemed, as many scholars had guessed in the twentieth century, a means of giving the plan extra weight. In a world where politics and religion, even in the west, were inextricably bound, it was necessary to ascribe a supernatural origin to the plan.

Indeed, Glogauer thought, it was more than likely that John believed his idea had been inspired by God, for the Greeks on the other side of the Mediterranean had not yet stopped arguing about the origins of inspiration—whether it began in a man's head or was placed there by the gods. That John accepted him as an Egyptian magician of some kind did not surprise Glogauer particularly, either. The circumstances of his arrival must have seemed extraordinarily miraculous and at the same time acceptable, particularly to a sect like the Essenes who practiced self-mortification and starvation and must be quite used to seeing visions in this hot wilderness. There was no doubt now that these people were the neurotic Essenes, whose ritual washing—baptism—and self-deprivation, coupled with the almost paranoiac mysticism that led them to invent secret languages and the like, was a sure indication of their mentally unbalanced condition. All this occurred to Glogauer the psychiatrist manqué, but Glogauer the man was torn between the poles of extreme rationalism and the desire to be convinced by the mysticism itself.

"I must meditate," John said, turning towards the cave entrance. "I must pray. You will remain here until guidance is sent to me."

He left the cave, striding rapidly away.

Glogauer sank back on the wet straw. He was without doubt in a limestone cave, and the atmosphere in the cave was surprisingly humid. It must be very hot outside. He felt drowsy.

## II

Five years in the past. Nearly two thousand in the future. Lying in the hot, sweaty bed with Monica. Once again, another attempt to make normal love had metamorphosed into the performance of minor aberrations that seemed to satisfy her better than anything else.

Their real courtship and fulfillment was yet to come. As usual, it would be verbal. As usual, it would find its climax in argumentative anger.

"I suppose you're going to tell me you're not satisfied again." She accepted the lighted cigarette he handed to her in the darkness.

"I'm all right," he said.

There was silence as they smoked.

Eventually, and in spite of knowing the result if he did so, he began to talk:

"It's ironic, isn't it?"

He waited for her reply. She would delay for a little while yet.

"What is?" she said, at last.

"All this. You spend all day trying to help sexual neurotics to become normal. You spend your nights doing what they do."

"Not to the same extent. You know it's all a matter of degree."

"So you say."

He looked at her face in the starlight from the window. She was a gaunt-featured redhead, with the calm, professional seducer's voice of the psychiatric social worker that she was. It was a voice that was soft, reasonable and insincere. Only occasionally, when she became particularly agitated, did her voice begin to indicate her real character. Her features never seemed to be in repose, even when she slept. Her eyes were forever wary, her movements rarely spontaneous. Every inch of her was protected, which was probably why she got so little pleasure from ordinary lovemaking.

"You just can't let yourself go, can you?" he said.

"Oh, shut up, Karl. Have a look at yourself if you're looking for a neurotic mess."

Both were amateur psychiatrists—she a psychiatric social worker, he just a reader, a dabbler, though he had done a year's study some time ago when he had planned to become a psychiatrist. They used the terminology of psychiatry freely. They felt happier if they could name something.

He rolled away from her, groping for the ashtray on the bedside table, catching a glance of himself in the dressing table mirror. He was a sallow, intense, moody Jewish bookseller, with a head full of images and unresolved obsessions, a body full of emotions. He always lost these arguments with Monica. Verbally, she was the dominant one. This kind of exchange often seemed to him more perverse than their lovemaking, where usually at least his role was masculine. Essentially, he realized, he was passive, masochistic, indecisive. Even his anger, which came frequently, was impotent. Monica was ten years older than he, ten years more bitter. As an individual, of course, she had far more dynamism than he had; but as a psychiatric social worker she had had just as many failures. She plugged on, becoming increasingly cynical on the surface but still, perhaps, hoping for a few spectacular successes with patients. They tried to do too much, that was the trouble, he thought. The priests in the confessional supplied a panacea; the psychiatrists tried to cure, and most of the time they failed. But at least they tried, he thought, and then wondered if that was, after all, a virtue.

"I did look at myself," he said.

Was she sleeping? He turned. Her wary eyes were still open, looking out of the window.

"I did look at myself," he repeated. "The way Jung did. 'How can I help those persons if I am myself a fugitive and perhaps also suffer from the *morbus sacer* of a neurosis?' That's what Jung asked himself. . . ."

"That old sensationalist: That old rationalizer of his own mysticism. No wonder you never became a psychiatrist."

"I wouldn't have been any good. It was nothing to do with Jung. . . ."

"Don't take it out on me."

"You've told me yourself that you feel the same—you think it's useless."

"After a hard week's work, I might say that. Give me another fag."

He opened the packet on the bedside table and put two cigarettes in his mouth, lighting them and handing one to her.

Almost abstractedly, he noticed that the tension was increasing. The argument was, as ever, pointless. But it was not the argument that was the important thing; it was simply the expression of the essential relationship. He wondered if that was in any way important, either.

"You're not telling the truth." He realized that there was no stopping now that the ritual was in full swing.

"I'm telling the practical truth. I've no compulsion to give up my work. I've no wish to be a failure. . . ."

"Failure? You're more melodramatic than I am."

"You're too earnest, Karl. You want to get out of yourself a bit."

He sneered. "If I were you, I'd give up my work, Monica. You're no more suited for it than I was."

She shrugged. "You're a petty bastard."

"I'm not jealous of you, if that's what you think. You'll never understand what I'm looking for."

Her laugh was artificial, brittle. "Modern man in search of a soul, eh? Modern man in search of a crutch, I'd say. And you can take that any way you like."

"We're destroying the myths that make the world go round."

"Now you say 'And what are we putting in their place?' You're stale and stupid, Karl. You've never looked rationally at anything—including yourself."

"What of it? You say the myth is unimportant."

"The reality that creates it is important."

"Jung knew that the myth can also create the reality."

"Which shows what a muddled old fool he was."

He stretched his legs. Doing so, he touched hers and recoiled. He scratched his head. She still lay there smoking, but she was smiling now.

"Come on," she said. "Let's have some stuff about Christ."

He said nothing. She handed him the stub of her cigarette and he put it in the ashtray. He looked at his watch. It was two o'clock in the morning.

"Why do we do it?" he said.

"Because we must." She put her hand to the back of his head and pulled it towards her breast. "What else can we do?"

† † †

*We Protestants must sooner or later face this question: Are we to understand the "imitation of Christ" in the sense that we should copy his life and, if I may use the expression, ape his stigmata, or in the deeper sense that we are to live our own proper lives, as truly as he lived his in all its implications? It is no easy matter to live a life that is modeled on Christ's, but it is unspeakably harder to live one's own life as truly as Christ lived his. Anyone who did this would . . . be misjudged, derided, tortured and crucified. . . . A neurosis is a dissociation of personality.*

(Jung: Modern Man in Search of a Soul)

† † †

For a month, John the Baptist was away and Glogauer lived with the Essenes, finding it surprisingly easy, as his ribs mended, to join in their daily life. The Essenes' township consisted of a mixture of single-story houses, built of limestone and clay brick, and the caves that were to be found on both sides of the shallow valley. The Essenes shared their goods in common and this sect had wives, though many Essenes led completely monastic lives. The Essenes were also pacifists, refusing to own or to make weapons—yet this sect plainly tolerated the warlike Baptist. Perhaps their hatred of the Romans overcame their principles. Perhaps they were not sure of John's entire intention. Whatever the reason for their toleration, there was little doubt that John the Baptist was virtually their leader.

The life of the Essenes consisted of ritual bathing three times a day, of prayer and of work. The work was not difficult. Sometimes Glogauer guided a plough pulled by two other members of the sect; sometimes he tended the goats grazing on the hillsides. It was a peaceful, ordered life; even its unhealthy aspects were so much a matter of routine that after a while Glogauer hardly noticed them for anything else.

Tending the goats, he would lie on a hilltop, looking out over the wilderness that was not a desert, but rocky scrubland sufficient to feed animals like goats or sheep. The scrubland was broken by low-lying bushes and by a few small trees along the banks of the river that doubtless ran into the Dead Sea. It was uneven ground. In outline, it had the appearance of a stormy lake, frozen and turned yellow and brown. Beyond the Dead Sea lay Jerusalem. Obviously Christ had not entered the city for the last time yet. John the Baptist would have to die before that happened.

The Essenes' way of life was comfortable enough, for all its

simplicity. They had given him a goatskin loincloth and a staff and,
except for the fact that he was watched by day and night, he appeared
to be accepted as a kind of lay member of the sect.

Sometimes they questioned him casually about his chariot—the
time machine they intended soon to bring in from the desert—and
he told them that it had borne him from Egypt to Syria and then to
here. They accepted the miracle calmly. As he had suspected, they
were used to miracles.

The Essenes had seen stranger things than his time machine.
They had seen men walk on water and angels descend from
heaven; they had heard the voice of God and His archangels as
well as the tempting voice of Satan and his minions. They wrote all
these things down in their vellum scrolls. They were merely a
record of the supernatural as their other scrolls were records of
their daily lives and of the news that traveling members of their
sect brought to them.

They lived constantly in the presence of God and spoke to God
and were answered by God when they had sufficiently mortified
their flesh and starved themselves and chanted their prayers
beneath the blazing sun of Judaea.

Karl Glogauer grew his hair long and let his beard come
unchecked. He mortified his flesh and starved himself and chanted
his prayers beneath the sun, as they did. But he rarely heard God
and only once thought he saw an archangel with wings of fire.

In spite of his willingness to experience the Essenes' halluci-
nations, Glogauer was disappointed, but he was surprised that
he felt so well considering all his self-inflicted hardships, and he
also felt relaxed in the company of these men and women who
were undoubtedly insane. Perhaps it was because their insanity
was not so very different from his own that after a while he
stopped wondering about it.

† † †

John the Baptist returned one evening, striding over the hills followed by twenty or so of his closest disciples. Glogauer saw him as he prepared to drive the goats into their cave for the night. He waited for John to get closer.

The Baptist's face was grim, but his expression softened as he saw Glogauer. He smiled and grasped him by the upper arm in the Roman fashion.

"Well, Emmanuel, you are our friend, as I thought you were. Sent by Adonai to help us accomplish His will. You shall baptize me on the morrow, to show all the people that He is with us."

Glogauer was tired. He had eaten very little and had spent most of the day in the sun, tending the goats. He yawned, finding it hard to reply. However, he was relieved. John had plainly been in Jerusalem trying to discover if the Romans had sent him as a spy. John now seemed reassured and trusted him.

He was worried, however, by the Baptist's faith in his powers.

"John," he began. "I'm no seer. . . ."

The Baptist's face clouded for a moment, then he laughed awkwardly. "Say nothing. Eat with me tonight. I have wild honey and locusts."

Glogauer had not yet eaten this food, the staple of travelers who did not carry provisions but lived off what they could find on the journey. Some regarded it as a delicacy. He tried it later, as he sat in John's house. There were only two rooms in the house, one for eating in, the other for sleeping in. The honey and locusts was too sweet for his taste, but it was a welcome change from barley or goat-meat. He sat cross-legged, opposite John the Baptist, who ate with relish. Night had fallen. From outside came low murmurs and the moans and cries of those at prayer.

Glogauer dipped another locust into the bowl of honey that

rested between them. "Do you plan to lead the people of Judaea in revolt against the Romans?" he asked.

The Baptist seemed disturbed by the direct question. It was the first of its nature that Glogauer had put to him.

"If it be Adonai's will," he said, not looking up as he leant towards the honey.

"The Romans know this?"

"I do not know, Emmanuel, but Herod the incestuous has doubtless told them I speak against the unrighteous."

"Yet the Romans do not arrest you."

"Pilate dare not—not since the petition was sent to the Emperor Tiberius."

"Petition?"

"Aye, the one that Herod and the Pharisees signed when Pilate the procurator did place votive shields in the palace at Jerusalem and seek to violate the Temple. Tiberius rebuked Pilate and since then, though he still hates the Jews, the procurator is more careful in his treatment of us."

"Tell me, John, do you know how long Tiberius has ruled in Rome?" He had not had the chance to ask that question again until now.

"Fourteen years."

It was 28 A.D.—something less than a year before the crucifixion would take place, and his time machine was smashed.

Now John the Baptist planned armed rebellion against the occupying Romans, but if the Gospels were to be believed, would soon be decapitated by Herod. Certainly no large-scale rebellion had taken place at this time. Even those who claimed that the entry of Jesus and his disciples into Jerusalem and the invasion of the Temple were plainly the actions of armed rebels had found no records to suggest that John had led a similar revolt.

Glogauer had come to like the Baptist. The man was plainly a hardened revolutionary who had been planning revolt against the Romans for years and had slowly built up enough followers to make the attempt successful. He reminded Glogauer of the resistance leaders of World War Two. He had a similar toughness and understanding of the realities of his position. He knew he would have only one chance to smash the cohorts garrisoned in the country. If the revolt became protracted, Rome would have ample time to send more troops to Jerusalem.

"When do you think Adonai intends to destroy the unrighteous through your agency?" Glogauer said tactfully.

John glanced at him with some amusement. He smiled. "The Passover is a time when the people are restless and resent the strangers most," he said.

"When is the next Passover?"

"Not for many months."

"How can I help you?"

"You are a magus."

"I can work no miracles."

John wiped the honey from his beard. "I cannot believe that, Emmanuel. The manner of your coming was miraculous. The Essenes did not know if you were a devil or a messenger from Adonai."

"I am neither."

"Why do you confuse me, Emmanuel? I know you are Adonai's messenger. You are the sign that the Essenes sought. The time is almost ready. The kingdom of heaven shall soon be established on earth. Come with me. Tell the people that you speak with Adonai's voice. Work mighty miracles."

"Your power is waning, is that it?" Glogauer looked sharply at John. "You need me to renew your rebels' hopes?"

"You speak like a Roman, with such lack of subtlety." John got up angrily. Evidently, like the Essenes he lived with, he preferred less direct conversation. There was a practical reason for this, Glogauer realized, in that John and his men feared betrayal all the time. Even the Essenes' records were partially written in cipher, with one innocent-seeming word or phrase meaning something else entirely.

"I am sorry, John. But tell me if I am right." Glogauer spoke softly.

"Are you not a magus, coming in that chariot from nowhere?" The Baptist waved his hands and shrugged his shoulders. "My men saw you! They saw the shining thing take shape in air, crack and let you enter out of it. Is that not magical? The clothing you wore—was that earthly raiment? The talismans within the chariot—did they not speak of powerful magic? The prophet said that a magus would come from Egypt and be called Emmanuel. So it is written in the Book of Micah! Are none of these things true?"

"Most of them. But there are explanations—" He broke off, unable to think of the nearest word to "rational." "I am an ordinary man, like you. I have no power to work miracles! I am just a man!"

John glowered. "You mean you refuse to help us?"

"I'm grateful to you and the Essenes. You saved my life almost certainly. If I can repay that . . ."

John nodded his head deliberately. "You can repay it, Emmanuel."

"How?"

"Be the great magus I need. Let me present you to all those who become impatient and would turn away from Adonai's will. Let me tell them the manner of your coming to us. Then you can say that all is Adonai's will and that they must prepare to accomplish it."

John stared at him intensely.

"Will you, Emmanuel?"

"For your sake, John. And in turn, will you send men to bring my chariot here as soon as possible? I wish to see if it may be mended."

"I will."

Glogauer felt exhilarated. He began to laugh. The Baptist looked at him with slight bewilderment. Then he began to join in.

Glogauer laughed on. History would not mention it, but he, with John the Baptist, would prepare the way for Christ.

Christ was not born yet. Perhaps Glogauer knew it, one year before the crucifixion.

† † †

*And the Word was made flesh, and dwelt among us (and we beheld his glory, the glory as of the only begotten of the Father), full of grace and truth. John bare witness of him, and cried, saying, This was he of whom I spake, He that cometh after me is preferred before me: for he was before me.*

*(John 1:14-15)*

† † †

Even when he had first met Monica, they had had long arguments. His father had not then died and left him the money to buy the Occult Bookshop in Great Russell Street, opposite the British Museum. He was doing all sorts of temporary work and his spirits were very low. At that time Monica had seemed a great help, a great guide through the mental darkness engulfing him. They had both lived close to Holland Park and went there for walks almost every Sunday of the summer of 1962. At twenty-two, he was already obsessed with Jung's strange brand of Christian mysticism.

She, who despised Jung, had soon begun to denigrate all his

ideas. She never really convinced him. But, after a while, she had
succeeded in confusing him. It would be another six months before
they went to bed together.

† † †

It was uncomfortably hot.

They sat in the shade of the cafeteria, watching a distant cricket
match. Nearer to them, two girls and a boy sat on the grass, drinking
orange squash from plastic cups. One girl had a guitar across her
lap and she set the cup down and began to play, singing a folksong
in a high, gentle voice. Glogauer tried to listen to the words. As a
student, he had always liked traditional folk music.

"Christianity is dead." Monica sipped her tea. "Religion is
dying. God was killed in 1945."

"There may yet be a resurrection," he said.

"Let us hope not. Religion was the creation of fear. Knowledge
destroys fear. Without fear, religion can't survive."

"You think there's no fear about these days?"

"Not the same kind, Karl."

"Haven't you ever considered the idea of Christ?" he asked her,
changing his tack. "What that means to Christians?"

"The idea of the tractor means as much to a Marxist," she replied.

"But what came first? The idea or the actuality of Christ?"

She shrugged. "The actuality, if it matters. Jesus was a Jewish
troublemaker organizing a revolt against the Romans. He was crucified for his pains. That's all we know and all we need to know."

"A great religion couldn't have begun so simply."

"When people need one, they'll make a great religion out of the
most unlikely beginnings."

"That's my point, Monica." He gesticulated at her and she drew
away slightly. "The idea preceded the actuality of Christ."

"Oh, Karl, don't go on. The actuality of Jesus preceded the idea of Christ."

A couple walked past, glancing at them as they argued.

Monica noticed them and fell silent. She got up and he rose as well, but she shook her head. "I'm going home, Karl. You stay here. I'll see you in a few days."

He watched her walk down the wide path towards the park gates.

The next day, when he got home from work, he found a letter. She must have written it after she had left him and posted it the same day.

*Dear Karl,*

*Conversation doesn't seem to have much effect on you, you know. It's as if you listen to the tone of the voice, the rhythm of the words, without ever hearing what is trying to be communicated. You're a bit like a sensitive animal that can't understand what's being said to it, but can tell if the person talking is pleased or angry and so on. That's why I'm writing to you—to try to get my idea across. You respond too emotionally when we're together.*

*You make the mistake of considering Christianity as something that developed over the course of a few years, from the death of Jesus to the time the Gospels were written. But Christianity wasn't new. Only the name was new. Christianity was merely a stage in the meeting, cross-fertilization metamorphosis of Western logic and Eastern mysticism. Look how the religion itself changed over the centuries, re-interpreting itself to meet changing times. Christianity is just a new name for a conglomeration of old myths and philosophies. All the Gospels do is retell the sun myth and garble some of the ideas from the*

*Greeks and Romans. Even in the second century, Jewish
scholars were showing it up for the mish-mash it was! They
pointed out the strong similarities between the various sun
myths and the Christ myth. The miracles didn't happen—
they were invented later, borrowed from here and there.*

*Remember the old Victorians who used to say that
Plato was really a Christian because he anticipated
Christian thought? Christian thought! Christianity was
a vehicle for ideas in circulation for centuries before
Christ. Was Marcus Aurelius a Christian? He was writing
in the direct tradition of Western philosophy. That's why
Christianity caught on in Europe and not in the East!
You should have been a theologian with your bias, not a
psychiatrist. The same goes for your friend Jung.*

*Try to clear your head of all this morbid nonsense and
you'll be a lot better at your job.*

*Yours,*
*Monica.*

He screwed the letter up and threw it away. Later that evening
he was tempted to look at it again, but he resisted the temptation.

### III

John stood up to his waist in the river. Most of the Essenes stood
on the banks watching him. Glogauer looked down at him.

"I cannot, John. It is not for me to do it."

The Baptist muttered, "You must."

Glogauer shivered as he lowered himself into the river beside
the Baptist. He felt light-headed. He stood there trembling, unable
to move.

His foot slipped on the rocks of the river and John reached out
and gripped his arm, steadying him.

In the clear sky, the sun was at zenith, beating down on his unprotected head.

"Emmanuel!" John cried suddenly. "The spirit of Adonai is within you!"

Glogauer still found it hard to speak. He shook his head slightly. It was aching and he could hardly see. Today he was having his first migraine attack since he had come here. He wanted to vomit. John's voice sounded distant.

He swayed in the water.

As he began to fall toward the Baptist, the whole scene around him shimmered. He felt John catch him and heard himself say desperately: "John, baptize *me!*" And then there was water in his mouth and throat and he was coughing.

John's voice was crying something. Whatever the words were, they drew a response from the people on both banks.

The roaring in his ears increased, its quality changing. He thrashed in the water, then felt himself lifted to his feet.

The Essenes were swaying in unison, every face lifted towards the glaring sun.

Glogauer began to vomit into the water, stumbling as John's hands gripped his arms painfully and guided him up the bank.

A peculiar, rhythmic humming came from the mouths of the Essenes as they swayed; it rose as they swayed to one side, fell as they swayed to the other.

Glogauer covered his ears as John released him. He was still retching, but it was dry now, and worse than before.

He began to stagger away, barely keeping his balance, running, with his ears still covered; running over the rocky scrubland; running as the sun throbbed in the sky and its heat pounded at his head; running away.

† † †

> *But John forbad him, saying, I have need to be baptized*
> *of thee, and comest thou to me? And Jesus answering*
> *said unto him, Suffer it to be so now: for thus it becometh*
> *us to fulfill all righteousness. Then he suffered him. And*
> *Jesus, when he was baptized, went up straightway out of*
> *the water: and, lo, the heavens were opened unto him,*
> *and he saw the Spirit of God descending like a dove, and*
> *lighting upon him: And lo a voice from heaven, saying,*
> *This is my beloved Son, in whom I am well pleased.*
>
> *(Matthew 3:14-17)*

† † †

He had been fifteen, doing well at the grammar school. He had read in the newspapers about the Teddy Boy gangs roaming South London, but the odd youth he had seen in pseudo-Edwardian clothes had seemed harmless and stupid enough.

He had gone to the pictures in Brixton Hill and started walking home to Streatham because he had spent most of the bus money on an ice cream. They came out of the cinema at the same time. He hardly noticed them as they followed him down the hill.

Then, quite suddenly, they had surrounded him: pale, mean-faced boys, most of them a year or two older than he. He realized that he knew two of them vaguely. They were at the big council school in the same street as the grammar school. They used the same football ground.

"Hello," he said weakly.

"Hello, son," said the oldest Teddy Boy. He was chewing gum, standing with one knee bent, grinning at him. "Where you going, then?"

"Home."

"Heouwm," said the biggest one, imitating his accent. "What are you going to do when you get there?"

"Go to bed." Karl tried to get through the ring, but they wouldn't let him. They pressed him back into a shop doorway. Beyond them, cars droned by on the main road. The street was brightly lit, with street lamps and neon from the shops. Several people passed, but none stopped. Karl began to feel panic.

"Got no homework to do, son?" said the boy next to the leader. He was redheaded and freckled and his eyes were a hard gray.

"Want to fight one of us?" another boy asked. It was one of the boys he knew.

"No. I don't fight. Let me go."

"You scared, son?" said the leader, grinning. Ostentatiously, he pulled a streamer of gum from his mouth, then replaced it and began chewing again.

"No. Why should I want to fight you?"

"You reckon you're better than us, is that it, son?"

"No." He was beginning to tremble. Tears came into his eyes. "'Course not."

"'Course not, son."

He moved forward again, but they pushed him back into the doorway.

"You're the bloke with the kraut name, ain't you?" said the other boy he knew. "Glow-worm or somethink."

"Glogauer. Let me go."

"Won't your mummy like it if you're back late?"

"More a yid name than a kraut name."

"You a yid, son?"

"He looks like a yid."

"You a yid, son?"

"You a Jewish boy, son?"

"You a yid, son?"

"Shut up!" Karl screamed. He pushed into them. One of them punched him in the stomach. He grunted with pain. Another pushed him and he staggered.

People hurrying by on the pavement glanced at the group as they went past. One man stopped, but his wife pulled him on. "Just some kids larking about," she said.

"Get his trousers down," one boy suggested with a laugh. "That'll prove it."

Karl pushed through them and this time they didn't resist. He began to run down the hill.

"Give him a start," he heard one of the boys say.

He ran on.

They began to follow him, laughing.

They did not catch up with him by the time he turned into the avenue where he lived. He reached the house and ran along the dark passage beside it. He opened the back door. His stepmother was in the kitchen.

"What's the matter with you?" she said.

She was a tall, thin woman, nervous and hysterical. Her dark hair was untidy.

He went past her into the breakfast room.

"What's the matter, Karl?" she called. Her voice was high-pitched.

"Nothing," he said.

He didn't want a scene.

† † †

It was cold when he woke up. The false dawn was gray and he could see nothing but barren country in all directions. He could not remember much about the previous day, except that he had run a long way.

Dew had gathered on his loincloth. He wet his lips and rubbed the skin over his face. As he always did after a migraine attack he felt weak and completely drained. Looking down at his naked body,

he noticed how skinny he had become. Life with the Essenes had
caused that, of course.

He wondered why he had panicked so much when John had
asked him to baptize him. Was it simply honesty—something in
him that resisted deceiving the Essenes into thinking he was a
prophet? It was hard to know.

He wrapped the goatskin about his hips and tied it tightly just
above his left thigh. He had better try to get back to the camp, find
John and apologize, see if he could make amends.

The time machine was there now, too. They had dragged it there,
using only rawhide ropes. If a good blacksmith could be found, or
some other metalworker, there was just a chance it could be
repaired. The journey back would be dangerous.

He wondered if he ought to go back right away, or try to shift
to a time nearer to the actual crucifixion. He had not gone back
specifically to witness the crucifixion but to get the mood of
Jerusalem during the Feast of the Passover, when Jesus was supposed to have entered the city. Monica had thought Jesus had
stormed the city with an armed band. She had said that all the
evidence pointed to that. All the evidence of one sort did point to
it, but he could not accept the evidence. There was more to it, he
was sure. If only he could meet Jesus. John had apparently never
heard of him, though he had told Glogauer there was a prophecy
that the Messiah would be a Nazarene. There were many prophecies, and many of them conflicted.

He began to walk back in the general direction of the Essene
camp. He could not have come so far. He would soon recognize the
hills where they had their caves.

Soon it was very hot and the ground more barren. The air wavered
before his eyes. The feeling of exhaustion with which he had awakened increased. His mouth was dry and his legs were weak. He was

hungry and there was nothing to eat. There was no sign of the range of hills where the Essenes had their camp.

There was one hill, about two miles away to the south. He decided to make for it. From there he would probably be able to get his bearings, perhaps even see a township where they would give him food.

The sandy soil turned to floating dust as his feet disturbed it. A few primitive shrubs clung to the ground and jutting rocks tripped him. He was bleeding and bruised by the time he began, painfully, to clamber up the hillside.

The journey to the summit (which was much farther away than he had originally judged) was difficult. He slid on the loose stones of the hillside, falling on his face, bracing his torn hands and feet to stop from sliding to the bottom, clinging to tufts of grass and lichen that grew here and there, embracing larger projections of rock when he could, resting frequently, both mind and body numb with pain and weariness.

He sweated beneath the sun. Dust stuck to the moisture on his half-naked body, caking him from head to foot. The goatskin hung in shreds. The barren world reeled around him, sky merging with land, yellow rock with white clouds. Nothing seemed still.

He reached the summit and lay there gasping. Everything had become unreal.

He heard Monica's voice, thought he glanced at her for a moment from the corner of his eye.

*Don't be melodramatic, Karl. . . .*

She had said that many times. His own voice replied now.

*I'm born out of my time, Monica. This age of reason has no place for me. It will kill me in the end.*

Her voice replied.

*Guilt and fear and your own masochism. You could be a brilliant psychiatrist, but you've given in to all your own neuroses so completely. . . .*

"Shut up!"

He rolled over on his back. The sun blazed down on his tattered body.

"Shut up!"

*The whole Christian syndrome, Karl. You'll become a Catholic convert next I shouldn't doubt. Where's your strength of mind?*

"Shut up! Go away, Monica."

*Fear shapes your thoughts. You're not searching for a soul or even a meaning for life. You're searching for comforts.*

"Leave me alone, Monica!"

His grimy hands covered his ears. His hair and beard were matted with dust. Blood had congealed on the minor wounds now on every part of his body. Above, the sun seemed to pound in unison with his heartbeats.

*You're going downhill, Karl, don't you realize that? Downhill. Pull yourself together. You're not entirely incapable of rational thought. . . .*

"Oh, Monica! Shut up!"

His voice was harsh and cracked. A few ravens circled the sky above him now. They called back at him in a voice not unlike his own.

*God died in 1945. . . .*

"It isn't 1945—it's 28 A.D. God is alive!"

*How you can bother to wonder about an obvious syncretistic religion like Christianity—Rabbinic Judaism, Stoic ethics, Greek mystery cults, Oriental ritual. . . .*

"It doesn't matter!"

*Not to you in your present state of mind.*

"I need God!"

*That's what it boils down to, doesn't it? Okay, Karl, carve your own crutches. Just think what you could have been if you'd come to terms with yourself. . . .*

Glogauer pulled his ruined body to its feet and stood on the summit of the hill and screamed.

The startled ravens wheeled in the sky and flew away.

The sky was darkening now.

† † †

*Then was Jesus led up of the Spirit into the wilderness to be tempted of the devil. And when he had fasted forty days and forty nights, he was afterward an hungred.*
*(Matthew 4:1-2)*

**IV**

The madman came stumbling into the town. His feet stirred the dust and made it dance and dogs barked around him as he walked mechanically, his face turned upwards to the sun, his arms limp at his sides, his lips moving.

To the townspeople, the words they heard were in no familiar language; yet they were uttered with such intensity and conviction that God himself might be using this emaciated, naked creature as his spokesman.

They wondered where the madman had come from.

† † †

The white town consisted primarily of double- and single-storied houses of stone and clay-brick, built around a marketplace fronted by an ancient, simple synagogue outside which old men sat and talked, dressed in dark robes. The town was prosperous and clean, thriving on Roman commerce. Only one or two beggars were in the streets and these were well fed. The streets followed the rise and fall of the hillside on which they were built—winding streets, shady and peaceful: country streets. There was a smell of newly cut timber in the air, and the sound of carpentry, for the town was chiefly famous for its skilled carpenters. It lay on the edge of the Plain of Jezreel, near the trade route between Damascus and Egypt, and wagons were always leaving it, laden with the work of the town's craftsmen. The town was called Nazareth.

The madman had found it by asking every traveler he saw where it was. He had passed through other towns—Philadelphia, Gerasa, Pella and Scythopolis, following the Roman roads asking the same question in his outlandish accent: "Where lies Nazareth?"

Some had given him food on the way. Some had asked for his blessing and he had laid hands on them, speaking in that strange tongue. Some had pelted him with stones and driven him away.

He had crossed the Jordan by the Roman viaduct and continued northwards towards Nazareth.

He had had no difficulty in finding the town, but it had been hard for him to force himself towards it. He had lost a lot of blood and had eaten very little on the journey. He would walk until he collapsed and lie there until he could go on, or, as had happened increasingly, until someone found him and gave him a little sour wine or bread to revive him.

Once, some Roman legionaries had stopped and with brusque kindness asked him if he had any relatives they could take him to. They had addressed him in pidgin-Aramaic and had been surprised when he replied in a strangely accented Latin that was purer than the language they spoke themselves.

They asked him if he was a Rabbi or a scholar. He told them he was neither. The officer of the legionaries offered him some dried meat and wine. The men were part of a patrol that passed this way once a month—stocky, brown-faced men, with hard, clean-shaven faces. They were dressed in stained leather kilts and breastplates and sandals, and had iron helmets on their heads, scabbarded short swords at their hips. Even as they stood around him in the evening sunlight, they seemed tense. The officer, softer-voiced than his men but otherwise much like them save that he wore a metal breastplate and a long cloak, asked the madman his name.

For a moment the madman had paused, his mouth opening and closing, as if he could not remember.

"Karl," he said at length, doubtfully: more a suggestion than a statement.

"Sounds almost like a Roman name," said one of the legionaries.

"Are you a citizen?" the officer asked.

But the madman's mind was wandering, evidently. He looked away, muttering to himself.

All at once, he looked back and said: "Nazareth?"

"That way." The officer pointed down the road cutting between the hills. "Are you a Jew?"

This seemed to startle the madman. He sprang to his feet and tried to push through the soldiers. They let him through, laughing. He was a harmless madman.

They watched him run down the road.

"One of their prophets, perhaps," said the officer, walking towards his horse. The country was full of them. Every other man you met claimed to be spreading the message of their god. They didn't make much trouble and religion seemed to keep their minds off rebellion. *We should be grateful,* thought the officer.

His men were still laughing.

They marched down the road in the opposite direction to the one the madman had taken.

† † †

Now the madman was in Nazareth and the townspeople looked at him with curiosity and more than a little suspicion as he staggered into the market square. He could be a wandering prophet or he could be possessed by devils. It was often hard to tell. The rabbis would know.

As he passed the knots of people standing by the merchants' stalls, they fell silent until he had gone by. Women pulled heavy woolen shawls about their well-fed bodies and men tucked in their cotton robes so that he would not touch them. Normally their instinct would have been to tax him with his business in the town, but an intensity about his gaze—a quickness and vitality about his face, in spite of his emaciated appearance—made them treat him with respect and they kept their distance.

When he reached the center of the marketplace, he stopped and looked around him. He seemed slow to notice the people. He blinked and licked his lips.

A woman passed, eyeing him warily. He spoke to her, his voice soft, the words carefully formed. "Is this Nazareth?"

"It is." She nodded and increased her pace.

A man was crossing the square. He was dressed in a woolen robe of red and brown stripes. A red skullcap rested on his curly, black hair. His face was plump and cheerful. The madman walked across his path and stopped him. "I seek a carpenter."

"There are many carpenters in Nazareth. The town is famous for them. I am a carpenter myself. Can I help you?" The man's voice was good-humored, patronizing.

"Do you know a carpenter called Joseph, a descendant of David? He has a wife called Mary and several children. One is named Jesus."

The cheerful man screwed his face into a mock frown and scratched the back of his neck. "I know more than one Joseph. There is one poor fellow in yonder street." He pointed. "He has a wife called Mary. Try there. You should soon find him. Look for a man who never laughs."

The madman looked in the direction in which the man pointed. Seeing the street, he seemed to forget everything else and strode towards it.

In the narrow street, the smell of cut timber was even stronger. He walked ankle-deep in wood shavings. From every building came the thud of hammers, the scrape of saws. Planks of all sizes rested against the pale, shaded walls of the houses and there was hardly room to pass between them. Many of the carpenters had their benches just outside their doors. They were carving bowls, operating simple lathes, shaping wood into everything imaginable. They looked up as the madman approached one old carpenter in a leather apron who sat at his bench carving a figurine. The man had gray hair and seemed shortsighted. He peered up at the madman.

"What do you want?"

"I seek a carpenter called Joseph. He has a wife—Mary."

The old man gestured with the hand holding the half-completed figurine. "Two houses along on the other side of the street."

† † †

The house the madman came to had very few planks leaning against it, and the quality of the timber seemed poorer than the other wood he had seen. The bench near the entrance was warped on one side and the man hunched over it repairing a stool seemed misshapen also. He straightened when the madman touched his shoulder. His face was lined and pouched with misery. His eyes were tired and his thin beard had premature streaks of gray. He coughed slightly, perhaps in surprise at being disturbed.

"Are you Joseph?" asked the madman.

"I've no money."

"I want nothing—just to ask a few questions."

"I'm Joseph. Why do you want to know?"

"Have you a son?"

"Several, and daughters, too."

"Your wife is called Mary? You are of David's line."

The man waved an impatient hand. "Yes, for what good either has done me."

"I wish to meet one of your sons. Jesus. Can you tell me where he is?"

"That good-for-nothing. What has he done now?"

"Where is he?"

Joseph's eyes became more calculating as he stared at the madman. "Are you a seer of some kind? Have you come to cure my son?"

"I am a prophet of sorts. I can foretell the future."

Joseph got up with a sigh. "You can see him. Come." He led the madman through the gateway into the house's cramped courtyard, crowded with pieces of wood, broken furniture and implements, rotting sacks of shavings. They entered the darkened house. In the first room—evidently a kitchen—a woman stood by a large clay stove. She was tall and bulging with fat. Her long, black hair, unbound and greasy, fell over large, lustrous eyes that still had the heat of sensuality. She looked the madman over.

"There's no food for beggars," she grunted. "He eats enough as it is." She gestured with a wooden spoon at a small figure sitting in the shadow of a corner. The figure shifted as she spoke.

"He seeks our Jesus," said Joseph to the woman. "Perhaps he comes to ease our burden."

The woman gave the madman a sidelong look and shrugged. She licked her red lips with a fat tongue. "Jesus!"

The figure in the corner stood.

"That's him," said the woman with a certain satisfaction. The madman frowned, shaking his head rapidly. "No."

The figure was misshapen. It had a pronounced hunched back and a cast in its left eye. The face was vacant and foolish, a little spittle on the lips. It giggled as its name was repeated. It took a crooked step forward. "Jesus," it said. The word was slurred and thick. "Jesus."

"That's all he can say." The woman sneered. "He's always been like that."

"God's judgment," said Joseph bitterly.

"What's wrong with him?"—a pathetic, desperate note in the madman's voice.

"He's always been like that." The woman turned back to the stove. "You can have him if you like. Addled inside and outside. I was carrying him when my parents married me off to that half-man. . . ."

"You shameless—" Joseph stopped as his wife glared. He turned to the madman. "What's your business with our son?"

"I wished to talk to him. I . . ."

"He's no oracle—no seer—we used to think he might be. There are still people in Nazareth who come to him to cure them or tell their fortunes, but he only giggles at them and speaks his name over and over."

"Are—you sure—there is not—something about him—you have not noticed?"

"Sure!" Mary snorted sardonically. "We need money badly enough. If he had any magical powers, we'd know."

Jesus giggled again and limped away into another room.

"It is impossible," the madman murmured. Could history itself have changed? Could he be in a dimension of time where Christ had never been?

Joseph appeared to notice the look of agony in the madman's eyes. "What is it?" he said. "What do you see? You said you foretold the future. Tell us how we will fare?"

"Not *now,*" said the prophet, turning away. "Not *now.*"

He ran from the house and down the street with its smell of planed oak, cedar and cypress. He ran back to the marketplace and stopped, looking wildly about him. He saw the synagogue directly ahead. He walked towards it.

The man he had spoken to earlier was still in the marketplace, buying cooking pots to give to his daughter as a wedding gift. He nodded towards the strange man as he entered the synagogue. "He's a relative of Joseph the carpenter," he told the man beside him. "A prophet, I shouldn't wonder."

The madman, the prophet, Karl Glogauer, the time traveler, the neurotic psychiatrist manqué, the searcher for meaning, the masochist, the man with a death wish and a messiah complex, the anachronism, made his way into the synagogue gasping for breath. He had seen the man he had sought. He had seen Jesus, the son of Joseph and Mary. He had seen a man he recognized without any doubt as a congenital imbecile.

† † †

"All men have a messiah complex, Karl," Monica had said.

The memories were less complete now. His sense of time and identity was becoming confused.

"There were dozens of messiahs in Galilee at the time. That Jesus should have been the one to carry the myth and the philosophy was a coincidence of history. . . ."

"There must have been more to it than that, Monica."

† † †

Every Tuesday in the room above the Occult Bookshop, the Jungian discussion group met for purposes of group analysis and therapy. Glogauer had not organized the group, but he had willingly lent his premises to it and had joined it eagerly. It was a great relief to talk with like-minded people once a week. One of his reasons for buying the Occult Bookshop was so that he could meet interesting people like those attending the Jungian discussion group.

An obsession with Jung brought them together, but everyone had special obsessions of his own. Mrs. Rita Blen charted the courses of flying saucers, though it was not clear if she believed in them or not. Hugh Joyce believed that all Jungian archetypes derived from the original race of Atlanteans who had perished millennia before. Alan Cheddar, the youngest, was interested in Indian mysticism, and Sandra Peterson, the organizer, was a great witchcraft specialist. James Headington was interested in time. He was the group's pride: Sir James Headington, wartime inventor, very rich and very well decorated for his contribution to the Allied victory. He had had the reputation as a great improviser during the war, but, after it, had become an embarrassment to the War Office, who thought him a crank. What was worse, he aired his crankiness in public.

Every so often, Sir James told the other members of the group about his time machine. They humored him. Most of them exaggerated their own experiences connected with their different interests.

One Tuesday evening, after everyone else had left, Headington told Glogauer that his machine was ready.

"I can't believe it," Glogauer said truthfully.

"You're the first person I've told."

"Why me?"

"I don't know. I like you—and the shop."

"You haven't told the government."

Headington had chuckled. "Why should I? Not until I've tested it fully, anyway. Serves them right for putting me out to pasture."

"You don't know it works?"

"I'm sure it does. Would you like to see it?"

"A time machine." Glogauer smiled weakly.

"Come and see it."

"Why me?"

"I thought you might be interested. I know you don't hold with the orthodox view of science. . . ."

Glogauer felt sorry for him.

"Come and see," said Headington.

He went down to Banbury the next day. The same day he left 1976 and arrived in 28 A.D.

††† 

The synagogue was cool and quiet with a subtle scent of incense. The rabbis guided him into the courtyard. They, like the townspeople, did not know what to make of him, but they were sure no devil possessed him. It was their custom to give shelter to the roaming prophets who were now everywhere in Galilee, though this one was stranger than the rest. His face was immobile and his body stiff, and tears ran down his dirty cheeks. They had never seen such agony in a man's eyes before.

††† 

"Science can say how, but it never asks why," he had told Monica. "It can't answer."

"Who wants to know?" she'd replied.

"I do."

"Well, you'll never find out, will you?"

† † †

"Sit down, my son," said the rabbi. "What do you wish to ask of us?"

"Where is Christ?" he said. "Where is Christ?"

They did not understand the language.

"Is it Greek?" asked one, but another shook his head.

*Kyrios:* The Lord.

*Adonai:* The Lord.

*Where* was *the Lord?*

He frowned, looking vaguely about him.

"I must rest," he said in their language.

"Where are you from?"

He could not think what to answer.

"Where are you from?" a rabbi repeated.

*"Ha-Olam Hab-Bah . . ."* he murmured at length.

They looked at one another. *"Ha-Olam Hab-Bah,"* they said.

*Ha-Olam Hab-Bah; Ha-Olam Haz-Zeh,* The world to come and the world that is.

"Do you bring us a message?" said one of the rabbis. They were used to prophets, certainly, but none like this one. "A message?"

"I do not know," said the prophet hoarsely. "I must rest. I am hungry."

"Come. We will give you food and a place to sleep."

He could only eat a little of the rich food and the bed with its straw-stuffed mattress was too soft for him. He was not used to it.

He slept badly, shouting as he dreamed, and, outside the room, the rabbis listened, but could understand little of what he said.

† † †

Karl Glogauer stayed in the synagogue for several weeks. He spent most of his time reading in the library, searching through the long scrolls for some answer to his dilemma. The words of the Testaments, in many cases capable of a dozen interpretations, only confused him further. There was nothing to grasp, nothing to tell him what had gone wrong.

For the most part, the rabbis kept their distance. They had accepted him as a holy man. They were proud to have him in their synagogue. They were sure he was one of the special chosen of God and they waited patiently for him to speak to them.

But the prophet said little, muttering only to himself in snatches of their language and snatches of the incomprehensible language he often used, even when he addressed them directly.

In Nazareth, the townsfolk talked of little else but the mysterious prophet in the synagogue, but the rabbis would not answer their questions. They told the people to go about their business, that there were things they were not yet meant to know. In this way, as priests had always done, they avoided questions they could not answer while appearing to have more knowledge than they actually possessed.

Then, one Sabbath, he appeared in the public part of the synagogue and took his place with the others who had come to worship.

The man reading from the scroll on his left stumbled over the words, glancing at the prophet from the corner of his eye.

The prophet sat and listened, his expression remote.

The chief rabbi looked uncertainly at him, then signed that the scroll should be passed to the prophet. Hesitantly, a boy placed the scroll into the prophet's hands.

The prophet looked at the words for a long time and then began to read. He read without comprehending at first what he read. It was the book of Esaias.

†††

*The Spirit of the Lord is upon me, because he hath*
*anointed me to preach the gospel to the poor; he hath*

*sent me to heal the brokenhearted, to preach deliver-*
*ance to the captives, and recovering of sight to the*
*blind, to set at liberty them that are bruised, To preach*
*the acceptable year of the Lord. And he closed the*
*book, and gave it again to the minister, and sat down.*
*And the eyes of all of them that were in the synagogue*
*were fastened on him.*

*(Luke 4:18-20)*

## V

They followed him now, as he walked away from Nazareth towards the Lake of Galilee. He was dressed in the white linen robe they had given him and though they thought he led them, they, in fact, drove him before them.

"He is our messiah," they said to those that inquired. And there were already rumors of miracles.

When he saw the sick, he pitied them and tried to do what he could because they expected something of him. Many he could do nothing for, but others, obviously in psychosomatic conditions, he could help. They believed in his power more strongly than they believed in their sickness. So he cured them.

When he came to Capernaum, some fifty people followed him into the streets of the city. It was already known that he was in some way associated with John the Baptist, who enjoyed huge prestige in Galilee and had been declared a true prophet by many Pharisees. Yet this man had a power greater, in some ways, than John's. He was not the orator that the Baptist was, but he had worked miracles.

Capernaum was a sprawling town beside the crystal lake of Galilee, its houses separated by large market gardens. Fishing boats were moored at the white quayside, as well as trading ships that plied the lakeside towns. Though the green hills came down from all sides to the lake, Capernaum itself was built on flat ground, sheltered by the hills. It was a quiet town and, like most others in Galilee, had a large population of gentiles. Greek, Roman and Egyptian traders walked its streets and many had made permanent homes there. There was a prosperous middle class of merchants, artisans and ship owners, as well as doctors, lawyers and scholars, for Capernaum was on the borders of the provinces of Galilee, Trachonitis and Syria and though a comparatively small town was a useful junction for trade and travel.

The strange, mad prophet in his swirling linen robes, followed by a crowd that was primarily composed of poor folk but also could be seen to contain men of some distinction, swept into Capernaum. The news spread that this man really could foretell the future, that he had already predicted the arrest of John by Herod Antipas and soon after Herod had imprisoned the Baptist at Peraea. He did not make the prediction in general terms, using vague words the way other prophets did. He spoke of things to happen in the near future and he spoke of them in detail.

None knew his name. He was simply the prophet from Nazareth, or the Nazarene. Some said he was a relative, perhaps the son, of a carpenter in Nazareth, but this could be because the written words for "son of a carpenter" and "magus" were almost the same and so the confusion had come. There was even a faint rumor that his name was Jesus. The name had been used once, or twice, but when they asked him if that was, indeed, his name, he denied it or else, in his abstracted way, refused to answer at all.

His actual preaching lacked the fire of John's. This man spoke gently, rather vaguely, and smiled often. He spoke of God in a strange way, too, and he appeared to be connected, like John, with the Essenes, for he preached against accumulating personal wealth and spoke of mankind as a brotherhood, as they did.

But it was the miracles that they watched for as he was guided to the graceful synagogue of Capernaum. No prophet before him had healed the sick and seemed to understand the troubles people rarely spoke of. It was his sympathy that they responded to, rather than the words he spoke.

For the first time in his life, Karl Glogauer had forgotten about Karl Glogauer. For the first time in his life he was doing what he had always sought to do as a psychiatrist.

But it was not his life. He was bringing a myth to life—a generation before that myth would be born. He was completing a kind of psychic circuit. He was not changing history, but giving history more substance.

He could not bear to think of Jesus as nothing more than a myth. It was in his power to make Jesus a physical reality rather than the result of a process of mythogenesis.

So he spoke in the synagogues—of a gentler God than most of his listeners had heard of—and where he could remember them, he told them parables.

And gradually the need to justify his actions faded and his sense of identity grew increasingly more tenuous and was replaced by a different sense of identity, where he gave greater and greater substance to the role he had chosen. It was an archetypal role, a role to appeal to a disciple of Jung, a role that went beyond a mere imitation. It was a role that he must now play out to the very last grand detail. Karl Glogauer had discovered the reality he had been seeking.

† † †

*And in the synagogue there was a man, which had a spirit of an unclean devil, and cried out with a loud voice, Saying, Let us alone; what have we to do with thee, thou Jesus of Nazareth? art thou come to destroy us? I know thee who thou art, the Holy One of God. And Jesus rebuked him, saying, Hold thy peace, and come out of him. And when the devil had thrown him in the midst, he came out of him, and hurt him not. And they were all amazed, and spake among themselves, saying, What a word is this! for with authority and power he commandeth the unclean spirits, and they come out. And the fame of him went out into every place of the country round about.*

(Luke 4:33-37)

† † †

"Mass hallucination Miracles, flying saucers, ghosts, it's all the same," Monica had said.

"Very likely," he had replied. "But *why* did they see them?"

"Because they wanted to."

"Why did they want to?"

"Because they were afraid."

"You think that's all there is to it?"

"Isn't it enough?"

† † †

When he left Capernaum for the first time, many more people accompanied him. It had become impractical to stay in the town, for the business of the town had been brought almost to a standstill by the crowds seeking to see him work his simple miracles.

He spoke to them in the spaces beyond the towns. He talked with intelligent, literate men who appeared to have something in common with him. Some were owners of fishing fleets—Simon, James and

John among them. One was a doctor, another a civil servant who had first heard him speak in Capernaum.

"There must be twelve," he said to them one day. "There must be a zodiac."

He was not careful in what he said. Many of his ideas were strange. Many of the things he talked about were unfamiliar to them. Some Pharisees thought he blasphemed.

One day he meet a man he knew as an Essene from the colony near Machaerus.

"John would speak with you," said the Essene.

"Is John not dead yet?" he asked the man.

"He is confined at Peraea. I think Herod is too frightened to kill him. He lets John walk about within the walls and gardens of the palace, lets him speak with his men, but John fears that Herod will soon find the courage to have him stoned, or decapitated. He needs your help."

"How can I help him? He is to die. There is no hope for him."

The Essene looked uncomprehendingly into the mad eyes of the prophet.

"But, master, there is no one else who can help him."

"I have done all that he wished me to do," said the prophet. "I have healed the sick and preached to the poor."

"I did not know he wished this. Now he needs help, master. You could save his life.'

The prophet had drawn the Essene away from the crowd.

"His life cannot be saved."

"But if it is not, the unrighteous will prosper and the Kingdom of Heaven will not be restored."

"His life cannot be saved."

"Is it God's will?"

"If I am God, then it is God's will."

Hopelessly, the Essene turned and walked away from the crowd.

John the Baptist would have to die. Glogauer had no wish to change history, only to strengthen it.

He moved on, with his following, through Galilee. He had selected his twelve educated men, and the rest who followed him were still primarily poor people. To them he offered their only hope of fortune. Many were those who had been ready to follow John against the Romans, but now John was imprisoned. Perhaps this man would lead them in revolt, to loot the riches of Jerusalem and Jericho and Caesarea. Tired and hungry, their eyes glazed by the burning sun, they followed the man in the white robe. They needed to hope and they found reasons for their hope. They saw him work greater miracles.

Once he preached to them from a boat, as was often his custom, and as he walked back to shore through the shallows, it seemed to them that he walked over water.

All through Galilee in the autumn they wandered, hearing from everyone the news of John's beheading. Despair at the Baptist's death turned to renewed hope in this new prophet who had known him.

In Caesarea they were driven from the city by Roman guards used to the wild men who roamed the country with their prophecies.

As the prophet's fame grew, they were banned from other cities. Not only the Roman authorities, but also the Jewish ones seemed unwilling to tolerate the new prophet as they had tolerated John. The political climate was changing.

It became hard to find food. They lived on what they could find, hungering like starved animals.

He taught them how to pretend to eat and take their minds off their hunger.

Karl Glogauer, witch doctor, psychiatrist, hypnotist, messiah.

Sometimes his conviction in his chosen role wavered and those following him were disturbed when he contradicted himself. Often, now, they called him the name they had heard, Jesus the Nazarene. Ordinarily, he did not stop them from using the name, but sometimes he became angry and cried a peculiar, guttural name:

"Karl Glogauer! Karl Glogauer!"

And they said, Behold, he speaks with the voice of Adonai. "Call me not by that name!" he would shout, and they would become disturbed and leave him alone until his anger subsided.

When the weather changed and the winter came, they went back to Capernaum, which had become a stronghold of his followers.

In Capernaum he waited the winter through, making prophecies.

Many of these prophecies concerned himself and the fate of his followers.

† † †

> *Then charged he his disciples that they should tell no man that he was Jesus the Christ. From that time forth began Jesus to shew unto his disciples, how that he must go unto Jerusalem, and suffer many things of the elders and chief priests and scribes, and be killed, and be raised again the third day.*
>
> *(Matthew 16:20-21)*

† † †

They were watching television at her flat. Monica was eating an apple. It was between six and seven on a warm Sunday evening. Monica gestured at the screen with her half-eaten apple.

"Look at that nonsense," she said. "You can't honestly tell me it means anything to you."

The program was a religious one, about a pop opera in a Hampstead Church. The opera told the story of the crucifixion.

"Pop groups in the pulpit," she said. "What a comedown."

He didn't reply. The program seemed obscene to him, in an obscure way. He couldn't argue with her.

"God's corpse is really beginning to rot now," she jeered. "Whew! The stink!"

"Turn it off, then," he said quietly.

"What's the pop group called? The Maggots?"

"Very funny. I'll turn it off, shall I?"

"No, I want to watch. It's funny."

"Oh, turn it off!"

"Imitation of Christ!" she snorted. "It's a bloody caricature."

A Negro singer, playing Christ and singing flat to a banal accompaniment, began to drone out lifeless lyrics about the brotherhood of man.

"If he sounded like that, no wonder they nailed him up," said Monica.

He reached forward and switched the picture off.

"I was enjoying it." She spoke with mock disappointment.

"It was a lovely swansong."

Later, she said with a trace of worrying affection, "You old fogey. What a pity. You could have been John Wesley or Calvin or someone. You can't be a messiah these days, not in your terms. There's nobody to listen."

## VI

The prophet was living in the house of a man called Simon, though the prophet preferred to call him Peter. Simon was grateful because the prophet had cured his wife of a chronic complaint. It had been a mysterious complaint, but the prophet had cured her almost effortlessly.

There were a great many strangers in Capernaum at that time, and many came to see the prophet. Simon warned the prophet that some were known agents of the Romans or the Pharisees. The Pharisees had not, on the whole, been antipathetic towards the prophet, though they distrusted the talk of miracles that they heard. However, the whole political atmosphere was disturbed and the Roman occupiers, from Pilate, through his officers, down to the troops, were tense, expecting an outbreak but unable to see any tangible signs that one was coming.

Pilate hoped for trouble on a large scale. It would prove to Tiberius that the emperor had been too lenient with the Jews about the matter of the votive shields. Pilate would be vindicated and his power over the Jews increased. At present he was on bad terms with all the Tetrarchs of the provinces—particularly the unstable Herod Antipas who had seemed at one time his only supporter. Aside from the political situation, his own domestic situation was upset in that his neurotic wife was having nightmares again and demanding far more attention from him than he could afford to give.

There might be a possibility, he thought, of provoking an incident, but he would have to be careful that Tiberius never learnt of it. This new prophet might provide a focus, but so far the man had done nothing against the laws of either the Jews or the Romans. There was no law that forbade a man to claim he was a messiah, as some said this one had done, and he was hardly inciting the people to revolt—rather the contrary.

Looking through his chamber window, with a view of the minarets and spires of Jerusalem, Pilate considered the information his spies had brought.

Soon after the festival that the Romans called Saturnalia, the prophet and his followers again left Capernaum and traveled through the country.

There were fewer miracles now that the hot weather had passed, but his prophecies were eagerly asked. He warned them of all the mistakes that would be made in the future, and of all the crimes that would be committed in his name.

Through Galilee he wandered, and through Samaria, following the good Roman roads towards Jerusalem.

The time of the Passover was nearing.

In Jerusalem, Roman officials discussed the coming festival. It was always a time of the worst disturbances. There had been riots during the last Feast of the Passover, and doubtless there would be trouble of some kind this year, too.

Pilate spoke to the Pharisees, asking for their cooperation. The Pharisees said they would do what they could, but they could not help it if the people acted foolishly.

Scowling, Pilate dismissed them.

His agents brought him reports from all over the territory. Some of the reports mentioned the new prophet, but noted that he was harmless.

Pilate thought that he might be harmless now, but if he reached Jerusalem during the Passover, he might not be so harmless.

† † †

Two weeks before the Feast of the Passover, the prophet reached the town of Bethany near Jerusalem. Some of his Galilean followers had friends in Bethany and these friends were more than willing to shelter the man they had heard of from other pilgrims on their way to Jerusalem and the Great Temple.

The reason they had come to Bethany was that the prophet had become disturbed at the number of the people following him.

"There are too many," he had said to Simon. "Too many, Peter."

Glogauer's face was haggard now. His eyes were set deeper into their sockets and he said little.

Sometimes he looked around him vaguely, as if unsure where he was.

News came to the house in Bethany that Roman agents had been making inquiries about him. It did not seem to disturb him. On the contrary, he nodded thoughtfully, as if satisfied.

Once he walked with two of his followers across country to behold Jerusalem. The bright yellow walls of the city looked splendid in the afternoon light. The towers and tall buildings, many of them decorated in mosaic reds, blues and yellows, were visible from several miles away.

The prophet turned back towards Bethany.

"When shall we go into Jerusalem?" one of his followers asked.

"Not yet," said Glogauer. His shoulders were hunched and he grasped his own chest as if cold.

Two days before the Feast in Jerusalem, the prophet took his men towards the Mount of Olives and a suburb of Jerusalem built on its side and called Bethphage.

"Get me a donkey," he told them. "A colt. I must fulfill the prophecy now."

"Then all will know you are the Messiah," said Andrew.

"Yes."

Glogauer sighed. He felt afraid again, but this time it was not physical fear. It was the fear of an actor about to make his final, most dramatic scene and unsure that he could do it well.

Cold sweat glistened on Glogauer's upper lip. He wiped it off.

In the poor light he peered at the men around him. He was still uncertain of some of their names. He was not interested in their names, particularly, only in their number. There were ten here. The other two were looking for the donkey.

They stood on the grassy slope of the Mount of Olives, looking towards Jerusalem and the great Temple lay below. There was a light, warm breeze blowing.

"Judas?" said Glogauer inquiringly.

There was one called Judas.

"Yes, master," he said. He was tall and good looking, with curly red hair and neurotic intelligent eyes. Glogauer believed him an epileptic.

Glogauer looked thoughtfully at Judas Iscariot. "I will want you to help me later," he said, "when we have entered Jerusalem."

"How, master?"

"You must take a message to the Romans."

"The Romans?" Iscariot looked troubled. "Why?"

"It must be the Romans. It can't be the Jews—they would use a stake or an axe. I'll tell you more when the time comes."

The sky was dark now, and the stars were out over the Mount of Olives. It had become cold. Glogauer shivered.

† † †

*Rejoice greatly, O daughter of Zion; shout, O daughter*
*of Jerusalem: behold, thy King cometh unto thee: he is*
*just and having salvation; lowly and riding upon an ass,*
*and upon a colt, the foal of an ass.*

*(Zechariah 9:9)*

† † †

*"Osha'na! Osha'na! Osha'na!"*

As Glogauer rode the donkey into the city, his followers ran ahead, throwing down palm branches. On both sides of the street jostled crowds, forewarned by the followers of his coming.

Now the new prophet could be seen to be fulfilling the

prophecies of the ancient prophets and many believed that he had come to lead them against the Romans. Even now, possibly, he was on his way to Pilate's house to confront the procurator.

*"Osha'na! Osha'na!"*

Glogauer looked around distractedly. The back of the donkey, though softened by the coats of his followers, was uncomfortable. He swayed and clung to the beast's mane. He heard the words, but could not make them out clearly.

*"Osha'na! Osha'na!"*

It sounded like "hosanna" at first, before he realized that they were shouting the Aramaic for "Free us."

"Free us! Free us!"

John had planned to rise in arms against the Romans this Passover. Many had expected to take part in the rebellion.

They believed that he was taking John's place as a rebel leader.

"No," he muttered at them as he looked around at their expectant faces. "No, I am the Messiah. I cannot free you. I can't . . ."

They did not hear him above their own shouts.

Karl Glogauer entered Christ. Christ entered Jerusalem. The story approached its climax.

*"Osha'na!"*

It was not in the story. He could not help them.

† † †

> *Verily, verily, I say unto you, that one of you shall betray me. Then the disciples looked one on another, doubting of whom he spake. Now there was leaning on Jesus' bosom one of his disciples, whom Jesus loved. Simon Peter therefore beckoned to him, that he should ask who it should be of whom he spake. He then lying on Jesus' breast saith unto him, Lord, who is it? Jesus answered,*

*He it is, to whom I shall give a sop, when I have dipped
it. And when he had dipped the sop, he gave* it *to Judas
Iscariot,* the son *of Simon. And after the sop Satan
entered into him. Then said Jesus unto him, That thou
doest, do quickly.*

(John 13:21-27)

††† 

Judas Iscariot frowned with uncertainty as he left the room and went
out into the crowded street, making his way towards the governor's
palace. Doubtless he was to perform a part in a plan to deceive the
Romans and have the people rise up in Jesus' defense, but he
thought the scheme foolhardy. The mood amongst the jostling men,
women and children was tense. Many more Roman soldiers than
usual patrolled the city.

†††

Pilate was a stout man. His face was self-indulgent and his eyes
were hard and shallow. He looked disdainfully at the Jew.

"We do not pay informers whose information is proved false," he
warned.

"I do not seek money, lord," said Judas, feigning the ingratiating
manner that the Romans seemed to expect of the Jews. "I am a
loyal subject of the Emperor."

"Who is this rebel?"

"Jesus of Nazareth, lord. He entered the city today. . . ."

"I know. I saw him. But I heard he preached of peace and
obeying the law."

"To deceive you, lord."

Pilate frowned. It was likely. It smacked of the kind of deceit he had
grown to anticipate in these soft-spoken people. "Have you proof?"

"I am one of his lieutenants, lord. I will testify to his guilt."

Pilate pursed his heavy lips. He could not afford to offend the Pharisees at this moment. They had given him enough trouble. Caiaphas, in particular, would be quick to cry "injustice" if he arrested the man.

"He claims to be the rightful king of the Jews, the descendant of David," said Judas, repeating what his master had told him to say.

"Does he?" Pilate looked thoughtfully out of the window.

"As for the Pharisees, lord . . ."

"What of them?"

"The Pharisees distrust him. They would see him dead. He speaks against them."

Pilate nodded. His eyes were hooded as he considered. The Pharisees might hate the madman, but they would be quick to make political capital of his arrest.

"The Pharisees want him arrested," Judas continued. "The people flock to listen to the prophet and today many of them rioted in the Temple in his name."

"Is this true?"

"It is true, lord." It was true. A half-dozen people had attacked the moneychangers in the Temple and tried to rob them. When they had been arrested, they had said they had been carrying out the will of the Nazarene.

"I cannot make the arrest," Pilate said musingly. The situation in Jerusalem was already dangerous, but if they were to arrest this "king," they might precipitate a revolt. Tiberius would blame him, not the Jews. The Pharisees must be won over. They must make the arrest. "Wait here," he said to Judas. "I will send a message to Caiaphas."

†††

> *And they came to a place which was named Gethsemane:*
> *and he saith to his disciples, Sit ye here, while I shall*
> *pray. And he taketh with him Peter and James and John,*
> *and began to be sore amazed, and to be very heavy; And*
> *saith unto them, My soul is exceeding sorrowful unto*
> *death: tarry ye here, and watch.*
>
> *(Mark 14:32-34)*

† † †

Glogauer could see the mob approaching now. For the first time since Nazareth he felt physically weak and exhausted. They were going to kill him. He had to die; he accepted that, but he was afraid of the pain to come. He sat down on the ground of the hillside, watching the torches as they came closer.

† † †

*"The ideal of martyrdom only ever existed in the minds of a few ascetics,"* Monica had said. *"Otherwise it was morbid masochism, an easy way to forgo ordinary responsibility, a method of keeping repressed people under control. . . ."*

*"It isn't as simple as that. . . ."*

*"It is, Karl."*

He could show Monica now. His regret was that she was unlikely ever to know. He had meant to write everything down and put it into the time machine and hope that it would be recovered. It was strange. He was not a religious man in the usual sense, but an agnostic. It was not conviction that had led him to defend religion against Monica's cynical contempt for it; it was rather *lack* of conviction in the ideal in which she had set her own faith, the ideal of science as a solver of all problems. He could not share her faith and there was nothing else but religion, though he could not believe in the kind of God of Christianity. The God seen as a mystical force of the mysteries of Christianity and other great religions had not been personal enough for him. His rational mind had told him that God did not exist in any personal form. His unconscious had told him that faith in science was not enough.

*"Science is basically opposed to religion,"* Monica had once said harshly. *"No matter how many Jesuits get together and rationalize their views of science, the fact remains that religion cannot accept the fundamental attitudes of science and it is implicit to science to attack the fundamental principles of religion. The only area in which there is no difference and need be no war is in the ultimate assumption. One may or may not assume there is a supernatural being called God. But as soon as one begins to defend one's assumption, there must be strife."*

*"You're talking about organized religion."*

*"I'm talking about religion as opposed to a belief. Who needs the ritual of religion when we have the far superior ritual of science to replace it? Religion is a reasonable substitute for knowledge. But there is no longer any need for substitutes, Karl. Science offers a sounder basis on which to formulate systems of thought and ethics. We don't need the carrot of heaven and the big stick of hell any more when science can show the consequences of actions and men can judge easily for themselves whether those actions are right or wrong."*

*"I can't accept it."*

*"That's because you're sick. I'm sick, too, but at least I can see the promise of health."*

*"I can only see the threat of death. . . ."*

† † †

As they had agreed, Judas kissed him on the cheek and the mixed force of Temple guards and Roman soldiers surrounded him.

To the Romans he said, with some difficulty, "I am the King of the Jews." To the Pharisees' servants he said: "I am the messiah who has come to destroy your masters." Now he was committed and the final ritual was to begin.

## VII

It was an untidy trial, an arbitrary mixture of Roman and Jewish law that did not altogether satisfy anyone. Its object was accomplished after several conferences between Pontius Pilate and Caiaphas and three attempts to bend and merge their separate legal systems in order to fit the expediencies of the situation. Both needed a scapegoat for their different purposes and so at last the result was achieved and the madman convicted, on the one hand of rebellion against Rome and on the other of heresy.

A peculiar feature of the trial was that the witnesses were all followers of the man and yet had seemed eager to see him convicted.

The Pharisees agreed that the Roman method of execution would fit the time and the situation best in this case and it was decided to crucify him. The man had prestige, however, so that it would be necessary to use some of the tried Roman methods of humiliation in order to make him into a pathetic and ludicrous figure in the eyes of the pilgrims. Pilate assured the Pharisees he would see to it, but he had them sign documents giving their approval to his actions.

† † †

*And the soldiers led him away into the hall, called Pretorium; and they call together the whole band. And they clothed him with purple, and platted a crown of thorns; and put it about his head, And began to salute him, Hail, King of the Jews. And they smote him on the head*

> *with a reed, and did spit upon him, and bowing* their
> *knees worshipped him. And when they had mocked him,*
> *they took off the purple from him, and put his own clothes*
> *on him, and led him out to crucify him.*
>
> *(Mark 15:16-20)*

† † †

His brain was clouded now, by pain and by the ritual of humiliation; by his having completely given himself up to his role.

He was too weak to bear the heavy wooden cross and he walked
behind it as it was dragged towards Golgotha by a Cyrenian whom
the Romans had press-ganged for the purpose.

As he staggered through the crowded, silent streets, watched by
those who had thought he would lead them against the Roman over-
lords, his eyes filled with tears so that his sight was blurred and he
occasionally staggered off the road and was nudged back onto it by
one of the Roman guards.

*"You are too emotional, Karl. Why don't you use that brain of
yours and pull yourself together?"*

He remembered the words, but it was difficult to remember who
had said them or who Karl was.

The road up the hillside was stony and he slipped sometimes,
recalling another hill he had climbed long ago. It seemed that he
had been a child, but the memory merged with others and it was
impossible to tell.

He was breathing heavily. The pain of the thorns in his head was
barely felt, but his whole body seemed to throb in unison with his
heartbeat. It was like a drum.

It was evening. The sun was setting. He fell on his face, cutting
his head on a stone, just as he reached the top of the hill. He
fainted.

† † †

*And they bring him unto the place Golgotha, which is,*
*being interpreted, The place of a skull. And they gave*
*him to drink wine mingled with myrrh: but he received*
*it not.*

*(Mark 15:22-23)*

† † †

He knocked the cup aside. The soldier shrugged and reached out
for one of his arms. Another soldier already held the other arm.

As he recovered consciousness Glogauer began to tremble violently. He felt the pain intensely as the ropes bit into the flesh of
his wrists and ankles. He struggled.

He felt something cold placed against his palm. Although it covered only a small area in the center of his hand, it seemed very
heavy. He heard another sound in rhythm with his heartbeats. He
turned his head to look at the hand.

The large iron peg was being driven into his hand by a soldier
swinging a mallet as he lay on the cross now horizontal on the
ground. He watched, wondering why there was no pain. The soldier
swung the mallet higher as the peg met the wood's resistance.
Twice he missed the peg and struck Glogauer's fingers.

Glogauer looked to the other side and saw a second soldier also
hammering in a peg. Evidently he missed the peg a great many
times because the fingers of the hand were bloody and crushed.

The first soldier finished hammering in his peg and turned his
attention to the feet. Glogauer felt the iron slide through his flesh,
heard it hammered home.

Using a pulley, they hauled the cross into a vertical position.
Glogauer saw that he was alone. There were no others being crucified that day.

He got a clear view of the lights of Jerusalem below. There was still a little light in the sky but not much. Soon it would be entirely dark. A small crowd looked on. One of the women reminded him of Monica. He called to her.

"Monica?"

But his voice was cracked and the word was a whisper.

The woman did not look up.

He felt his body dragging at the nails supporting it. He thought he felt a twinge of pain in his left hand. He seemed to be bleeding very heavily.

It was odd, he reflected, that it should be he hanging here. He supposed that it was the event he had first come to witness. There was little doubt, really. Everything had gone perfectly. The pain in his left hand increased.

He glanced down at the Roman guards playing dice at the foot of his cross. They seemed absorbed in their game. He could not make out the markings of the dice.

He sighed. The movement of his chest threw extra strain on his hands. The pain was quite bad now. He winced and tried to ease himself back against the wood.

The pain spread through his body. He gritted his teeth. It was dreadful. He gasped and shouted. He writhed.

There was no longer any light in the sky. Heavy clouds obscured stars and moon.

From below came whispered voices.

"Let me down," he called. "Oh, please let me down!"

Pain filled him. He slumped forward, but nobody released him.

A little while later he raised his head. The movement caused a return of the agony and again he began to writhe on the cross.

"Let me down. Please. Please stop it!"

Every part of his flesh, every muscle and tendon and bone filled with an almost impossible degree of pain.

He knew he would not survive until the next day as he had thought he might. He had not realized the extent of his pain.

† † †

*And at the ninth hour Jesus cried with a loud voice, saying, Eloi, Eloi, lama sabachthani? which is, being interpreted, My God, my God, why hast thou forsaken me?*

*(Mark 15:34)*

† † †

Glogauer coughed—a dry, barely heard sound. The soldiers below the cross heard it because the night was now so quiet.

"It's funny," one said. "Yesterday they were worshiping him. Today they seemed to want us to kill him—even the ones who were closest to him."

"I'll be glad when we get out of this country," said another.

† † †

He heard Monica's voice again. *"It's weakness and fear, Karl, that's driven you to this. Martyrdom is a conceit. Can't you see that?"*

Weakness and fear.

He coughed once more and the pain returned, but it was duller now.

Just before he died he began to talk again, muttering the words until his breath was gone. "It's a lie. It's a lie. It's a lie."

Later, after the servants of some doctors who believed it to have special properties stole his body, there were rumors that he had not died. But the corpse was already rotting in the doctors' dissecting rooms and would soon be destroyed.

† † †

### Author's Commentary

As a child, most of my exposure to religion was incidental, via the
Anglican Church. I attended a church only once—to be chris-
tened, for convention's sake, even though my mother's background
was secular and Jewish. My father's family had been Methodists
since the eighteenth century when they left Yorkshire for better
weaving prospects in the Wamering and Oxford areas. As the city
grew around them, they became Londoners by default. My great-
great-etc. aunt Rachel wrote and published poetry with the
Methodist press. In a poem about the Apocalypse, she shows the
Jews refused Heaven because they fail to accept the Messiah.

Demagogues interested me, as did the manner in which they
conform to what the crowd of the day demands. I was actually
thinking about Hitler, one Easter, and chatting about him with wife
and friends over the kitchen table in Ladbroke Grove. In the end,
though, I chose Jesus, maybe because of then current news about
the recently unearthed Dead Sea Scrolls. Then I read the Bible,
both Testaments, reread the New a few times, and devoured everything I could on the period, including speculative books about
Christ. Because I had no religion, I had no religious axe to grind—
which is not to say that I was not deeply interested in such matters,
a fact that I hope comes through in Karl's obsessive quest for spiritual certainty. Although I lacked Karl's hang-ups, I made use of a
fair bit of autobiographical material, including every single bad
experience I'd had as a kid. But, having had a fairly happy childhood, I ran out early!

The only reference I found to an historical Jesus was a Roman
author's mention of a simpleton. I no longer recall my precise source;
like most writers, once I have used the research in a story, my head
clears for the next batch of research. But that is why, when Karl
finds Jesus, he is a simpleton. I meant no offence to religious people

and in fact had no overtly religious acquaintances. Such people did not exist in my circle, and it was not until I came to America that I realized religion was not dead—for me, a type of time travel, like going back to the Dark Ages.

Frankly, I found little spirituality in most expressions of American Christianity, which struck me as aggressive and more derivative of ignorance and uncertainty than of a reasoned belief system. Also, given what I have witnessed of late from self-proclaimed Christians in both the US and the UK, I have no cause to change my mind. Indeed, given the current situation in the Middle East, I now firmly believe that religion is no longer the opium, but the crack of the people.

† † †

*And had He lived?*

# SEQUEL ON SKORPIÓS
## Michael Bishop

### i.

Yeshua has died, an old man with tangled nose hairs and rotten teeth. I place two of Caesar's denarri on his eyes, to blind his death-stare. Soon, in this Ionian island's fierce heat, his body will release the first odors of its corruption.

Many people believe that Yeshua died forty years ago on a cross on Skull Mount outside Jerusalem. Many believe that two days later he rose from his tomb, not as a ghost but as a death-changed cutting of God's selfsame vine. In truth, Yeshua did not die on that cross, and so had no call to come alive again. Our plot entailed bribing two Roman soldiers and so much risk that even now I marvel that we accomplished it.

In our hovel on Skorpiós, the dead Yeshua hardly resembles the young rabbi whom the soldiers scourged that day, pressing a mock crown onto his head and scarring his back with flails. The crown's thorns and those flails dripped with an opiate I had boiled out of a desert root. This substance helped Yeshua endure the pain of crucifixion and lapse by the gradual slowing of his heart into a limpness akin to death.

One bribed soldier argued against breaking Yeshua's legs. "He's gone," he said. "Why waste more effort on him?" When another legionary crowed, "For the fun of it," our soldier, to stymie a worse assault, stabbed Yeshua under the ribs with his spear, delivering another does of opiate. This sustained his deathlike slumber until Sunday morning.

But on Friday evening, Joseph of Arimathea came with an ox cart and several women to Skull Mount, to take Yeshua from the cross. I also came, in woman's garb, and wrestled him into the car. Later, I carried him into the garden tomb. After I laid him out there, Mary, Mary of Magdala, and Joanna massaged his body with spices and bound him in clean linen strips.

Tonight Yeshua's aged corpse has none of his younger self's poignant beauty. (What foolishness, attempting to reform the corrupt Judean religion by shamming a death and a return!) In its fleeing slumber, his crucified body had appeared ready to soar out of itself on viewless wings. How did so lovely a man dwindle into this grizzled wreck?

In this wise:

On that long-ago Sunday, Joseph and I crept into the tomb through a hidden tunnel. When Yeshua awoke, we unwrapped his body, robed him, and led him back out to a juniper grove several hundred paces away. From there, Yeshua fled, at length reaching Nazareth in Galilee. Meanwhile, some soldiers moved the tomb's stone (for a rumor had spread, that someone would steal the body) and found nothing inside but Yeshua's discarded wrappings.

Later, on a Galilean mountain where the rabbi had given his most famous sermon, we feigned a resurrection event. Even more people believed. When the Romans came to investigate, Yeshua and I hiked to Tyre and boarded a Greek merchant ship, yielding the preaching of his gospel to an army of beloved dupes.

† † †

## ii.

Cephas, the brothers Boanerges, the man once named Saul, and many others carried our false good tidings (believing them implicitly) to the Gentiles, to every major city on the jagged northern shore of the Middle Sea. Soon, colonies of Christ followers pocked the coastlands, suffering the scorn of pagan neighbors but infecting many others with belief. Yeshua, whom some of these evangels would have recognized even in disguise, avoided his old comrades.

We settled in a small village on Skorpiós. I made and sold rare medicines. Yeshua carpentered or fished. He nearly undid us, though, by urging baptism on amazed pagans and casting his cryptic parables before them like pearls.

And then a fishing accident left Yeshua unable to move any body part but his eyes. If God had chosen Yeshua (as Yeshua had always said, even during our Passover ruse), why had this paralyzing injury befallen him? I could not believe that God would so cruelly humble his anointed son, but my affection for Yeshua led me to serve him as physician and slave. I fed and cleaned him, turned him to keep him from growing pallet sores. Beyond assisting in his lie, though, what I had done to render myself this imposter's keeper?

Observing me at work, an islander asked me why I did not abandon Yeshua and return to Palestine. I recalled Yeshua's admonitions to visit the sick, to go to the prisoner, and I stayed. The plealess dignity of his gaze also spoke to me. Heal yourself, I silently begged him. Meanwhile, my ministry to him stretched into years. Often I prayed that he would die. His eyes, though, kept me from denying him food, or the solacing rubdown, or the occasional clumsy story.

Travelers to our village sometimes told me of the spread throughout Asia Minor, Greece, and Italy of a queer Judean sect trumpeting a savior who had died but who now lived again as an emblem of eternal hope. I said nothing in contradiction, even though the savior himself, eating and eliminating, mocked this hope every time I rubbed ointment on his sores or added fresh ticking to his pallet. My faith in the man had died long ago, even before the accident at sea.

† † †

### iii.

This morning, in his seventy-third or –fourth year, long after most other chronic invalids have passed on, Yeshua in fact died. I have leisure to write. The dead do not rise. Even worse, God does not preside.

Yeshua's corpse, its aroma unbearably high, sits propped against the parapet in mute witness to God's silence. I should bury the man, but the act has no urgency for me, even in this heat. Does it matter that our lives have no follow-on, that we sleep rather than soar? Tonight, as Yeshua's corruption rises, mere oblivion seems a gift.

† † †

### iv.

God forgive me, I burned him on the beach. I made an oven of stones and torched his tenantless body. The smoke climbed both sweet and foul into the evening sky. His skull failed to burn. More disturbing to me, so did his heart.

If only in the here and now we have hope in Yeshua, we who

loved him constitute the most pitiable people on earth—as I, a slave in bondage to a lie partly of my own devising, have known for years. And now

† † †

## coda

Yeshua has appeared to me. Without even opening a door, he stood before the table in my hovel cupping his unburnt heart in his hands. He laid the heart on my table. He looked like an old man, but an old man in perfect health with a strange bronze nimbus about him. He said to me, after years of invalid muteness, "Congratulations, Lebbeus," and vanished as startlingly as he had come.

I do not know what this means. But Yeshua's heart still rests on my table, and I did not visit the beach to fetch it here. (Nor have I gone mad, like those from whom Yeshua once evicted demons.) Meanwhile, his heart smells sweet, less like braised flesh than new roses, and what I begin to know is that I must open my own to its fragrance.

† † †

### Author's Commentary

The year 1996 was my first as writer-in-residence at LaGrange College, a Methodist-affiliated liberal arts institution twenty miles north of my home in Pine Mountain. On the recommendation of my friend and colleague, John Kessel, author of *Good News from Outer Space* (Tor, 1989) and *Corrupting Dr. Nice* (Tor, 1997), among other titles, I used *Writing Fiction: A Guide to Narrative Craft* by Janet Burroway as my creative-writing text. Fairly late in the course, I asked my students to undertake a difficult assignment from this text requiring them to write a story in which one of their most cherished beliefs proves *untrue*.

As I had done with them that semester on every other assignment, I wrote my own story, "Sequel on Skorpiós," the one you've just read. One pro-life student did a piece in which abortion turns out the only viable option for a young woman in circumstances most of us would regard as dire. Another student, believing that one true love (and one only) exists for each person in the world, produced a story in which her central character finds *two* perfect soul mates. And I—well, *I* tackled the crucial identifying events and tenets of the Christian faith: the historicity of the Crucifixion and the absolute authenticity of the Resurrection.

I like my brief story. However, honesty compels me to confess that "Sequel on Skorpiós" initially accepts, but finally sidesteps, Burroway's challenge. Later, I paid for my bet hedging. The evident fact that "Sequel" offers a deliberate contrast to the Gospel accounts of the Crucifixion upset some parents at a private school to which I had been invited to speak; and so I had to tell a go-between employed by the institution that these troubled parents, and the student who had brought "Sequel on Skorpiós" to their notice, had not misunderstood my narrative's *events*, but that they had indeed misunderstood its *meaning*. In brief, unlike my students, I had failed Burroway's assignment. On the other hand, I take heart from my "failure."

††††

*A game of transcultural telephone, a Japanese pietà . . .*

# SHIMABARA
## Karen Joy Fowler

The sea, the same as now. It had rained, and we can imagine that too, just as we have ourselves seen it—the black sky, the ocean carved with small, sharp waves. At the base of each cliff would be a cloud of white water.

At the top of the cliffs was a castle and, inside the castle, a fifteen-year-old boy. Here is where it gets tricky. What is different and what is the same? The story takes place on the other side of the world. The boy has been dead more than three hundred and fifty years. There was a castle, but now there is a museum and a mall. A Japanese mall is still a mall; we know what a mall looks like. The sea is the same. What about a fifteen-year-old boy?

The boy's mother, Martha, was in a boat on the sea beneath the cliffs. Once a day she was taken to shore to the camp of Lord Matsudaira for interrogation. Then she could see the castle where her son was. The rest of the time she lay inside the boat with her two daughters, each of them bound by the wrists and the ankles, so that when she was allowed to stand, her legs, through disuse, could hardly hold her up. Add to that the motion of the boat. When she walked on land, on her way to interrogation, she shook and pitched. The samurai thought it was terror, and of course there was that, too.

Perhaps Martha was more concerned about her son in the castle than her daughters on the boat. Perhaps a Japanese mother three hundred and fifty years ago would feel this way. In any case, all their lives depended on her son now. As she lay on the boat, Martha passed the time by counting miracles. The first was that she had a son. On the day of Shiro's birth, the sunset flamed across the entire horizon, turning the whole landscape red, then black. Later, when Shiro was twelve, a large, fiery cross rose out of the ocean off the Shimabara Peninsula and he was seen walking over the water toward it. He could call birds to his hands; they would lay eggs in his palms. This year, the year he turned fifteen, the sunset of his birth was repeated many times. The cherry blossoms were early. These things had been foretold. Martha remembered; she summoned her son's face; she imagined the sun setting a fire each night behind Hara Castle. The worst that could happen was that her son prove now to be ordinary. The wind that had brought the rain rocked the boat.

Thirty-seven thousand Kirishitan rebels followed Shiro out of Amakusa to the Shimabara Peninsula and the ruin of Hara Castle. *Kirishitan* is a word that has been translated into Japanese and come back out again, as in the children's game of telephone. It goes in as Christian, comes out Kirishitan.

The rebels made the crossing in hundreds of small boats, each with a crucifix in the bow. A government spy stood in the cold shadow of a tree and watched the boats leave. He couldn't count the rebels. Maybe there were fifty thousand. Maybe twenty thousand. Of those, maybe twelve thousand were men of fighting age. The spy grew weak from hunger and fatigue. Just to stand long enough to watch them all depart required the discipline and dedication of a samurai.

General Itakura Shigemasa pursued the rebels through Amakusa, burning the villages they'd left behind. Many of the remaining inhabitants died in the fires. Those who survived, Itakura put to death anyway. He had the children tied to stakes and then burned alive. It was a message to the fifteen-year-old Kirishitan leader.

Although Hara Castle had been abandoned for many years, it was built to be defended. The east side of the castle looked over the sea; on the west was a level marsh, fed by tides, which afforded no footing to horses, no cover to attackers. North and south were cliffs one hundred feet high. Only two paths led in, one to the front, one to the rear, and neither was wide enough for more than a single man. On January 27, 1637, after ten days of repairs, the rebels occupied Hara Castle.

They hoisted a flag. It showed a goblet, a cross, a motto, and two angels. The angels were fat, unsmiling, and European; the motto was in Portuguese. LOVVAD SEIA O SACTISSIM SACRAMENTO: Praised be the most holy sacrament. In March, when Martha knelt in Lord Matsudaira's camp to write Shiro a letter, there were one hundred thousand Bakufu samurai between her and her son.

† † †

January, February, March, and early April passed in a steady storm of negotiations. The air above Shimabara was full of words wound around the shafts of arrows. One landed in the camp outside the castle. "Heaven and earth have one root, the myriad things one substance. Among all sentient beings there is no such distinction as noble and base," the arrow said. An arrow flew back. "Surrender," it asked, but obliquely, politely, confining itself, in fact, to references to the weather.

January and February were muddy. General Itakura commanded the Bakufu forces. Government agents tried to dig a tunnel into the castle, but the digging was overheard. The rebels filled the tunnel with smoke and regular deposits of urine and feces until the diggers refused to dig farther.

Itakura planned to pummel the castle walls with cannonballs so large it took twenty-five sweating men to move each one to the front lines. The last days of January were spent pulling and pushing the cannonballs into place, but it proved a Sisyphean labor in the end since no cannon, no catapult, was large enough to launch them.

More letters flew across on arrow shafts. "The samurai in Amakusa cannot fight," the letters from inside the castle said. "They are cowards and only good at torturing unarmed farmers. The sixty-six provinces of Japan will all be Kirishitan, of that there is no doubt. Anyone who does doubt, the Lord Deus with His own feet will kick him down into Inferno; make sure this point is understood." "Surrender," said the arrows going in, but the penmanship was beautiful; the letters could almost have been framed. Meanwhile, Lord Matsudaira Nobutsuna and a fleet of sixty ships were moving up the coast from Kyushu, bringing Martha to her son.

General Itakura received a letter from his cousin in Osaka. "All is well. When Lord Matsudaira arrives, the castle, held as it is by mere peasants, will not last another day." Itakura translated this letter immediately as mockery. He decided to attack before the reinforcements arrived.

His first try was on February 3, a mousy, hilarious effort; his second on New Year's Day, February 14. Itakura himself led the bold frontal attack across the marsh and was killed by a rebel sharpshooter. After his death, he was much condemned for inappropriate bravura. He had laid the government open to more ridicule, dying as he had at the hands of farmers.

The night before his death Itakura wrote a poem.

*When only the name remains of the flower*
*that bloomed on New Year's Day,*
*remember it as the leader of our force.*

He attached it to an arrow and shot it out over the ocean in the direction of Lord Matsudaira's fleet and the moon.

On February 24, the Commissioner of Nagasaki transmitted Lord Matsudaira's request that the Dutch ship *de Ryp* begin a bombardment of the castle from the sea. The shelling lasted two weeks until, on March 12, the shogunate canceled the request. Two Dutch sailors had been killed; one, shot in the topmast, fell to the deck and landed on the other. A storm of arrows left the castle. "The government agents," these arrows said, "are better at squeezing taxes out of starving farmers, better at keeping account books, than at risking their lives on the field of battle. This is why they have to depend on foreigners to do their fighting. We in Hara Castle are armed with faith. We cannot be killed and we will slay all village magistrates and heathen bonzes without sparing even one; for judgment day is at hand for all Japan."

The Dutch commissioner, Nicolaus Coukebacker, sent a defensive letter by boat back to Holland. "We were, of course, reluctant to fire upon fellow Christians, even though the rebels in question are Roman Catholics and the damage the rebellion has done to trade conditions in Nagasaki has been severe. Our bombardment was, in any case, ineffectual." He was too modest. The outer defenses had been weakened.

On March 5, in the middle of the lull provided by the Dutch bombardment, a letter flew into the government camp from one Yamada Emonsaku of Hara Castle. Expressing his reverence for the rule of hereditary lords in particular and governments in general, Yamada assured them he had never been a sincere Kirishitan.

He then outlined a lengthy plan in which he offered to deliver Shiro to the Bakufu alive. "Please give me your approval immediately, and I will overthrow the evil Kirishitans, give tranquillity to the empire, and, I trust, escape with my own life." An answer asking for further information was sent back, but Yamada did not respond.

The invisible men, the *ninjutsuzukai*, went into Hara Castle and returned with information. The rebel leader had a mild case of scabies. While he'd been playing a game of *go*, an incoming cannonball had ripped the sleeve of his coat. His divinity had never seemed more questionable. The letter to Yamada had been easily intercepted. He was bound in a castle room under a sentence of death.

Around their ankles, the invisible men wore leads that unwrapped as they walked. If they were killed their bodies could be dragged back out. You might think such cords would have given them away, but you are more inclined to believe in the fabulous skills of the ninjutsuzukai than that a boy has walked on water. Not a single ninjutsuzukai was lost.

Lord Matsudaira judged that the rebel position was weakening. After the silly death of Itakura, he had settled on the inglorious strategy of blockade. The strategy appeared justified. The ninjutsuzukai said that the rebels were living in holes they had excavated under the castle. There was not enough to eat.

† † †

Matsudaira wrote a letter. The letter spoke of the filial piety owed to parents. It assured Shiro of Matsudaira's reluctance to hurt Shiro's family and said further that Matsudaira knew a fifteen-year-old boy couldn't possibly be leading such a large force. "I am pleased, therefore, to offer a full pardon to the boy, asking only that he surrender, recant, and identify the real leader of the rebellion. I look forward to a joyful family reunion."

Martha knelt in the mud beside Matsudaira and wrote as he directed. "We know that you have forced conversions on some of your followers. If you let those hostages go, Lord Matsudaira will allow your family to join you in Hara Castle. All who surrender may depend on the traditional magnanimity of the Bakufu; no one who freely recants will be punished. Indeed, rice lands will be given to those who surrender!" Matsudaira gestured with one hand that Martha was to finish the letter herself. "For myself, I ask only to see you again. Perhaps we could speak. Lord Matsudaira is willing. Don't forget your family on the outside who wish only to be with you."

These letters were carried into the castle by Shiro's young nephew and little sister. The Bakufu had dressed them in kimonos with purple bursts of chrysanthemums. They wore embroidered slippers brought up the coast by boat for the occasion. Small as they were, the narrow path to the castle held them both, but the path was muddy from the rain, and the children wanted to save their shoes, so they stepped slowly and sometimes, when puddles narrowed the path even more, one did go before the other. Inside the shining kaleidoscope of armor and sunlight, Martha saw the small bobbing chrysanthemums and, high above them, the flag over Hara Castle. "Now we will know what kind of a son you have," Lord Matsudaira told her. "If you have the wrong kind, only you are to blame for what happens next."

Soon the tiny figures disappeared from view. Martha counted slowly, trying to guess at the exact moment they would enter the castle. The path was very long and their steps so small. The ocean sobbed behind her. The sun through the trees moved down her face to her hands. If she could send Shiro one more message she would ask him to keep the children. She imagined the wish like a small, shining stone in Shiro's hand. He rubbed it with his fingers, feeling it, understanding it. He threw it into the air, as he would any other stone, but it became the bird whose shadow passed over Martha's face, the shadow Shiro's answer to her.

Martha struggled to keep her mind on the miracles. Left to itself, her memory immediately chose the most ordinary of moments. A little boy throwing stones. A pair of arms around her neck. A game of hiding. His face when he slept.

Matsudaira had tea prepared. He drank and attended to his mail. He discussed Hara Castle with several of his officers. They were all agreed that the rebellion could not have held out at any other spot. It was a wonderful castle, and after they had taken it they must be sure to destroy it completely. Fire, first, but then the stonework must be carefully dismantled. The unit from Osaka was charged with this.

Matsudaira decided to change the passwords. He sent out the new codes. Now the sentries were to inquire "A mountain?" "A river" would be the correct reply. In an optimistic mood, he selected a password to signal the start of an attack. It, too, would be in the form of a question. "A province?" "A province!" was also the answer. He had a meal of rice balls and mullet. While he was eating, Martha heard a shout. The children were returning. Shiro had written a letter, which his nephew gave to Matsudaira. "Frequent prohibitions have been published by the Shogun, which have greatly distressed us. Some among us there are who consider the hope of future life as of the highest importance. For these there is no escape. Should . . . the above laws not be repealed, we must incur all sorts of punishments and torture; we must, our bodies being weak and sensitive, sin against the infinite Lord of Heaven; and from solicitude for our brief lives incur the loss of what we highly esteem. These things fill us with grief beyond our capacity. There are no forced converts among us, only outside, among you.

We are protected by Santa Maria-sama [Mary], Sanchiyago-sama [Jesus], and Sanfuranshisuko-sama [St. Francis]."

To his mother Shiro sent a large parcel of food containing honey, bean-jam buns, oranges, and yams. He had given his little sister his ring to wear.

The ninjutsuzukai had reported starvation. Scavengers from the castle had been seen on Oe beach, searching for edible seaweeds. The bodies of rebel dead had been cut open and their stomachs contained only seaweed and barley. The unexpected sight of bean-jam buns sent Matsudaira into a rage. "Your son thinks very little of you," he said. "Very little of his sisters. All you ask is to speak with him. What kind of a son is this?"

Martha was filled with grief beyond her capacity. The largest part of it was only the fact that her daughter and her grandson had been allowed to see Shiro and she had not. In Shiro's presence she would have endured anything. "God is feeding him," she told Matsudaira. "He is stronger than you can imagine. God will change him into a bird to fly away from your soldiers. You will never kill my son."

This display angered Matsudaira even more. "Take her back to the boat," Matsudaira told the soldiers. "Take her and bind her below where she can't watch the sun set or see the castle. Her son doesn't love her enough to see her. What kind of a mother is this?"

††† 

When it came, the final attack was a mistake. On April 12 a fire was misread as a signal. The Nabeshima division rushed forward, soon joined by others. The rebels were completely out of ammunition and the sentries too weak from hunger to hold their posts. The agents easily penetrated the outer perimeter. In the inner rings, the women and children defended themselves with stones and cooking pots. They held out for two more days and nights of steady fighting. On April 15, the defenses collapsed.

By nightfall the government had set up tables to count and collect heads. The count was at 10,869. Headless bodies covered the fields about the castle, clogged the nearby rivers. By April 16, only one person from the castle had survived. As a reward for his letter of March 5, Yamada Emonsaku was spared. Eventually he would be taken back to Edo to serve in Lord Matsudaira's house as his assistant.

The *kubi-jikken*, or head inspection scene, is a traditional element of feudal literature. Martha saw Shiro one more time. The soldiers collected every head that might belong to a fifteen-year-old boy and summoned Martha to identify her son. "He is not here," she told them. Her daughters had been killed and her grandson. Their heads would be displayed in Nagasaki. Her own death was very close now. "He was sent by heaven and heaven has protected him. God has transformed him to escape you." There were many possible heads. She rejected them all. Finally Lord Sasaemon held up a recent victim. The boy had been dressed in silks.

Martha began to weep at once, and once she began there was no reason to stop. She thought of her son throwing stones, playing hiding games, his face when he slept. She took the head and held it in her lap. We can imagine this moment, if we let ourselves, as a sort of Japanese pietà, the pietà translated, like the word Kirishitan, into Japanese and out again. "Can he really have become so thin?" Martha asked.

✝ ✝ ✝

Every mother can easily imagine losing a child. Motherhood is always half loss anyway. The three-year-old is lost at five, the five-year-old at nine. We consort with ghosts, even as we sit and eat with, scold and kiss, their current, corporeal forms. We speak to people who have vanished and, when they answer us, they do the same. Naturally, the information in these speeches is garbled in the translation.

I myself have a fifteen-year-old son who was once nine, once five, once fit entirely inside me. At fifteen, he speaks in monotones, sounds chosen deliberately for their minimal content. "Later," he says to me, leaving the house, and maybe he means that he will see me later, that later he will sit down with me, we will talk. At fifteen, he has a whole lot of later.

Me, not so much. To me, later is that time coming soon, when he will be made up almost entirely of words: letters in the mailbox, conversations on the phone, stories we tell about him, plans he tells to us. And you probably think I would have trouble imagining that thirty-seven thousand people could follow him to their deaths, that this is the hard part, but you would be wrong. No other part of the story, except for the sea, is so easy to imagine.

Isn't it really just a matter of walking on water? To me, today, this seems a relatively insignificant difference, but of course it is the whole point—along with starvation and persecution, peasant messianism and ronin discontent. Was the boy in the castle God, or wasn't he? Who saw him walking on water? Who says the sunsets were his?

The story comes to us over time, space, and culture, a game of telephone played out in magnificent distances. Thirty-seven thousand Kirishitans and one hundred thousand Bakufu samurai were willing to die, arguing over the divinity of Amakusa Shiro. But what does this mean to us? Nothing is left now but the flag and the words.

"An angel was sent as messenger and the instructions he transmitted must therefore be passed on to the villagers," the rebels wrote to someone and, eventually, to us. "And the august personage named Lord Shiro who has these days appeared in Oyano of Amakusa is an angel from Heaven."

Within one moment, anything is possible. Only the passage of time makes our miraculous lives mundane. For a single moment any boy can walk on water. An arrow can hang in the sky without falling. Martha kneels to write a letter. The sun is in her face. Negotiations continue. CNN is filming. The compound will never be taken. There are children inside.

† † †

## Author's Commentary

The first time I heard the story of Amakusa Shiro and the siege of Hara Castle I was in college. I'd attended a lecture on the Christian missionaries in Asia and the messianic movements, the score of Christ's little brothers, they left in their wake. The point of the lecture, as I recall it, was the conundrum these Christians created for the missionaries. How should they be regarded? Was this successful missionary work or not? When the imperial powers moved to put these messiahs down, what role should the missionaries play? Hara Castle, my professor said, might never have been taken if the Dutch had not helped, allying themselves with the shogunate rather than the Kirishitan movement. I hardly noticed Shiro's age when I first heard the story, perhaps because I was not so very much older myself.

In 1993 the FBI laid siege to the Branch Davidian ranch known as Mount Carmel near Waco, Texas. This siege, prompted by rumors of child abuse and illegal weapons, lasted fifty-one days and ended in the death of seventy-six people, twenty-seven of them children. I watched some of this on television, and then I went to the library, to search again for the story of the Shimabara rebellion. By 1993 I was myself a mother. This time through, the story for me was profoundly about Martha and Shiro, about me and my son, and about the people who hung banners from the roofs and windows of Mount Carmel asking for help from the world outside, and who died when the compound was taken.

†††

*If a god is judged, who renders the judgment?*

# THE PALE, THIN GOD
## Mike Resnick

He stood quietly before us, the pale thin god who had invaded our land, and waited to hear the charges.

The first of us to speak was Mulungu, the god of the Yao people.

"There was a time, many eons ago, when I lived happily upon the earth with my animals. But then men appeared. They made fire and set the land ablaze. They found my animals and began killing them. They devised weapons and went to war with each other. I could not tolerate such behavior, so I had a spider spin a thread up to heaven, and I ascended it, never to return. And yet *you* have sacrificed yourself for these very same creatures."

Mulungu pointed a long forefinger at the pale thin god. "I accuse you of the crime of Love."

He sat down, and immediately Nyambe, the god of the Koko people, arose.

"I once lived among men," he said, "and there was no such thing as death in the world, because I had given them a magic tree. When men grew old and wrinkled, they went and lived under the tree for nine days, and it made them young again. But as the years went by men began taking me for granted, and stopped worshiping me and making sacrifices to me, so I uprooted my tree and carried it up to heaven with me, and without its magic, men finally began to die."

He stared balefully at the pale thin god. "And now you have taught men that they may triumph over death. I charge you with the crime of Life."

Next Ogun, the god of the Yoruba people, stepped forward.

"When the gods lived on Earth, they found their way barred by impenetrable thorn bushes. I created a *panga* and cleared the way for them, and this *panga* I turned over to men, who use it not only for breaking trails but for the glory of war. And yet you, who claim to be a god, tell your worshipers to disdain weapons and never to raise a hand in anger. I accuse you of the crime of Peace."

As Ogun sat down, Muluku, god of the Zambesi, rose to his feet.

"I made the earth," he said. "I dug two holes, and from one came a man, and from the other a woman. I gave them land and tools and seeds and clay pots, and told them to plant the seeds, to build a house, and to cook their food in the pots. But the man and the woman ate the raw seeds, broke the pots, and left the tools by the side of a trail. Therefore, I summoned two monkeys, and made the same gifts to them. The two monkeys dug the earth, built a house, harvested their grain, and cooked it in their pots." He paused. "So I cut off the monkeys' tails and stuck them on the two men, decreeing that from that day forth they would be monkeys and the monkeys would be men."

He pointed at the pale thin god. "And yet, far from punishing men, you forgive them their mistakes. I charge you with the crime of Compassion."

En-kai, the god of the Maasai, spoke next.

"I created the first warrior, Le-eyo, and gave him a magic chant to recite over dead children that would bring them back to life and make them immortal. But Le-eyo did not utter the chant until his own son had died. I told him that it was too late, that the chant would no longer work, and that because of his selfishness, Death will always have power over men. He begged me to relent, but because I am a god and a god cannot be wrong, I did not do so."

He paused for a moment, then stared coldly at the pale thin god. "You would allow men to live again, even if only in heaven. I accuse you of the crime of Mercy."

Finally Huveane, god of the Basuto people, arose.

"I, too, lived among men in eons past. But their pettiness offended me, and so I hammered some pegs into the sky and climbed up to heaven, where men would never see me again." He faced the pale thin god. "And now, belatedly, you have come to our land, and you teach that men may ascend to heaven, that they may even sit at your right hand. I charge you with the crime of Hope."

The six fearsome gods turned to me.

"We have spoken," they said. "It is your turn now, Anubis. Of what crime do you charge him?"

"I do not make accusations, only judgments," I replied.

"And how do you judge him?" they demanded.

"I will hear him speak, and then I will tell you," I said. I turned to the pale thin god. "You have been accused of the crimes of Peace, Life, Mercy, Compassion, Love, and Hope. What have you to say in your defense?"

The pale thin god looked at us, his accusers.

"I have been accused of Peace," he said, never raising his voice, "and yet more Holy Wars have been fought in my name than in the names of all other gods combined. The earth has turned red with the blood of those who died for my Peace.

"I have been accused of Life," he continued, "yet in my name, the Spaniards have baptized Aztec infants and dashed out their brains against rocks so they might ascend to heaven without living to become warriors.

"I have been accused of Mercy, but the Inquisition was held in my name, and the number of men who were tortured to death is beyond calculation.

"I have been accused of Compassion, yet not a single man who worships me has ever lived a life without pain, without fear, and without misery.

"I have been accused of Love, yet I have not ended suffering, or disease, or death, and he who leads the most blameless and saintly life will be visited by all of my grim horsemen just as surely as he who rejects me.

"Finally, I have been accused of Hope," he said, and now the stigmata on his hands and feet and neck began to glow a brilliant red, "and yet since I have come to your land, I have brought famine to the north, genocide to the west, drought to the south, and disease to the east. And everywhere, where there was Hope, there is only poverty and ignorance and war and death.

"So it has been wherever I have gone, so shall it always be.

"Thus do I answer your charges."

They turned to me, the six great and terrible deities, to ask for my judgment. But I had already dropped to my knees before the greatest god of us all.

††† 

## Author's Commentary

Back in the mid-1990s I wrote a lot of well-received science-fiction stories about Africa, including some Hugo winners. Because I had been there a number of times and had enormous respect and affection for the peoples of Africa, I had always tried to treat their religious beliefs with equal respect.

One day an ardent young born-again Christian accosted me and accused me of suggesting in my stories that the pantheon of African deities was somehow greater or more important than Jesus. He wanted me to write a story showing Jesus' primacy. (I think his exact words were that he wanted me to "prove that Jesus was greater than all the other gods," a desire that struck me as just a bit strange, for, if you believe in Jesus, you aren't supposed to believe in any other gods.)

Anyway, Jane Yolen had just asked me for another of my African stories for her anthology *Xanadu*, so I decided to borrow some African folk myths, take the young man at his word, prove his point—and show him its consequences.

Not surprisingly, I never heard from him again.

✝ ✝ ✝

*An insurrection, a legend, and a kiss . . .*

# THE INQUISITOR GENERAL

## Fyodor Dostoyevsky

### *i. insurrection*

After a brisk walk, Alyosha halted outside the Metropolis, a tavern on the square. As a matter of propriety, his cassock prevented him from entering the place. At that moment, though, his older brother Ivan flung open a second-story window and asked him to join him upstairs.

"In respect to Father Zosima," Alyosha said, "I probably shouldn't."

"But I'm in a private room," Ivan assured him. "Please come up."

Alyosha obeyed and found his brother at dinner—not in a private room, but at a table behind a set of wooden screens. How different from the cloisters at the monastery! The cries of waiters, the popping of corks, the clacking of billiard balls, and the wheeze of an organ perturbed Alyosha's hearing, heightening his unease.

Ivan ordered him fish soup, hot tea, and cherry jam, and the two men, long riddles to each other but each ready to learn something new about his sibling, fell into an intense, far-reaching discussion. For months, Alyosha had longed for some opportunity to learn from

Ivan what he believed, or whether he believed at all, for in their green youth only matters of eternal significance—the so-called "great" questions—had possessed any real meaning for either of them. Still, Alyosha prayed that what Ivan held sacred, or scorned as nonsense, would not lead him to laugh at his expense or to thrust Ivan outside the pales of salvation.

As if he had intuited this concern, Ivan said, "Why would I laugh at you? I bear an extraordinary fondness for a Russian youth named . . . Alyoshenka."

"Ah, you exempt me from our great national pastime of philosophical nitpicking!" Alyosha grinned. "Thank you. Now begin. After all, the eternal questions *warrant* such nitpicking, and yesterday at Father's you said there is no God."

"Solemn boy, I said that to tease you. In fact, I love life and accept the existence of God. What I reject is God's created *world*."

"Why? Tell me why."

Here Ivan launched a defense of the principles by which he lived, advancing in particular the suffering of children—of blameless innocents—as proof that if Satan does not exist, humanity has created him in its own likeness.

"Ah," said Alyosha, "just as that old sinner Voltaire once claimed we invented God?"

"Well, if that's so, yours must be a fine God indeed." Ivan chuckled mordantly, but not unkindly. "But hear me: I collect anecdotes, from books and newspaper stories, about bestial human acts, especially our treatment of children, whom many adults exult in torturing. To all other persons, such adults behave in a civilized way, but they take an obscene sexual gratification from tormenting children, whose very defenselessness—the angelic trust they put in those they cannot escape or appease—stirs the blood of these vile monsters."

Ivan catalogued examples: a five-year-old whose educated parents flogged and kicked her, locked her up in an outhouse on winter nights, and rubbed her face with slimy filth from its pit; a seven-year-old whose father beat her with a birch rod bristling with twigs because the branches stung her so severely, but who won a case in which he stood accused of cruelty because the judge and the public wished to uphold the right of parents to discipline their offspring; and an eight-year-old boy on whom an aristocratic general sicced a pack of dogs, to tear him apart before his mother because the boy, tossing a rock in play, had hurt the paw of the general's favorite hound.

"Tell me, Alyosha: What did that general deserve—to be shot to satisfy our moral cravings for justice?"

Alyosha smiled, but in a sickly way. "To be shot," he murmured.

"Ah!" cried Ivan. "Even the novice monk agrees. See there, Alexei Fyodor, a petty demon crouches in your heart too!"

The young monk sought to recover. "I misspoke absurdly, but—"

"That 'but' makes my case, Alyosha. The world rests on absurdities, and I'm nearly persuaded that nothing would exist or occur without them. We know what we know!"

"What do *you* know?"

Ivan assumed a thoughtful expression. "I harangued you about children only to make my case more vivid. In all humility, what *I* know is that I have no idea why God arranged the world as He did. Maybe humanity itself must stand to blame. It received paradise, it wanted freedom, and it pilfered fire from heaven . . . despite its awareness that none of these 'boons' would yield it happiness. We needn't pity humanity, brother mine. Suffering exists, it multiplies, and none is guilty: *this* I know. But what comfort may I take from such knowledge? I want justice—not in some remote time and place, but *here and now on earth*, justice I can see myself.

"Surely, Alyosha, I haven't suffered to enrich the soil of God's future harmony for somebody else. And children? If all must suffer to pay for eternal harmony in the hereafter, what have children to do with this horrid matter? I don't understand why they should suffer or pay for the harmony. If truth trembles in the idea that children must share in the burden of their parents' crimes, such a truth—despite the truth of solidarity of sin among people—well, it doesn't belong to this world, and thus it confounds my sense of justice.

"Oh, Alyosha, if children's sufferings must add to the total sum necessary to pay for truth, the truth isn't worth it. I don't want that mother whose landlord set the dogs on her son to embrace the old devil! She dare not forgive him! Let her forgive him for her own suffering heart, but not for the suffering of her mutilated son! She hasn't the right. And if she dare not forgive, what of eternal harmony? Well, I don't want harmony. For love of my own kind, I don't want it. It lies outside our means to pay so much, and so I respectfully return to God my entrance ticket to His costly paradise."

"*'Respectfully'*?" said Alyosha, despite himself. "That's insurrection."

"I'm sorry you call it that. Imagine you're creating a fabric of human destiny, with the end in view of humanity's ultimate happiness. Would you agree to weave this fabric if finishing it meant torturing an innocent child to death? Tell me the truth."

"No," Alyosha whispered. "I wouldn't."

"And can you embrace the idea that those for whom we weave this fabric would willingly take their joy from this tiny victim's tears, and that doing so they would remain happy forever?"

"No, I can't." Alyosha leaned forward. "But you forget there's one Being in God's created world who does have the right to forgive, and who can forgive indeed, everything and all, for everyone.

He shed His innocent blood to this end, for all and everything, and you've forgotten Him, Ivan."

"On the contrary: Why didn't you mention Him earlier? Most arguments on your side bring Him up immediately." Ivan lifted his chin. "About a year ago, I wrote a poem featuring Him—don't laugh, Alyosha—and if you have the time, I'll recite it."

"A poem?"

"A legend, really: a poem in prose. I wrote it in a frenzy of inspiration, without writing it down, but I recall it nearly word for word. Will you hear it? If so, you'll be my first . . . listener."

"I'm all ears." Alyosha smiled, whether at this trite remark or at the thought of his brother's "legend" he could not have said.

††† 

### ii. the legend

"I set my story in Spain, in Seville, during the Inquisition, when agents of the Church of Rome lit fires every day to the glory of God, for *'in their splendid auto-da-fé / believers burnt heretics.'* Of course, this coming was *not* the one during which He will manifest at the Apocalypse, but rather a silent comment on the activity of the inquisitors and their confreres, who on the 'hot pavements' of Seville, only a day before, had roasted almost a hundred dissenters and apostates, *ad majorem gloriam Dei*. The cardinal with the title Inquisitor General had presided—in the presence of the king, the court, the caballeros, the other cardinals, the most delightful beauties of the nobility, and the city's entire rapturous population.

"The Being whom you adore, Alyosha, came unobserved, at first, to these agitated Andalusians, and yet all who saw Him knew Him for Himself. (I believe this part of the poem the most poignant, for the people all recognize Him, and He accepts their adulatory mobbing with ungodly humility.) Walking among them, He bestows on all and sundry the same compassionate smile, a gaze as radiant as the sun's. His robe conducts healing to whoever touches it, and He holds out His hands and blesses alike the lowly and the mighty. An old blind man who begs Him for aid has his sight restored, and children sing alleluias: along His path they drop rose and camellia petals. 'It is He!' many in the crowd proclaim. 'It can be no other!'

"Before the steps of the grand cathedral, He spies some pall-bearers carrying the small white coffin of the young daughter of a prominent knight. The child lies embedded in flowers. Her mother falls at His feet crying, 'If it is You, resurrect her!' Despite the reproachful looks of the priest coming to meet the group, the pall-bearers lay the coffin at His feet. *'Talitha cumi,'* He prompts: 'Sweet maid, arise.' And, wide-eyed and smiling, the child sits up, a nosegay of white roses in her hands.

" *'Alleluia, alleluia,'* murmur the people, some sobbing, where-upon the Inquisitor General, a tall ninety-year-old cardinal of gaunt demeanor, passes the steps—not in the scarlet regalia he wore yes-terday to burn the enemies of Roman Catholicism, but rather in a humble cassock akin to your own, Alyosha—and sees the child's resurrection. A look of implacable outrage crosses his face, and he orders the 'holy guard' at his back to seize the Interloper. No one has the courage to resist; indeed, the people bow to the cardinal as he impersonally blesses them, and as his guards escort the Pris-oner away."

"A cardinal has Christ arrested?" Alyosha blurted. "What a mistake!"

"Call it a fantasy instead," Ivan said, lightly chuckling. "But if modern realism has so seduced you that you can't abide fantasy, feel free to assume mistaken identity. Maybe the ancient cardinal has succumbed to senility or delusion. But in addressing the Prisoner, as you will soon hear, the Inquisitor General voices aloud what he has privately thought for most of his ninety years."

"All right." Alyosha gripped his own shoulders. "Go ahead."

"The Prisoner finds himself, during that day and the succeeding hot night of laurel and lemon scents, in a dungeon of the Inquisitorial Court; then, in pitch darkness, its door creaks open and the old cardinal enters carrying a lamp. By its fitful glow he squints into the Prisoner's face.

" 'It's You, isn't it?' Getting no answer, he sets the lamp on a table. 'Remain silent. You have no right to add a syllable to what You spoke before. Why, then, do You return to impede our work? Do You know what I have planned tomorrow? Whether You are He or a lying double, You'll die in flames as our chief heretic, and those who kissed Your robe today, tomorrow at my nod will toss kindling on your pyre.'"

"The Inquisitor wants to *burn* the Son of God?" cried Alyosha. "The body and soul of our faith?"

Ivan ignored this outburst. "The old man rebukes Him again for returning, scolds Him for compromising our 'freedom of faith' with miraculous 'signs.' He declares that although the Prisoner once promised to make people free, the Church has completed His work by persuading them that they possess perfect freedom, even as it leads them to set that freedom meekly at the feet of its priests and popes. He claims that he and his cohorts have defeated and buried the concept of freedom, to make people happy. He notes that Christ had ample warning that our species, created and born rebels, could never achieve happiness if free to act on its own basest impulses, so thank God that on His departure He bequeathed the Church the right *to bind and unbind*. What an outrage, then, that He now considers revoking that power!"

Alyosha asked, "What does the cardinal mean, 'ample warning'?"

"Why, that's the crux of his argument, little brother. 'Satan,' the old man rebukes his Prisoner, 'tempted You in the wilderness. *Tempted!* But Your rejection of his three offers merits grief rather than praise. Don't You see that his asking those three questions is a greater miracle than resurrecting a child? Those questions not only perfectly fit the occasion of Your fast but also summarized and foretold all subsequent world history. In them, Satan harmonized the contradictions of human nature, which, fifteen hundred years later, we see as brilliantly divined, prophesied, and fulfilled. For just as You can neither add to nor subtract from Your words in the Gospels, we can neither augment nor diminish the dread spirit's questions.

" 'Bread,' the Inquisitor General said. ' "Bread," Satan said, "turn these stones in this parched land to bread and people will flock to You like sheep, grateful but atremble lest You one day *cease* to provide." But You declined, thinking freedom worthless if one can buy obedience with bread. You said, *"Man shall not live by bread alone, but by every word spoken by the mouth of God."* Noble, but unwise! Didn't You know that for the procurement of bread Satan would grapple with You in the hearts of Your people and wrest them away, so that even sages say, "Neither crime nor sin exists—only hunger," and the people lift before You a banner beseeching, *"Feed us before asking for virtue"*? Under this banner they will destroy Your temple and build a new Tower of Babel. Like the fabled tower, this one will remain unfinished, but You could have prevented it and thus saved Your people a thousand or more years of suffering. They will come to us, the Church, begging for food because those who promised them fire from heaven reneged, and we shall finish the tower by feeding them in Your name. *"Better to eat as slaves,"* they will say, *"than to starve as citizens."* These weak angry insurgent beings—the greater part of humanity—will

never believe Your bread of heaven attainable, even if a sad
minority follows You willingly, striving to forego material bread for
the heavenly.

" 'Well and good, but what of the sinful majority who love You?
*We* care for these, who regard us as gods because *we* take Your
heavy freedom and rule over them as Your servants—although, for
their sake, we work to keep You from returning, and lie to them to
preserve them from freedom. For this deceit, we suffer profoundly.
Satan's first question has this import: Had You chosen bread over
freedom, You would have fed our species' hunger for a god we
could worship in common. For this phantasm, a dream that *might*
have come true, we have maimed or killed those of other beliefs
while challenging them to adopt ours and live. So it will go on until
all gods vanish, when we will set up and genuflect before shabby
grim-faced idols.

" 'You knew this about us all along. You could have gathered us
under the one flag guaranteeing a universal communion, that of
earthly bread, but You disavowed it in favor of human freedom and
the bread of heaven. What folly. People want only to give their
freedom to a kind authority that can still their consciences. If this
authority appears, why, they will toss aside Your bread and follow
that power anywhere.

" 'In that,' the Inquisitor General continues, 'You didn't err.
People desire not only life, but a cause to live for. Without it, we
would rather kill ourselves, despite bread aplenty. But You, instead
of taking our freedom, enlarged it! You forgot that most of us prefer
peace, even death, to freedom of choice between Good and Evil.
Nothing, I admit, exalts us more than freedom of conscience, but
nothing causes us greater uncertainty and suffering. And You, who
could have set our consciences at ease forever, activated those
vague mechanisms, even though we lack the spiritual strength to

use them as You would like, with just Your exacting figure as our
guide. Didn't You know that we—or most of us, for I say "we" in
solidarity with the weak—would renounce Your image and truth if
forced to bear the onus of free choice? Given the pain and confusion that You have laid upon us, many will cry that no truth dwells
in You at all.

"'No one deserves more blame for undermining Your kingdom.
After all, what did Satan offer? The only forces able to capture, for
their own happiness, the consciences of our frailest rebels: *miracle*,
*mystery*, and *authority*. As an example, You waved off all three.
When Satan set You atop the temple and said, "Cast Yourself off,"
so that angels might bear You up in witness to Your faith, you said,
*"It is written again, You shall not tempt the LORD your God,"* and,
like God, did well to say so.

"'But do we feeble humans resemble gods? Though You refused,
aware that God would let you strike the earth that You came to
redeem, and that Satan would rejoice, few mortals could do as You
did. During the soul's darkest nights, we—*they*—seldom reject a
miracle to embrace the free verdict of the heart. You hoped that we,
too, would spurn miracle and cling to God, but weak humans seek
God less than they do the miraculous. Not finding it, we—*they*—
worship feats of sorcery and witchcraft, still seeing themselves as
rebels and heretics, atheists and infidels.

"'When, at Golgotha, these people mocked, "Step down, and we
will believe!" You didn't come down from the Cross. Desiring their
free allegiance, You declined—so as not to enslave them by a miracle. But You thought too well of these insurgent slaves, who, after
fifteen hundred years, must have revealed to even You the febrile
baseness of their natures. Could they do what You did? By
assuming so, You stopped feeling for them. You asked too much.
Respecting them less, You would have shown more love, relieving

them of the yoke of conscience. Everywhere now, they arrogantly flout our power—like schoolchildren, barring the teacher and rioting in the classroom. At length, they will pay dearly. In their riots they will soak the earth in blood, only to realize that although they delight in insurgency, they lack the strength to sustain it. They will see that by making them rebels, God mocked their impotence, and, disillusioned, they will curse Him, increasing their unhappiness, for even the vilest won't tolerate blasphemy and will find a way to punish it—as *I* well know. Despite what You sacrificed for our freedom, then, our lives partake of commotion and despair.

" 'St. John of Patmos envisioned that in the first resurrection, 144,000—twelve tribes squared, and multiplied by a thousand— would arise: those who faithfully endured the wilderness, bearing Your Cross and grubbing roots and locusts, followers who acted more like gods than men. Take pride in them, yes, but remember that these strong sons and daughters constitute only a *remnant*. What of the teeming and defiant weak? Must You disinherit them? If so, then You give heavenly bread only to the elect.

" 'And if *that* is so, You embody a mystery beyond comprehension. And if You endorse a mystery, why can't *we* proclaim one, affirming that only mystery matters—not love or the heart's free choices, but a mystery all must embrace, even against the alarms of conscience? And so, by that assertion, we reclaimed Your teaching by grounding ours on *miracle, mystery,* and *authority*. Praise the Adversary that we've done so, freeing the multitudes from freedom and allowing their weakness the release of sin, with our full sanction—for we act out of a greater, a more practical, tenderness than the rigorous love with which You obstruct our work.

" 'Shall I tell You *our* defining mystery?

" 'You make no answer—perhaps because You already know it. Hear me, then: We do not labor for You; we labor with *him*, the dire spirit whose three challenges You withstood, being not only *from* God but also *of* him. And there You have it, our mystery, the fact of our alignment with the Devil, ever since a Frankish king gave several moieties of land to the pope, thus profaning what even You may have once approved as holy. For eight centuries, then, we have sided with that fallen savant.

" 'From a high place, he showed You the world's kingdoms and promised them to You for the paltry coin of Your worship, but you replied, *"Avaunt, Satan!"* Such nobility and righteousness! But we accepted his offer for You—Rome and the sword with which to defend her—and called ourselves sole kings of the planet. True, we haven't achieved what we then proclaimed, but if *You* had taken Caesar's sword, we might have long ago attained our three most urgent desires: a god to worship, a hammock for our consciences, and a way to gather our species into one concordant hive.

" 'Throughout history, people have longed for a universal state. The more highly organized the state the less satisfied its citizens— for, more exquisitely than others, such a populace craved an all-encompassing union. Irresistible Tamerlanes and Genghis-Khans spun like hurricanes across the earth, subjugating all they could in pursuit of this dream, but if You had accepted Caesar's purple, *You* would have founded that state and fulfilled our dream, for who but the One who gives us bread and salves our consciences can reign in everlasting peace?

" 'You declined. We accepted. And ever since, God's outcast savant has had our allegiance. The rebels who embrace free thought, free science, and the philosophies of godless unrestraint, they will have their day—ages of chaos and cannibalism in which to continue building their Tower of Babel. Eventually, though, they'll crawl back to us with empty bellies and bloody mouths, so that we may lift over them a cup bearing the legend, *"Mystery."*

Only then, for the rebels as for the Church's sinful millions, will there begin a credible reign of peace and contentment.

" 'You "love" Your elect, but *we* comfort everyone. Hence, all will scurry to us, including many of the elect disgusted by Your failure to return, for we will persuade them that real freedom comes from surrendering it to us. Recalling the chaos to which freedom tied them, they will believe us. Some, fierce in their freed consciences, may first destroy themselves and others, but most will lick our feet, saying, *"You alone know His mystery. Save us from ourselves!"*

" 'They will take bread from our hands, not transfigured stones, and rejoice in its ordinariness, recalling that once even the bread they baked turned to rock, and they will understand the value of surrender. You, Captive, sent the flock wandering on crooked paths, but we shall gather them again, show them they are mere children, and prove again that in their childishness also abides happiness. We shall permit them even sin, and in the confessional shrive them of their most agonizing secrets. All will dwell in ignorant bliss, except for the enlightened hundred thousand who oversee their blinkered lives: we who for their sake bear the curse of the knowledge of Good and Evil—we who preserve the mystery. Our disciplined remnant will labor so that multitudes may frolic. Of course, they will die in Your name and find nothing beyond this life but darkness. Never fear, though: We shall harbor our secret and draw them to us with a promise of heavenly life, although if such a reward awaits anyone, it hardly awaits *them*.

" 'Prophecy says You will return in triumph with Your glorious elect, but we will declare that although they have redeemed only themselves, we have saved all. And we who have achieved this victory will say to You: *"Judge us if You can. Judge us if You dare."*

Remember, Sir: I too lived on thorns and grasshoppers. Like You, I treasured freedom and strove to stand with the resolute of God. But, finally awake, I decried my insanity and rejoined the holy remnant that has corrected Your work. I left the proud to lift the obscure, for their happiness, and what I prophesy *will* occur, bringing about our indisputable dominion.'

"The Inquisitor General fell silent, exhausted. Then he shook himself and said, 'Tomorrow, at my behest, the sinful weak will heap cinders on the pile on which I will burn You for coming to foul our work. I have spoken.' "

† † †

### iii. the kiss

In the tavern's upper room, Ivan stopped talking and smiled.

Alyosha, releasing his objections, said, "What nonsense! Your poem extols rather than convicts Jesus. And our Orthodoxy has no such absurd concept of human freedom as your arrogant cardinal frames it. Only Rome and the worst of Catholics—inquisitors, Jesuits—put forth such trash! And your self-abnegating Inquisitor, nobly suffering for blasted humanity, exists only in your dreams, a blasphemous fantasy!"

"Whoa," said Ivan, laughing. "Slow down."

"If such people exist—a cabal of a hundred thousand atheistic sages—they do so from lust of power and material greed, not from 'love' of the weak!"

"Wait. Why couldn't there be among the Jesuits and inquisitors one sorrowful soul who loved humanity and who realized that attaining perfection and freedom meant nothing, if millions of others could never attain them? And so turned back and joined the caring clever?"

"Utter bunk! They have no feelings, cleverness, or mysteries, and just one secret, a nauseating one: atheism! Your Inquisitor no longer believes in God!"

"Ah, you've guessed it. But isn't his atheism a kind of suffering, for a man who spent much of his life in the wilderness without ever losing his love of humanity? As an old man, he decides that only the challenges of Satan can create for the poor and the weak a supportable life. Therefore he must lead them to ultimate destruction in Jesus' name, disguising what he knows so that on their journeys they may think themselves saved and so taste happiness. Don't you see the old man's secret knowledge and deliberate sacrifice as tragic? Can't you credit him with a heartbreaking portion of goodness?"

"Ivan—!" Alyosha felt a pang in his own heart.

"I tell you, brother, that I think such a one has always stood at the forefront of the Roman Church. In his noble obstinacy and love, he stands with a league of such persons established centuries ago to guard the weak and ignorant, to bring them bliss, and to help them abide until Judgment." Ivan paused. "But enough. I sound critic-stung."

"Now I see," Alyosha whispered. "Ivan, you don't believe in God."

Ivan smiled with gentle irony.

"Surely, Ivan, you didn't end your poem with the old man's ugly threat?"

"No, I didn't. Throughout his monologue, the Inquisitor yearned for the Prisoner to break His silence, if only to scold him. But only after he said, 'I have spoken,' did the Prisoner change His expression, from curious to sad. Then He approached the cardinal and kissed his leprous-looking lips. He had no other answer."

"Your poem ends with this mysterious kiss?"

"Not quite. The cardinal shudders, goes to the door, cracks it, and says, 'Go. And never return—*never!*' Into the alley he ushers the Prisoner, who quietly departs."

"And the old man?"

"The kiss kindles in his chest, but he clings to his conviction."

"As you do to yours, Ivan—though I'd call it a delusion rather than an idea."

Ivan laughed. "Easy. It's only a student's silly fantasy. I don't plan to join the old cardinal and the Jesuits in correcting Christ's work. Rather, I hope to live to thirty"—Ivan was now twenty-three— "and then dash my cup to the ground."

"But with such a hellish vision in your heart, how will you survive?"

"In the old Karamazov way, with the strength of the Karamazov baseness."

"Do you mean because 'All is lawful'? Is *that* what you mean?"

Ivan blanched, a little. "Yes: 'All is lawful.' " He added, "I had hoped to have your love, but now I fear that if I fail to disown the saying 'All is lawful,' you won't fail to disown me." Alyosha continued to stare. "Come, dear hermit, speak."

Alyosha leaned across the table and kissed Ivan softly on the lips.

"You *plagiarist!*" Ivan shouted. "But thank you—*thank you*— for your thievery. You honor me."

Together the brothers trod downstairs and briefly conferred outside the tavern. Ivan promised that if he decided to "dash his cup to the ground," he would return from his journeying, even from the American heartland, for one more talk with Alyosha. He urged Alyosha to hasten back to the monastery to see about Father Zosima, for if Father Zosima died in his absence, Alyosha would resent Ivan forever.

To some degree reconciled, the brothers exchanged a final kiss. Then Ivan turned on his heel and hurried purposefully away.

† † †

## Editor's Commentary

*The Brothers Karamazov*, which Fyodor Dostoyevsky published in January 1880, rests among my favorite novels. The section known as "The Grand Inquisitor"—here called "The Inquisitor General" to distinguish my adaptation from its appearances in unabridged translations—spoke to me so strongly that I modeled part of my first science fiction novel, *A Funeral for the Eyes of Fire* (1975), on it. Later, largely because "The Grand Inquisitor" led to my desire to compile a book of Christ fictions, I deliberately sought out tales that painted a variegated portrait of Christ. Such an anthology, I thought, would stand witness to the persistence of his impact and to the variety of responses he still elicits—from believers, skeptics, and deniers.

In *The Brothers Karamazov*, Dostoyevsky set himself the task of refuting Ivan's indictment of God in "The Grand Inquisitor," but long feared that his answer—Father Zosima's sermon in Book VI— was insufficient. According to Geir Kjetsaa, Norwegian author of *Fyodor Dostoyevsky: A Writer's Life* (1987), in December 1879 Dostoyevsky read "The Grand Inquisitor" to some students at St. Petersburg University, prefacing it with an introduction in which he explained that young Ivan, an atheist depressed by his unbelief, writes "a curious, fantastic poem" showing Christ in colloquy with a leader of the Catholic Church, the Inquisitor General. Ivan regards this man as "a true and genuine servant of Christ," despite his atheism, which derives from a Catholic worldview grown distant from the original Apostolic faith. What the poem implies, Dostoyevsky told the students, "is that if the Christian faith is combined and corrupted with the objectives of the world, then the meaning of Christianity will perish" (339). Inevitably, driven by "reason," humanity will adopt unbelief as its credo and set aside the exalted idea of the Church in favor of a new Tower of Babel, in whose shadow human beings will act like herd animals, creating behind the façade of "social love" what Dostoyevsky labeled "an open contempt for humanity" (339).

Kjetsaa asserts that, in writing *The Brothers Karamazov*, the author discovered a powerful truth, "that it is only by *loving life* that man can grasp its meaning" (344). He also contends that the "idea of love as a precondition for a true understanding of life's meaning is one of the main themes" of the novel, and that human beings who suffer must "seek an answer to the problem of life's meaning that is different from the one arrived at with theoretical arguments," i.e., they must unfold to life and allow it to "speak to them" (344). Father Zosima represents one who has embraced love and who eloquently speaks for it, asserting, as Constance Garnett phrases it in her translation (Signet Classic Edition, 1960) that "love is a teacher . . . hard to acquire . . . dearly bought . . . won slowly by long labor. For we must love not only occasionally, for a moment, but forever" (295), words that in the context of the novel identify not only Father Zosima, but also Dostoyevsky, as persons who have journeyed beyond mere rationality into mysticism, for both believe that to embrace love fully one must also embrace suffering—and that by voluntarily accepting suffering, one will receive an answer, and likely an answer suggesting one's own guilt in the promulgation of evil. For a harrowing example, think of the autumn 2006 shooting of ten girls in an Amish schoolhouse in Nickel Mines, Pennsylvania.

Such a problem admits of no easy solution, for which reason Dostoyevsky wrote a novel hundreds of pages long. Look, however, into *Love's Endeavor, Love's Expense: The Response of Being to the Love of God* by W. H. Vanstone (London, 1977), in which the author argues that trying to suppose that God wills some "greater good" in the deaths of innocents (whether at Aberfan in Wales or at Nickel

Mines, Pennsylvania) leaves us grasping only "an alleged 'good' . . . tainted, compromised, and unacceptable: like Ivan Karamazov we would have no part in it and would 'hand in our ticket'" (65). But if God, like Dostoyevsky, qualifies as a creative artist, as Vanstone recurrently asserts, then these disasters represent moments when "the step of creative risk was the step of disaster: the creative process passed out of control" (65). Earlier, though, Vanstone has also informed us that the demand on the artist is to overcome the unforeseeable problem—to handle it in such a way that it becomes a new and unforeseen richness in his work. The artist fails not when he confronts a problem but when he abandons it: and he proves his greatness when he leaves no problem abandoned. Our faith in the Creator is that he leaves no problem abandoned and no evil unredeemed. (64) Further, to assume that God had a prefigured purpose in either of these disasters, or in any outbreak of evil, "is to destroy the basis for any real analogy between divine and human creativity, and to exclude from the activity of God all the precariousness and all the poignancy of love" (65). In short, Vanstone supposes a God as vulnerable in His creative action as human artists in their analogous activities.

*The Brothers Karamazov* is a great novel, "The Inquisitor General" a profoundly challenging constituent of that novel, and Vanstone's *Love's Endeavor, Love's Expense*, which I have unsatisfactorily excerpted here, perhaps the best response to Ivan's outrage at the suffering of innocents that I have ever read. I owe my acquaintance with this eye-opening little book to my friend Randy Loney, and I urge anyone troubled by either *The Brothers Karamazov* or "The Inquisitor General" to seek it out and sample its comforting exegeses of problems seemingly impervious to rational solution.

† † †

*May even Jesus sin . . . by essaying a compassionate deed?*

# THE SIN OF JESUS
## Isaac Babel

Arina had a little room by the grand stairway near the guest rooms, and Sergei, the janitor's assistant, had a room near the service entrance. They had done a shameful deed together. Arina bore Sergei twins on Easter Sunday. Water flows, stars shine, muzhiks feel lust, and Arina again found herself in a delicate condition. She is in her sixth month, the months just roll by when a woman is pregnant, and Sergei ends up being drafted into the army—a fine mess! So Arina goes to him and says, "Listen, Sergunya, there's no point in me sitting around waiting for you. We won't see each other for four years, and I wouldn't be surprised if I had another brood of three or four by the time you come back. Working in a hotel, your skirt is hitched up more often than not. Whoever takes a room here gets to be your lord and master, Jews or whatever. When you come back from the army my womb will be worn out, I'll be washed up as a woman, I don't think I'll be of any use to you."

"True enough," Sergei said, nodding his head.

"The men who want to marry me right now are Trofimich the contractor, he's a rude roughneck, Isai Abramich, a little old man, and then there's the warden of Nilolo-Svyatskoi Church, he's very feeble, but your vigor has rattled my soul to pieces! As the Lord is my witness, I'm all chewed up! In three months I'll be rid of my burden, I'll leave the baby at the orphanage, and I'll go marry them."

When Sergei heard this he took off his belt and gave Arina a heroic beating, aiming for her belly.

"Hey!" the woman says to him. "Don't beat me on the gut, remember it's your stuffing in there, not no one else's!"

She received many savage wallops, he shed many a bitter tear, the woman's blood flowed, but that's neither here nor there. The woman went to Jesus Christ and said:

"This and that, Lord Jesus. Me, I'm Arina, the maid from the Hotel Madrid & Louvre on Tverskaya Street. Working in a hotel, your skirt is hitched up more often than not. Whoever takes a room there gets to be your lord and master, Jews or whatever. Here on walks a humble servant of Yours, Sergei the janitor's assistant. I bore him twins last year on Easter Sunday."

And she told him everything.

"And what if Sergei didn't go to the army?" the Savior pondered.

"The constable would drag him off."

"Ah, the constable," the Savior said, his head drooping. "I'd forgotten all about him. Ah!—and how about if you led a pure life?"

"For four years!" the woman gasped. "Do you mean to say that everyone should stop living a life? You're still singing the same old tune! How are we supposed to go forth and multiply? Do me a favor and spare me such advice!"

Here the Savior's cheeks flushed crimson. The woman had stung him to the quick, but he said nothing. You cannot kiss your own ear, even the Savior knew that.

"This is what you need to do, humble servant of the Lord, glorious maidenly sinner Arina!" the Savior proclaimed in all his glory. "I have a little angel prancing about up in heaven, his name is Alfred, and he's gotten completely out of hand. He keeps moaning, 'Why, O Lord, did you make me an angel at twenty, a fresh lad like me?' I'll give you, Arina, servant of God, Alfred the angel as a husband for four years. He'll be your prayer, your salvation, and your pretty-boy, too. And there's no way you'll get a child from him, not even a duckling, because there's a lot of fun in him, but no substance."

"That's just what I need!" maid Arina cried. "It's their substance that has driven me to the brink of the grave three times in two years!"

"This will be a sweet respite for you, child of God, a light prayer, like a song. Amen."

And thus it was decided. Alfred, a frail, tender youth, was sent down, and fluttering on his pale blue shoulders were two wings, rippling in a rosy glow like doves frolicking in the heavens. Arina hugged him, sobbing with emotion and female tenderness.

"My little Alfredushka, my comfort and joy, my one-and-only!"

The Savior gave her instructions that, before going to bed, she had to take off the angel's wings, which were mounted on hinges, just like door hinges, and she had to take them off and wrap them in a clean sheet for the night, because at the slightest frolic the wings could break as if they were made of infants' sighs and nothing more.

The Savior blessed the union one last time, and called over a choir of abbots for the occasion, their voices thundering in song. There was nothing to eat, not even a hint of food—that wouldn't have been proper—and Arina and Alfred, embracing, descended to earth on a silken rope ladder. They went to Petrovka, that's where the woman dragged him to, she bought him lacquered shoes, checkered tricot trousers (by the way, not only was he not wearing pants, he was completely in the altogether), a hunting frock, and a vest of electric-blue velvet.

"As for the rest, sweetie," she said, "we'll find that at home."

That day Arina did not work in the hotel, she took the day off. Sergei came and made a big to-do outside her room, but she wouldn't open, and called out from behind her door, "Sergei Nifantich, I'm busy washing my feet right now and would be obliged if you would distance yourself with all that to-do!"

He left without saying a word. The angelic power was already taking effect.

Arina cooked a meal fit for a merchant—ha, she was devilishly proud, she was! A quart of vodka, and even some wine, Danube herring with white potatoes, a samovar filled with tea. No sooner had Alfred eaten this earthly substance than he keeled over into a deep sleep. Arina managed to snatch his wings off their hinges just in time. She wrapped them up, and then carried Alfred to her bed.

Lying on her fluffy eiderdown, on her frayed, sin-ridden bed, is a snow-white wonder, an otherworldly brilliance radiating from him. Shafts of moonlight mix with red rays and dart about the room, trippling over their feet. And Arina weeps, rejoices, sings, and prays. The unheard-of, O Arina, has befallen you in this shattered world, blessed art thou among women!

They had drunk down the whole quart of vodka. And it was pretty obvious, too. As they fell asleep, Arina rolled over onto Alfred with the hot, six-month gut that Sergei had saddled her with. You can imagine the weight! It wasn't enough that she was sleeping next to an angel, it wasn't enough that the man next to her wasn't spitting on the wall, or snoring, or snorting—no it wasn't enough for this lusty, crazed wench! She had to warm her bloated, combustible belly even more. And so she crushed the Lord's angel, crushed him in her drunken bliss, crushed him in her rapture like a week-old infant, mangled him beneath her, and he came to a fatal end, and from his wings, wrapped in the sheet, pale tears flowed.

Dawn came, the trees bowed down low. In the distant northern woods, every fir tree turned into a priest, every fir tree genuflected.

The woman comes again before the throne of the Savior. She is strong, her shoulders wide, her red hands carrying the young corpse.

"Behold, Lord!"

This was too much for Jesus' gentle soul, and he cursed the woman from the bottom of his heart.

"As it is in the world, Arina, so it shall be with you!"

"But Lord!" the woman said to him in a low voice. "Was it I who made my body heavy, who brewed the vodka, who made a woman's soul lonely and stupid?"

"I do not wish to have anything further to do with you," Lord Jesus exclaimed. "You have crushed my angel, you trollop, you!" And Arina was hurled back down to earth on a purulent wind, to Tverskaya Street, to her sentence at the Madrid & Louvre. There all caution had been thrown to the winds. Sergei was carousing away the last few days before he had to report as a recruit. Trofimich, the contractor, who had just come back from Kolomna, saw how healthy and red-cheeked she was.

"Ooh what a nice little gut!" he said, among other things.

Isai Abramich, the little old man, came wheezing over when he heard about the little gut.

"After all that has happened," he said, "I cannot settle down with you lawfully, but I can definitely still lie with you."

Six feet under, that's where he should be lying, and not spitting into her soul like everyone else! It was as if they had all broken loose from their chains—dishwashers, peddlers, foreigners. A tradesman likes to have some fun.

And here ends my tale.

Before she gave birth—the remaining three months flew by quickly—Arina went out into the backyard behind the janitor's room, raised her horribly large belly to the silken skies, and idiotically uttered, "Here you are, Lord, here is my gut! They bang on it as if it were a drum. Why, I don't know! And then, Lord, I end up like this again! I've had enough!"

Jesus drenched Arina with his tears. The Savior fell to his knees.

"Forgive me, my Arinushka, sinful God that I am, that I have done this to you!"

"I will not forgive you, Jesus Christ!" Arina replied. "I will not!"

† † †


### Editor's Commentary

What is there to say? The temptation, of course, is to judge Arina rather than Jesus, and to lay the blame for this perplexing episode on her.

Resist, the Savior might well advise us, that temptation.

† † †

*A case, as Flannery O'Connor might have put it, of mystery and manners.*

# THE DETECTIVE OF DREAMS

## Gene Wolfe

I was writing in my office in the rue Madeleine when Andrée, my secretary, announced the arrival of Herr D_____. I rose, put away my correspondence, and offered him my hand. He was, I should say, just short of fifty, had the high, clear complexion characteristic of those who in youth (now unhappily past for both of us) have found more pleasure in the company of horses and dogs and the excitement of the chase than in the bottles and bordels of city life, and wore a beard and mustache of the style popularized by the late emperor. Accepting my invitation to a chair, he showed me his papers.

"You see," he said, "I am accustomed to acting as the representative of my government. In this matter I hold no such position, and it is possible that I feel a trifle lost."

"Many people who come here feel lost," I said. "But it is my boast that I find most of them again. Your problem, I take it, is purely a private matter?"

"Not at all. It is a public matter in the truest sense of the words."

"Yet none of the documents before me—admirably stamped, sealed, and beribboned though they are—indicates that you are other than a private gentleman traveling abroad. And you say you do not represent your government. What am I to think? What is the matter?"

"I act in the public interest," Herr D_____ told me. "My fortune is not great, but I can assure you that in the event of your success you will be well recompensed; although you are to take it that I alone am your principal, yet there are substantial resources available to me."

"Perhaps it would best if you described the problems to me?"

"You are not averse to travel?"

"No."

"Very well then," he said, and so saying launched into one of the most astonishing relations—no, *the* most astonishing relation—I have ever been privileged to hear. Even I, who had at first hand the account of the man who found Paulette Renan with the quince seed still lodged in her throat; who had received Captain Brotte's testimony concerning his finds amid the Antarctic ice; who had heard the history of the woman called Joan O'Neal, who lived for two years behind a painting of herself in the Louvre, from her own lips—even I sat like a child while this man spoke.

When he fell silent, I said, "Herr D_____, after all you have told me, I would accept this mission though there were not a *sou* to be made from it. Perhaps once in a lifetime one comes across a case that must be pursued for its own sake; I think I have found mine."

He leaned forward and grasped my hand with a warmth of feeling that was, I believe, very foreign to his usual nature. "Find and destroy the Dream-Master," he said, "and you shall sit upon a chair of gold, if that is your wish, and eat from a table of gold as well. When will you come to our country?"

"Tomorrow morning," I said. "There are one or two arrangements I must make here before I go."

"I am returning tonight. You may call upon me at any time, and I will apprise you of new developments." He handed me a card. "I am always to be found at this address—if not I, then one who is to be trusted, acting in my behalf."

"I understand."

"This should be sufficient for your initial expenses. You may call me should you require more." The cheque he gave me as he turned to leave represented a comfortable fortune.

I waited until he was nearly out the door before saying, "I thank you, Herr Baron." To his credit, he did not turn; but I had the satisfaction of seeing a red flush rising above the precise white line of his collar before the door closed.

Andrée entered as soon as he had left. "Who was that man? When you spoke to him—just as he was stepping out of your office—he looked as if you had struck him with a whip."

"He will recover," I told her. "He is the Baron H_____, of the secret police of K_____. D_____ was his mother's name. He assumed that because his own desk is a few hundred kilometers from mine, and because he does not permit his likeness to appear in the daily papers, I would not know him; but it was necessary, both for the sake of his opinion of me and my own of myself, that he should discover that I am not so easily deceived. When he recovers from his initial irritation, he will retire tonight with greater confidence in the abilities I will devote to the mission he has entrusted to me."

"It is typical of you, monsieur," Andrée said kindly, "that you are concerned that your clients sleep well."

Her pretty cheek tempted me, and I pinched it. "I am concerned," I replied; "but the Baron will not sleep well."

† † †

My train roared out of Paris through meadows sweet with wild flowers, to penetrate mountain passes in which the danger of avalanches was only just past. The glitter of rushing water, sprung from on high, was everywhere; and when the express slowed to climb a grade, the song of water was everywhere too, water running and shouting down the gray rocks of the Alps. I fell asleep that night with the descant of that icy purity sounding through the plainsong of the rails, and I woke in the station of I_____, the old capital of J_____, now a province of K_____.

I engaged a porter to convey my trunk to the hotel where I had made reservations by telegraph the day before, and amused myself for a few hours by strolling about the city. Here I found the Middle Ages might almost be said to have remained rather than lingered. The city wall was complete on three sides, with its merloned towers in repair; and the cobbled streets surely dated from a period when wheeled traffic of any kind was scarce. As for the buildings—Puss in Boots and his friends must have loved them dearly: there were bulging walls and little panes of bull's-eye glass, and overhanging upper floors one above another until the structures seemed unbalanced as tops. Upon one grey old pile with narrow windows and massive doors, I found a plaque informing me that though it had been first built as a church, it had been successively a prison, a customhouse, a private home, and a school. I investigated further, and discovered it was now an arcade, having been divided, I should think at about the time of the first Louis, into a multitude of dank little stalls. Since it was, as it happened, one of the addresses mentioned by Baron H_____, I went in.

Gas flared everywhere, yet the interior could not have been said to be well lit—each jet was sullen and secretive, as if the proprietor in whose cubicle it was located wished it to light none but his own wares. These cubicles were in no order; nor could I find any directory or guide to lead me to the one I sought. A few customers, who seemed to have visited the place for years, so that they understood where everything was, drifted from one display to the next. When they arrived at each, the proprietor came out, silent (so it seemed to me) as a specter, ready to answer questions or accept a payment; but I never heard a question asked, or saw any money tendered—the customer would finger the edge of a kitchen knife, or hold a garment up to her own shoulders, or turn the pages of some moldering book; and then put the thing down again, and go away.

At last, when I had tired of peeping into alcoves lined with booths still gloomier than the ones on the main concourse outside, I stopped at a leather merchant's and asked the man to direct me to Fräulein A_____.

"I do not know her," he said.

"I am told on good authority that her business is conducted in this building, and that she buys and sells antiques."

"We have several antique dealers here, Herr M_____—"

"I am searching for a young woman. Has your Herr M_____ a niece or a cousin?"

"—handles chairs and chests, largely. Herr O_____, near the guildhall—"

"It is within this building."

"—stocks pictures, mostly. A few mirrors. What is it you wish to buy?"

At this point we were interrupted, mercifully, by a woman from the next booth. "He wants Fräulein A_____. Out of here, and to your left; past the wigmaker's, then right to the stationer's, then left again. She sells old lace."

I found the place at last, and sitting at the very back of her booth Fräulein A_____ herself, a pretty, slender, timid-looking young woman. Her merchandise was spread on two tables; I pretended to examine it and found that it was not old lace she sold but old clothing, much of it trimmed with lace. After a few moments she rose and came out to talk to me, saying, "If you could tell me what you require? . . ." She was taller than I had anticipated, and her flaxen hair would have been very attractive if it were ever released from the tight braids coiled round her head.

"I am only looking. Many of these are beautiful—are they expensive?"

"Not for what you get. The one you are holding is only fifty marks."

"That seems like a great deal."

"They are the fine dresses of long ago—for visiting, or going to the ball. The dresses of wealthy women of aristocratic taste. All are like new; I will not handle anything else. Look at the seams in the one you hold, the tiny stitches all done by hand. Those were the work of dressmakers who created only four or five in a year, and worked twelve and fourteen hours a day, sewing at the first light, and continuing under the lamp, past midnight."

I said, "I see that you have been crying, Fräulein. Their lives were indeed miserable, though no doubt there are people today who suffer equally."

"No doubt there are," the young woman said. "I, however, am not one of them." And she turned away so that I should not see her tears.

"I was informed otherwise."

She whirled about to face me. "You know him? Oh, tell him I am not a wealthy woman, but I will pay whatever I can. Do you really know him?"

"No." I shook my head. "I was informed by your own police."

She stared at me. "But you are an outlander. So is he, I think."

"Ah, we progress. Is there another chair in the rear of your booth? Your police are not above going outside your own country for help, you see, and we should have a little talk."

"They are not our police," the young woman said bitterly, "but I will talk to you. The truth is that I would sooner talk to you, though you are French. You will not tell them that?"

I assured her I would not; we borrowed a chair from the flower stall across the corridor, and she poured forth her story.

"My father died when I was very small. My mother opened this booth to earn our living—old dresses that had belonged to her own mother were the core of her original stock. She died two years ago, and since that time I have taken charge of our business and used it to support myself. Most of my sales are to collectors and theatrical companies. I do not make a great deal of money, but I do not require a great deal, and I have managed to save some. I live alone at Number 877 _____strasse; it is an old house divided into six apartments, and mine is the gable apartment."

"You are young and charming," I said, "and you tell me you have a little money saved. I am surprised you are not married."

"Many others have said the same thing."

"And what did you tell them, Fräulein?"

"To take care of their own affairs. They have called me a man-hater—Frau G_____, who has the confections in the next corridor but two, called me that because I would not receive her son. The truth is that I do not care for people of either sex, young or old. If I want to live by myself and keep my own things to myself, is it not my right to do so?"

"I am sure it is; but undoubtedly it has occurred to you that this person you fear so much may be a rejected suitor who is taking revenge on you."

"But how could he enter and control my dreams?"

"I do not know, Fräulein. It is you who say that he does these things."

"I should remember him, I think, if he had ever called on me. As it is, I am quite certain I have seen him somewhere, but I cannot recall where. Still . . ."

"Perhaps you had better describe your dream to me. You have the same one again and again, as I understand it?"

"Yes. It is like this. I am walking down a dark road. I am both frightened and pleasurably excited, if you know what I mean. Sometimes I walk for a long time, sometimes for what seems to be only a few moments. I think there is moonlight, and once or twice I have noticed stars. Anyway, there is a high, dark hedge, or perhaps a wall, on my right. There are fields to the left, I believe. Eventually I reach a gate of iron bars, standing open—it's not a large gate for wagons or carriages, but a small one, so narrow I can hardly get through. Have you read the writings of Dr. Freud of Vienna? One of the women here mentioned once that he had written concerning dreams, and so I got them from the library, and if I were a man I am sure he would say that entering that gate meant sexual commerce. Do you think I might have unnatural leanings?" Her voice dropped to a whisper.

"Have you ever felt such desires?"

"Oh, no. Quite the reverse."

"Then I doubt it very much," I said. "Go on with your dream. How do you feel as you pass through the gate?"

"As I did when walking down the road, but more so—more frightened, and yet happy and excited. Triumphant, in a way."

"Go on."

"I am in the garden now. There are fountains playing, and nightingales singing in the willows. The air smells of lilies, and a cherry tree in blossom looks like a giantess in her bridal gown. I walk on a straight, smooth path; I think it must be paved with marble chips, because it is white in the moonlight. Ahead of me is the *Schloss*—a great building. There is music coming from inside."

"What sort of music?"

"Magnificent—joyous, if you know what I am trying to say, but not the tinklings of a theater orchestra. A great symphony. I have never been to the opera at Bayreuth; but I think it must be like that—yet a happy, quick tune."

She paused, and for an instant her smile recovered the remembered music. "There are pillars, and a grand entrance, with broad steps. I run up—I am so happy to be there—and throw open the door. It is brightly lit inside; a wave of golden light, almost like a wave from the ocean, strikes me. The room is a great hall, with a high ceiling. A long table is set in the middle and there are hundreds of people seated at it, but one place, the one nearest me, is empty. I cross to it and sit down; there are beautiful loaves on the table, and bowls of honey with roses floating at their centers, and crystal carafes of wine, and many other good things I cannot remember when I awake. Everyone is eating and drinking and talking, and I begin to eat too."

I said, "It is only a dream, Fräulein. There is no reason to weep."

"I dream this each night—I have dreamed so every night for months."

"Go on."

"Then he comes. I am sure he is the one who is causing me to dream like this because I can see his face clearly, and remember it when the dream is over. Sometimes it is very vivid for an hour or more after I wake—so vivid that I have only to close my eyes to see it before me."

"I will ask you to describe him in detail later. For the present, continue with your dream."

"He is tall, and robed like a king, and there is a strange crown on his head. He stands beside me, and though he says nothing, I know that the etiquette of the place demands that I rise and face him. I do this. Sometimes I am sucking my fingers as I get up from his table."

"He owns the dream palace, then."

"Yes, I am sure of that. It is his castle, his home; he is my host. I stand and face him, and I am conscious of wanting very much to please him, but not knowing what it is I should do."

"That must be painful."

"It is. But as I stand there, I become aware of how I am clothed and—"

"How are you clothed?"

"As you see me now. In a plain, dark dress—the dress I wear here in the arcade. But the others—all up and down the hall, all up and down the table—are wearing the dresses I sell here. These dresses." She held one up for me to see, a beautiful creation of many layers of lace, with buttons of polished jet. "I know then that I cannot remain; but the king signals to the others, and they seize me and push me toward the door."

"You are humiliated then?"

"Yes, but the worst thing is that I am aware that he knows that I could never drive myself to leave, and he wishes to spare me the struggle. But outside—some terrible beast has entered the garden. I smell it—like the hyena cage at the *Tiergarten*—as the door opens. And then I wake up."

"It is a harrowing dream."

"You have seen the dresses I sell. Would you credit it that for weeks I slept in one, and then another, and then another of them?"

"You reaped no benefit from that?"

"No. In the dream I was clad as now. For a time I wore the dresses always—even here to the stall, and when I bought food at the market. But it did no good."

"Have you tried sleeping somewhere else?"

"With my cousin who lives on the other side of the city. That made no difference. I am certain that this man I see is a real man. He is in my dream, and the cause of it; but he is not sleeping."

"Yet you have never seen him when you are awake?"

She paused, and I saw her bite at her full lower lip. "I am certain I have."

"Ah!"

"But I cannot remember when. Yet I am sure I have seen him— that I have passed him in the street."

"Think! Does his face associate itself in your mind with some particular section of the city?"

She shook her head.

When I left her at last, it was with a description of the Dream-Master less precise than I had hoped, though still detailed. It tallied in almost all respects with the one given me by Baron H_____; but that proved nothing, since the baron's description might have been based largely on Fräulein A_____'s.

††† 

The bank of Herr R_____ was a private one, as all the greatest banks in Europe are. It was located in what had once been the town house of some noble family (their arms, overgrown now with ivy, were still visible above the door), and bore no identification other than a small brass plate engraved with the names of Herr R_____ and his partners. Within, the atmosphere was more dignified—even if, perhaps, less tasteful—than it could possibly have been in the noble family's time. Dark pictures in gilded frames lined the walls, and the clerks sat at inlaid tables upon chairs upholstered in tapestry. When I asked for Herr R_____, I was told that it would be impossible to see him that afternoon; I sent in a note with a sidelong allusion to "unquiet dreams," and within five minutes I was ushered into a luxurious office that must once have been the bedroom of the head of the household.

Herr R_____ was a large man—tall, and heavier (I thought) than his physician was likely to have approved. He appeared to be about fifty; there was strength in his wide, fleshy face; his high forehead and capacious cranium suggested intellect; and his small, dark eyes, forever flickering as they took in the appearance of my person, the expression of my face, and the position of my hands and feet, ingenuity.

No pretense was apt to be of service with such a man, and I told him flatly that I had come as the emissary of Baron H_____, that I knew what troubled him, and that if he would cooperate with me I would help him if I could.

"I know you, monsieur," he said, "by reputation. A business with which I am associated employed you three years ago in the matter of a certain mummy." He named the firm. "I should have thought of you myself."

"I did not know that you were connected with them."

"I am not, when you leave this room. I do not know what reward Baron H_____ has offered you should you apprehend the man who is oppressing me, but I will give you, in addition to that, a sum equal to that you were paid for the mummy. You should be able to retire to the south then, should you choose, with the rent of a dozen villas."

"I do not choose," I told him, "and I could have retired long before. But what you just said interests me. You are certain that your persecutor is a living man?"

"I know men." Herr R_____ leaned back in his chair and stared at the painted ceiling. "As a boy I sold stuffed cabbage-leaf rolls in the street—did you know that? My mother cooked them over wood she collected herself where buildings were being demolished, and I sold them from a little cart for her. I lived to see her with half a score of footmen and the finest house in Lindau. I never went to school; I learned to add and subtract in the streets—when I must multiply and divide I have my clerk do it. But I learned men. Do you think that now, after forty years of practice, I could be deceived by a phantom? No, he is a man—let me confess it, a stronger man than I—a man of flesh and blood and brain, a man I have seen somewhere, sometime, here in this city—and more than once."

"Describe him."

"As tall as I. Younger—perhaps thirty or thirty-five. A brown, forked beard, so long." (He held his hand about fifteen centimeters beneath his chin.) "Brown hair. His hair is not yet grey, but I think it may be thinning a little at the temples."

"Don't you remember?"

"In my dreams he wears a garland of roses—I cannot be sure."

"Is there anything else? Any scars or identifying marks?"

Herr R_____ nodded. "He has hurt his hand. In my dream, when he holds out his hand for the money, I see blood in it—it is his own, you understand, as though a recent injury had reopened and was beginning to bleed again. His hands are long and slender—like a pianist's."

"Perhaps you had better tell me your dream."

"Of course." He paused, and his face clouded, as though to recount the dream were to return to it. "I am in a great house. I am a person of importance there, almost as though I were the owner; yet I am not the owner—"

"Wait," I interrupted. "Does this house have a banquet hall? Has it a pillared portico, and is it set in a garden?"

For a moment Herr R_____'s eyes widened. "Have you also had such dreams?"

"No," I said. "It is only that I think I have heard of this house before. Please continue."

"There are many servants—some work in the fields beyond the garden. I give instructions to them—the details differ each night, you understand. Sometimes I am concerned with the kitchen, sometimes with livestock, sometimes with the draining of a field. We grow wheat, principally, it seems; but there is a vineyard too, and a kitchen garden. And of course the house must be cleaned and swept and kept in repair. There is no wife; the owner's mother lives with us, I think, but she does not much concern herself with the housekeeping—that is up to me. To tell the truth, I have never actually seen her, though I have the feeling that she is there."

"Does this house resemble the one you bought for your mother in Lindau?"

"Only as one large house must resemble another."

"I see. Proceed."

"For a long time each night I continue like that, giving orders, and sometimes going over the accounts. Then a servant, usually it is a maid, arrives to tell me that the owner wishes to speak to me. I stand before a mirror—I can see myself there as plainly as I see you now—and arrange my clothing. The maid brings rose-scented water and a cloth, and I wipe my face; then I go in to him.

"He is always in one of the upper rooms, seated at a table with his own account book spread before him. There is an open window behind him, and through it I can see the top of a cherry tree in bloom. For a long time—oh, I suppose ten minutes—I stand before him while he turns over the pages of his ledger."

"You appear somewhat at a loss, Herr R____—not a common condition for you, I believe. What happens then?"

"He says, 'You owe . . .'" Herr R____ paused. "That is the problem, monsieur, I can never recall the amount. But it is a large sum. He says, 'And I must require that you make payment at once.'

"I do not have the amount, and I tell him so. He says, 'Then you must leave my employment.' I fall to my knees at this and beg that he will retain me, pointing out that if he dismisses me I will have lost my source of income, and will never be able to make payment. I do not enjoy telling you this, but I weep. Sometimes I beat the floor with my fists."

"Continue. Is the Dream-Master moved by your pleading?"

"No. He again demands that I pay the entire sum. Several times I have told him that I am a wealthy man in this world, and that if only he would permit me to make payment in its currency, I would do so immediately."

"That is interesting—most of us lack your presence of mind in our nightmares. What does he say then?"

"Usually he tells me not to be a fool. But once he said, 'That is a dream—you must know it by now. You cannot expect to pay a real debt with the currency of sleep.' He holds out his hand for the money as he speaks to me. It is then that I see the blood in his palm."

"You are afraid of him?"

"Oh, very much so. I understand that he has the most complete power over me. I weep, and at last I throw myself at his feet—with my head under the table, if you can credit it, crying like an infant.

"Then he stands and pulls me erect and says, 'You would never be able to pay all you owe, and you are a false and dishonest servant. But your debt is forgiven, forever.' And as I watch, he tears a leaf from his account book and hands it to me."

"Your dream has a happy conclusion, then."

"No. It is not yet over. I thrust the paper into the front of my shirt and go out, wiping my face on my sleeve. I am conscious that if any of the other servants should see me, they will know at once what has happened. I hurry to reach my own counting room; there is a brazier there, and I wish to burn the page from the owner's book."

"I see."

"But just outside the door of my own room, I meet another servant—an upper-servant like myself, I think, since he is well dressed. As it happens, this man owes me a considerable sum of money, and to conceal from him what I have just endured, I demand that he pay at once." Herr R_____ rose from his chair and began to pace the room, looking sometimes at the painted scenes on the walls, sometimes at the Turkish carpet at his feet. "I have had reason to demand money like that often, you understand. Here in this room.

"The man falls to his knees, weeping and begging for additional time; but I reach down, like this, and seize him by the throat."

"And then?"

"And then the door of my counting room opens. But it is not my counting room with my desk and the charcoal brazier, but the owner's own room. He is standing in the doorway, and behind him I can see the open window, and the blossoms of the cherry tree."

"What does he say to you?"

"Nothing. He says nothing to me. I release the other man's throat, and he slinks away."

"You awaken then?"

"How can I explain it? Yes, I wake up. But first we stand there; and while we do I am conscious of . . . certain sounds."

"If it is too painful for you, you need not say more."

Herr R_____ drew a silk handkerchief from his pocket, and wiped his face. "How can I explain?" he said again. "When I hear those sounds, I am aware that the owner possesses certain other servants, who have never been under my direction. It is as though I have always known this, but had no reason to think of it before."

"I understand."

"They are quartered in another part of the house—in the vaults beneath the wine cellar, I think sometimes. I have never seen them, but I know—then—that they are hideous, vile and cruel; I know too that he thinks me but little better than they, and that as he permits me to serve him, so he allows them to serve him also. I stand—we stand—and listen to them coming through the house. At last a door at the end of the hall begins to swing open. There is a hand like the paw of some filthy reptile on the latch."

"Is that the end of the dream?"

"Yes." Herr R_____ threw himself into his chair again, mopping his face.

"You have this experience each night?"

"It differs," he said slowly, "in some details."

"You have told me that the orders you give the under-servants vary."

"There is another difference. When the dreams began, I woke when the hinges of the door at the passage-end creaked. Each night now the dream endures a moment longer. Perhaps a tenth of a second. Now I see the arm of the creature who opens that door, nearly to the elbow."

I took the address of his home, which he was glad enough to give me, and leaving the bank made my way to my hotel.

† † †

When I had eaten my roll and drunk my coffee the next morning, I went to the place indicated by the card given me by Baron H_____, and in a few minutes was sitting with him in a room as bare as those tents from which armies in the field are cast into battle. "You are ready to begin the case this morning?" he asked.

"On the contrary. I have already begun; indeed, I am about to enter a new phase of my investigation. You would not have come to me if your Dream-Master were not torturing someone other than the people whose names you gave me. I wish to know the identity of that person, and to interrogate him."

"I told you that there were many other reports. I—"

"Provided me with a list. They are all of the petite bourgeoisie, when they are not persons still less important. I believed at first that it might be because of the urgings of Herr R____ that you engaged me; but when I had time to reflect on what I know of your methods, I realized that you would have demanded that he provide my fee had that been the case. So you are sheltering someone of greater importance, and I wish to speak to him."

"The Countess—" Baron H____ began.

"Ah!"

"The Countess herself has expressed some desire that you should be presented to her. The Count opposes it."

"We are speaking, I take it, of the governor of this province?"

The Baron nodded. "Of Count von V____. He is responsible, you understand, only to the Queen Regent herself."

"Very well. I wish to hear the Countess, and she wishes to talk with me. I assure you, Baron, that we will meet; the only question is where it will be under your auspices."

† † †

The Countess, to whom I was introduced that afternoon, was a woman in her early twenties, deep-breasted and somber-haired, with skin like milk, and great dark eyes welling with fear and (I thought) pity, set in a perfect oval face.

"I am glad you have come, monsieur. For seven weeks now our good Baron H____ has sought this man for me, but he has not found him."

"If I had known my presence here would please you, Countess, I would have come long ago, whatever the obstacles. You then, like the others, are certain it is a real man we seek?"

"I seldom go out, monsieur. My husband feels we are in constant danger of assassination."

"I believe he is correct."

"But on state occasions we sometimes ride in a glass coach to the *Rathaus*. There are uhlans all around us to protect us then. I am certain that—before the dreams began—I saw the face of this man in the crowd."

"Very well. Now tell me your dream."

"I am here, at home—"

"In this palace, where we sit now?"

She nodded.

"That is a new feature, then. Continue, please."

"There is to be an execution. In the garden." A fleeting smile crossed the Countess's lovely face. "I need not tell you that that is not where the executions are held; but it does not seem strange to me when I dream.

"I have been away, I think, and have only just heard of what is to take place. I rush into the garden. The man Baron H_____ calls the Dream-Master is there, tied to the trunk of the big cherry tree; a squad of soldiers faces him, holding their rifles; their officer stands beside them with his saber drawn, and my husband is watching from a pace or two away. I call out for them to stop, and my husband turns to look at me. I say: 'You must not do it, Karl. You must not kill this man.' But I see by his expression that he believes that I am only a foolish, tenderhearted child. Karl is . . . several years older than I."

"I am aware of it."

"The Dream-Master turns his head to look at me. People tell me that my eyes are large—do you think them large, monsieur?"

"Very large, and very beautiful."

"In my dream, quite suddenly, his eyes seem far, far larger than mine, and far more beautiful; and in them I see reflected the figure of my husband. Please listen carefully now, because what I am going to say is very important, though it makes very little sense, I am afraid."

"Anything may happen in a dream, Countess."

"When I see my husband reflected in this man's eyes, I know— I cannot say how—that it is this reflection, and not the man who stands near me, who is the real Karl. The man I have thought real is only a reflection of that reflection. Do you follow what I say?"

I nodded. "I believe so."

"I plead again: 'Do not kill him. Nothing good can come of it . . .' My husband nods to the officer, the soldiers raise their rifles, and . . . and . . .'"

"You wake. Would you like my handkerchief, Countess? It is of coarse weave; but it is clean, and much larger than your own."

"Karl is right—I am only a foolish little girl. No, monsieur, I do not wake—not yet. The soldiers fire. The Dream-Master falls forward, though his bonds hold him to the tree. And Karl flies to bloody rags beside me."

††† 

On my way back to the hotel I purchased a map of the city; and when I reached my room I laid it flat on the table there. There could be no question of the route of the Countess's glass coach— straight down the Hauptstrasse, the only street in the city wide enough to take a carriage surrounded by cavalrymen. The most probable route by which Herr R_____ might go from his house to his bank coincided with the Hauptstrasse for several blocks. The path Fräulein A_____ would travel from her flat to the arcade crossed the Hauptstrasse at a point contained by that interval. I need to know no more.

Very early the next morning I took up my post at the intersection. If my man were still alive after the fusillade Count von V_____ fired at him each night, it seemed certain that he would appear at this spot within a few days, and I am hardened to waiting. I smoked cigarettes while I watched the citizens of I_____ walk up and down before me. When an hour had passed, I bought a newspaper from a vendor, and stole a few glances at its pages when foot traffic was light.

Gradually I became aware that I was watched—we boast of reason, but there are senses over which reason holds no authority. I did not know where my watcher was, yet I felt his gaze on me, whichever way I turned. So, I thought, you know me, my friend. Will I too dream now? What has attracted your attention to a mere foreigner, a stranger, waiting for who-knows-what at this corner? Have you been talking to Fräulein A_____? Or to someone who has spoken to her?

Without appearing to do so, I looked up and down both streets in search of another lounger like myself. There was no one—not a drowsing grandfather, not a woman or a child, not even a dog. Certainly no tall man with a forked beard and piercing eyes. The windows then—I studied them all, looking for some movement in a dark room behind a seemingly innocent opening. Nothing.

Only the buildings behind me remained. I crossed to the opposite side of the Hauptstrasse and looked once more. Then I laughed.

They must have thought me mad, all those dour burghers, for I fairly doubled over, spitting my cigarette to the sidewalk and clasping my hands to my waist for fear my belt would burst. The presumption, the impudence, the brazen insolence of the fellow! The stupidity, the wonderful stupidity of myself, who had not recognized his old stories! For the remainder of my life now, I could accept any case with pleasure, pursue the most inept criminal with zest, knowing that there was always a chance he might outwit such an idiot as I.

For the Dream-Master had set up His own picture, and full-length, and in the most gorgeous colors, in His window. Choking and sputtering I saluted it, and then, still filled with laughter, I crossed the street once more and went inside, where I knew I would find Him. A man awaited me there—not the one I sought, but one who understood Whom it was I had come for, and knew as well as I that His capture was beyond any thief-taker's power. I knelt, and there, though not to the satisfaction I suppose of Baron H____, Fräulein A____, Herr R____, and the Count and the Countess von V____, I destroyed the Dream-Master as He has been sacrificed so often, devouring His white, wheaten flesh that we might all possess life without end.

Dear people, dream on.

††††

## Author's Commentary

For something like thirty years now I've been teaching writing—for Clarion East and Clarion West, Haystack, Florida Atlantic U., Columbia College, and so on. I've learned to know would-be writers pretty well, and one of the things I've learned is that just about all of them will tell you that evil is scarier than good, more interesting than good, and sexier than good. That is what every last one of them believes, and every last one of them is wrong.

The perpetual puzzle is not Lucifer—anyone who tries will exhaust him pretty quickly—but Christ, the God-man. His disciples, who saw Him, ate with Him, and talked with Him, did not understand Him. What's more, they *knew* that they did not; the gospels make that very plain. Although separated from Him by two thousand years, we are quick to assume that we know Him through and through, this Prince of Peace who got along so well with Roman soldiers and drove out the moneychangers with a whip. Who would not grant His mother an interview. Who withered the fig tree, though it was not the season for figs. G. K. Chesterton said it was a good thing He told us He was meek and humble of heart since we would not have guessed it otherwise.

He was a human being, and not less of a human being because He was so much more. If we could examine Him today, we would find that He had human DNA. He would have a human blood type, Type O or Type A or whatever, and could give a transfusion to a man or woman with the same blood type. (I cannot even begin to speculate on what the result of such a transfusion might be.) His mother was a human woman, and through her He was descended from the first man as well as the first woman.

So am I. So are you.

He knew how terribly easy it would be for us to see Him merely as a god in human form, scarcely different from some Greek divinity come down from Mount Olympus to seduce a shepherdess. He knew it; and thus He, who was in fact the Son of God, insisted over and over again that He was the Son of Man.

As indeed He was.

Once we came to arrest Him with swords and clubs. Why then shouldn't He be the quarry in a detective story? How many millions have sought Him! And how many millions have found Him!

If I have dishonored or displeased Him by my little tale, I am most heartily sorry for it; but I feel certain that He will forgive me. After all, He is a fine short-story writer Himself.

✝ ✝ ✝

*Under the Big Sky pampas, the Sea of Faith floods in.*

# THE GOSPEL ACCORDING TO MARK

## Jorge Luis Borges

The incident took place on the Los Alamos ranch, south of the small town of Junín, in late March of 1928. Its protagonist was a medical student named Baltasar Espinosa. We might define him for the moment as a Buenos Aires youth much like many others, with no traits worthier of note than the gift for public speaking that had won him more than one prize at the English school in Ramos Mejía and an almost unlimited goodness. He didn't like to argue; he preferred that his interlocutor rather than he himself be right. And though he found the chance twists and turns of gambling interesting, he was a poor gambler because he didn't like to win. He was intelligent and open to learning, but he was lazy; at thirty-three he had not yet completed the last requirements for his degree. (The work he still owed, incidentally, was for his favorite class.) His father, like all the gentlemen of his day a freethinker, had instructed Espinosa in the doctrines of Herbert Spencer, but once, before he set off on a trip to Montevideo, his mother had asked him to say the Lord's Prayer every night and make the sign of the cross, and never in all the years that followed did he break that promise. He did not lack courage; one morning, with more indifference than wrath, he had traded two or three blows with some of his classmates that were trying to force him to join a strike at the university. He abounded in debatable habits and opinions, out of a spirit of acquiescence; his country mattered less to him than the danger that people in other countries might think Argentines still wore feathers; he venerated France but had contempt for the French; he had little respect for Americans but took pride in the fact that there were skyscrapers in Buenos Aires; he thought that the gauchos of the plains were better horsemen than the gauchos of the mountains. When his cousin Daniel invited him to spend the summer at Los Alamos, he immediately accepted—not because he liked the county but out of a natural desire to please, and because he could find no good reason for saying no.

The main house at the ranch was large and a bit run-down; the quarters for the foreman, a man named Gutre, stood nearby. There were three members of the Gutre family: the father, the son (who was singularly rough and unpolished), and a girl of uncertain paternity. They were tall, strong, and bony, with reddish hair and Indian features. They rarely spoke. The foreman's wife had died years before.

In the country, Espinosa came to learn things he hadn't known, had never even suspected; for example, that when you're approaching a house there's no reason to gallop and that nobody goes out on a horse unless there's a job to be done. As the summer wore on, he learned to distinguish birds by their call.

Within a few days, Daniel had to go to Buenos Aires to close a deal on some livestock. At the most, he said, the trip would take a week. Espinosa, who was already a little tired of his cousin's *bonnes fortunes* and his indefatigable interest in the vagaries of men's tailoring, stayed behind on the ranch with his textbooks. The heat was oppressive, and not even nightfall brought relief. Then one morning toward dawn, he was awakened by thunder. Wind lashed the casuarina trees. Espinosa heard the first drops of rain and gave thanks to God. Suddenly the wind blew cold. That afternoon, the Salado overflowed.

The next morning, as he stood on the porch looking out over the flood plains, Baltasar Espinosa realized that the metaphor equating the pampas with the sea was not, at least that morning, an altogether false one, though Hudson had noted that the sea seems the grander of the two because we view it not from horseback or our own height, but from the deck of a ship. The rain did not let up; the Gutres, helped (or hindered) by the city dweller, saved a good part of the livestock, though many animals were drowned. There were four roads leading to the ranch; all were under water. On the third day, when a leaking roof threatened the foreman's house, Espinosa gave the Gutres a room at the back of the main house, alongside the toolshed. The move brought Espinosa and the Gutres closer, and they began to eat together in the large dining room. Conversation was not easy; the Gutres, who knew so much about things in the country, did not know how to explain them. One night Espinosa asked them if people still remembered anything about the Indian raids, back when the military command for the frontier had been in Junín. They told him they did, but they would have given the same answer if he had asked them about the day Charles I had been beheaded. Espinosa recalled that his father used to say that all the cases of longevity that occur in the country are the result of either poor memory or a vague notion of dates—gauchos quite often know neither the year they were born in nor the name of the man that fathered them.

In the entire house, the only reading material to be found were several copies of a farming magazine, a manual of veterinary medicine, a deluxe edition of the romantic verse drama *Tabaré*, a copy of *The History of the Shorthorn in Argentina*, several erotic and detective stories, and a recent novel that Espinosa had not read— *Don Segundo Sombra*, by Ricardo Güiraldes. In order to put some life into the inevitable after-dinner attempt at conversation, Espinosa read a couple of chapters of the novel to the Gutres, who did not know how to read or write. Unfortunately, the foreman had been a cattle drover himself, and he could not be interested in the adventures of another such a one. It was easy work, he said; they always carried along a pack mule with everything they might need. If he had not been a cattle drover, he announced, he'd never have seen Lake Gómez, or the Bragado River, or even the Núñez ranch, in Chacabuco. . . .

In the kitchen there was a guitar; before the incident I am narrating, the laborers would sit in a circle and someone would pick up the guitar and strum it, though never managing actually to play it. That was called "giving it a strum."

Espinosa, who was letting his beard grow out, would stop before the mirror to look at his changed face; he smiled to think that he'd soon be boring the fellows in Buenos Aires with his stories about the Salado overrunning its banks. Curiously, he missed places in the city he never went, and would never go: a street corner on Cabrera where a mailbox stood; two cement lions on a porch on Calle Jujuy a few blocks from the Plaza del Once; a tile-floored corner grocery-store-and-bar (whose location he couldn't quite remember). As for this father and his brothers, by now Daniel would have told them that he had been isolated—the word was etymologically precise— by the floodwaters.

Exploring the house still cut off by the high water, he came upon a Bible printed in English. On its last pages the Guthries (for that was their real name) had kept their history. They had come originally from Inverness and had arrived in the New World—doubtlessly as peasant laborers—in the early nineteenth century; they had intermarried with Indians. The chronicle came to an end in the eighteen-seventies; they no longer knew how to write. Within a few generations they had forgotten their English; by the time Espinosa met them, even Spanish gave them difficulty. They had no faith, though in their veins, alongside the superstitions of the pampas, there still ran a dim current of the Calvinist's hard fanaticism. Espinosa mentioned his find to them, but they hardly seemed to hear him.

He leafed through the book, and his fingers opened it to the first verses of the Gospel According to St. Mark. To try his hand at translating, and perhaps to see if they might understand a little of it, he decided that would be the text he read the Gutres after dinner. He was surprised that they listened first attentively and then with mute fascination. The presence of gold letters on the binding may have given it increased authority. "It's in their blood," he thought. It also occurred to him that throughout history, humankind has told two stories: the story of a lost ship sailing the Mediterranean seas in quest of a beloved isle, and the story of a god who allow himself to be crucified on Golgotha. He recalled his elocution classes in Ramos Mejia, and he rose to his feet to preach the parables.

In the following days, the Gutres would wolf down the spitted beef and canned sardines in order to arrive sooner at the Gospel.

The girl had a little lamb; it was her pet, and she prettied it with a sky blue ribbon. One day it cut itself on a piece of barbed wire; to stanch the blood, the Gutres were about to put spiderwebs on the wound, but Espinosa treated it with pills. The gratitude awakened by that cure amazed him. At first, he had not trusted the Gutres and had hidden away in one of his books the two hundred forty pesos he'd brought; now, with Daniel gone, he had taken the master's place and begun to give timid orders, which were immediately followed. The Gutres would trail him through the rooms and along the hallway, as though they were lost. As he read, he noticed that they would sweep away the crumbs he had left on the table. One afternoon, he surprised them as they were discussing him in brief, respectful words. When he came to the end of the Gospel According to St. Mark, he started to read another of the three remaining gospels, but the father asked him to reread the one he'd just finished, so they could understand it better. Espinosa felt they were like children, who prefer repetition to variety or novelty. One night he dreamed of the Flood (which is not surprising) and was awakened by the hammering of the building of the Ark, but he told himself it was thunder. And in fact the rain, which had let up for a while, had begun again; it was very cold. The Gutres told him the rain had broken through the roof of the toolshed; when they got the beams repaired, they said, they'd show him where. He was no longer a stranger, a foreigner, and they all treated him with respect; he was almost spoiled. None of them liked coffee, but there was always a little cup for him, with spoonfuls of sugar stirred in.

That second storm took place on a Tuesday. Thursday night there was a soft knock on his door; because of his doubts about the Gutres he always locked it. He got up and opened the door; it was the girl. In the darkness he couldn't see her, but he could tell by her footsteps that she was barefoot, and afterward, in the bed, that she was naked—that in fact she had come from the back of the house that way. She did not embrace him, or speak a word; she lay down beside him and she was shivering. It was the first time she had lain with a man. When she left, she did not kiss him; Espinosa realized that he didn't even know her name. Impelled by some sentiment he did not attempt to understand, he swore that when he returned to Buenos Aires, he'd tell no one of the incident.

The next day began like all the others, except that the father spoke to Espinosa to ask whether Christ had allowed himself to be killed in order to save all mankind. Espinosa, who was a freethinker like his father but felt obliged to defend what he had read to them, paused.

"Yes," he finally replied. "To save all mankind from hell."

"What *is* hell?" Gutre then asked him.

"A place underground where souls will burn in fire forever."

"And those that drove the nails will also be saved?"

"Yes," replied Espinosa, whose theology was a bit shaky. (He had worried that the foreman wanted to have a word with him about what had happened last night with his daughter.)

After lunch they asked him to read the last chapters again.

Espinosa had a long siesta that afternoon, although it was a light sleep, interrupted by persistent hammering and vague premonitions. Toward evening he got up and went out into the hall.

"The water's going down," he said, as though thinking out loud. "It won't be long now."

"Not long now," repeated Gutre, like an echo.

The three of them had followed him. Kneeling on the floor, they asked his blessing. Then they cursed him, spat on him, and drove him to the back of the house. The girl was weeping. Espinosa realized what awaited him on the other side of the door. When they opened it, he saw the sky. A bird screamed; *it's a goldfinch*, Espinosa thought. There was no roof on the shed; they had torn down the roof beams to build the Cross.

† † †

## Editor's Commentary

In his seminal study about Christ fictions, *Fictional Transfigurations of Jesus*, Theodore Ziolkowski notes that the most famous novel of the literary genre that he terms *imitatio Christi* (in which the "hero" decides to live life in accordance with the tenets modeled or commanded by Jesus in the Gospels) is the "Bible Belt classic, *In His Steps* (1896)" by Charles M. Sheldon. An inspirational tome that inspired millions, *In His Steps* prompted Glenn Clark, a half century later, to write a sequel, *What Would Jesus Do?* (1950), the title of which become a watchword among young believers in the late twentieth and early twenty-first centuries.

The medical student Baltasar Espinosa probably never read the first of these two titles and had no opportunity to read the second. Indeed, Espinosa's in-his-steps journey derives from a horrific inadvertence. And the power of "The Gospel According to Mark" derives both from this inadvertence and the well-intentioned but abominable act that the Gutres family carries out in the name of Mark's protagonist. Was Borges deliberately writing about the evil that human beings do one another out of religious faith? I don't know, but the ramifications of the Gutres' ignorance and of Espinosa's cluelessness echo across our planet even today.

† † †

*A parable in the tradition of the Parable Maker . . .*

# RAGMAN
## Walter Wangerin Jr.

I saw a strange sight. I stumbled upon a story most strange, like nothing in my life, my street sense, my sly tongue had ever prepared me for.

Hush, child. Hush, now, and I will tell it to you.

### † † †

Even before the dawn one Friday morning I noticed a young man, handsome and strong, walking the alleys of our City. He was pulling an old cart filled with clothes both bright and new, and he was calling in a clear, tenor voice: "Rags!" Ah, the air was foul and the first light filthy to be crossed by such sweet music.

"Rags! New rags for old! I take your tired rags! Rags!"

"Now, this is a wonder," I thought to myself, for the man stood six feet four, and his arms were like tree limbs, hard and muscular, and his eyes flashed intelligence. Could he find no better job than this, to be a ragman in the inner city?

I followed him. My curiosity drove me. And I wasn't disappointed.

Soon the Ragman saw a woman sitting on her back porch. She was sobbing into a handkerchief, sighing, and shedding a thousand tears. Her knees and elbows made a sad X. Her shoulders shook. Her heart was breaking.

The Ragman stopped his cart. Quietly, he walked to the woman, stepping round tin cans, dead toys, and Pampers.

"Give me your rag," he said so gently, "and I'll give you another."

He slipped the handkerchief from her eyes. She looked up, and he laid across her palm a linen cloth so clean and new that it shined. She blinked from the gift to the giver.

Then, as he began to pull his cart again, the Ragman did a strange thing: he put her stained handkerchief to his own face; and then *he* began to weep, to sob as grievously as she had done, his shoulders shaking. Yet she was left without a tear.

"This *is* a wonder," I breathed to myself, and I followed the sobbing Ragman like a child who cannot turn away from mystery.

"Rags! Rags! New rags for old!"

In a little while, when the sky showed grey behind the roof tops and I could see the shredded curtains hanging out black windows, the Ragman came upon a girl whose head was wrapped in a bandage, whose eyes were empty. Blood soaked her bandage. A single line of blood ran down her cheek.

Now the tall Ragman looked upon this child with pity, and he drew a lovely yellow bonnet from his cart.

"Give me your rag," he said, tracing his own line on her cheek, "and I'll give you mine."

The child could only gaze at him while he loosened the bandage, removed it, and tied it to his own head. The bonnet he set on hers. And I gasped at what I saw, for with the bandage went the wound! Against his brow it ran a darker, more substantial blood—his own!

"Rags! Rags! I take old rags!" cried the sobbing, bleeding, strong, intelligent Ragman.

The sun hurt both the sky, now, and my eyes; the Ragman seemed more and more to hurry.

"Are you going to work?" he asked a man who leaned against a telephone pole. The man shook his head.

The Ragman pressed him: "Do you have a job?"

"Are you crazy?" sneered the other. He pulled away from the pole, revealing the right sleeve of his jacket—flat, the cuff stuffed into the pocket. He had no arm.

"So," said the Ragman. "Give me your jacket, and I'll give you mine."

Such quiet authority in his voice!

The one-armed man took off his jacket. So did the Ragman— and I trembled at what I saw: for the Ragman's arm stayed in its sleeve, and when the other put it on he had two good arms, thick as tree limbs, but the Ragman had only one.

"Go to work!" he said.

After that he found a drunk, lying unconscious beneath an army blanket, an old man, hunched, wizened, and sick. He took that blanket and wrapped it round himself, but for the drunk he left new clothes.

† † †

And now I had to run to keep up with the Ragman. Though he was weeping uncontrollably, and bleeding freely at the forehead, pulling his cart with one arm, stumbling for drunkenness, falling again and again, exhausted, old, old, and sick, yet he went with ter- rible speed. On spider's legs he skittered through the alleys of the City, this mile and the next, until he came to its limits, and then he rushed beyond.

I wept to see the change in this man. I hurt to see his sorrow. And yet I needed to see where he was going in such haste, perhaps to know what drove him so.

The little old Ragman—he came to a landfill. He came to the garbage pits. And then I wanted to help him in what he did, but I hung back, hiding. He climbed a hill. With tormented labor he cleared a little space on that hill. Then he sighed. He lay down. He pillowed his head on a handkerchief and a jacket. He covered his bones with an army blanket. And he died.

Oh, how I cried to witness that death! I slumped in a junked car and wailed and mourned as one who has no hope—because I had come to love the Ragman. Every other face had faded in the wonder of this man, and I cherished him; but he died. I sobbed myself to sleep.

I did not know—how could I know?—that I slept through Friday night and Saturday and its night, too.

But then, on Sunday morning, I was wakened by a violence.

Light—pure, hard, demanding light—slammed against my sour face, and I blinked, and I looked, and I saw the last and first wonder of all. There was the Ragman, folding the blanket most carefully, a scar on his forehead, but alive! And, besides, that, healthy! There was no sign of sorrow or of age, and all the rags that he had gathered shined for cleanliness.

Well, then I lowered my head and, trembling for all that I had seen, I myself walked up to the Ragman. I told him my name with shame, for I was a sorry figure next to him. Then I took off all my clothes in that place, and I said to him with dear yearning in my voice: "Dress me."

He dressed me. My Lord, he put new rags on me, and I am a wonder beside him. The Ragman, the Ragman, the Christ!

✝ ✝ ✝

## Editor's Commentary

At a Saturday morning breakfast of United Methodist Men, I first heard this story read as a devotional by my friend Lamar Hamric. In a brief piece that he calls "An Invocation," which begins his book *Ragman: And Other Cries of Faith* (HarperSanFrancisco, 2004), Walter Wangerin Jr. writes, "In the oily streets, damp with rain and human sin, lit by a single light, I see your face reflected, O God, your incarnation's in the streets. I see the city, and I cannot help but see you" (ix).

And I cannot help but hazard that the city of which Wangerin speaks is the City of God implicit in our world.

✝ ✝ ✝

*What if God were one of us?*

# CHRISTUS DESTITUTUS

## Bud Webster

Jesus lay dying in a five-dollar flop. Dark against the sheets, his face and hands were marked and bent by every day of his seventy years; his thin body barely made a dent in the old mattress.

None of the beds in the shelter's clinic were empty. There was no shortage of old men too poor for the hospitals or for whom there was no room elsewhere. Once, he had tended the hopeless old men in these beds; now, he was just one more of them.

"Yeshua bar-Yosef." The voice was lifeless; the words a statement, not a question. It was his birth name: no one had called him that for two thousand years.

He opened his eyes.

"Oh," he said, "it's you. What are you doing here?"

The old man glanced down the aisle at the floor supervisor. If he'd heard the voices, he gave no sign. The words weren't English—weren't any Earthly tongue—but it wouldn't matter anyway; there was always the low murmur of voices here. Some patients prayed; some babbled, or cried out in pain. If you were here long enough, you got used to it.

Vic wouldn't see the angel standing over the old man's bed.

† † †

"I am here for you," the angel said.

"Yeah, well, I didn't call for you. Go away."

"It is not permitted."

"By who? Him? Screw Him," the old man said hotly. "It's not His life. It never was. Leave me alone, Uriel."

"It does not have to be your time."

"Bullshit. It's been my time for the past twenty centuries. It's *always* been my time. Go away and let me die in peace."

"It is not permitted. You know this."

The old man sighed; his lungs crackled, and it turned into a coughing fit. "'Angelic compassion'," he finally managed. "You're inhuman. You can't know."

"What can I not know?"

"What your compassion is for, that's what. What a joke." The old man reached for a chipped mug on the table next to the bed. The messenger watched, but did nothing to help.

The cup shook as he lifted it to his lips, spilling water on the worn blanket.

"Here, Pete. Lemme help ya." The supervisor, alarmed by the old man's coughing, had hurried over. He cranked the head of the bed to a sitting position and held the cup so the old man could drink. "You okay now? You want me to call Father Nicholas?"

"Nah, Vic. I'm as okay as I can be, I guess. Thanks."

"Hey, 's all right. You'd do th' same." Patting the old man's hand, he returned the cup to the little table and walked back to his desk.

"That, Uriel. *That's* compassion. That's *humanity*." He shook his head against the pillow. "I pity you, all of you, because you'll never know."

The Messenger said nothing.

"They've had many names for you. Cherubim, Seraphim,

Principalities, all those dancing-on-the-head-of-a-pin names. You know what name fits you best? Aliens. Strangers. You don't touch humanity at any given point, did you know that? You don't love, don't hate, eat, fart, or fuck. You've been given dominion over humanity since the very beginning, and you haven't had the slightest idea in all that time what you were dealing with." The old man chuckled. "No wonder the human race is so screwed up."

"It is our lot. There is no justification, no explanation. It just is."

"'Why, daddy?'" the old man replied in a high, quavery voice. Then, much lower, "'Because, that's why.' What a crock."

The Messenger blinked. "You blaspheme."

"Then take your goddam flaming sword and run my ass out of the goddam garden, Uriel. Who has better reason to blaspheme?"

"It is not permitted."

"Yeah, right, I don't have a fucking permit. So sue me."

They were silent for a few moments. Finally, the old man spoke. "You really want to know why, Messenger?"

The angel shrugged. "Perhaps."

"You were there at Golgotha."

"I was there."

"Then you saw what happened. Didn't it ever occur to you to ask why? Shit, He destroyed Sodom. He let Joshua bring down Jericho by blowing rams' horns. He gave it to Moses to part the Red Sea. Did you ever stop to wonder why He didn't just bring me down off that goddam cross once He'd made His point?" The sound the old man made might have been a laugh.

"'Goddam cross' is right," he went on. "He turned His back on me. I took the sins of the whole world on my bleeding shoulders because it was His Will, and He turned His almighty face away from me because I made Him want to puke. *He left me there to die alone*, Uriel! He abandoned me because I did what he put before me to do, because He couldn't stand to see what He'd made me become." A tear leaked from the corner of one eye.

"Why did He do that? It was all His idea, His . . . *Plan.* I did what I was supposed to do. Hell, even *Judas* did what he was supposed to do." He turned his blazing eyes on the Messenger. "And where is the thirteenth disciple now, Uriel?" he asked softly. "What tree in hell bears his name and sorrow?"

The Messenger gazed down at the old man, but showed no signs of feeling. "It is not for us to know . . ." it began.

"It was for *me* to know, goddamn it! I was His 'only begotten son,' or had you forgotten that?"

"I forget nothing."

The old man sank back against the pillow. "Leave me the Hell alone, Uriel. You can't do anything for me and I can't do anything for you."

The angel looked around impassively, then said, "There are humans present. This is no concern of theirs."

"The hell you say."

"We must not attract undue attention."

"Then fix it! You're the frigging supernatural entity here, you want this to be private, *you* do something about it. Take us to Limbo or someplace. I don't care, as long as I can get Vic's attention if I need to."

"To take you out of this reality would be pointless. I am to stay with you until your death, and my time is limited. However, as of now, none can hear us."

"Try to imagine how comforting *that* is," the old man said.

There was a palpable silence, and then the Messenger spoke: "You have confused us with this manifestation. After almost two millennia, why did you choose this time and place?"

"I needed time to think. Time to cool off. I stayed dead a long time, Uriel." The old man sighed. "Time goes by fast when you're having fun. After nineteen hundred years or so, give or take a decade, I decided to try again, on my own."

"You deliberately chose an anonymous path when your Second Coming would have been celebrated. Most of humanity would have followed you."

The old man shook his head. "I didn't want that. I wanted to see if I could make it work without all the church stuff, just by being what I could be." He picked idly at the thin, worn blanket. "I wanted friends, not followers. I helped a lot of people in small ways. It turned out I had a real talent for healing—how's that for irony, Messenger?—and I went all over the place. I worked in hospitals, rode with rescue squads, I was even an army corpsman. Hell, I've been here almost twenty years. I just wanted to help." He shrugged and the sheets whispered against his thin back. "It's all I ever wanted to do.

"It seemed to work. People got better, were grateful. They passed along the favors to others, donated time and money to the shelter, made the world a slightly better place than it might have been otherwise.

"I've lived a lot longer this time, too. And you know the best part, Uriel? Nobody will come along after I'm dead this time to piss in it so they like the taste. No Crusades in my name, no Inquisition, no pogroms. No 'ethnic cleansing.' If He really had wanted to do this thing right, He'd have gathered an army of 'unnecessary manifestations' and set us loose all over the world. But then," he continued wearily, "there wouldn't have been a Big Book with His name in it and all those ludicrous stories."

"You avoid the question."

"I'm under no obligation to answer it. I've paid those dues. Look," he continued, "He came to me when I was just a kid. I was smart enough to have attracted some attention among the rabbis, and I asked a lot of questions that some of them weren't comfortable with. God gave me a vision one night, and promised me a lot of things—immortality, the ability to really help people, whatever it would take for His Plan to work." He shook his head. "I said yes. What did I know? I was just a kid."

"That was then. What of now?"

"Okay. You want reasons?" the old man asked quietly. "Renewal. Recompense. Requital. Restitution." With each word his voice grew stronger. "Release. Rectification. Revenge. Resurrection." Then, softer: "Redemption."

"Is this proper?"

"You ask stupid questions, Uriel, and insult both our intelligence. Vic!" he called out to the supervisor. "Ask God about proper, Uriel. Was it proper for Him to go off in a sulk because he didn't like the way His experiment turned out? Because He couldn't handle the enormity of what he'd done?" He struggled to raise himself. "Job. That poor bastard didn't know how well off he was. *Vic!*"

Vic hurried over. "Whataya need, Pete?"

"I gotta piss, man. Can you get me to the can?"

"Yeah, sure." He helped the old man sit up, then put his arm across the bony shoulders and half-carried him to the bathroom. The Messenger looked on dispassionately.

After seating the old man on the toilet, Vic said, "Now, you call me when you're done. Don't try an' make it back by y'self, ok?"

"Ok, Vic. I'll call you if I need you." He smiled wanly as Vic left.

The flow from the old man's bladder was slow and painfully hot; he didn't have to look to know that it was tinged with blood.

The Messenger appeared in front of him.

"Oh, this is a good one, all right," the old man muttered. "Uriel in the urinal. What are you doing here, Messenger?"

Something about the angel's bearing betrayed uncertainty. "You left after your resurrection. We watched you walk away from your disciples, leaving them frightened and puzzled, full of questions. You did nothing to answer those questions."

"That was Paul's job, and he was welcome to it. Hell, he wrote most of the New Testament and let the rest of them take the credit— or the blame. I just wanted out." He leaned his head back against the wall. "I'd had enough of the cult, enough of the adoration and the praise. It's not what I wanted, ever."

"You went to Hell."

"Heh. Yeah, I went *all* to Hell." He closed his eyes. "I was furious. I wanted to kick ass and take names. I couldn't take it out on the poor bastards who hung me up. They didn't know what they were doing. So, I harrowed Hell."

"The marks remain. The gates have never been rebuilt."

"Yeah, well. Milton was impressed. What's your point, Uriel?"

"Where did you get such power?"

The old man glared. "I had it. Not that I wanted it. When I let Him . . . recruit me, He charged me like a battery. There was plenty left."

"Even after He had abandoned you?"

"Look, He set all kinds of shit in motion that day. Earthquakes, an eclipse, storms. It doesn't just dissipate. Once you manifest on the physical plane, you have to deal with physical laws. How much power do you think it takes to rise after three days? Just because He turned away doesn't mean He turned it off like some kind of heavenly circuit breaker."

"You could have used the power to search for Him."

"And then what? Reasoned with Him? Begged Him to take me back? Beat the living shit out of Him?" The old man reached behind himself and flushed. His hand trembled. "What you are to Humanity, He is to me; there's no common point for discussion." Eyes closed, he slumped wearily against the toilet back.

"Ah, God, I'm so tired . . . so fucking tired. Why are you here, Messenger? I didn't ask for you."

The angel didn't answer for a moment. "There is an imbalance. It must be corrected."

"What kind of imbalance?" the old man asked dully.

"An impermissible one. One that concerns the entirety of humanity."

"Great. Well," he said after a moment, "what? C'mon, I'm old and tired, and I just want to die and have done with it. What's so important?"

"You were wrong."

"Wrong about what?"

"Your crucifixion and its consequences."

The old man's eyes opened, and he turned to focus on the other's face. "What are you telling me, Messenger?"

The angel stared with cold eyes. "Are you so arrogant that you believe He turned His back on you alone? He deserted all of us."

"I don't understand. All's right with the world, isn't it? Doesn't that mean God's in His heaven?"

"Your jest is meaningless and out of place."

"Yeah, well, you guys were never known for your sense of humor. Explain yourself."

"My statement was clear. God has abandoned His throne. There is no existing physical or metaphysical plane that we have not searched. He went where none of us could follow."

The old man stared as the enormity of this sank in. He passed a shaking hand over his eyes. "This . . . you can't be serious. You can't have looked *every*where."

"We have. Our search was systematic and complete. There is no place in existence in which God can be found. He is gone."

A look of sick horror passed over the old man's face. "When? When did He leave?"

"Does it matter? He is gone."

"*When*, goddam it!"

"Golgotha."

"Golgotha! But . . .the souls in heaven, are they gone, too? Did he at least pull the plug and let them go?"

"He did not. The souls remain."

"But without Him, with just you there, they couldn't survive. Not and stay sane."

"They survive. They are not . . . whole."

"Oh . . . oh, my . . ." There were no words to express what the old man felt. He raised his head, tears now falling freely. "What about Hell?"

"All mad, demons and lost souls alike."

"Purgatory?"

"All mad."

"Even limbo? Even the righteous heathen? And . . . Oh, God, the children! Even the children?"

"Mad. There was no one," the angel said, "capable of maintaining sanity after He left. Do you understand?" The angel stared at the old man. "Do you understand all that this means?"

Eyes again closed, the old man nodded his head. "They don't have anyone to guide them, to help them make sense of what's happened. Their Heavenly Father, the one who made all the promises, isn't there to counsel them, to make them safe." Hopelessly, he looked at the angel. "Do they know they've been abandoned?"

"How could they not know? God is gone."

"And you . . . you waited *two thousand years* to tell me this?"

"Our time does not pass as yours. Our search was extensive, it required much more time than that." The angel's voice was ice. "It passed no more quickly for those who are lost."

"How long?" the old man said between clenched teeth. "How long has it been for them?"

"Eternity."

Jesus wept. Slumped against a toilet in a New York shelter for the homeless, his thin body wracked with sobs, he wept for the souls of the dead; lost now, lost always, lost forever.

"Do you understand all that this means?" the angel repeated.

"*Yes*, goddamit, I know! He walked out on the whole human race, walked out on all His promises, and plans, and against His sworn word. I *know* what it means." His head sagged against his chest. "Just let me die and get it over with. I'm tired."

"You do *not* understand. God is gone. His place must not remain empty."

The words sank in slowly. Jesus raised his head, eyes wide with shock. "What?"

The angel looked at him without emotion. "You spoke of compassion. You said that you pitied us, that we would never know what it meant. You were wrong."

The old man said nothing; he just stared.

"Those who are lost, those who will come, need guidance. We cannot give it. They cannot give it to themselves. There is only you. We can no longer allow them to suffer."

"No! It's too much! I've *earned* dying, damn it!"

"You will take His place."

"I said no! I won't do it!"

The angel looked down at the old man with cold eyes: burning cold, inhuman eyes. "I will tell you as I once told Ezra. Go weigh for me the weight of fire, or measure for me a blast of wind, or call back for me the day that is past. Can you do these things?"

The old man's voice shook with helpless rage. "You know I can't! I never could! I wasn't born with power, He wasn't my real Father!" He tried to bring himself under control, but his hands and head shook as if palsied, and his face was as blotched as the tiles beneath his bare feet.

"I was given this choice once before, Messenger, and I took it even though I knew it would kill me. This time I'm refusing the cup!" His voice became petulant. "You can't make me do it, you son of a bitch!"

"You had choice in Gethsemane. Here and now, you do not. I am not here to bring you back, or to convince you, but to tell you what will be." The air around the angel grew bright and hot as it spoke. "You will die. You will ascend. You will take the throne. There is nothing else. God is gone, and you have no choice."

"Bastard . . . bastard . . ." The ancient voice was whisper-thin now, cracked and broken like spun glass. "Let me die . . ."

"Yes." The angel placed a hand on Jesus' brow.

And the old man's hands stopped shaking; his head fell back against the wall; his worn body sagged slowly in place; and he died.

† † †

Back at his desk, Vic grew worried. Pete had been in the toilet a long time, and there was no sound. Not wanting to disturb the other patients, he got up and hurried around to make sure everything was okay. He tapped softly on the door.

"Yo, Pete. You need help?" There was no answer. "Pete!" he said louder.

Alarmed, he eased the door open just far enough to look in; he didn't want to embarrass the old man if he'd just fallen asleep on the john.

What he saw made him curse softly and rush to the old man's side. He felt the thin wrist, then turned and ran out of the bathroom and down the hall to Father Nicholas's room. He returned moments later with the priest behind him.

"I couldn't find a pulse, padre. Oh, jeez, what a way to go . . ." His voice was thick with grief; the old man had been well loved.

Father Nicholas checked for a pulse, then closed the eyes and began Last Rites. Vic stood to one side, unashamed tears on his cheeks.

The priest finished the sacrament, then went to phone for an ambulance. Vic followed, his eyes pleading for comfort, for sense.

"Why'd he hafta die in *there*, padre? Why'd he hafta go in the can?"

The priest patted Vic's shoulder. "I know, I know. It's a bad place to end, especially for a man like Pete. But it's okay, Vic." He turned to look one last time at the body sprawled on the toilet. "It's okay. He's with God now."

† † †

## Author's Commentary

I was raised a Southern Baptist in Roanoke, Virginia, in the early 1950s. That meant Sunday School plus morning and evening services, and Wednesday night Prayer Meeting and Church Supper (to this day I can't abide ham salad); later on, there was Royal Ambassadors on Tuesday nights and choir practice on Thursdays. In the summer, there was Vacation Bible School with Bible Drills (your Bible was your sword) and pictures painstakingly constructed from macaroni.

In our hallway at home hung a print of a well-known painting of Jesus, hands folded in prayer in Gethsemane, a halo around his head done in gold; at night, light reflected off that halo and silhouetted His face, so that when I awoke in the night with my evil thoughts, there was this great and terrible EYE staring at me: an unearthly eye, inhuman and implacable, cold and omnipotent— probing, searching, finding every sliver of anger, every crime, every flaw, every bad wish I had . . . and not forgiving *any of it*.

I recall my mother catching me in some small lie, probably

about a broken dish or spilt grape juice. She shook her head sadly. "Every time you lie, the Devil chips off a piece of your soul. If you tell too many lies, he'll have it all." Then she told me it would be all right as long as I kept Jesus inside me. I had just read something in school about undercooked pork and parasites; the image wasn't comforting.

"Christus Destitutus" is a very personal story, far more personal than I had ever planned for it to be. It has a subtext I will not mention here for all its truthfulness, because I myself didn't see it until my not-wife, Mary, showed it to me (it took my feet out from under me—had I not been near a chair, I would have fallen), and it has little to do with this book's theme. The story is so personal, in fact, that I find I'm unable to address it academically.

Jesus is, in fact, inescapable, for better or worse, whether you see him as the Son of God, the Sacrifice to end all sacrifices—or as a cold, unforgiving eye in the hallway, counting down your childish sins.

Jesus was inside me. And I was afraid.

†††

# SLOW DANCING WITH JESUS
## Gardner Dozois & Jack Dann

Jesus Christ appeared at Tess Kimbrough's door dressed in a white tuxedo with a blue cummerbund and matching bow tie. His chestnut-brown hair was parted in the middle and fell down past his shoulders, and his beard and mustache were close-cropped and neatly combed.

Tess's mother answered the door. "Come right inside. Tess will be down in a jiffy." She led Jesus into the front room. "Tess," she called, "your date is here."

Upstairs, Tess checked the bobby pins that held her French twist together and smoothed imaginary wrinkles out of her dress. It was the emerald green one, with dyed-green shoes to match, that her urbane and sophisticated mother had helped her pick out, and she was somewhat nervous about it. But then, she was so nervous anyway that her teeth were chattering. She told her image in the mirror that this was going to be the most perfect night of her life, but the image in the mirror didn't look convinced. She practiced breathing evenly for a moment, flaring her nostrils. Then she walked down the stairs to meet Jesus, remembering not to look at her feet, and trying to maintain good posture.

Jesus stood up as she entered the room and presented her with a corsage, a small orchid on a wristlet. She thanked him, kissed her mother goodbye, promised that she'd be back at a reasonable hour, and then she was sitting beside Jesus in the leatherette seat of his Thunderbird convertible. Jesus refrained from laying rubber in the front of Tess's house, as most kids would have done; instead he shifted smoothly and skillfully through the gears. Tess momentarily forgot about being nervous as the wind rushed by against her face and she thought that she was actually—right now—going to the prom.

"How are you doing?" Jesus asked. "Do you want a cap or something so the wind won't mess your hair?"

"No, thanks," Tess said shyly. She was almost afraid to look at him, and kept stealing sidelong glances at him when she thought his attention was elsewhere.

"You nervous?"

Tess glanced at him again. "You mean, about the prom?"

"Uh-huh," Jesus said, executing a highspeed turn with an easy, expert grace. The buildings were going by very fast now.

"Yeah . . . I guess so."

"Don't be," Jesus said, and winked.

Tess felt herself blushing, but before she could think of something to say, Jesus was bringing the car to a smooth stop in the lower parking lot of the high school. A kid whose Vaseline-smeared hair was combed back into a ducktail opened the door for Tess, and then slid into the driver's seat when Jesus got out. Jesus gave him a five-dollar tip.

"Jeez, thanks," the boy said.

Cinders crunched under their feet as they crossed the parking lot toward the open fire door of the gym, which was now framed by paper lanterns glowing in soft pastel colors. Tess walked hesitantly and slowly now that they were really here, already beginning to feel the first sick flutterings of panic. Most of the kids didn't like her—she had long ago been classified as uncool and, worse, a "brain"—and she didn't see any reason why they'd start to like her now . . .

But then Jesus was surrendering their tickets at the door, and it was too late to flee.

Inside the gym, the bleachers had been pulled back from the dance floor and the basketball nets had been folded up. Paper streamers hung from rafters and water pipes, herds of slowly jostling balloons bumped gently against the ceiling, and crepe-paper roses were everywhere. The band—five sullen, young men in dark-red jackets that had "The Teen-Tones" written on them in sequins—had set up in the free-throw zone and were aggressively but unskillfully playing "Yakety Yak." Kids in greasy pompadours, crew cuts, and elephant trunks milled listlessly around the dance floor, looking stiff and uncomfortable in their rented suits. Only a few couples were dancing, and they jerked and twitched in lethargic slow motion, like people slowly drowning on the bottom of the sea.

Most of the girls were still standing by the refreshment tables on the other side of the room, where the punch bowls were, and Tess made her way toward them, feeling her stomach slowly knot with dread. Already she could see some of the kids smirking at her and whispering, and she heard a girl say loudly, "Just look at that *dress!* What a nerd!" One of the class clowns made a yipping, doggy noise as she passed, and someone else broke up into high-pitched, asthmatic laughter. Blindly, she kept walking. As she came up to the group around the punch bowls, her friend Carol gave her an unenthusiastic smile and said, "Hey, lookin' good," in an insincere voice. Vinnie, Carol's bullet-headed boyfriend, made a snorting sound of derision. "I just don't understand why you have anything to do with that dog," he said to Carol, not even making a pretense of caring whether Tess could hear him or not. Carol looked embarrassed; she glanced at Tess, smiled weakly, and then looked uneasily away—she genuinely liked Tess, and sometimes hung out with her after school (in the classic teen configuration, encountered everywhere, of one pretty girl and a "dog" doing things together), but as a captain of cheerleaders she had her own status to worry about and under the circumstances she'd lose face with the cool kids if she stuck up too vigorously for Tess. "I mean, *look* at her," Vinnie complained, still speaking to Carol as if Tess weren't there. "She's *so* uncool, you know?"

Tess stood frozen, flushing, smiling a frozen smile, feeling herself go hot and freezing-cold by turns. Should she pretend that she hadn't heard? What else could she do? The clown had drifted over, and was making yipping noises again. . . .

Jesus had been a few steps behind her coming through the crowd, but now he stepped up beside her and took her arm, and all the other kids suddenly fell silent. "Leave her alone," Jesus said. His voice was rich, strong, resonant, and it rang like a mellow iron bell in the big, empty hall. "She's here with *me.*" Vinnie's mouth dropped open, and Carol gasped. All the kids were gaping at them, their faces soft with awe. Tess was intensely aware of Jesus' strong, warm fingers on the bare flesh of her arm. Jesus seemed to have grown larger, to have become huge and puissant, a giant, and his rugged, handsome face had become stern and commanding. He radiated strength and warmth and authority, and an almost tangible light—a clear and terrible light that seemed to reveal every zit and pimple and blackhead in the sallow, shallow faces of her tormentors, each slack mouth and weak chin and watery eye, a light that dwindled them to a petty and insignificant group of grimy children. "She's here with me," Jesus repeated, and then he smiled, suavely, jauntily, almost rakishly, and winked. "And if *I* say she's cool, believe it, she's cool."

Then, before anyone could speak, Jesus had taken Tess's hand and led her onto the dance floor, and they were dancing, slow dancing, while the band played "A Million to One." She had never been able to dance before, but now she danced with effortless skill, swirling around and around the floor, following Jesus' lead, moving with beauty and flowing, silken grace, shreds of torn paper roses whispering around her feet. One by one the other couples stopped dancing and stood silently to watch them, until they were surrounded by a ring of pale, gaping, awed faces, small as thumbnails and distant as stars, and they drifted and danced within that watching ring as the band played "Goodnight, My Love" and "Twilight Time" and "It's All in the Game."

After the dance, Jesus drove her home and kissed her goodnight at her door, gently but with authority, and with just the slightest sweet hint of tongue.

Tess let herself in and went upstairs to her room, moving quietly so that her mother wouldn't realize that she was back. She switched on a soft light and stared at herself in the mirror; her flesh was tingling, and she was sure that she must be glowing in the darkness like freshly hammered steel, but her face looked the same as always, except perhaps for the expression around the eyes. She sat down at her night table and took her diary out from the locked, secret drawer. She sat there silently for a long while, near the open window, feeling the warm, night breeze caress her face and smelling the heavy, sweet perfume of the mimosa trees outside. A dog was barking out there somewhere, far away, at long intervals and cars whined by on the highway, leaving a vibrant silence in their wake. At last she opened her diary, and in a bold neat hand wrote, *"Dear Diary, Tonight I met—Him. . . ."*

†††

## Authors' Commentaries

### Gardner Dozois:

This story resulted from a social evening when Susan Casper, Jack Dann, and I went out to dinner at Dave Shore's (a family-style Jewish restaurant that I still miss twenty years after its closing) with friends Bob Walters and Tess Kissinger, two local artists. During dinner, conversation turned to Tess's weird and wonderful dreams, of which she has a seemingly inexhaustible supply. At my insistence, she related my favorite, in which, as an unpopular teenager, she found Jesus taking her to her high-school prom, at which he told all the kids who had been scorning her, "She's here with me. And if *I* say she's cool, she's cool."

Jack took fire with this idea and, after a razor-thin pause to ask a bemused Tess if she minded our stealing her dream, decided that we would write it as a story that very night and began working it out in the cab on the way home. And as soon as he got to our apartment, he rushed to my battered stand-up Remington typewriter, whipped a piece of paper into it, and began to type.

Jack is a fearless writer of great ambition, unafraid of plunging into any writing project, no matter how daunting its creative challenge. Already, in the cab going home, I had been getting cold feet, daunted by the subtle technical difficulties that we would have to overcome. Alone, I would have thought about it for a day or so, decided it was too difficult, and dropped it. But with Jack pounding away on my typewriter in my living room (also the kitchen), I could no longer opt out. Jack wrote furiously for over an hour, taking the story from its opening scene to the point where Jesus and Tess arrive outside the gym. Then he stood and made a sweeping gesture toward the typewriter, as if to say, "Your turn."

I did take my turn, and finished the story, but in two days rather than a little over an hour. The biggest challenge was to make it more than a sacrilegious joke, like a Monty Python routine. I wanted it to evoke a young girl's longing dreams, at once sad and funny— bittersweet, strange, and wistful. Because this mood was a difficult one to create, so fragile that one false step would shatter it, I was careful where I placed my metaphorical feet, avoiding anything too facile or too obvious, too ha-ha Monty Pythonish. I carefully shaped every detail; I even worked out which songs the characters dance to and the order in which they should be played.

Everybody told us that we had no chance to sell this story. Instead, it sold on our second attempt, to *Penthouse* fiction editor Kathy Green, whom we should salute for taking a chance on risky material during a conservative and repressive time (does that sound familiar?) in American society. If she had not bought it, I doubt that anyone else would have.

### Jack Dann:

Ah, yes, I, too, miss Dave Shore's: some of the best *Yiddishe* cooking in North America. And I remember Tess describing her strange, ultraviolet dreams, dreams at once affecting, beautiful, and frightening. And Gardner is spot on: When Tess told us her dream about going to the senior prom with Jesus, *this* Jewish boy went wild. The image that flashed in my mind was as strong and distinct and three-dimensional as anything I had ever experienced. I *saw* Jesus: well-coifed, shoulder-length, chestnut-brown hair parted in the middle; short beard neatly clipped; face tanned, handsome, and sensitive. He wears a one-button white tuxedo jacket, black trousers, and a pale blue cummerbund. He pulls up in front of Tess Kimbrough's house in a vintage, white 1955 Thunderbird convertible. He is movie-star cool; he is James Dean, Marlon Brando, Kirk Douglas, and John Fitzgerald Kennedy all rolled into one. And, to make it even sweeter, he's the Son of God! And she . . . she is a plain girl with acne, the girl no one wants to be seen with, much less take out on a date. (I should hasten to add that Tess was—and is—the absolute antithesis of a plain Jane. I had, in fact, flashed back to my own adolescence when I had acne so bad that, in the summers, I would not take off my T-shirts at the beach, lest people see the reefs of ugly acne sores on my back and shoulders.)

God, I had to write that story—to transform that numinous, coruscating, three-dimensional image into a painting on the page. Once I shook myself out of that fugue state of creative yearning and intention, I did indeed see that Tess looked completely bemused. And Gardner . . . well, Gardner looked embarrassed. (However, he often looked like that when we were in public together.)

But I just couldn't let the story go.

So, generous entrepreneurs that we were, we made a deal with Tess. Let *us* write the story and when (and *if!*) it sells, we'll . . . buy you dinner.

As Gardner recounts, we went home, and I sat down and banged away furiously on Gardner's old Remington, trying to tease out and trap the ideas and images before they dissipated into the light-bulb glow of that soft summer Philadelphia night. At least, I *think* it was summer.

Gardner did write the story through to the end. We passed it back and forth, I think; but he had indeed caught the tender poignancy and yearning of adolescence. I remember arguing that the hint of tongue in the last kiss might be construed as sacrilegious; but, after all these years, I think Gardner was right. He maintained exactly the right balance on the tightrope, and the ending—Gardner at the top of his form—is a perfect pirouette.

†††

*When magicians hitchhike, beware the destination.*

# ON THE ROAD TO NEW EGYPT
## Jeffrey Ford

One day when I was driving home from work, I saw him there on the side of the road. He startled me at first, but I managed to control myself and apply the brakes. His face was fixed with a look somewhere between agony and elation. That thumb he thrust out at an odd angle was gnarled and had a long nail. The sun was setting and there were red beams dancing around him. I stopped and leaned over to open the door.

"You're Jesus, right?" I said.

"Yeah," he said and held up his palms to show the stigmata.

"Hop in," I told him.

"Thanks, man," he said as he gathered up his toga and slipped into the front seat.

As I pulled back out onto the road, he took out a pack of Camel Wides and a dark blue Bic lighter. "You don't mind, do you?" he asked, but he already had a cigarette in his mouth and was bringing a flame to it.

"Go for it," I said.

"Where you headed?" he asked.

"Home, unless you're here to tell me different," I said, forcing a laugh.

"Easy, easy," he said.

After a short silence, Christ took a couple of deep drags and blew the smoke out the partially opened window.

"Where are you going?" I asked.

"You know, just up the road a piece."

We stopped at a red light and I looked over at him. That crown of thorns must have itched like hell. I shook my head and said, "Wait till I tell my wife about this."

"She religious?" he asked.

"Not particularly, but still, she'll get the impact."

He smiled and flicked some ashes into his palm.

We drove on for a while through the vanishing light past fields of pumpkins and dried corn stalks. A few minutes later, night fell, and I put on the lights. I didn't see it at first, but a possum darted out into the road right in front of the car. Bump, bump, we were over it in a microsecond. I looked at Christ.

He shrugged as if to say, "What can you do?"

". . . and Heaven?" I asked as the car traveled into a valley where the trees from either side of the road had, above, grown together into a canopy.

"Angels, blue skies, your relatives are all there. The greats are there. Basically everybody is there. It gets a little tense sometimes, a little close."

"You said that 'basically' everybody is in Heaven," I said. "Who isn't?"

"You know," he said, "those other people."

We kept going past the fences of the horse farms, the edges of barren fields, until Christ had me stop at McDonalds and order him a quarter pounder with cheese and a chocolate shake. I paid for it with my last couple of dollars.

He said, "I'll pay you back in indulgences."

"Hey, it's on me," I said.

He wolfed that burger like the Son of Man that he was.

"So what have you seen in your travels?" I asked.

"You name it," he said, sucking at his shake. "The human drama."

"Do you ever stop anywhere?"

"Sometimes. I'm always on the look out for an old Howard Johnson." There was a short pause and then he said, "Could you step on it a little, I have to be in New Egypt by eight."

"Sure thing," I said and put down the pedal. "You meeting someone?"

"I've been seeing this woman there on and off for the past couple of years. Every once in a while I'll appear, give her a little push and then split by sunup."

"She must be pretty special."

"Yeah," he said and took out a flattened wallet. "Here she is."

He showed me an old photo of this forty-five-year-old ex-blonde-bombshell in a leopard bikini.

"Nice," I said.

"Nice isn't the word for it," he said with a wink.

"What's she do?" I asked.

"A little of this and a little of that," he said.

"No, I mean where does she work?"

"At the funeral parlor. She sews mouths and lids shut. She lives in a small house in the center of town. When I get there, she's usually in bed. I step out of the armoire, minus the robe, and slip between the sheets with her. We eat of the fruit of the knowledge of good and evil for a few hours and then lie back, have a smoke."

"Does she know who you are?"

"I hope by this time she's figured it out," he said.

"She'll end up going to the tabloids with the story," I warned.

"Screw it, she already has. We were in that one recently with Bigfoot on the cover and the story about the woman who turned to stone on page three."

"I missed that one, but I remember the cover."

All of a sudden Christ sat straight up and pointed out the windshield. "Whoa, whoa," he said, "pull over like you're going to pick this guy up."

Only when he spoke did I see the shadowy figure up ahead on the side of the road. I could tell it was a guy and that he was hitchhiking. I passed by him a few feet and then pulled over to the shoulder. We could hear him running toward the car.

"O.K., peel out," Christ said.

I did and we left that stranger in the dust.

"I love that one," said the Savior.

A few minutes passed and then I heard a hatchet of a voice from the backseat. "You fuckers," it said. I looked in the rear view mirror and there was the Devil—horns, red skin, cheesy whiskers in a goatee. As I looked at him his grin turned into a wide smile.

Jesus reached back and offered a hand.

"Who's the stiff at the wheel?" asked the Devil.

"You mean fat boy, here?" Christ said and they both burst out laughing. "He's cool."

"Nice to meet you," said the Devil.

I reached back and shook a hand that was a tree branch with the power to grip. "Name's Jeff," I said.

"I am legion," he hissed.

Then he stuck his head into the front seat and shot a little burp of flame into the air. Christ doubled over with silent laughter. "I got a bag of Carthage Red on me, you got any papers?" the Devil asked, putting his hand on Christ's shoulder.

"Does the Pope shit in the woods?" asked the Son of God.

The Devil got the papers and started rolling one in the backseat. "Jeff, you ever try this shit?"

"I never heard of it."

"It's old, man, it'll make you see God."

"By the way," Christ said, interrupting, "whatever happened with that guy in Detroit?"

"I took him," said the Devil. "Mass murderer, just reeking evil. He hung himself in the jail cell. They conveniently forgot to remove his belt."

"I thought I told you I wanted him," said Christ.

"I thought I cared," said the Devil. "Anyway, you get that old woman from Tampa. She's going to make canonization. I guarantee it."

"I guess that's cool," he said.

"Eat me if it isn't," said the Devil. They both started laughing and each patted me on the back. The Devil lit up the enormous joint he had created and the odd pink smoke began to permeate the car.

It tasted like cinnamon and fire, and at the first toke I was stunned. Paranoia set in instantly, and I slowed the car down to about thirty. I drove blindly while in my head I saw the autumn afternoon woods of my childhood. It was so still and the leaves were silently falling. I thought of home and it was far away.

When my mind returned to me at a red light, I noticed that the radio was on. New Age music, a piano, and some low moaning formed a backdrop to the conversation of my passengers.

"What do you think?" Christ had just asked.

"I think this music has to go," said the Devil. His fingers grew like snakes from the backseat, and he kept pressing the scan button on the radio till he came to the oldies station. "Backseat memories," he said.

Somehow it was decided that we would go to Florida and check

out the lady who was going to become a saint. "Maybe she'll pop a
miracle," said the Devil.

"No sweat," said Christ.

"My wife's expecting me home around nine," I said.

The Devil laughed really loud. "I'll tell you what I'll do," he
said. "I'll split myself in two and half of me will go to your house
and boff your wife till we get back."

Christ leaned over and put his hand on my knee. "Don't be an
idiot," he said to me with a smile. "I have to be in New Egypt by
eight."

"You can do things?" I asked.

"Look," said Christ, nodding toward the windshield, "we're
there. Just make a right at this corner. It's the third house on the
left."

I looked up and saw that we were in a suburban neighborhood
with palm trees lining the side of the road. The houses were all one-
story ranch styles and painted in pastel colors. When I pulled the
car over in front of the house, I could hear crickets singing quickly
in the night heat.

Before we got out, the Devil leaned into the front seat and said
to Christ, "I'll make you a bet she doesn't do a miracle while
we're here."

"Bullshit," said Christ.

"What do you want to bet?" asked the Devil.

"How about him," said the Savior and pointed that weird thumb
at me.

"Quite the high roller," said the Devil.

As we were walking up the driveway to the front door, the Devil
lagged a little behind us. I leaned over, and, in a whisper, asked
Christ if he thought she would perform.

He shrugged and rolled his eyes. "Have faith, man," he said.
"Sometimes you win, sometimes you lose."

"I heard that," said the Devil. "I don't like whispering."

We walked right through the front door and into the living room where a woman was sitting in front of the television. At first, I thought she was deaf, but it soon became clear that we were completely invisible to her in every way.

The Devil walked up behind me and handed me a sixteen-ounce Rolling Rock. "There she is in all her splendor," he said as he handed a beer to Christ. "Doesn't look like much of an opportunity here unless she's gonna get better looking."

We stood and stared at her. She was about sixty-five with short hair dyed brown and was wearing a flowered bathrobe. On the coffee table in front of her was an ashtray with a lit cigarette in one of the holders. In her left hand was a glass of dark wine. As the daily reports of mayhem and greed came through the box, she shook her head from time to time and sipped her drink.

"What's she done?" I asked.

"She brought a kid back from the dead a few months ago," said the Devil. "A girl was hit by a car outside a local grocery store. Mrs. Lumley, here, was present and just touched the girl's hand. The kid got right up off the stretcher and walked away."

"Strange shit," said Christ. "We don't really know how it works."

"You mean," I said, "that you can't make her do a miracle?"

"Not exactly," said Christ.

"That's a bitch, isn't it?" said the Devil. "Now drink your beer and calm down."

The Devil walked around behind Mrs. Lumley's chair and used two fingers to make horns behind her head. Christ went to pieces over that one. I even had to laugh while we watched her pick her nose. She was at it for a good five minutes. Christ applauded her every strategy, and the Devil said, "The one that got away."

"We better sit down. This may take a few minutes," said Christ.

The Devil and I sat down on the couch and Christ took an old rocker across from us. The evil one rolled another huge joint and listened intently to the report on the television of a murder/suicide out in California. Mrs. Lumley began singing "The Whispering Wind" to herself between sips of wine, and Christ hummed a duet with her.

"I've had more fun in church," said the Devil, passing me the joint. Again, I tasted the cinnamon and fire, and took big gulps of beer to soothe my throat.

Christ begged off and just rocked contentedly in his chair.

The news eventually went off and *Jeopardy* came on the television. "Wait till I get my hooks into this asshole," the Devil said, nodding toward the host of the show.

"He's yours," said Christ. "It's on me." Then he pointed his finger at Mrs. Lumley and made her change the channel to a *Star Trek* rerun.

While we waited for something to happen, the Devil showed me a trick. He took a big draw of Carthage Red and then exhaled it in a perfect globe of smoke. The globe hovered in the air before my eyes and turned crystal clear. Then it was filled with an image of my wife and kids reading bedtime stories. When I reached for it, it popped like a soap bubble.

"Parlor tricks," said Christ.

Eventually, Mrs. Lumley got up, turned off the set and went into her bedroom. We followed her as far as the door, where we looked in at her. She was kneeling next to the bed, saying her prayers.

"I hope you like the heat," the Devil said to me.

Then Christ said, "Look."

Mrs. Lumley was lying on the floor and her body was twitching. A steady groan came through her clenched teeth. In seconds, her skin had become a metallic blue and her head had doubled in size. Fangs, claws, gills, audibly popped from her features. She turned her head to face us, and I could feel she was actually seeing us with her expanding eyes.

"Shit," said the Devil and turned and ran toward the door.

"Let's get out of here," said Christ and he too turned and ran. I followed close behind.

When we got outside the Devil was sticking his head out of the backseat window of the car. "Move your asses," he yelled. I ran around and got in the driver's seat as fast as I could. Mrs. Lumley growled from the lawn, some kind of rapidly changing blue creature. I hit the gas.

"What the fuck was that supposed to be?" said Christ, catching his breath, as he passed us each a cigarette.

"Your old man is out of his mind," said the Devil. "It's all getting just a little too strange."

"Tell me about it," said Christ. "Remember, I warned you back when they first walked on the moon."

"This is some really evil shit, though," said the Devil.

"The whole ball of wax is falling apart," said Christ.

"I actually had a breakout in the ninth bole of Hell last week," said the Devil. "A big bastard—he smashed right through the ice. Killed one demon with his bare hands and broke another one's back."

"Did you get him?" I asked.

"One of my people said she saw him in Chicago."

"Purgatory is spreading like the plague," said Christ.

The Devil leaned up close behind me and put his claw and on my shoulder. I could feel his hot breath on my nape. "His old man is reading Nietzsche," he whispered, his tongue grazing my earlobe.

"What's he saying?" Christ asked me.

"Which way am I supposed to turn to get out of this development?" I asked.

Just then there was an abrupt bump on the top of the car. It startled me and I swerved, almost hitting a garbage can.

"You gotta check this out," said the Devil. "Saint Lumley of the Bad Trips is flying over us."

"Punch the gas," yelled Christ, and I floored it. I drove like a maniac, screeching around corners, and the pastel ranches flew by.

"We're starting to lose her," the Devil called out.

"What are you carrying?" Christ asked.

"I've got a full minute of fire," said the Devil. "What have you got?"

"I've got The Machine of Eden," said Christ.

"Uhh, not the fucking Machine of Eden," said the Devil and slammed my seatback.

"What do you mean?" said Christ.

"When was the last time that thing worked?"

"It works," said Christ.

"Pull off and go through the gate up on your right," said the Devil. "We've got to take her out or she'll dog us for eternity."

"I don't like this at all," said Christ.

After passing the gate, I drove on a winding gravel road that led to the local landfill. There were endless moonlit hills of junk and garbage. I parked and we got out.

"We've got to get up on the top of that hill before she gets here," said Christ, pointing to a huge mound of garbage.

I scrabbled up the hill, clutching at old car seats and stepping on dead appliances. Startled rats scurried through the debris. When I reached the top I was sweating and panting. Christ beat me, but I had to reach back down and help the Devil up the last few steps.

"It's the hooves," he said, "they're worse than high heels."

"There's some cool old stuff here," said Christ.

"I saw a whole carton of *National Geographic* I want to snag on the way out," said the Devil.

Off in the distance, I saw the shadow of something passing in front of the stars. It was too big to be a bird. "Here she comes," I yelled and pointed. They both spun around to look. "What do I do?" I asked.

"Stay behind us," said Christ. "If she gets you, it's going to hurt."

The next thing I knew, we three were backed against the edge of the hill with a steep drop behind us and Mrs. Lumley had landed. Her blue skin shone in the moonlight like armor, but there were tufts of hair growing from it. She had this amazing aqua body and an eight-foot wingspan, but with the exception of the gills and fangs, she still had the face of a sixty-five-year-old woman. She moved slowly toward us, burping out words that made no sense.

When she got within a few feet of us, Christ said, "Smoke 'em if you got 'em," and the Devil stepped forward. Tentacles began to grow from her body toward him. One managed to wrap itself around his left horn before he opened his mouth and gave her a minute of fire. The flames came like a blowtorch and stopped her cold. When she was completely engulfed in the blaze, the tentacles retracted, but she would not melt.

As soon as the evil one finished and was coughing out big clouds of gray smoke, she opened her eyes and the tentacles began again to grow from her sides. I looked over and saw that Christ was holding something in his right hand. It appeared to be a television remote control, and he was furiously pushing buttons.

The Devil had jumped back beside me and his hand was clutching my arm. He had real fear in his serpent eyes, yet he could not help but laugh at Christ messing around with The Machine of Eden.

"What's with the cosmic garage-door opener?" he shouted.

"It works," said Christ as he continued to nervously press buttons. Then I felt one of the tentacles wrapping itself around my ankle. Mrs. Lumley opened her mouth and crowed like a rooster. Another of the blue snake appendages was entwining itself around the Devil's mid-section. We both screamed as she pulled us toward her.

"Three," Christ yelled and a beam of light shot out of the end of the Machine. The next thing I noticed was the sound of celestial voices singing in unison. Mrs. Lumley took the blast full in the chest and began instantly to shrivel. Before my eyes, like a special effect for a crappy science-fiction movie, she turned into a tree. Leaves sprouted, pink blossoms grew, and with the end of the singing, pure white fruit hung on the lower branches.

"Not fun," said the Devil.

"I thought she was going to suck your face off," said Christ.

"What exactly was she," I asked, "an alien?"

Christ shook his head. "Nah," he said, "just a fucked-up old woman."

"Is she still a saint?" I asked.

"No, she's a tree," he said.

"You and your saints," said the Devil and plucked a piece of fruit. "Take one of these," he said to me. "It's called *The Still Point of the Turning World*. Only eat it when you need it."

I picked one of the white pears off the tree and put it in my pocket before we started down the junk hill. The Devil found the box of magazines and Christ came up with a lamp made out of seashells. We piled into the car and I started it up.

I heard Christ say, "Holy shit, it's eight o'clock," and the next thing I knew I was on my usual road back in Jersey. The car was empty but for me, and I was just leaving New Egypt.

††† 

## Author's Commentary

I have been teaching at Brookdale Community College in Monmouth County, New Jersey, for eighteen years. My drive to work and back requires two hours each way and often feels like an infernal odyssey—perhaps the result of a sin I can no longer remember committing. But, each teaching day, those four hours behind the wheel give me plenty of time to daydream.

Along my route lies a town called New Egypt. From the first time I saw its sign, its biblical overtones insured that eventually I would use it in a story. The impetus for "On the Road to New Egypt" came from the town's name and an article in the *Weekly World Star* or one of those "hyperbolic" newspapers one sees at grocery-store checkout counters. You know, "President Walks with Aliens on White House Lawn," "Woman Turns to Stone," "Co-Workers' Farts May Be Injurious to Your Health." One day as I pushed my purchases along the conveyor belt, the cover on one such rag caught my eye: a picture of Jesus walking down the street in a modern suburban setting. I never read the article, but my quick glimpse of that photo stayed with me, and these elements conspired to get my story percolating.

Another contributing idea was the legend of the hitchhiking Jesus. Perhaps you've heard stories of this phenomenon: Someone picks up a longhaired hitchhiker and discovers over the course of the ride that it is Jesus. Just when the driver catches on, the passenger disappears—no doubt a modern variation of the Wandering Jew theme.

With all this story stuff in my head, I started thinking about Jesus. Who was Jesus to me? I had been a Catholic as a kid, but that was long gone. Many of my religious friends often said, "You have to develop your own relationship with Jesus," which made sense if you initially bought the concept. If God took the trouble of incarnating as a specific individual in human history, surely he would try to reach people as individuals. The question for me became, "Who is my Christ?" And then: "What if Christ was a lot like me and my friends?" Say the Son of God had personal troubles, business problems, a parent acting out, fun-loving but unreliable friends, and the prospect of confronting worldly situations out of his control? Say Jesus had to face the chaos of everyday life—the ups, the downs, the good times, the bummers?

These ideas inform my Jesus in "On the Road to New Egypt." I wasn't trying to be facetious when I made The Devil his good friend—I really had a sense that, over the eons, through all of the trials and tribulations of working for the same overbearing boss, they would at least have become drinking buddies.

†††

*Is it worth* anything *to enact one's authentic being?*

# UNDERSTANDING ENTROPY
## Barry Malzberg

So I go to Martin Donner's bedside in the room they have staked out for him in Florida, and I ask him the crucial question: If you had known, I say, if you had known that it would end this way, that you would be dying of a hundred wounds, of the tuberculosis, of the pneumocystitis, of the parasites and the kidney breakdown and the hepatitis, the jaundice, the venerium and the shattering of the pancreas, if you had known that five years after the positive diagnosis and three years after the first episode of the pneumonia you would be lying here, eighty-two pounds, filled with morphine that doesn't work anymore—oh, nothing works but that isn't quite the point, is it, they are trying—with your lover and your daughters and your wife and the doctors circling in the outer room and coming in now and then to inspect your reeking corpus, some of them weeping, others taking your pulse and monitoring your breathing: if you had known this fifteen years ago, Martin Donner, if you had known everything that would happen to you and that it would end this way, would you have left your wife and children to their lives and your history and gone out to Fire Island, Cherry Groves, the baths and the bathhouses and the quick and the scuffled, the long and the grievous affairs full time, no longer sneaking it around? Would you if you had known? Or would you have stayed in your marriage in the suburbs, Martin Donner, and played with your daughters and watched them grow and claimed your wife with closed eyes in the marriage bed and nothing more, *nothing* more because you would never know when the dogs truly came into the basement and snuffled up the stairs? Oh maybe once a year you might let some man tend to you with rubber gloves in a bank vault, but otherwise nothing, nothing, nothing at all? If you could have seen that it would end this way, Martin, what would you have done? Tell me the truth now. Do you know the truth? Because I need, I need, I need to know now, it affects my own situation.

He stares at me. He is relatively lucid now, it comes and it goes, in and out, back and forth, the pounding on the chest has loosened the phlegm, the morphine has momentarily quelled the cough; he thinks that he can think, although this is not necessarily the issue, and he thinks, of course, that I am a hallucination. Hallucination is common in this late-life condition, although the dementia has not affected him as fully as it might in a few more hours or (if he lasts that long, he probably will not) days. I don't know, he says, his eyes are strangely lustrous, the only motion, the only thing in his face not quiescent, the rest is dead, bland, sunken, a canvas upon which has been embedded the full and perfect features of the dead, the shades and valleys and small tablelands upon which the dead walk until at last they sleep. Yes, Martin Donner says, I do know, I can answer that. He thrashes weakly, the ganglia in his shattered nerves trying to pull into alignment. I wouldn't have done it, he says. I would not have died this way. It is not worth it. I *thought* it was worth it, that it was worth any price to be what you are, to live expressly and fully, but it is not; this is unbearable, I am sinking, I am sinking in disgrace, I wet myself, I humiliate myself, I see with the visions and dreams of such inextinguishable horror ... no, he says, *no*, and his voice is momentarily stronger, he screams in the room, *no*, he says, I would not have left them, I would have stayed there and I would have died, I would have died in a thousand ways, but it is the difference between metaphor and truth, they are *not* the same, once I thought they were but no, no, no, no, no, he says uncontrollably, the word ratcheting uncontrollably, and he sinks into the steaming sheets, his eyes fluttering, closed, and the coughing, the moaning, the turgid phlegm passes again through his desiccated and shattered cavities. *No*, he says, and *no*, I think, his answer is no and momentarily there is a kind of settling; I can feel my own realignment and a sense of history colliding with imminence merging with the steaming and impenetrable future, but of course this fusion cannot last and I am in Martin Donner's bedroom fifteen years earlier, the bedroom on the second floor of the suburban colonial in one of the nicest areas of a nicer suburb in these sets of anterooms to the city, and I have put the question again. I have put it to him calmly and without sinister intent and then have used my powers—the powers granted me by the old and terrible antagonist who nonetheless, and this is undeniable, always plays fair, as fairly as Martin did not with his wife and daughters and friends and family through all the years up to this point. I show him the bottles, the tubing, the arc and density of the room, the harsh and desperate light and it is uncommonly vivid; I have placed all my powers in the service of this adumbration. O yes, Martin says, seeing it all, oh yes, I see now. Yes, he says, it is worth it. I would do this. I would not be deterred. It is worth it. It is worth anything to expressly enact what you are, what you must be, the full and alarming necessities of the soul. So I do not care, he says. I am going, I am going to leave, if this is my destiny, so be it. His features congeal with conviction, unlike his face in the room of his

death, they recede and pulsate, project and flutter with light, there
is light all through him. Worth it, he says, worth it to be what one
is. How many years until this happens? he says. Not that it matters.
But I want to know.

Seventeen, I say. Seventeen years and not all of them will be
happy. Your daughters will weep and one of them will hate you,
there will be many betrayals, also other illnesses, earlier illnesses,
small and larger betrayals, a terrible bout with hepatitis. Dis-
graceful venereal conditions. I don't care, he says, seventeen years
is a good time. In seventeen years here, lying here, sneaking
around, pounding myself into myself, I will be dead, I will have
killed myself anyway. No, he says, there is no question, there is no
argument. I have made my choice. He closes his eyes, smiles,
thinking evidently that he is dreaming. Such dialogues are common
inside Martin in this crucial time; he thinks that he is constructing
a worst-case venue but is nonetheless being firm. Yes, he says, I
will do this. His breathing, irregular, levels out. As I withdraw, he
thinks that he is making passage into dreamless slumber. As he
recedes he feels, I know, a kind of imminence, and perhaps it is my
question, no less than anything else, that has led him to this reso-
lution. It is difficult to work within such difficult and speculative
borders without being overwhelmed by my own relative helpless-
ness and stupor.

† † †

But of course this is in only partial quest of verification. I move
through the channels of recorded (and possible) time, asking
Martin Donner this question at various places within the con-
tinuum. I discuss this with him at Cherry Grove in 1978 at a tea
dance while he is hanging shyly against the walls, yes, he says, of
course it is worth it; I ask him this in 1986 when, thunderously, the

implications of the positive diagnosis begin to come through to him and he closes his eyes as I make the forced pictures in his head, showing him what it would be like: I don't know, he says, I don't know, I am in shock, I am in agony here, I can't give you a false or real answer, can take no position, how can I tell? Maybe I shouldn't have done it, I don't know, I don't know. Take the question to him in Chicago two years later; he is attending a class reunion with his lover, partial remission, he feels in control of himself, some benignity, perhaps illusory but the moment can be extended, he feels, as so many other moments have been extended. I would have done it again, he says, knowing what I know, I would have wanted it this way still; I would not have treated it differently, I would not exchange these years for anything. Ask him and ask him, up and down the line, sometimes an enthusiastic, desperate yes, other times more tentative, a no at the end and tracking back from that *no* mostly for the six to eight months before this special, spectacular extended agony; his position then is not fixed any more than it might have been twenty, thirty years ago when Martin refused to respond to the messages flicking like trap shots from the basement of his sensibility. Nothing is sure, nothing is firm. Mostly yes, an occasional no, more *no* as the end is approached, but even then at some of the moments of the worst anguish, a soft, insistent yes. It is not fixed, nothing is fixed, the human condition is not fixed. The price we will pay for fully expressing what we are does seem indeterminate then. It resonates, this confusion, against my own uncertainty, and I understand then, staring at and through all of this, that there can be no answers from Martin, none at all. If Martin is the voice and tensor of all possibility, then there is *no* possibility, no singularity.

Understanding this does not surprise me but fills me with a desperate and irreparable weakness; I would not have had it this way,

I would have wanted surer answers. Everyone wants answers if not *the* answer, even I. I return to my old antagonist on the desert and hand him the helmet and the simulating device and the other armaments of our translation, our bargain, our possibility. I have wrestled and wrestled, I say, I have wrestled you through all the avenues of this life and I do not know, I am stunned and pinned, dislocated and shattered. Martin is not the answer; he can provide me with no firm basis at all.

Of course, my old antagonist says. His ruddy skins glow with sympathy or perhaps it is only health. Or vindication. You see, he says, you are left with it just as I said, you are left with all of this on your own. *You* must decide what price to pay and whether that is correct and no one can know. He backs away from me, horns a rapier, fine eyes glints of purpose in the night. Now, he says, *now* you must decide. *You*, not Martin Donner, who is only a paradox or a metaphor, *you* must make that decision. It is the fortieth day, he says. Soon it will be the fortieth night. You must now turn in the way you must, and there will be no returning.

Yes, I say, yes, I understand that. Before me, closing my eyes like Martin in the hallucinatory daze, I see the traps, the sights, the visions of my own circumstance: the donkey, the cobblestones, the crowds, Pilate's smooth and terrible judgment, the hanging and the darkness. I see and I see and I see and in the iron spikes of the sun of Golgotha, alone and under the darkness, I see too the expanding and necessitous heart of God.

† † †

## Author's Commentary

"Understanding Entropy" was written in memory of Henry Walter Weiss (2/10/ 40–11/3/91), whom I knew for more than forty years and who for a substantial part of my life was my best friend. A graduate of Dartmouth and Oxford Colleges, Henry graduated from Harvard Law in 1965 and practiced in New York and New Jersey for a quarter of a century. He died in Florida very bravely, after a long illness. He was not only best friend but also my attorney, and if that isn't an oxymoron, then there is no such thing as the Science Fiction and Fantasy Writers of America.

I miss Henry a lot. I hope the story does not dishonor him.

† † †

*A park for a stable, a gazebo for a crèche . . .*

# MURMUR'S LAWS
## Jack Slay Jr.

When he first stepped into the gazebo, we figured he couldn't be more than nine, ten at the most. Some of us remembered him trembling, not so much from fright as from nervousness, trepidation. Maybe because of the half dozen people milling about; certainly because of what he was about to announce. Others of us said he stepped boldly forth and spoke without a glitch or hiccup.

Whichever way it happened, all of us—even those of us not there—remembered what he said, that first Law. "No murder," he said.

The sky was a swirl of angry blue, a storm approaching. Clouds ate the sun, darkening the park, a small plot of grass perched on the verge of town. In the center stood a rotting gazebo; behind it, a dying tree reached its skeletal branches skyward.

"All types," the boy said, "of premeditated killing."

He looked like any other ten-year-old until you stepped a little closer. Then it seemed as if his features didn't quite come together. His arms were too long and his face too broad. His eyes, blue as ice, were wide and spaced far apart. His mouth was huge, taking up the entire lower half of his face, his teeth like small stones. He looked boyish, gentle—but also strange, otherworldly.

Later, rumors sprouted about his oddness. There had been star showers the night before and some of us whispered of aliens and planetary visitations. Some spoke of the end of Times, a second coming. Still others remembered him from town, a small boy living with his mama just a street or two over.

Stretch, Georgia, is a small town. We take life as it's handed to us, swallowing the strange with the everyday. We have a courthouse on the square, a crumbling statue of a Confederate soldier, a new high school, a fire station. A quarter-century ago we were mostly farmers and mill workers, laborers who actually labored; we've changed with the rest of the world, and today we're mostly white collar with a country club and a cotillion dance every spring. Mostly, though, we've remained unchanged in the last century, going our ways, doing our things. Then came this boy.

No one believed him, of course. No one else heard that first Law, only a handful of us in the park that early spring day. He said we had a month to let the Law sink in and, if necessary, to adjust our ways.

From that first day we called him Murmur, it's what we heard him say through a crackling microphone. Some said they heard his name as Murrmann, Pat or Bob or Bill, but to us he was forever Murmur, a wisp that became a gale.

Murmur ended his conference saying he'd be back. Then he stepped from the gazebo and into a green Ford Truce; a woman drove him away. We stood there, looking at one another, smiling bemusedly. *Such talk*, we said, *such hope!*

† † †

A month passed and we had all but forgotten the boy and his Law. In the meantime, the world rolled as it always had, as did we, occasionally grumbling and passing the day as we had every day before. We strove, we endured.

A week before Murmur's second conference, exactly four weeks since the first one, a man stepped out of the shadows of an ATM over in Pine Mountain and leveled a .45 into the temple of a woman named Bonita Langley. It left a small ringworm-shaped bruise, a picture of it in the paper the next morning. He demanded her money, she refused, he pulled the trigger—and the gun backfired, taking off most of the right side of his head (no picture of that). No one thought of Murmur and his Law. A couple days later, over in Vidalia, a man named Jim Turner tried to poison his wife—except he got their toddies mixed up and drank the strychnine-laced bloody mary he'd fixed for her.

We knew little of murder in Stretch; we had long ago learned to live with what, and who, we didn't like. But we began to take notice after the fourth or fifth fumbled murder. Like a virus, the Murder Law spread through the state. When it hit Atlanta, the day before Murmur's second conference, CNN ran a dozen stories of guns misfired, of blunt instruments doubled back into their wielders, of blades snapped. The *Atlanta Constitution* ran a headline a week later, No Killings, the first time the city had had a murder-free week in years. But no one connected any of this to the small, oddly shaped boy in our gazebo.

† † †

We remembered instantly—as if we had never disremembered, as if a veil had been rent—the moment he stepped into the gazebo and spoke into the same black microphone. "The end of rape," he said. "You have two weeks," he said. A woman stood just behind him, the one from the Truce, silent, staring into the sky.

More of us were in the park that morning, not because we'd remembered the conference or had an inkling of Murmur, but because it was Saturday, a fine spring day, and the park had called us. Even the children listened, his voice like birdsong. We clapped after his statement and thought *what if*, smiling at his innocence, those bright ice-blue eyes, while inwardly wincing at our own jaded reckonings with the world.

Murmur grinned shyly and, waving, stepped down from the gazebo. He and the woman—we figured she had to be his mama: the same gangly arms, the same oversized mouth—waved again and ducked into their car. They drove away and we returned to our strolls and games.

✝ ✝ ✝

Two weeks later rapes stopped.

Over in Atlanta, the Buckhead Rapist met Murmur's Rape Law when his equipment got hung in his zipper as he pried open the legs of his sixth victim. His cries caught the attention of nearby police. Similar incidents occurred through the South: Knoxville caught their own serial rapist when his intended victim kicked him out of her car and backed over him, squashing his intended weapon. We read stories from as far away as Virginia, all reporting incidences of spontaneous genital combustion, all the victims male but for a single woman in Spartanburg, South Carolina. Her date said she'd tried to do things he didn't care to do.

We chuckled over these stories, delighted by the ironic justice, but only slowly did we think of Murmur.

We put two and three together, considering the *if* of the Murder Law, the Rape Law. We began to talk, quietly at first. Word spread quickly, rumor passing in whispers like a family secret. People grew delirious with the possibility. They became bold again, venturing out past dark, cutting through alleys and byways, taking back the dusk.

We looked for Murmur, of course, but quickly learned that he didn't live a street or two over—that, in fact, he seemed to live nowhere, that no one seemed to have known him before that spring day in the park.

††† 

Two weeks to the minute from his last conference, Murmur returned. We were ready, waiting with our hopes and wishes—and so was most of the rest of the state.

CNN and a number of local news affiliates sent crews with shoulder-mounted cameras and a batch of microphones, all trained on the gazebo. People, mostly strangers bedecked in bermuda shorts and odd hats, milled about, crowding us into the corners of our own park. Someone had festooned the gazebo with loops of red, white, and blue balloons, now bobbing in the spring breeze. A buzz of excitement filled the park, all of us on tiptoes, waiting.

The Murder Law reached the Rockies; the Rape Law rolled not far behind it, settling for the moment somewhere in Nebraska.

Murmur appeared behind the microphones as from nowhere, his face pale, a quiet smile parting his lips. His mama, just behind him, looked taken aback by the crowd, a bit worn and frazzled. Murmur, too, seemed surprised by it. He hesitated, then spoke firmly into the mikes.

"No more abuse," he said. "Child, spousal, otherwise."

The crowd hushed, as though his words had paralyzed them.

"No abuse," he repeated. "Physical, sexual, mental, emotional. No more abuse." He paused again, and again seemed ready to say something else.

The crowd remained still.

Then Murmur shrugged and said, "A week." He took his mama's hand and together they stepped off the gazebo and into a car we could not see. Silence hung in the park. Then, as one, we cheered, applause like thunder rolling through the park. For minutes the roaring filled us with the sheer happiness, the *joy* of its sound, its power. We stomped and hollered and pounded one another on the back; we whooped and jumped and knew how wonderful life was, our faces nearly split in half and aching with grins as big as Murmur's.

When the park quieted, Murmur was gone, slipped away into the gathering darkness. Even the news people had missed him. We reveled on, celebrating Murmur's world, thinking little now of the boy, rejoicing in the Laws and not the hows and whys.

✝ ✝ ✝

Not quite two days later the rumors began, of his health, of how ill he had looked at the conference. We'd been far in the back, behind the cavalry of camera crews and visitors, but we, too, remembered his paleness, his pauses. He'd looked poorly, we recalled, not as *there*.

Because of the outsiders, we told one another; because of the onslaught and excitement. We satisfied ourselves—and knew the first creeping of fear, for Murmur, for ourselves, for our given new world.

We waited for his return and watched the Murder Law, like an unfurling wave, wash across the West Coast, riding down into Mexico and up into Canada. It swept into the Pacific and headed into the Eastern Hemisphere. The Rape Law surged just behind it. Within a week they'd covered the world.

Then, in a single blinding flash, the Abuse Law also swept the world.

✝ ✝ ✝

For the next three months, Stretch, along with the rest of our planet, caught itself up in the celebration of untainted life. As

Murmur had said in our gazebo, abuse—physical, sexual, mental, emotional—halted.

Clumsy children, those constantly battered and swollen from tumbling down stairs and walking into unopened closets, appeared unbruised and smiling; women's safe homes across the country emptied and, eventually, closed. The occasional man came into work unlimping, his face free of the marks he'd said the razor, the cat, or an untrimmed hedge alongside his driveway had made.

We lived in a fresh world—mornings bright and clear, twilights safe.

We celebrated, as did the rest of the world: all-night parades, citywide picnics, parties encompassing whole counties. We spoke to strangers and gave lifts to hitchhikers. We slept with doors unlocked and windows flung open to the cool night winds.

Naturally, we had our share of naysayers—contemporary Cassandras, like Old Man Warner and his wife Mildred, wailing about population explosions and natural selection and the planet in peril. "We're on the Road to Eternity," they wailed. "The world's at end!"

We glued ourselves to CNN, fascinated with quarter-hourly reports on what they called the Millennium Miracles. One report spotlighted a scientist out in Colorado who went on about entropy and the necessity of chaos; otherwise, he said, we encountered the horror of equilibrium and ultimately the inevitable heat death of the universe. He made it sound terrible, ghastly, a universal meshing of stagnated lives. We gladly gave him his fifteen minutes, nodding our heads, listening attentively before returning to our parades and picnics, dragging him with us.

We shouted at the naysayers: Take it to Murmur!

Corollaries developed, apparently built-in deductions of Murmur's Laws. In late May two men over in Alabama decided to rob the Second National Bank in a wayside town. It seemed a sure thing: they couldn't be murdered in the process. They stormed into the bank waving guns (both later discovered to be clipless) and shouting obscenities. The bank guard drew his own sidearm and, in a combination of instinct and panic, shot both would-be robbers, taking each down with a single shot. Someone later said it had not appeared that the guard had been aiming his gun in even the general direction of the hapless robbers.

An afternoon or so later, a young woman killed her husband up in one of those New England states, maybe Vermont. She said he was coming after her with a leather strop, something he'd done before but not since the Third Law. He was drunk, out of his mind and raving, she said. As he charged, she pulled a butcher knife from the dish drain and held it out, a warning. He tripped over the cat, and the blade, she said, slipped easily between his ribs, finding his heart.

Signs, the Caustics screamed, of the Laws crumbling. Glitches and mistakes, they wailed, omens of the end. We saw them as corollaries and amendments. We ignored them, happy, continuing our days and ways, beyond striving, beyond enduring, waiting, impatiently now, for Murmur's next Law, anticipating, imagining what new wonder he'd unfold for us.

††††

By midsummer Stretch rocked with people, thousands upon thousands flocking to hear the next Law. They came from the world over, crowding into our small, one-light town, bringing their own hopes and dreams to the heart of the world's celebration. Stretch burst at the seams, spilling into neighboring towns, flooding the adjoining counties. And still they came, packing the motels, crowding the streets, stripping away everything that could be bought or toted. When they'd filled every room for a hundred miles, they slept on our lawns and in our garages; when they'd eaten every grocery clean, they pled at our doors and beneath our windows. Vendors made fortunes. Everybody sported a bright white Murmur tee shirt, baseball cap, or bumper sticker, each emblazoned with the alien gaze of Murmur. We called in the National Guard to direct traffic, even though traffic had stood stock-still through half the state for over a week. And still they poured into Stretch, all to see Murmur, to hear his Law, to shout his name, to touch, if they could, the hem of his jeans, the frayed seam of his tee shirt.

He hadn't appeared for three months, a long silence. People tried to track him. The news lived on supposed sightings and suspect interviews with this strange boy we'd misnamed Murmur, a name taken up and shouted by the world. No one found anything, as if he didn't exist outside the realm of his Laws, our gazebo. No one looked too hard or too long, though, suspecting, as we all did, that finding Murmur would disrupt the magic, eradicate the mojo.

When he finally did reappear, it was like before, as if from nowhere, stepping shakily into the gazebo. His name, in awed whispers, flashed through the crowd like wildfire. Murmur, we said, he's come. The name whipped along, through the park and into the streets where the crowds had long since spilled. It carried past the square and through the town, into the county and across the state. He's back! we said. He's *here*!

He looked worse, our Murmur. If there had been doubt and rumor before, none existed now. He appeared deathly ill, his skin like chalk, his body wasted. His face was skull-like and his hair, once a bright sun-blond, hung lifeless and thin, like an old man's. Even from the rear of the park we saw tiny spasms jerking his body.

His mama laid a hand on his shoulder. He pressed a gaunt cheek to her hand and stepped to the microphones. He smiled.

That slow smile lit us; we found its strength and knew our Murmur had returned, that his word would soon make this great given world even better. Someone far away cheered, a lone cry of spirit, and we caught it up, shouting our joy at this boy, screaming our delirium skyward.

Murmur remained silent, looking out over the throng, smiling his gentle, stone-toothed smile. After several minutes, he slowly raised his hand (it, too, shook: an old man's hand) and the crowd fell silent. His mama stepped beside him and slipped a clear plastic bowl over his mouth and nose. He breathed deeply and the tremors slowly ceased. Oxygen? we heard someone ask, fear heavy as rain in that voice. He turned back to the microphones and said, "No more addictions, no more highs."

The crowd stood still, waiting for more. A few shuffled impatiently.

"Two days," he said, stepping back, and his mama took his elbow and led him from the gazebo.

The crowd seemed unsure. A few groans, clearly audible in the summer heat, filtered through the park. No highs, no addictions, we mumbled. What did he mean? We looked at one another as if someone else might have an answer.

A platoon of reporters moved toward Murmur, shouting his name, endless queries behind the whys and hows of his life and Laws. He smiled his trembling smile, waved a birdlike hand, and climbed with his mama into their car. The crowd surged forward and then quickly parted as the car emerged, sputtering and backfiring. We touched it as it cruised past, to feel the tingle of his Laws in the dented metal. Through the sun-sparkled windshield, we saw Murmur huddled in the back seat, staring at his clasped hands in his lap. His mama at the wheel, their car disappeared into the throngs.

Two days later the Law fell into effect. No addictions. No highs. We found that alcohol still proffered its moments of numbing ease, that nicotine retained its acrid bite, that drugs kept their nirvanic snap—but only briefly. Worse, desire was suddenly gone, the desire, the *need* for the escape intoxicants brought. They had been regulated, by the fingering of a single Law, to a momentary rush, an infinitesimal buzz of freedom, of loss—and then nothing, instantly subsumed by the everyday trot of everyday feelings: each pill, each hypodermic, each lung-filling drag just the same. No altered euphorias, no euphoric alterings.

No highs. No addictions.

The world groaned. It was the first Law whose teeth nipped at our own secret walks of life. He's taken something now, we said: more than we'd asked for.

The Caustics yawped, See! *See!* We continued to ignore them, hating them for hating our given new world.

The Law's corollary, too, we soon learned, had bite. Murmur gave no solace to the addicted, those already in the quagmire of prefabricated moods. They lived without their escapes and preferred realities; cut off from their buzzes and highs, they struggled, lost, in a vast world of cold turkey, freezing.

Some handled it, gritting their teeth, clenching their fists, and moving into the celebration of our new world. Others didn't. For the first time in months, the media bloated itself on stories of death. Pre-Murmur addicts dropped like flies denied their sugar, curling up like overgrown fetuses. The Caustics railed and the rest of us had our first doubts, an oily feeling slipping into our minds.

The Caustics—now a thousandfold more than their original wheedling number—began to politic for control, their platforms based on the horror of a perfect world, on the fallibility of utopia. Too good is doom, became their cry; seemingly, much of the world listened—even, we feared, some of us.

Then, catching us unaware, he returned, stumbling up to the gazebo on stick legs, clutching a microphone, his face an unlined mummy's. He looked more alien than ever, flung from outer reaches, up-washed from the deeps. He shielded the sun with a clawlike hand, and his eyes found ours; he smiled and bowed his head.

We *knew* him then, recognized him in the grip of a creature we'd known too often. We'd seen it in our grandfathers and great aunts, their wasted bodies curled beneath the quilts, their breath hot and fetid against our last kisses. We'd smelled its cheesy odor in the corridors of our hospital and nursing home, had heard its death rattle in our houses, coming from the depths of our fathers and sisters and even our very own children. We'd encountered this creature too often, smiting it occasionally, more often losing to its power.

Meeting his eyes—gummed almost shut, swollen and discolored—for that brief instant, we knew that Murmur had met the creature as well. He was eaten with it.

He looked out over the crowd, *his* crowd, and the park fell quiet. Even the birds and squirrels paused.

"No more hate—please." His voice cracked: hope fissuring.

A world without hate? we asked. Countries without wars, cities without strife, neighbors without feuds? We trembled at the thought, quaked at the possibility.

"Now," Murmur said.

The world paused, considered utopian dreams; then the Caustics rallied, uniformly railing, bringing with them, it seemed, most of the world, a world that could not see itself without hatred for something. Hatred, they shouted, was human necessity. It was instinct, the collective unconsciousness, the subatomic bond that held us intact. To allow, to *be allowed*, that cold passion to flow through our thoughts, our veins, our selves was human essence. To *not hate* should be choice, the Caustics, now legion, screamed—not Law.

There erupted what we later called the World Riots, a planet-wide resistance, a tremendous yammering against the Laws. Rioters, the young, the old, the angry and fed-up, stormed through, trashing cities across the globe, driven to frenzy by the impossible thought of an impossibly perfect world. They screamed at the sky; they smashed into stores and houses. But no one was murdered or raped, no one was abused, emotionally or physically, no one got drunk or stoned. It was (we decided after things had settled, after the world had turned its steady way into the next day) a rather docile riot.

Fear, we later said, should have been the last law: Murmur should have said No more fear—fear of the unknown, fear of possibility.

† † †

Murmur appeared a final time, a shadow of the boy we'd met last spring. It was a rainy day in early fall, the clouds dense and gray, the first chill heavy in the air. Few were in the park, only a handful of us, true believers. We drew near, as close as we'd ever been.

Murmur smiled down, the smile cracking his lips, opening the lesions on his face.

"No more cancer," he said, his voice little more than a whisper. His breath hitched in his chest. Blood like tears ran from his eyes. He nodded and smiled again. Then he said, "All," and stepped off the gazebo and walked away. No one followed him. In the sky appeared a double rainbow: twin ribbons the color of promise.

We knew that things must happen as they did. Murmur had crossed a boundary. He'd interrupted the natural world, attempting, we knew, to make even the natural order of things better. We asked why, of course. Then the magic broke, the mojo snapped, and the world flowed back into itself. People once again, as they had from the primordial ooze, murdered and raped and abused one another. Hate fed us, and highs let us sleep.

Even now, we few true believers, the Murmurers, remember him, to ourselves and to others, speaking the wonders of a perfect world, a utopia beyond all utopias, beyond even a madman's dreams. Passersby and rare listeners nod and perhaps stare blankly before walking on—a world as green and lovely as what we speak too unreal, too perfect, too far beyond their beliefs.

We speak on, in this tiny park, stopping whoever will listen, telling Murmur's tale, and always, always watching the skies, hope fluttering in our hearts like a moth batting against the glassed flame.

† † †

### Author's Commentary

Like many stories, "Murmur's Laws" began as daydream: What would I do if I could change the world? What miracles would I wring from the clouds? Ideas began to coalesce as I read Karen Joy Fowler's *Sarah Canary*, and bits of her fabulous alien occasionally clung to my own mysterious stranger. But Murmur, an odd boy hanging out in a rundown Georgia gazebo, began to cultivate his own needs and traits, most obviously a decided messianic complex. He moved and acted as I envisioned Jesus doing in the Gospels. Hence, Murmur serves as answer to that ubiquitous pop question: What would Jesus do?

The key to Murmur, though, lies not in his affinity with Jesus or in his apparent miracles. Most of the changes he speaks into law are changes that *we* could bring about if we set our heads aright. As everyday people, we could abolish rape and murder and abuse. As mere humanity, we could forge a better world. Only when

Gore Vidal smiled his distant, deep smile. "Now look, Larry. You know what the wars between religions were about, don't you? About which side had the better imaginary friend."

King laughed uncomfortably as he got the point. "I've heard that joke."

Vidal grimaced with mock mercy. "Okay, let's be fair. It was about which side had the one true imaginary friend."

King shrugged. "Same difference. So you think faith is a sham?"

Gore Vidal said, "I'm sure that I could make a better defense of faith than mere insistence."

As Larry King hesitated before the poised intellect of his guest, someone who might have been taken for Jesus in a lineup appeared slowly in the chair next to Gore Vidal.

The audience gasped. Larry King stared. Gore Vidal looked over and said wearily, "Magic tricks? I'm going to be part of a magic show? Good God, give me a break."

Larry King reached over and grabbed Vidal's wrist. "But you . . . didn't you see him just fade in? That's what he did, that's what he did! Faded right in next to you!"

Vidal sighed and pulled his wrist free. "Fade in? I had to type that in my scripts for ten years so I could make enough money to live as I please." Then he glanced over at the smiling man sitting next to him and said, "Good evening, Sir. I don't know why you're here, but I hope they're paying you enough. My name is Gore Vidal."

"Yes, I know," the bearded, smiling man said through yellowing teeth.

Just as Larry King began to say, "Look here, buddy, I don't know how you got in here, but the soup kitchen's down the street," the visitor disappeared.

In the twinkling of an eye, before Gore Vidal had a chance to look at him again.

Murmur messes with the natural order—when he asks for his only genuinely Christlike miracle—do things actually fall apart.

Finally, a secret deep in the story's heart: Bob Murrmann was a hometown friend, an easygoing guy I could count on for anything. Several years ago, doctors detected spots on one of his lungs. As I began this story, Bob's battle with cancer reached its valiant height. He succumbed about the time I finished "Murmur's Laws." To my good friend Bob Murrmann, then, I dedicate this story.

† † †

*Lord of the celebrity circuit . . .*

# THE COMING OF CHRIST T
# JO
## George Zebro

---

*By 2001 a.d. some 44 percent of Americans believed th*
*I would be coming back in the new millennium. Tha*
*better than the ten just men my Father tried to find.*

—Jesus Chr

✝✝✝

"Well, you know, God is at best an exaggeration," sa Vidal to his talk show host.

"What do you mean?" Larry King asked.

"You know—omnipotent, omniscient, biggest, b extremes. Imaginative exaggerations each." He crossed and sat back with a sigh.

"Don't you believe in God, Mr. Vidal?" Larry King a hushed voice.

"Believe? Oh, come now, Mr. King, I shan't be dragged can of worms."

"It's certainly more than that," King said.

"Faded right out!" King exclaimed. "Right on out there . . ."

"There's no soup kitchen down the street," Gore Vidal said as Christ the Joker came to all parts of the world.

He came to ridicule, not to teach or save, following the principle that a good horselaugh is the best weapon against stupidity.

Heads of state found themselves floating naked above their capital cities, screaming as pigeons alighted on these human dirigibles.

At Grant's Tomb in New York City, Jesus walked up to a cop on the beat while eating a hot dog and wiped his mustard-covered hand on the back of the policeman's blue uniform. The Irish cop turned around, and Jesus finished the job on the front of the uniform.

"Now look here, friend," the cop said. "I'll be runnin' you in for that!"

"Oh, come now. If you've heard my parable about the mustard seed, you'll know why I did it."

"Is that a fact?" the cop said as he reached out to arrest the empty air.

On Wall Street, Jesus appeared on the main floor of the stock exchange and scrambled the big board. Amidst the shouts and moans that followed, he unscrambled the board, then with a hand motion sent it into chaos again, just so there would be no mistaking that he had done the deed.

"Terrorist!" cried the money mob, clearing a circle around the Nazarene.

"Put it back!" a lone voice pleaded from some private hell.

As all eyes looked to the salvation of the big board, the chaos continued.

Simultaneously at the Vatican, Jesus appeared in the Pontiff's earthly garden.

"Who are you?" the Pope demanded, putting away his Palm Pilot.

"Who do I look like?" Jesus asked.

"I think you had better leave," said the Pontiff, looking around for his guards.

"Very well," Jesus said, and dissolved.

When the guards arrived, they found the Pope buck naked, attempting to cover himself with a few fern branches.

At Donald Trump's third wedding reception, Jesus appeared at the champagne fountain and turned all the waiting bottles into boxed wines.

At the annual conference of American governors, combined in this year with a convention of prison wardens, Jesus replaced the keynote speaker, William Bennett, and said, "The measure of a criminal justice system is whether it commits new crimes against the convicted. Fresh crimes harm those who commit them as much as they harm the punished. Surely you can understand that much?"

Then he did a magic trick—the destruction of all documents, physical and electronic, by which 60 percent of all people incarcerated were imprisoned. "Thus I free the undeserving," he said to the delegates, "and there will be nothing you can do about it. The lawyers will do their work with a good conscience."

"Who do you think you are!" Mayor Rudolph Giuliani cried from the middle row.

Jesus raised his right hand and said, "I am who *will* be."

"What's that?" Rudy asked.

"As my father *was* when the Burning Bush spoke," Jesus continued. "He was who *is*, and I am who *will* be."

"Ah, shut up, Giuliani!" a voice cried out. "You'd arrest Jesus, Mary, and Joseph if they came to New York."

Rudy said, "The homeless are not, I repeat, not those holy figures." The audience booed.

Jesus raised a hand. "The mayor of New York forgets that what he does to the least of mine he does to me."

Suddenly silent, the audience shrank back from the intruder. Giuliani rolled his eyes, insisting to himself that no one powerful would show solidarity with the weak and worthless without a political motive. Only legends and myths did that. Tricksters he did not have to worry about.

Silently, Jesus looked at the audience—as he did on Wall Street, and in the Papal Garden of the Vatican where the Pontiff prayed on all fours, and in a thousand other places throughout the world. At Grant's Tomb he leaped into the cop's arms and kissed him on the lips. The policeman let him go. Jesus did not fall.

"Lord have mercy!" cried the wardens and governors, still shrinking from the hand that seemed raised to strike.

Jesus popped back in on *Larry King Live*.

Gore Vidal crossed his legs and said, "You know, you're quite good. You remind me of a novel I once wrote called *Messiah*. But there's one fatal flaw in your act."

Jesus lowered his hand and turned to the famous author. "Flaw?" Jesus asked. "Act? There can be no flaw."

Gore Vidal sat back and smiled.

"Well, aren't you going to tell me?" Jesus asked.

"Don't you know everything?"

"I don't pry," Jesus said.

Vidal leaned forward. "Exactly what I mean. You cannot be Jesus Christ, despite your tricks. But you do have his persona right. At least I've always liked to believe that Jesus was an annoying character, even to his friends."

Jesus sat back and gazed with interest at the man of wit. "So why am I not he?"

"As you said," Vidal explained, "you don't pry. Now if theism were true, and God—your Dad, I suppose—made us all, then the first thing he would do is to convince us of his nonexistence. At the very least he would make of his being a thing of doubt. This would then leave room for moral freedom and faith. After all, everyone bets on a certainty, and you wouldn't like to be worshiped as a sure thing. There's no test in that."

"Go on," Jesus said.

"Therefore, God's absence is the best proof we have of his existence." Vidal yawned. "That is, if you wish to play theological games."

"So what does all this have to do with me not being myself?" Jesus asked.

Gore Vidal grinned, and there was a twinkle in his eye as he asked, "Now, you're sure you don't want to pry into my mind and find out—and prove something to me?"

"No," Jesus said.

"Well, there you have it. Since you've interfered with human affairs, you cannot be God or his Son. An interfering God is inconceivable, so you can't be Jesus."

"I interfered once before," Jesus said.

"So people say. For my part a God of second thoughts cannot be God. Therefore you're a very clever impostor. For all I know you're David Coppersteel . . . or some such magician."

"Don't get him angry!" a woman cried from the audience.

Elsewhere throughout the world, Jesus continued his guerrilla raids, playing pranks upon humanity in place of exhortations, teachings, or plagues. These last had always been later explained as natural events anyway, so they had never done any good. Even great theologians had marked them as "physical evils" having nothing to do with God, whose evils would surely have been "intentional."

This time Jesus had begun with slapstick. But he quickly began to see that perhaps something stronger was needed—irony, even bitter black comedy.

Maybe.

He thought about this as he sat next to Gore Vidal, and in a thousand other locations. Humor, it had been said by these very same creatures who had been set in motion by his father (creation was hardly the word for what he had done), was the highest form of reason. It provoked sudden, unexpected exposures of stupidity. Unfortunately, these insights lasted only long enough to produce very slow net progress in human affairs. These creatures might very well destroy themselves before self-improvement kicked in decisively.

"Mercy!" cried the peoples of the world, as ironic bitterness pierced their lives in a million ways. "Why teach us in this way? Why did you not make us right to begin with, oh Lord?"

Jesus answered that to do so would have simply created the so-called angels all over again. Then, as with the angels, it would have been necessary to give them free will, so that they would escape the triviality of guaranteed goodness. And look what happened when the angels had been set free. One faction stayed loyal. The other set up shop elsewhere. Both continued to meddle. No, he was not yet ready to give up on goading humanity to see the right—which was permitted—and have them choose it for themselves. It was risky, but maybe it would come out right this time; after all, not all the angels had chosen wrongly.

Jesus adjusted the time, enabling him to sit next to Gore Vidal even as his plan of provocation played throughout the world.

After a few unmeasured moments that might have been years, or miniature infinities, Gore Vidal said, "Okay, I do sense that you're doing something to the world, to my mind, and perhaps to time itself. I would consider it good manners if you would at least be up front about it. Of course, I can't think of you as the traditional Christ. That would be beneath whoever or whatever you are."

The man was brilliant, Jesus thought. For a man, that is. That was the trouble with these experiments. It was impossible to know where they might lead; yet they had to be left to run their course to have any value.

"I've always suspected," the brilliant and intuitive man continued, "that humankind was some kind of put-up job. Will you confirm this?"

"Mercy!" the unprotectedly satirized cried in Christ's mind.

"Watch it," the Father said within him. "I wouldn't want to have to try to drown them a second time."

What the brilliant and remarkably intuitive man had said made Jesus think that it would be better to tell these creatures the complete truth about who they were and where they came from. That way they would at last be disabused of their misguided ideas about the powers of the Trinity. The brilliant and witty man sitting next to him was right. Show these creatures any great unexplained power and they tended to exaggerate.

"We have hundreds of callers," Larry King said.

The speakerphone crackled. "How do we know you're God, or Christ, or whatever?" asked a male voice, and a baldheaded little man in pajamas was suddenly sitting in Larry King's lap.

The man got up and dropped to his knees with conviction.

"See that?" Jesus said to Gore Vidal. "It would have been better for him to doubt and find his faith, but you people always need a convincer."

The man vanished.

"But very shortly many will doubt I did that," Jesus said, "even if they replay the scene."

"Well," Gore Vidal said, "you do admit that it's a shabby miracle, since there are countless ways to explain it. A miracle must be made of sterner stuff. It must be inexplicable."

Larry King pulled himself together and said, "Is this why you've come, to nudge us into goodness . . . again?"

Jesus sighed. "I'm of three minds about it, and maybe I should lose all patience. We've tried to help you by visiting your scale of life, but it did no good then and might do no good this time either. Laughter doesn't seem to open your eyes, except fleetingly, and then you forget to live the lesson. So I will let you all know how things are, just who and what you are."

"Really?" Gore Vidal asked, eyes wide as his skepticism warred with his growing wonder.

Jesus said, "Starting over at the manger wouldn't work today. You're not children anymore."

"I quite agree," Gore Vidal said. "The lessons of that Bronze Age document, the Bible, have rarely instructed us to do more than kill each other."

Disturbed by Gore Vidal's critical attitude (he couldn't tell which side the writer was on), King shifted in his chair and gazed at Jesus, determined to humor his mad guest. "So what did you . . . you or your Father, and that third thing, think you were doing when . . . you created the universe?"

"The universe?" Jesus said. "Hardly that. A world."

"All right, a world," King said.

"Being creative," Jesus said. "You can understand that, I suppose," he added, glancing at the brilliant and intuitive man next to him. "I've now reentered your scale of existence from what you would call a much larger one. You are an escaped creation, but we've left you to yourselves because we consider it wrong to destroy anything self-sustaining, however humble. It's a matter of before and after. After is very different. It's later."

King's jaw dropped. "You've got to be kidding, buddy."

"Not at all," Jesus said. "You're only a quantum fluctuation in a superspace vacuum, scarcely more than a greasy spot on the wall in one of our oldest cities. But we have let you be. Our mistake was to make you free too early in the game. And of course you don't like freedom. You want to be told what to do all the time, as if your own decisions, especially those about how you should treat each other, don't count unless they have some kind of divine pedigree. And you yearn for enforcers."

"But you say you're Christ," King said. "So you know what's right and wrong."

"See what I mean?" Jesus said to Gore Vidal. "Yes and so what?"

"And you punish us when we die, right?" King asked.

"Of course not," Jesus said. "Most of you just dissipate into nothing."

King stared at him.

"What?" Jesus asked. "Isn't that bad enough? To go and not to know, I mean."

Gore Vidal had a sick took on his face and held his stomach, as if he was about to hurl.

"Are you all right?" Jesus asked.

"No," Gore Vidal grunted and bent forward.

Jesus touched his forehead. "There, is that better?"

The brilliant and intuitive man sat back. "Yes, thank you."

"How did you do that!" King asked.

"No more difficult than putting a Band-Aid on a cut," Jesus said. "You'd call it a kind of channeling."

Shaken, Gore Vidal asked, "How . . . do you power all these miracles?" and rubbed his chin.

Jesus said, "We lay off the energy expenditure to another scale."

"Oh, I see," Gore Vidal said. "So it's paid for."

"Yes. Supernatural in your eyes, but quite something for something rather than something for nothing. It's pay as you go, even if you do rob Peter to pay Paul." Jesus smiled.

"Can anyone learn?" Gore Vidal asked.

"In principle, yes."

"This scale . . . of things," King said, "does it go on forever?"

"Yes, it does. How else could we lay off the energy we need to do things? It's a standing infinity."

King looked confused, so Jesus said, "Things get bigger forever, and they get smaller forever. Got it?"

"And you made us, and kept this from us?" King asked.

"You'd only have destroyed yourselves sooner," Jesus said. "You have to grow into that level of power usage. Some of you know about vacuum energy and the impossibility of zero-fields. But you've always ignored your best minds, except when they make weapons for you."

Larry King took a deep breath.

Gore Vidal fidgeted. "I was not a good science student," he confessed.

"Another caller!" King cried. "Go ahead, you're on!"

"Do animals have souls?" a woman asked, then burst into tears.

"What is it, dear?" Jesus asked.

"My cat Dino died a few days ago, and my minister . . . well, I asked him where my cat was now, and my minister said *nowhere!* Because animals don't have souls. He said that about Dino, for Christ's sake!"

Jesus said, "Animals have as much soul as all living things, because they're part of the same evolutionary programs we made. It doesn't matter whether it's pigeons or people. They achieve their share of soul, however small."

Gore Vidal looked at him as if to say that this wasn't much of an answer, because it still left the soul undefined, but it seemed to console the woman, who heard what she wanted to hear and cried out, "I knew it! Thank you so much," and hung up. Jesus looked at Gore Vidal, as if he knew what the man of wit was thinking, and said, "You do have to earn a soul, my dear man. It must be built up in the complexities of learning and response to life, along with a good memory. A soul must be deserved."

"Are you now prying?" Vidal asked.

"No, your objection was plain on your face."

"Let me ask you something," King said. "From what you've said about these levels, or scales—then there may be someone . . . above you?"

"Of course," Jesus said. "But they haven't visited us."

"No, no," King said, "that's not what I meant. I mean is there someone above it all? I mean a God, a real one above all the levels of infinity?"

"You've got to be kidding," Jesus said. "That's not even a question."

"It certainly is," Larry King insisted, smoothing back his hair.

Gore Vidal leaned forward and said, "Larry, keep in mind that by the meaning of the word *infinity* it goes on forever, up and down from us. There can't be an overall God, just the infinity. An overall God would limit it, and then would himself have to be an additional infinity."

"Oh," King said, then sat back looking confused. "No," he said after a moment, "there can't be an infinity. And how could you know if there was one?" He laughed. "Count it? Measure it?"

"That's a puzzle," Jesus said. "If we could travel indefinitely in scale, up and down through the multiverses, we might still never know whether they went on forever, since we might reach the last one in the next jump. After an eternity of travel, we would still not be certain."

"There," Larry King said to Gore Vidal, "I knew it!"

"However," Jesus said, "the principle that you call induction would suggest, after a while, that one is facing an infinity. Besides, an infinite superspace is necessary to explain universes, to avoid the problem of origin, which then becomes inexplicable in finite systems. Local origins are acceptable, but there must be an inconceivable infinite vastness to support local origins. All reality is local."

Gore Vidal smiled. "Either God always existed and is the ground of being, or the universe always existed and needs no explanation, in the same way that we would not ask where God came from. Choose one. Or are they both one and the same?"

Jesus looked at him. "I wish you people were as bright when it comes to your violent history and treatment of one another."

"So is there life after death?" Larry King asked.

"Mostly no," Jesus said. "You'll have to gain the glory of greater life spans on your own."

"Will you help us?" Gore Vidal asked, looking at Jesus with eyes that knew their mortality.

"I tried to give you life once," Jesus said, "but you misunderstood and turned it into all kinds of mystical jargon."

"Jargon?" Larry King asked.

"Words like divine love, grace, providence became meaningless as they were enlisted to serve your thieving power politics."

King sat back, looking appalled.

Jesus continued, "According to your Bible, my Dad supposedly said to me, in so many words if not exactly, 'I'll forgive them their sins, now and forever, if you're willing to die for this humanity on the cross. Just speaking up for them won't be enough. I'll know you mean it when you actually suffer and die for them. Of course, later on we'll get you up again, but you will have experienced the human pain.' And so on, as if my coming was a mission of some kind." Jesus paused, then said, "But of course he said no such thing to me. I was not a sacrifice for your salvation, which still seems a long ways off to me. You got this Lamb of God sacrifice idea from your agricultural festivals, or some such."

"If Christ has not been raised," Gore Vidal intoned, "then our preaching is in vain and your faith is in vain. Corinthians 15:14, I believe."

"But you did rise?" King asked, ignoring him.

"Yes, yes," Jesus said. "But what happened to me back then was a complete accident, later embellished."

"But you did get up from the dead," King insisted.

"What else could I do?" Christ said. "Later it seemed that maybe it would set a good example, encourage you to thinking about the shortness of your lives and spur you to getting yourselves a decent life span, for a start, and more later."

"Huh?" King asked.

"I wanted to set a good example," Christ said.

"Let me get this straight," King said, sounding dazed. "The way you talk suggests that you . . . made us somewhere, like on a table somewhere, in some large corner beyond our stars."

Jesus nodded. "We made a program, with every initial condition specified, then let it run. It wasn't the most impressive phenomenal realization of the noumena that I've seen. We might have started with a better Word. Still, you did get away from us, and there is much to be said for independence of action. While some of you do think, you're mostly hopeless."

"Oh, come now," Gore Vidal said. "Here I must side with Larry and say that you don't expect us to believe that our whole universe of stars and galaxies is some greasy spot on a wall?"

"One of you actually guessed something like the truth," Jesus said, "a mystic named . . ."

But even as Gore Vidal named the noumenously inclined scribbler, Jesus was also at a nearby hospital-hospice telling jokes to the sick and dying. At first a few of the patients laughed, but as the jokes found their mark one man cried out:

"I'm pissed off! They say you're Jesus Christ and you've been appearing all over the world. So you should be performing miracles instead of crackin' funnies." He looked around at the suddenly silent ward. "We're dyin' here! You should help us!"

Jesus raised a hand and said, "A laugh is nothing to sneeze at, my friends. Laughter has curative powers."

Slowly, the chain reaction started, and the sick ward chuckled, laughed, then roared explosively.

Gore Vidal sat back smugly and said, "So you've come to pillory us for our sins?"

Jesus said, "I've come to make you laugh, to wake you up."

"What's pillory?" Larry King asked.

"You're doing it to yourself," said Gore Vidal.

Jesus shouted, "Laughter is divine, a kind of grace born of the unexpected, invasive understanding that steals into us and cannot be denied. A revelation, no matter how trivial the joke."

"What does he mean?" King demanded.

"I tried other ways of helping you think for yourselves," Jesus continued. "I revealed myself in various ways, to different people. But it did no good. They made the same thing of my good advice."

"And what was that?" Larry asked him.

"Religion," Jesus said. "The bureaucratization of ethics."

"What's wrong with religion?" King demanded. "You, of all people . . ."

"It's only a wish-fulfillment way out of your difficulties, death among them. You'll have to work harder than just imagining a better place to go to. You'll have to learn enough to make one for yourselves."

"Tell me," Gore Vidal began, "how is it that you do miracles, given that you're not what we really mean by God?"

"I say again, they're not miracles," Jesus insisted. "Not in the sense that natural laws are inexplicably suspended. When you visit another scale, you can go around, behind, below, lower scales . . . and well, open doors in the physical laws."

Gore Vidal looked skeptical, as if he had just awakened. "All this you've made us think you've done, it's some kind of hypnosis, isn't it? And it's not really happening."

He waited, as if expecting the illusion to dissolve.

"It's the best I can do to explain it to your level of understanding," Jesus said.

Larry King guffawed. "Well, he certainly put you in your place!" He was still trying to do a tube show, even though human reality itself was in the balance and about to be found wanting.

"So what will come of your visit, this time?" Gore Vidal asked.

"We might just have to let you go," Jesus said, "let you dissolve into nothing."

"What!" King cried.

"So you've come to threaten us," Gore Vidal asked, "rather than make us laugh? We're supposed to die laughing, I suppose."

"Don't underrate nothingness," Jesus said. "It's a great peace. There are vast stretches of it in the up-and-down scales. Still, it's hard to achieve. Something always persists, some suffering echo of a bad job, impossible to erase, since one would have to achieve what some of your finest today would call a zero-point field."

"A what?" King asked.

"A hard wipe," Jesus said, clicking his tongue.

"Erase us?" Larry King cried. "How cruel! Who do you think you are?"

"Might we not appeal our case to your father?" Gore Vidal asked, "or to some being above your . . . scale, who might be more . . . of a

God than you are? Maybe there's a God above all the scales, or outside them?"

Jesus sighed, then said, "I don't think so. Why do you say it's cruel? Your misery will be at an end. I will prevent a future of suffering damnation for humanity, going on as it has in pain."

"But you can't see all futures," Gore Vidal said, "so maybe in some we'll succeed."

"You're right about that," Jesus said. "There is an infinity of possible futures. To see or try to change them, or prevent them, would put me in search mode forever. You're quite a bright fellow, but no, I mean this world right here."

"And by damnation you mean nothing more than our continued, fragile existence?"

"Of course," Jesus said. "As one of your great ones said, 'First you dream, then you die.'"

"Did it ever occur to you," King began, "that we might wish to continue as we are?"

"Everything occurs to me," Jesus said. "Evil always wishes to perpetuate itself. Have some faith in me when I tell you that you'll be much happier as nothing."

"That's sheer sophistry," Gore Vidal said. "We won't be around to appreciate a state of nothing."

"Trust *me*," Jesus said. "I'll know you're better off. Appreciate the thought now, while you can. You won't be able to later. You know, bright as you are, for a man, you really should listen more closely. Worlds teeter on a Word."

King took a deep breath. "Are you flesh and blood, now?"

"If you doubt it," Jesus said as he took a Smith & Wesson revolver from under his armpit and slid it across the table to Larry King, "you can shoot me through the head." King caught the weapon before it landed in his lap. "Feel free," Jesus said. "That's what you're supposed to do, act freely, even if it looks to me like repetitive motion."

King put the black gun gently on the table. "Let me ask you if there's any point to the universe, I mean from your perspective . . . uh, in the scale . . . of things." He stared at the gun.

"Oh, I don't think there are *things* really. It's all nearly nothing to begin with, with no beginning or end, needing no explanation of anything except local origins. The only thing that really seems to matter is being the right size."

"Right size?" King asked, his eyes still worrying the gun before him.

"Morally and physically, we're bigger than you, since we know how things have gone in the scale below us, at least down to several trillion levels."

"And above?" asked Gore Vidal.

"We do not inquire upward," Jesus said impatiently.

"Ah—so you fear something after all, or someone?"

"No, we just don't care to know more of what's there. What good would it do us?"

"But you do know?" Gore Vidal said.

"Hierarchies," Jesus answered, "—endless, petrified hierarchies from endless duration. I prefer the humilities of below."

"And you ignore the true God who rules above it all!" Larry King added belligerently.

"No," Jesus said. "An eternal being would be an absurd mystery to itself. I am that I am. An all-powerful, eternal, and even all-knowing being would still be unable to answer the question, why am I like this? Such a being would be an enigma to itself"

"But that doesn't rule it out, does it?" King asked, delighted by his own cleverness.

Gore Vidal smiled and said, "Well, I suppose that would all depend on what the meaning of the word *is* . . . is, wouldn't it?"

"We already have eternal existence," Jesus said. "It's the unique, infinite superspace—the *mysterium tremendum.* You've heard the story—the roof of the world . . . is supported by seven pillars, and the seven pillars are set on the shoulders of a genie whose strength is beyond thought. And the genie stands on an eagle, and the eagle on a bull, and the bull on a fish, and the fish swims in the sea of eternity!"

*"Mysterium tremendum!"* King exclaimed ecstatically.

"Latin," Vidal added, "for a right smart piece of time, as Lionel Barrymore once said about eternity."

Jesus said, "The most important part of that story is the infinite sea, in which the fish swims. Without that infinity, nothing would be possible."

"I see," Gore Vidal said. "The buck stops there, since the infinity simply is, and needs no further explanation. It always was."

Jesus said, "That is what the word *is* truly means."

"I think I see what you mean," Larry King added.

"Wait a minute," Gore Vidal said. "I know that story. It's from *The Thief of Bagdad,* a 1940 movie!"

"Yes," Jesus replied. "I've seen quite a few. They're so much better than the shapeless dramas that are your lives. I've even seen some of the movies you wrote."

Gore Vidal waited to hear what Jesus might say about his movies, but after a few moments of silence asked, "And my novels? Read any?"

"No," Jesus said, "no novels. I do envy the best moviemakers their godlike eye."

Gore Vidal grimaced. "Who do you fear?" he asked, pressing the question as if he had discovered something.

"Unpleasant, unkind people, if you must know," Christ said. "One of us got like that and fled upward into the scales a long time ago. We don't know what he's doing there, and we don't care as long as he stays away."

"One of you?" King asked. "Could that by any chance be Satan?"

"We don't know his name anymore," Jesus said with a wave of his hand.

"I don't quite understand this fleeing upward," Gore Vidal said, "despite your pilfered fish story. Who inhabits the upward?"

"It's all pretty mysterious," Jesus said. "The same infinity, the infinity! It's a kind of endless horror of unknowing for us who know so much, a cloud without edges. It's the one thing all our knowledge can't encompass. Not even our deep travelers will ever dive to the top or bottom of physical infinity."

"Deep travelers?" asked Gore Vidal.

Jesus smiled and pointed to himself.

"Then why do any of you bother . . . to travel?" King asked.

"It might still not be an infinity," Jesus said. "The idea haunts many of us, that infinity might only seem to be one, and that at any moment the end may not be far off."

"And if you came to the end of it," King asked, "what would you learn? That there's more beyond?" He laughed, proud of himself for getting it.

"Alas, yes. No matter how far we travel, the end may be an infinite way off. And if we found it suddenly nearby, there would likely be more beyond it."

"You've said *we* rather often," Gore Vidal said. "Who is this *we?*"

"The Trinity," Jesus said. "And each of us is also made up of quite a few lessers. We've been massing for a long time now."

"Massing?" Gore Vidal asked.

"We share each other," Jesus said. "You've had some imitative experience of that in your worship of cultural idols."

"Another caller!" King cried. "Go ahead, you're on."

A deep voice said over the loud crackle. "Hi, I'm from North Carolina . . ."

"Let me fix that for you," Jesus said, and the interference died.

"Thanks! Lookee here, I've been dead for donkey's years now, and suddenly here I am in my fallin' down old house with my dead girlfriend, who just said to me, 'Jesse Helms, how did we get back here?' "

"How do you think?" Jesus asked.

"My question is this. How can you be Jesus Christ? From what I've experienced firsthand you're just some kind of powerful alien . . . or some hogwash like that."

"So what's your question?" King asked.

"Who does he think he is, coming here and doing all these crazy things? Shoot him through the head and see what he does!"

"Go right ahead," Jesus said, pointing at the gun on the table.

"Don't get him mad, Jesse!" a woman's voice cried out. "He'll send us to hell!"

There was a long silence.

"Call his bluff, King!" Helms cried. "Do it and settle this crap once and for all."

"Lordy, lordy," chuckled Gore Vidal.

"Jesus! Jesus!" cried the crowd in Central Park. "What can we do?"

"First," Jesus said, "you get a big needle. As big as you can find, so you'll have a chance, at least. Then you get a very small camel— I'm trying to be helpful—then pass the beast through the eye of the needle—and you're home free."

Gore Vidal said, "Jesus, that's a really bad one."

"But Lord, Lord!" cried the mob. "We can't do that. No one can."

"It's a parable," Jesus said.

"Easy for you to say, Lord!" the mob cried.

"But remember," Jesus said, "I am who will be. And you can do the same."

"Mercy, Lord!" cried the crowd. "Save us!"

Larry King asked, "What about eternal life?"

"Aren't you going to shoot me?" Christ asked.

"Read his mind," Gore Vidal said.

"Can't tell which possible world this might be," Jesus countered in what seemed a moment of confusion. "But to answer your question. Eternal life? A nice ambition—a prerequisite to any kind of civilized life—but no one will give it to you. Certainly I won't. You'll have to accomplish all that on your own—or you won't know what to do with it."

"Providing you let us live," Gore Vidal said, using the word that might or might not be related to providence.

"Shoot him!" cried Jesse Helms over the crackle-free phone line.

"How can we achieve eternal life on our own?" King asked.

"You'll have to learn how."

"You've done it, then?" King asked.

"A long time now. It's a basic of truly intelligent life. But don't rush things. There are virtues to having a beginning and an end— certain qualities of dynamism. True, they must be paid for by being brief. Short lives in intelligent species are a way of shuffling the genes until something worth permanence emerges."

"Hmmm," said Gore Vidal wonderingly. "But not always . . ."

"And you can raise the dead?" King asked.

"That's part of it," Jesus said.

"No use in shooting you, is there?"

"Shoot him!" Helms cried. "So we'll know he's a goddamn liar!"

"It's worse if he's telling the truth," said Gore Vidal.

"You're forgetting the Trinity," Jesus said, shaking his finger at the camera.

"He's got backup," Gore Vidal said with a smile.

"Eternal life is a matter of bending time," Jesus said.

"Please demonstrate?" King asked, picking up the gun and

pointing it at him. "Correct me if I'm wrong, but I get the feeling you want me to use this. You will get up from the dead, won't you?"

"I'll show you once more before I leave. Try not to get it all wrong." He stood up and faced the host's desk.

King hesitated, and his hand trembled.

"Here, give me that," Jesus said, grabbing the gun by the barrel and pulling it up to his chest.

"Wait a minute!" King cried as he let go and crashed back into his chair.

The gun fired, opening up Jesus' chest. The bullet came out through his back, whizzed over Gore Vidal's head, and shattered a studio light. A sudden shadow covered the scene. Jesus fell forward across the veneer wood desk and lay there for a moment.

Then he stood up and smiled.

And in the next twinkling of an eye, Jesus Christ rose into the air and vanished with a whoosh, abandoning Jesse Helms to the prison of this life and leaving Larry King with an open and locked jaw.

Trembling uncontrollably, Gore Vidal leaped up from his chair and shouted, "My Lord! My Lord! Take me with you!"

† † †

After three days of solemnity, during which the world sought to explain away the Millennial Coming of Christ the Joker, the man buried in Grant's Tomb arose, walked marveling to the public library on Fifth Avenue, and asked a pedestrian, "What happened?"

No one had noticed his blue Union general's attire.

Jesus appeared at his side, presented Ulysses S. Grant with his favorite cigar, and lit it for him with a flutter of flame from nowhere.

"Thank you," Grant said, taking a puff. "How do you do that? Who are you?" There was another man beside Jesus, heavyset, gray-haired, and pale, looking a bit shaken but relieved.

"Deep travelers, like yourself now," Jesus said. "You'd better come with us."

Grant looked at him inquiringly, and then at his companion. "You think that would be best?" he asked as he flicked the ash from his cigar.

Jesus nodded. "You and Mr. Vidal are about the best to be had from . . . here."

The two men looked at each other, and the shadows fled from their faces.

Then Jesus took them by the hand and together the threesome slipped downward through worlds-within-worlds, searching the lower infinities, where swimmers from above would always be gods.

† † †

### Author's Commentary

"The Coming of Christ the Joker" deals with the ideals that have been read into Christ's message of human reform, and so rarely practiced. We don't know who he was or what he stood for (even the Gospels contradict his message of peace); he might have been someone else entirely. Of course, I don't believe a word of it— except for the ideals, the same ones that have been disgraced in all revolutions, in all times; secular or religious, the reforms seem to make no difference.

† † †

*If life were an Easter pageant . . . as maybe it is.*

# PASSION
## John M. Williams

The climax approached.

In the narthex, Maurice, his face gone bloodless, his body glazed with sweat, stood in a world of private agony as two young women with clipboards and headsets touched up the bloodstreaks on his forehead and attached a strip of flesh-colored padding to his shoulder. To the side, a couple of Roman soldiers waited with the cross—hollow, and fitted with a little wheel at the foot.

Down in the orchestra pit of the cavernous sanctuary the conductor lured a tragic chorus into the slowly darkening room—spellbinding the audience.

Meanwhile, Maurice, raising his hands to hold off the soldiers, sucked several short gasps out of the air. The stage manager watched him, talking tersely into her headset mike. *Timing, people—all in the timing.* Here and there in the sanctuary, silhouetted heads turned to look.

Matters grew more dire by the minute. Maurice grabbed two desperate handfuls of his chest and, his ashen features contorting, sank like a collapsing umbrella to his knees. A communal gasp escaped the little group—the attendants, the costumed soldiers

and onlookers, Simon the Cyrene. For those few seconds the line
between reality and drama, never what you'd call crisp, wavered,
and they watched the performance—but when he toppled, his face
seized by a ghastly grin, they looked at one other and somebody
said, "I think something's wrong."

"Yeah something's wrong," he gasped. "*Hello*—I'm dying."

"It's too early," someone said.

"Call an ambulance!" a more authoritative voice called.

The narthex turned to a confusion of voices and feet while,
below, the conductor looked peevishly over his shoulder and
kept repeating section S, thinking *This is inexcusable, absolutely
inexcusable.*

"What do we do?" someone asked the stage manager, who curtly
gestured for silence, listening to her earplug.

"Find another Jesus—quick," she reported after a moment, and
everybody looked at somebody else. "Who has a beard, please?"

Within ten seconds the process of elimination had brought all
eyes to Arnold, a five-year-veteran Robed Onlooker, whose dark
hair and beard framed his angular features and black eyes.

"Me?" he said.

"Yes, you," answered the stage manager, "we have no choice"—
and knelt to dislodge the crown of thorns from the gasping Maurice.

"Ow!" he cried, not from the thorns (rubber), but from the bump
of his discarded head hitting the floor.

"Quiet, please," said the stage manager.

Arnold looked around, but indeed no one else seemed to fit the
bill. He opened his mouth to protest—

"Make-up!" The stage manager whisked his headdress away and
plopped the thorny crown on.

The music repeated, repeated. Outside, a distant siren wailed.

"Take off your robe, please," the stage manager directed Arnold, then snapped over her shoulder, "Somebody get those rags off JC!" She turned back to Arnold, in whose eyes an odd resignation had already settled. He unfastened his robe and stood waiting in sandals and gym shorts.

The siren bore down on them. The stricken Maurice lay on the floor in a pose like someone trying to scale a wall, in boxers.

A costume girl lifted his rags and tucked them around Arnold's midsection while make-up applied the new recruit's bloodstreaks and stripes, and the soldiers lowered the cross onto the pad on his bony shoulder.

The stage manager inscribed a tight circle with her hand. "Okay, people—let's move!"

And the procession began. As everyone moved down the aisle, the star laboring amid them, some of the audience turned to others perplexed, while others seemed too entranced to notice, and back in the vacated narthex the paramedics burst through the door. Manger Scene, looking desperately after this transfigured *man*, this *Arnold*, lingered just long enough to point out—unnecessarily— the prostrate Maurice to the medical crew, then hurried to catch up the rear.

Things got a little blurry.

Bam bam bam went the hammer.

Disgruntled thieves hanging overlong to either side, the center cross finally rose heavenward from its slot. Arnold, aboard, plundered his memory—*Forgive them, Father . . . surely this day . . . into thy hands . . . Eloi, Eloi, lama sabachthani*—though this last went counter to the church's official position (closely argued by the Reverend Dr. Blaine Larney in his book *Lying Tongues and "Dinosaur" Bones*) that English had been spoken in ancient Palestine.

God, the view! High in the rear of the sanctuary, faces of the crew glowed bluely in the control booth, as "darkness covered the sun" and the full orchestra sawed and thundered beneath him. All of them, everybody in the world, on one side—then me, thought Arnold: a weighty reflection. *Behold the Lamb of God* . . . He surveyed the ocean of faces, many and one, pierced unexpectedly by the tragedy of each—being born, living, dying—so brave, so sad. He blinked away the warm tears and caught the eye of that young woman, looking longingly up at him.

It was finished, the tympani and cymbals said.

He got through the denouement with surreptitious cue cards, until the ultimate moment when the hoist reared him towards Paradise through clouds of dry ice, and he stood there white-robed and resplendent and raised his nail-pierced hands to the unendurable light, tasting joy's infinite pain.

What if you *were* God, he thought. Would it just hit you every now and then: Hey, I'm *God*? And how would you know there wasn't one above you? The *real* God—but how would *He* know? And so on.

† † †

As he walked, lightheaded, to the back, people crowded the corridors, reaching out to touch him. He stopped in the Fellowship Hall and began to sign the programs thrust at him. So hungry! Little sucking mouths of the Life Force. And then *her*—the one from the foot of the cross—buffeted to the side and holding his eye piningly.

At last he escaped into a side room and sat down with a long groan, still robed, his face gleaming with sweat. He closed his eyes and drifted—back through the extraordinary sensations of the last hour—until some time later a voice roused him from his fatigue.

"Thank you," said the Reverend Ron Barksdale, "for filling in. I understand it was a bit of—what do they call it?" he smiled "—a forced conscription. But you rose to the occasion."

Arnold looked up and nodded. "Maurice?"

"He died."

Arnold stared at him.

"For two minutes. They managed to resuscitate him. On the table. I understand he's resting in his room now."

Overloaded with that information, Arnold found himself alone again, dreading the exertion of the walk home. He sighed to his feet—though when he opened the door, people throughout the Hall converged excitedly toward Him, robed and brown-tressed in the doorway. Three young men at the threshold pushed and elbowed one other as if fighting for a rebound.

"Hey, no fair!" complained one. "I was first!"

"No you weren't," returned the one accused. "I was right *there*!"

"Stop poking me!" added the third.

"*Please*," Arnold pleaded and held up his arms. What *was* that beaming in everyone's face? A kind of ecstatic desperation.

Someone took his shoulders, pulled him back into the room, and locked the door.

Glenda, the costume lady.

"You can use that door," she said, pointing to the far corner of the room. "It opens into that alley between the buildings."

"Thanks. Do you know where my clothes are?"

"No," she exhaled an harassed sigh. "I'm sorry."

"It's okay."

He slipped into the cool spring evening. Just as the door hissed shut behind him someone stepped out of the shadow of the air conditioner unit, and stood there.

*Her*.

"See, I was right," she said.

"About what?"

"About you coming this way."

"I remember you," he replied.

"I remember *you*."

"I mean—before. We were both Onlookers." She smiled. "It's your first time?" he asked.

"And last," she glowered. "I came to try out for one of the women who discover the empty tomb. Wrong! They have a waiting list. You've got to be married to the cousin of somebody that sucked off a deacon to have a chance."

"What's your name?"

"Manger Scene."

They started walking. The exertion in the fresh air energized Arnold.

"It's my last time too," said Arnold.

"To be Jesus?"

"To be anything."

"How come?"

"I only did it to make Mother happy."

"Oh," said Manger Scene. "Is she . . ."

"She passed away."

"Oh. When?"

"Three months ago."

"I'm sorry."

He nodded.

"Both my parents are—passed away."

He looked at her. "Well, I'm sorry too."

"It's funny when they die, isn't it?" she said. "You know they're going to. Then they do."

"Yeah," he said. "They do."

"I think it's sort of their job to do it first, don't you? So you'll know it's okay."

"Maybe so."

"Did you see her much?"

"Before she died?"

"Yeah."

"I always ate supper with her."

"Oh, so you *really* miss her then. Unless you're too weak with hunger."

"I get by."

"My father died five years ago," Manger Scene said. "But he'd moved to Texas with some woman and we didn't see him too much."

"Who's we?"

"Me and Venison—my brother. I sort of live with him. Do you think they're up there somewhere looking at us?"

"Your father and that woman?"

"No, anybody's parents—after they die."

"I don't know."

"And they can watch you going to the bathroom and stuff?"

"I doubt that," Arnold said. "But I did figure she'd get in touch with me somehow—like in a dream or something. But she hasn't."

"You don't dream about her?"

"No—I do. Regular dreams. I mean *communicate*—appear at the foot of the bed or something. Now I'm thinking that's why being dead is so famous. They don't."

"You don't believe they're somewhere else?"

"*She* did."

"Do you?"

"Yeah, they're somewhere else. They're who they were."

At the end of the alley they stepped out into the yellow-lighted, mostly empty parking lot. Suddenly at a clamor from the building they stopped and turned. The three fellows from inside came dashing toward them, one in a purple bike helmet pushing a bike, racing each other.

"Ow!" the biker cried, momentarily tangled up in his bike. "Stop pushing!"

The other two reached Arnold, still robed and standing in the half-light, and Manger Scene, watching curiously. The bikers stopped, breathing heavily. Then the third arrived and they all looked at one another.

"What's your names?" asked Arnold.

One, with straight oily hair and smudged glasses, said, "I'm Verl." He pointed to the one standing beside him, sweepingly coiffed, a wad of keys hanging from his belt. "That's Turk."

"I'm Turk."

"And that's Buzzy," Verl said, pointing to the baby-faced, blue-whiskered biker.

"Buzzy, Turk, and Verl," said Arnold.

"Verl, Turk, and Buzzy," confirmed Manger Scene.

Verl nodded. "Turk, Verl, and Buzzy."

"Well, good," said Arnold. "Where are you headed?" He started walking again.

"Nowhere," replied Verl, as they fell in alongside. "How about you?"

"Me? I'm going home."

"Where do you live?"

"Same place I always have. That's a nice bike you have," he said to Buzzy.

"It's a little bit broken."

"Ha!" Verl spat. "It's a rolling hunk of junk."

"Oh yeah? It's better than your bike!" Buzzy returned.

"I don't have a bike."

"See?"

"Oh come on. You can't say your bike is better than my bike if I don't *have* a bike. It doesn't make any sense."

"Yes it does. Everybody's bike if they don't have one is the one they would have and you don't so mine is better."

Verl rolled his eyes.

"What's wrong with it?" Arnold asked.

"It's kind of wobbly."

"Where?"

"Well, sort of everywhere. But see—the handlebars jiggle."

"You want me to look at it?"

"Well, if you want to."

"He means fix it, Buzzy," explained Turk.

"Can you fix it?"

"I can look at it."

Buzzy looked confused.

"Just say yes," Verl said.

"Yes."

They had reached the edge of the vast lot, and now started down the shadowy sidewalk of Pearle Street. The occasional passing car slowed; one or two beeped their horns.

"We're glad you're the new Jesus," said Verl.

"I'm not the new Jesus."

"But we want you to be. From now on."

"You've already got a Jesus."

"Ugh!"

"What's wrong with Maurice?"

"We like you better."

"Yeah, well, he's been it for, like, ten years or something."

"He's prissy and conceited and fake," said Manger Scene.

"So?"

"So you should be it."

"I don't want to." A half-hearted protest—Arnold had become preoccupied with Buzzy's bike. "I'm going to see if I can find a new bushing for that," he said.

Buzzy smiled and looked at Verl and Turk to make sure they'd heard, but they acted like they hadn't.

Another block and Arnold stopped at a driveway leading to a

small, white, green-shuttered house. An old pick-up loaded with
ladders and toolboxes rested in a weak circle of porch light.
Mechanical refuse littered the weedy yard as though something had
crashed there—and just visible out back, an old leaning garage and
several sheds seemed in the process of disgorging more of the same.

"Well—here we are," he said.

"You live here?" asked Verl.

"Yep."

They hesitated, standing in place looking at the house, only its
upper half visible behind the crazy shrubs.

"I was thinking about fixing something to eat," Arnold said.
"Anybody hungry?"

They shifted around and mumbled.

"Come on in—and I'll see about those handlebars."

"World-Go-Round Repair Service," said the truck door. "'The
Handyman Can'."

Manger Scene pulled a Walkman from her pocket. "Can you fix
radios?"

He took it and turned it over in his hand. "What's wrong with it?"

"It doesn't work."

"I'll look at it."

† † †

In the kitchen they decided on grilled cheese sandwiches and
canned chili. It was either that or macaroni and cheese and tuna
fish. Arnold handed out beers from the refrigerator.

"Imagine that," Verl said in high amusement. "Jesus drinking
beer."

"I'm not Jesus. And so what—it's just beer."

Later, in the living room, the robed repairman patiently dismantled Buzzy's handlebars, examining each piece, emitting an occasional grunt of discovery—then spent ten or fifteen minutes,

shadowed by an inquisitive Buzzy, combing through the garage and sheds in search of materials. He had to improvise—but then, he always did—and before long, as they sat around eating and depleting his beer stash, he had the handlebars tight and straight, then went over the whole antique machine with a wrench and oil can.

Buzzy beamed.

They talked a while—but Arnold, once he sat down and relaxed, felt exhaustion overtaking him, and the last thing he remembered was trying to stay awake.

† † †

When he opened his eyes the next morning, the sun nibbling at the shades, he realized that he was on the sofa, still in the robe. Very comfortable, he reflected: I see why they wore these things. Nice, simple apparel for the day—*and* portable bedcovers for night, with nothing cramped underneath. Nice and loose—ah-h. Then—oh yeah: *them.* He rolled over, hardly even wondering if he'd dreamed it all—and there she was: folded into his stuffed armchair, a beach towel over her, mouth half open, asleep. Of the others, only a bit of mechanical evidence on the coffee table and his foggy memory remained.

He looked at Manger Scene, seeing her really for the first time—gazing at her face, oblivious and serene. On the TV set beside her sat her little silent radio, like a child's dead hamster.

Trying to be quiet, he rose stiffly, visited the bathroom—now there's something you never thought about when you thought about robes—then went into the kitchen to make coffee. As the coffeemaker began to gurgle, he looked for something better than the usual to eat, briefly considered macaroni and cheese with Log Cabin, but decided against it and took his coffee and a box of Trix to his messy workbench in the living room. As he eased the radio from the TV, Manger Scene rustled about and sleepily worked her

mouth, but slumbered on. About thirty minutes later, a burst of
headphone static rasped into the room and Manger Scene bolted up
like someone had plugged her in.

Arnold quickly dialed it to a station and turned it down. "Sorry."

"You fixed it."

"It was the switch."

She blinked several times, half stunned, half amazed. "How'd
you do it?"

"I just went around it and it worked, so it was the switch. What
I did, I just put you another one on. I screwed it on right here—"
he showed her "—so the old one won't work anymore. Just use this
new one now."

She rose and came over and looked. A miniature toggle switch
had been screwed with almost microscopic screws to the plastic
casing, with wire disappearing into a tiny, newly drilled hole. She
gazed in astonishment.

"Thanks," she said, and clicked it a few times.

"You want some coffee?"

She did; they sat down in the living room, sharing the Trix.

"I hope you're not upset with me," she said.

"What for?"

"For staying here."

"No—but you should have gotten in my bed."

"I hardly know you."

"Well, I wasn't in it."

"I know."

"But don't you think your brother will be worried about you?"

"Worried?" She laughed. "The question is, will he even notice?"

"What does he do?"

"He's ineffectual." Arnold looked at her curiously. "Sort of a
hippie."

"How does he live?"

"Grows pot."

Arnold nodded.

"Anyway, I told you I just *sort of* live with him."

"What about the rest of the time?"

"Well—I do what I can. I never said I was Miss Perfect. Even the foxes have holes and all that. Do you like living by yourself?"

"How do you know I live by myself?"

"Well," she answered, holding out her hands. "I don't *see* anybody else. Unless there's some kind of funny room in the back." He smiled mysteriously. "And of course there's just one toothbrush. None of the usual junk in the bathroom. The toilet lid was up when we got here. One plate in the sink. No white Zinfandel in the refrigerator."

"Sounds like you're the observant type."

She shrugged. "So you have to cook for yourself now, huh?"

"I try."

"What's wrong with this picture? Jesus doing the cooking."

"I'm not Jesus."

She looked unconvinced. "You will be."

"No I won't."

"You're going to disappoint all those people?"

"All what people?"

"You blew them away, Jesus. You don't even know."

"Well—they needed me—I did it—I'm done."

"What if Prissy-Butt has another heart attack?"

Arnold shrugged. "Well, I hope he doesn't."

"I hope he does."

"You don't mean that."

"Yes I do. I don't like him." He looked at her oddly. "Do you?"

"No. But that's no reason to wish he was dead."

"Why not?"

"Just because I don't like him?"

"Look at animals. If they don't like something they kill it."

"They *eat* it."

"Yeah, sometimes. Just to get rid of it. But not always. I had a cat that would bite the feet off mice and then play with them as they flopped around. She never ate them. And a dog that killed squirrels and just left them. He didn't want to eat them either—they just bugged him."

"He was obeying his instinct."

"That's what I'm saying. I'm obeying mine. Like cavemen. If somebody got on your nerves you smashed their head in. Killing what bothers you is natural."

"Well, we're not cavemen anymore. And we're not animals."

"People aren't animals? You ever cut one open?"

"No. Have you?"

"No. But there's a few I'd like to."

"Anyway," Arnold protested, "why just because animals do it, or cavemen, does that make it right?"

"Because it's *natural*," Manger Scene replied.

"So natural means not thinking?"

"You think animals don't think?"

"They don't think they think."

"Which is why they don't make mistakes," claimed Manger Scene.

"What? That's crazy," Arnold objected. "*My* cat can't tell a litter box from the floor. That's not a mistake?"

"It just doesn't care."

"Or how about a possum that stops in the middle of the road? Or my parakeet when I was ten that flew into the window?"

"That's because of people. Things *people* put in the way. Have you ever seen a deer trip? Or a squirrel jump and miss a limb? Or a bird take a wrong turn and end up in a bad neighborhood?"

"But why is your dog so happy when it realizes you didn't *mean* to step on him? And why do they think it's *us* that can't do anything wrong? Or take that radio. When it was broken, when it got fixed it thought it was broken."

She furrowed her brow.

"If we're animals too, how come everything we do is wrong?"

"I thought I was saying something else."

He reflected. "Maybe you were."

Just then, a recent subliminal disturbance crossed the line into audibility and they looked at each other then rose in unison and went to the front door.

Arnold opened it onto a crowd of about fifty people, streaming down the sidewalk and up his drive, with toasters, weed-eaters, radios, microwave ovens, vacuum cleaners, and toys in their arms. In the vanguard Buzzy came pushing his bike, trying to maneuver ahead of Turk with a waffle iron, and Verl with a singing Santa Claus.

At the sight of Arnold they all cheered.

"Jesus! Jesus! Jesus!" they chanted.

Arnold stood on his small porch, robed, gazing in amazement over the scene.

"They've come for their Jesus," said Manger Scene.

"I'm not Jesus," Arnold replied and raised his arms.

The crowd immediately hushed, except for a momentary disturbance up front.

"Quit pushing me!"

Arnold glanced down—the commotion ceased—then back up. The crowd had converged into a semicircle in front of the house— shorter people in the back jumping up and down for a better look.

"What?" said Arnold.

"Stop bending my bike!"

"I'm not bending your bike!"

"Shut up!" cried Verl, who looked up at Arnold. "We want you to be Jesus from now on."

"See?" said Manger Scene.

The crowd exploded: "Jesus! Jesus!"

Arnold raised his arms and the people instantly fell quiet again. He looked over their hopeful expectant faces, and the feeling of last night again cut through his heart. Who ever asked to be in this fix, trapped in whatever you grow up to be, lost and lonely?

"It's not my decision," he said.

"We want you!"

Roar.

He turned to Manger Scene. "What should I do?"

"Tell them something."

"What?"

"I don't know—you're Jesus. I'll go order some pizza."

When she went inside, he turned back to the sea of souls and their wounded flotilla of appliances. "What do you want from me?" he asked.

Silence. Then a voice called out, "Meaning!"

Arnold frowned. "Meaning?" he said. "I don't have any meaning. There isn't any meaning. Nothing *means* anything."

Silence. They stared at him.

"Can you fix my boy's fire truck?" a man asked, holding it out.

"What's wrong with it?"

"It stopped making all the noises, and two wheels came off."

"I'll look at it."

Everyone exploded in a clamor, holding up their apparati, pushing closer.

"Stop! Stop!" pleaded Arnold.

They stopped and Arnold, breathing heavily, regarded them, thinking.

"Have you ever thought—if you couldn't see or hear or smell or feel—and you were just sitting there somewhere? That was it? What would you think? What would you do? Then one day somebody came along and put a spoonful of honey in your mouth—have you ever thought about that?"

They stared.

"Well, that's what everything's like."

They kept staring. Then, like a flock of birds rising from a field, a cheer burst from them.

"And what if the phone rings in the middle of the night—and it wakes you up and you answer it—and all you hear is somebody hang up? What do you think? You're not just mad—you don't just hate. You *make up* somebody to hate. Because when you need to hate somebody, it doesn't matter if they're there or not."

Silence.

"Right?"

Cheer.

"And remember—whatever you think of, that's not it. Does water have to *try* to flow? Does something have to *try* to fall if you drop it? Does fire *try* to burn?"

Cheer.

"And you know you couldn't love spring if there wasn't any winter—so what's the point of being alive if you never had to be dead? Because when you boil it all down, there isn't really any difference between always and never."

Cheer.

"The best thing you can do for your friend is go get your colonoscopy first. And the same is true when you die."

Cheer.

"The only reason you ever try to tell somebody something is because there *is* somebody. If we were all one thing, there wouldn't be anything to say. And nobody would ever hurt anybody if they could feel it too."

Cheer.

"And don't let them tell you life is cheap just because it is. You need to always remember—one day, if there was anybody, they'd point to this burnt-out piece of rock floating in the middle of nowhere and say: *right there* is where it all was—*right there* is where it all happened—and I'd try to tell you about it, but you wouldn't believe me if I did. Friends, we all played our part in that, and that's something we can be proud of!"

Roar.

They pressed closer with their appliances just as Manger Scene reappeared.

"Does anybody want pizza?" she cried.

Thunderous roar.

"How about a cold keg of beer?"

Even more thunderous.

"It's coming! Let's all be patient—and remember: render unto Little Caesar's."

Laughter.

"So Buzzy here's going to pass his helmet around, and I want you to dig deep in those pockets, friends. Dig down in those pockets and bring out a big handful of love!"

Cheer.

"And we're going to eat and we're going to drink, and we're going to make a joyful noise. Can I get an amen?"

"Amen!"

As the helmet made its round, Arnold sat down and puzzled over Verl's Santa Claus. A few minutes later Buzzy came back with the take and handed it to Manger Scene. She counted it and then stood and faced the crowd again.

"Friends," she said, holding up the helmet. "The good Lord doesn't raise His voice. He whispers. Sometimes He's maybe just a little bit *too* quiet. I'm going to be honest with you, friends—this isn't enough to keep the wolf from the door. Do you want the wolf at your door?"

"No!"

"Or I should say, *his* door"—pointing to Arnold—"because if you don't, *he'll* have to. Is it right to expect him to pay for you?"

Murmur.

"Let's try it one more time for Jesus!"

† † †

By mid-afternoon, the keg drained dry and pizza boxes littering the yard, the gathering had spilled into and through the house and out into the back. Arnold, who hadn't bothered to change clothes, had spent most of the day at his workbench inside, going from job to job like one working his way through a series of amusing riddles, often stepping out to browse among the milling crowd in the back yard in search of some gadget or tool that might have a name and might not. The crowd dwindled, and about four o'clock he stood up and stretched with a loud groan.

"Folks," he announced to the people waiting around the room with their devices, "I'm very tired—and if I don't go see about Mrs. Simkins's gutters this afternoon she'll act hurt and make me feel guilty."

Groan.

"I'll get to everything—I'm just going to have to do it another day."

By the time he got a shower and changed, the gathering had all but dispersed—just a few stragglers left, and Manger Scene.

"I need to go see about Venison," she said.

"Your brother?"

She nodded. "He's a little odd—did I tell you that?"

"I think so. Are you worried about him?"

"No—not worried. It's just—sometimes—if I don't see him for a few days, he sort of stops eating. He won't keep anything in the freezer because he thinks it hurts to be in there and he doesn't want anybody to do it to him."

"Well, for heaven's sake go check on him," said Arnold who noticed, backing his truck down the driveway, a makeshift sign on a pizza box jabbed into the ground.

"Thank you Jesus."

† † †

Arnold wondered if they would call and want their robe back but they didn't so when he got home he slipped into it again, then wore it to bed. When he awoke the next morning, he lay groggily luxuriating in its laxness—but only for the few seconds it took him to realize he wasn't alone.

He jerked, struck at the sight of the wave-shaped swell beside him, a quadrant of smooth exposed shoulder and splayed hair buried in the pillow. His movement startled his bedmate awake, and she sat up holding the sheet about her, staring back, until a smile stole over her face.

"Hi."

"Hi."

A bulging Army duffel bag leaned against the wall on Manger Scene's side like a drunk.

For a minute they could come up with nothing to replace the silence.

"Well, come on," Manger Scene finally said, "you're *Jesus*, man. You ought to be getting laid."

"Well," he answered. "Okay."

A while later they sat in bed passing the box of Trix between them.

"How was your brother?" Arnold asked.

"Crazy and getting crazier all the time. Like me."

"Like everybody."

"Yeah, but you do sort of wonder what's going to happen. All those drugs—when you're young, it's just, whatever—then you're not so young anymore and it's just weird—but what about when you *really* get old?"

"Well, what about when anybody gets old?—it's the same problem."

"Do you think everybody's lonely?"

He shrugged. "Well, when they're not, I think it's just because they found a way not to be for a while."

"You got any brothers or sisters?"

"Yeah, one of each. They're older than me—they're both out west."

"They left you to take care of Mother."

"No, not really. It just worked out that way."

"They say babies don't know they're a different thing from their mother."

"Yeah, and it's the saddest day of their life when they find out they are."

"Except, like you said, if they didn't, they wouldn't have anybody to love."

"They wouldn't need anybody to love."

"There wouldn't even *be* any love—would there?"

"Probably not. There wouldn't even be any be."

"Being's weird, isn't it?"

"Not any weirder than not being. Unless you are."

"You know what I think the weirdest thing about being dead is?" she said.

"What?"

"You can't ever say or do anything new again. Like you—talking to you right now—you can say anything and it'll be the first time. But when you're dead everything you said you already said."

"Unless they come to you in a dream."

"She still hasn't?"

Arnold shook his head. "You know what scares me? Not dying just because it's dying—but realizing it wasn't yours—it never was—it's somebody else's and they just let you inside for a minute—like being in a rich person's house."

"You need to steal a vase or something," she said—then they heard the noise outside. "They're back."

Streaming up the driveway again—with their worn-out blenders and cracked computers, a few pushing invalid lawnmowers—they formed a rough file converging on the porch. Arnold stepped down the steps—the first woman in line clutched a clock radio, a look of angelic desperation on her face.

"What's wrong with it?" Arnold asked.

"Station won't change," she said, fighting tears. "It's stuck on country music."

"I'll look at it."

Behind her a man held an oscillating fan, its cord carefully wrapped around its base.

"What's the matter with it?"

"You have to push the blades to make it start, and it makes a noise. I . . . I don't know what to do."

"Sometimes they just wear out," said Arnold, and came to the next man, who carried nothing broken but had his arm around an unusual-looking woman.

Her hair was twisted into odd spikes, extra lips lipsticked onto each cheek, one lens of her glasses painted blue, a huge eyeball painted on the other, band-aids stuck haphazardly all over her, two shirts on, the buttons of one buttoned into the holes of the other, masking tape holding it all together, a purple skirt and lime-green pants, one flip-flop, one combat boot, one elbow-length white glove. Every now and then she made an odd face, emitted some curious sound, or gestured strangely with her arms.

"What's the matter with her?" asked Arnold.

"She says God makes her do it."

Arnold looked deep into her eyes, meeting the fervid harassed soul alive within.

"The Lord directs all things," she said.

"Yeah?"

"His will controls everything."

"What does that mean?"

The man answered for her. "She thinks everything she does God has already decided it and makes her do it." The woman stared indecipherably at Arnold. "*Everything*," emphasized the man.

"Even scratching an itch?"

"It was the Lord's will that put that itch there," the woman interjected.

Arnold considered that, then said, "If you go to the store . . . "

"The Lord's will, not mine," she said.

"And buy some chicken soup . . . "

"The Lord's will."

"Then suddenly decide to turn down aisle three instead of aisle four . . . "

"He has some reason for it."

"Lady, I got to tell you—that's *crazy*. You think he keeps up with every breath, every cell, every electron?"

"He controls everything."

"But why would he do it twice?"

She stared thunderstruck at him. "Because it's His *will*," she insisted. She raised her left arm above her head. "The Lord made

do it"—again—"the Lord made me do it"—again—"the Lord
ade me do it—"

"Stop that!" cried Arnold.

She froze, looking at him aghast, then emitted a mournful groan.
"Oh-h-h-h—"

Whap! She stopped, utterly shocked, and stared at her kindly-
eyed robed slapper. Light came burning into her eyes as the blood
rose in her face.

"I'm telling you to stop all this," he told her. "Give yourself
some peace. Why would God think up a crazy world like that?"

She just stared.

"You've got to let go of whatever holds you back. Everybody
knows that. Now I want you to walk—somewhere—it doesn't
matter where—and then come back here. Not because anybody's
telling you to—but just because *you* want to. Okay?"

"But *you're* telling me to."

"But you don't *have* to, unless you want to—see the difference?"

At last she blinked. "Just walk?" she asked, a tremor in her voice.

"Only if you want to."

Then, ever so slowly, she took a tentative step into the terra
incognita just around her, then brought her other foot up even and
stood there, an odd joy experimenting with her features.

"Ha!" she laughed. Then took another uncertain step and
stopped again. "I'm doing it!" she quaveringly exclaimed. With the
brave wobble of one who has just cast off polio braces she made her
way to a dogwood tree halfway across the yard, reached out and
grasped a branch for support.

She looked radiantly over her shoulder at Arnold. "It was just me!"

The crowd, swollen to a small throng, burst into applause.

She lurched her way back—fell into the man's arms—the crowd
cheered again.

"I'm free!" she cried. "But—" her expression turned ardently desperate—"is He listening to me think?"

Arnold raised his arms and addressed not just her but the whole gathering. "I tell you, *nobody* is listening to you think. Not if you don't want them to. That's just you—it's personal, it's private, and nobody else can hear it."

Cheer.

"Who wants Hot Wings?" Manger Scene cried from the porch.

Big cheer.

† † †

And so, as the spring slowly wore into summer, the pattern established in those days after Easter was set—but shifted to the weekends, when the throngs would return with eager souls and broken gadgets, and Arnold, his hair, his beard knowing no blade, and grown to be one with his robe, would tinker and mingle. The sweet savor of roasted meat saturated the neighborhood, and old kegs went back for new beer, routinely.

Then fall came, and as the evenings grew cool huge bonfires appeared in the back yard, brightening the circle of faces who stayed late into the night—then driving out the cold as winter set in.

Christmas, with its own pageant and live-action Nativity on the church lawn, came and went, and the New Year brought nothing particularly new but a long series of wet raw days, somewhere on a nondescript mid-afternoon of one of which, a small delegation made its way into the administrative wing of the church, and announced itself in the pastor's office.

Mrs. Puerco, the executive secretary, disappeared into the inner sanctum as Verl, Buzzy, and Turk jostled for the same spot on the naugahyde furniture, finally reached a truce, and sat scowling at the dry reading matter. Buzzy chewed on his fingers.

"Stop that!" hissed Verl as Mrs. Puerco returned and announced that the Reverend Barksdale would see them shortly. Then ignored them.

About ten minutes later Verl saw something flickering around the peephole of the minister's door—cut his eyes away, then back, and sure enough, the door opened. Rev. Barksdale, in shirtsleeves and tie, a sheen on his manicured nails, stood there looking with low-grade curiosity at the group, who sprang in unison to their feet.

"Yes? How can I help you?"

"We wanted to ask you something," said Verl.

The minister sized them up a moment longer. "Well—come in."

After a tussle over who would sit where, they wound up in three chairs facing the aircraft carrier of the pastor's desk, and the sheepskin-framed Reverend himself, who sat back and teepee'd his fingers under his nose.

"We want Arnold to be the new Jesus," said Verl.

Rev. Barksdale eyed him acutely, then barely nodded. "Hmph," he grunted.

Turk and Buzzy sat forward in their chairs, staring in silence. "We've got a petition," Verl went on, "with three hundred names."

Something like a smile played over the Reverend's face. "Our congregation is twelve thousand," he rejoined.

"It's still a lot."

Rev. Barksdale shrugged. "Not exactly a majority."

"We haven't even asked everybody."

"Well," smiled Rev. Barksdale, "something tells me there would be significant *other* sentiment on the matter."

"Arnold's the best," blurted Buzzy.

"Why?" asked Rev. Barksdale. "Why do you say that?"

"Because He's nice and He talks to you and He does things for you and He shares—and now I have somewhere to go and something to do."

"Ah—*you* have."

"Well?"

"You realize, of course," Rev. Barksdale countered, "that Maurice is an Elder in this church. A leader. But are you aware that he headed the Building Fund Drive last year, and raised eight hundred and fifty-four thousand, nine hundred and seventeen dollars and thirty-nine cents? And all he asks in return is the opportunity to serve. What is your *Arnold*—hmm? What has he done? What has he given?"

"He helps you," argued Verl. "I used to be so shy I was afraid to do anything—now I'm not shy at all. He makes you feel okay."

"Feel okay. Hmmm." Rev. Barksdale chuckled.

"And I don't have those funny thoughts anymore," said Turk. "Anyway, not all the time. Not since I met Him."

"Stop capitalizing that H. And you attribute these—*improvements*—to this *Arnold*?"

They all nodded.

"Well," Rev. Barksdale said, smiling. "I'm sure Mr. Arnold is a capital fellow. That's not the issue. The issue—for *me*—is the integrity of this church—by which I mean its *wholeness*. I seek above all a single, unified purpose and vision. I *loathe* division, discord, disagreement."

"We're not the only ones," said Verl.

"Yes, I see that." Rev. Barksdale sighed. "I've heard what you have to say. I don't know that I can—*do*—anything, but I will take it up in prayerful reflection. I would certainly find any kind of division in the church—*regrettable*."

"Water doesn't try to flow," said Turk. "And fire doesn't try to burn."

Rev. Barksdale paused, hands poised on his chair arms. "Ooh," he said, then showed them out.

† † †

Manger Scene was desperate. She had no idea where to look and, having no car, couldn't drive there.

A pleasant, breezy February afternoon—she'd been with Venison for three days and lost track of Arnold's doings. She only knew his truck was gone.

Then it struck her to check his answering machine. Somebody's dryer. A leaking kitchen drain. Then Mrs. Rickett: please finish that painting on the porch.

"I bet that's where he is," Manger Scene said to herself. An outside day.

Three Ricketts in the phone book—had to be the one on Barker Avenue, about a block from where Arnold's mother had lived. People on Willow Pointe Circle and Wild Ginger Lane don't need their porches painted. Yet.

She saw the truck, backed up the driveway, about a block away. Hearing some commotion from the far side of the house, she cut across the front lawn and, sure enough, saw the ladder with Arnold on it at the back corner. As she approached, a barrage of suction-cup arrows rained from the hedges, most wobbling harmlessly to the ground, or clattering against the ladder, except for one that grazed the painter on the leg.

"Agh!" he cried. "You got me! I'm dead!"

Delighted chittering from the hedges.

"Arnold?"

He turned his head and saw Manger Scene.

"What?" She didn't look right. "What's the matter?"

"Venison," she said. "He's—well, can you come?"

† † †

A small cabin on the edge of town by a stagnant pond—somewhere in the hardly rememberable past somebody in the family's idea of a getaway cottage, many years neglected, then claimed by the rootless heir.

He sat on his bed, in the far dim corner of the one room, backed as far as he could get from something, huddled there in tee shirt and underwear, knees against his chest, staring at them as they came in.

"It's just us," said Manger Scene.

He didn't respond but kept his wild eyes locked on them as they slowly approached. It was not until they advanced to a certain point that he flinched, drew himself a bit more into the corner, watching them with his searing eyes.

"Venison," said Arnold. "What's the matter?"

Venison only stared.

"Talk to me. Tell me."

The terrorized rigor mortis of his expression transformed schizophrenically into a malignant smile.

He hacked a spiritless laugh. "Whatever you do—just don't die—that's all I can tell you."

Arnold gazed in astonishment at him, then turned to Manger Scene.

"He says he died last night."

"I *did* die last night!"

Arnold considered him for a moment. "You dreamed you died?"

"What difference does it make? I know where I was."

The room for a short span fell silent.

"Tell him," said Manger Scene.

Venison's face turned hard.

"Tell me what?" asked Arnold.

"Tell you what it was like. What he saw."

Arnold turned to Venison, whom the terror had reclaimed.

"Just don't die—if you know what's good for you."

"How can you not die?"

Venison laughed. "You can't."

"Tell me what you saw."

"Saw? I didn't see anything. I didn't hear anything. There wasn't anything to see or hear—understand? There's nothing!" He sat breathing in short wild gasps.

"You mean—"

"I mean it's a joke, a trap—all of this!" He swept a bony arm around. "The only reason it's here is just so you'll *know*—don't you get it? Prepared a place—remember? Oh, you're going to love it—your own hollowed-out hole in a rock—not enough room to turn over—it's dark, it's cold—and you're there forever! Do you hear me? Forever!"

Arnold stared. Manger Scene wept.

Venison calmed a bit and sat breathing in slow, labored heaves. "Just stay alive as long as you can. That's all I can tell you."

† † †

He would not be unpersuaded or consoled. They left him, but the encounter slid into their hearts like a shard of glass. At Arnold's house they sat in silence until Arnold walked outside into the front yard, breathed deeply for several minutes, then came back in and, though it was hardly five o'clock, lay down on his bed and tried to be nothing.

Haunted but dreamless, the attempt. When a sound jarred him awake, he sensed and, from the full light outside, saw that it was late the next morning. The sound proved to be the telephone, and Manger Scene, excavating through her half disemboweled duffel bag, stopped to answer it.

"Yes." She listened. "Just a minute." She covered the mouth-piece, handing him the receiver. "My underwear's gone again," she said.

"I'll talk to him." Arnold took the phone.

"Yes." He looked at the floor. "What time?" He looked some more. "Yeah, I guess so." He hung up.

"The church," said Manger Scene, and Arnold nodded. "What do they want?"

"Barksdale wants to see me."

"What about?"

Arnold shrugged. "She didn't say."

† † †

The standard ten-minute wait: Arnold, in blue jeans, his hair and beard untouched, sat drawing surreptitious glances from Mrs. Puerco as he became engrossed in a recent article in *Glory*—about how one could begin the process of selecting color schemes for heaven—and could hardly put it down until the door opened and the Rev. Barksdale appeared, appraising his visitor.

"Arnold."

"Yes," replied Arnold and remained seated.

"Well—come in."

He did, and they considered each other across the desk.

"I don't want any divisions in my church," Barksdale began. "It's not healthy, it's not productive, and I'm going to find a way to avoid it if I can."

Arnold nodded.

"So it's very clear what the Lord is asking you to do."

Arnold cut his eyes up. "What?"

"Step aside."

"Step aside? From what? I didn't choose anything."

"But it seems to've chosen you—so for the good of the church, unchoose."

"What is the church?"

"You're sitting in it."

"Wrong. Come on, they tell you that in first-grade Sunday school. The church is the people."

"Yes," Barksdale wearily agreed, "it's the people. But there are people and there are people—and a lot of the people I'm talking about are not happy."

"But the ones I'm talking about are."

"But who *are* they?"

"You know."

"Yes, I do. Do you?"

"Sure. The nobodies."

At that, a door behind the minister opened. "The nobodies," a voice scathingly repeated—and Maurice, hair no less flowing than Arnold's, and beard well established, emerged in a business suit and came around the desk. "Let's stop and examine for just a moment what that actually means."

Barksdale glanced at him.

"Just take twenty names from this *list* at random,"—Maurice held up the revised petition—"and add up the sum of their pledges, as I did—"

"Their pledges?" Arnold returned indignantly. "I thought that was private."

"It was. You add them up and get—drum roll, please—just over three thousand dollars. *Annual* pledges. *Twenty* people. *Three* thousand dollars."

"So?"

"*So?* Friend, I've written checks to this church for that sum. *Personal checks.*"

"Are you talking about money?"

"Oh for God's sake." Maurice laughed and looked at Arnold. "You know something? I can't see anything you are. Tell me—are you a praying man?"

"Not really, but I'm pretty good at wishing."

Maurice snorted. "What do you believe?"

"Oh, I guess nothing—only the wishing. Believing just gets in the way."

Maurice laughed. "Gets in the *way*?"

"You know—like trying to look at your own face." Maurice stared with incredulous scorn. "It's just best not to care. Then everything kind of goes its own way. When you don't care, what you were afraid of usually won't even happen. And if it does—well, you don't care."

Barksdale followed the conversation, back and forth.

"So that explains it," said Maurice. "Aren't you going to ask what *I* believe?"

"I hadn't planned on it."

"What I believe is very simple."

"I bet."

"I believe this is a world where hard work counts, and that the things hard work accomplishes should not be pissed away by dreamers and losers. I believe in honesty. I believe in responsibility. I believe in decency. I believe in—and I know this is pretty radical—*right and wrong*. And I believe Jesus Christ died for my sins."

"Or it wouldn't count?"

"Look, I don't give a damn for your puns or whatever they are, okay? I know it's not popular—you'll roll your eyes and sneer—but I'll say it anyway: What Jesus Christ was, was a good businessman."

"He was?"

"Yes he was. He came to earth with a product and a marketing strategy. He understood his clientele and he tried to eliminate the competition. Everything he said and everything he did was geared toward moving that product. And what was that product? Only the best product there is: *life*."

"Who was his clientele?"

"Whoever had ears to hear."

"Man, he was just talking to the Jews. Trying to tell them it wasn't working."

"What wasn't working?"

"God wasn't working. He was dead. They needed a new one."

"*What?*"

"The dudes in the fancy robes, you know. Going into the little room. Wasn't getting it done. Because if it *was*—what were these pigs doing here bossing us around? Do you know why he didn't blow up the Romans?"

"Blow up the Romans? Yes. Because he was the Prince of Peace."

"The Prince of Blow You to Pieces. What do you think coming with a sword means? The reason he didn't blow them up was because he couldn't: they didn't have bombs and airplanes back then."

"*What are you implying?*"

"That you wouldn't recognize him if he came today. Back then, he used the only power he had."

"Which was—"

"If you have no power, you make having no power your power."

Maurice turned to Barksdale. "I won't stand here and listen to this blasphemy. Do what you need to do."

Barksdale smiled weakly. "I'm—I'm just concerned about this division—"

"There is no division! Just take care of the situation, *Reverend*."

"Did you ever stop to think," Arnold asked, "out of all the places in the world, how lucky you are to have been born a five-minute air-conditioned ride from Absolute Truth?"

"Yes." Slam.

Barksdale sighed. "For the good of the church," he said. "I hope you'll see where your duty lies."

† † †

If not his duty, certainly his inclination.

But his followers left him no choice. Relentless, the pressure they applied—as the first signs of spring sprouted around them.

Then the first posters appeared: Airbrushed Maurice, eyes daring the camera, forearm propped against a cross, garment half open. "Maurice: A Jesus of All Time, A Jesus for Our Time," it said, and added below: "Genuine. Dependable. Wise."

Answered about a week later by a stunning close-up action shot from the previous pageant: thorn-crowned, blood-streaked Arnold, cross digging into his shoulder: "Arnold: Remember the Feeling," it urged—then at the bottom added: "Look into those brown eyes and go crazy, girl!"

The weeks slid past, and the crowds at Arnold's house grew. Word of Maurice's preparations across town reached them daily. Here and there things got ugly: fistfights in parking lots, shouting matches on the streets, menacing phone calls in the night, poisoned pets, drive-by shootings. Oh, there will be tribulations in the end times, some thought. And Maurice, raven-tressed and robed, could often be seen about town surrounded by his Galilean entourage, letting the children come unto him, healing the sick.

At last the occasion arrived—Easter itself—and the day, as if sensing its own importance, did not disappoint: a cool golden dawn that ripened into the sort of spring day God obviously had in mind from the start.

That afternoon the other robed Lamb, half willing, sat in his living room on the couch as his faithful milled about, and Verl, Turk, and Buzzy formed a jostling triangular bodyguard around him.

Manger Scene never left his side. "You know," he confided during a moment's respite, "I've discovered I prefer the simple life."

"Everybody with sense does," she said. "It's just, you can't always have sense."

"That's true."

And so, about six o'clock, the procession began—an energized vanguard of his admirers leading the way up Pearle Street, thoroughly disrupting traffic. Police arrived and, in fluorescent vests, took positions at key intersections—as the joyful throng, the robed and chestnut-locked Arnold conspicuous in the middle, came like a lava flow up the road. Verl and Turk sandwiched him while behelmeted Buzzy rode in festive circles around them on his bike.

About a block from the church, a spontaneous cheer from up ahead thundered the air, and they glanced at one other. Then another cheer, and another. The source revealed itself when they reached the edge of the already overflowing parking lot: an excited mob at the north end of the portico giving way to another advancing robed and sandaled party, Maurice in white serenely in the center, hand raised in blessing.

"Are we afraid of them?" Verl called out.

"No-o-o!" they roared.

Drawing an immediate responding roar—then as the upstarts cut across the Red Sea of the parking lot, both sides fell into a decibel contest. When throng met throng near the doors, pandemonium broke out, and briefly the threat of violence charged the air. But, despite a few random punches at the fringes, the opponents sieved through the row of doors and formed into fervid camps at facing ends of the vestibule.

Arnold, his face warm and a cold sweat icing his body, half intoxicated, half frightened, sat down to catch his breath. Manger Scene fanned his face while some of his more spirited followers engaged in shouting matches across the no-man's-land between themselves and the opposing legions.

Eventually, as the tension built, the head deacon appeared midway between them and raised his arms.

The crowd jeered.

"Listen!" he called.

The crowd jeered louder.

"You need to listen! This isn't going to work!"

The crowd bellowed defiantly, but Arnold cried, "Let him speak!" and they grudgingly left off.

"There are some things there can't be two of," the deacon argued, "and this is one of them. We know that, you know that. And I don't want to have to point out that you are outnumbered—significantly—so I won't. But I will remind you that we've got a full house in there—paying customers who came to see this show—and they're *going* to see it, *with the proper cast*. You're all here illegally and you need to go out those doors the way you came, or we'll have no choice but to show you out."

An earthshaking defiant outcry—spiced with Bronx cheers, boos, and howls.

"They can't stop us!" a voice called above the din. "Come on—let's go first!"

And with an approving hurrah they burst into the sanctuary, and as five thousand heads turned to look, Arnold, swept up in the flow, crowned and wheeling his cross, made his entrance to an explosion of applause. House lights immediately went down—a spot hit him—and the orchestra lunged into a dark fanfare.

As he labored down the aisle, hands reached to touch him. Verl, Turk, and Buzzy fluttered about trying to push them away. People strained to see—some cried, drinking the rich emotion like cream—while below awaited the bitter cup and Calvary. Arnold floated away from the scene into the repose of a timeless place where self-consciousness dissipated before the inexorable events. Those around him, Manger Scene, the audience, turned airy and only vaguely real, and he could not even feel the exertion of his legs.

A violent eruption jarred this odd serenity. Arnold needed a moment to register its reality then stopped, turned his head with all the others, and there—arms outstretched in a spotlight at the head of the opposing aisle—stood the radiant Maurice. An explosive cheer vibrated the church, the orchestra blared like Gabriel. Someone handed him his cross, and to a deafening roar he started down the aisle pulling it with one arm as though it were balsa wood—not toiling like his counterpart, but striding with ease. When he drew even with Arnold, arrested in his tortured, glacial progress, he stopped to look over the heads of the spectators in the center section at him.

The volume of the noise doubled.

Then Maurice turned, proceeded to the stage, bounced up the three short steps, tossed his cross lightly aside—then strode center stage and, stepping into the spotlight, gestured "come on." The crowd went wild.

Arnold resumed his own advance, reached the front, panted up the steps, and with the help of many eager hands, disburdened himself of his cross, then drew stiffly erect. Like many things, maybe everything, the decisive moment itself, measured against the anticipation and the aftermath, was an act of flickering brevity.

Arnold took a few steps forward, and Maurice immediately paced around him in a circle. The crowd. The music. Sweeping spotlights. Arnold followed Maurice with his eyes, chary and incredulous, flinching as Maurice made little feints toward him— drawing some snare pops from below, cymbal crashes, and the lust of the crowd—then abruptly, striking out of the hypnotic lull like a snake, Maurice caught Arnold at the waist and flipped him over his shoulder, full over backwards in a body slam—then sprang, pinned his yelping prey, and locked his right arm behind him.

"Aggh!" cried Arnold, feeling his arm about to be ripped from its socket. His legs kicked wildly as he struggled to free himself, and the congregants screamed bloodily.

Maurice held him for a few seconds, solidifying his point, then let go. Groaning in spectacular pain, Arnold lay for a few moments and then slowly rose on his elbows—but just as he reached his knees, Maurice crept up and seized him in a headlock. The audience feasted loudly—and when Maurice pulled the squirming pretender to his feet and paraded him up and down the stage, they exploded. Arnold went dizzy, and just when he thought he'd lose consciousness, the pressure around his neck relaxed, and he buckled to his knees like a dropped towel. Instantly Maurice flattened him, pinned him—the crowd registered the finality and bellowed approval—a roar that reached a maniacal level when Maurice straddled Arnold and raised his arms. Dimly, Arnold felt the painful sucking of the hoard feeding on his humiliation.

Verl, Turk, and Buzzy hightailed it, and the suddenly not-so-teeming crowd of Arnoldians evaporated. Only Manger Scene rushed to the fallen light of her world and threw her arms around him.

"So it's not fake?" she said.

"Fake, hell," he grimaced. "My damn shoulder—"

"I'll look at it. Come on—let's get out of here."

But the touching spectacle of her helping him to his feet and hobbling with him to the side door formed such a minor distraction to the greater show—Maurice triumphantly mounting the cross and holding out his hands for the winning nails—that hardly anybody noticed.

† † †

May—lovely May: the grass a delicate green, the air scented with mint, wildflowers scattered like laughter over the earth.

The big black car pulled just into the end of the driveway and delicately parked. Ten or fifteen other cars sat parked about the yard at odd angles.

As the driver, hair and beard recently trimmed, in shirt and tie but no jacket, got out and started circumspectly for the house, a few people drinking beer by the side door stopped talking and stared. A few yards before the front steps, the man nodded curtly at them, and another group drifted curiously around from the back, watching in silence; then the driver looked intently at the door. From behind it came the buzz of a gathering and the muted sounds of a ballgame on TV.

He knocked.

An odd sound to those within—but the person nearest the door opened it, and instantly the room, except for the droning of the TV, fell deathly quiet.

"May I come in?"

The opener glanced inward, apparently got a nod, and stepped back. The visitor came in, and everyone—sitting, standing, leaning from the kitchen, holding beers—just stared. Empty bottles and cans, abandoned paper plates of food and chip bags covered every surface. Arnold, his own hair uncut, still preferring the robe, sat beside Manger Scene (no baseball fan, headphoned to her Walkman) on the couch, between Verl, Turk, and Buzzy.

The man cleared his throat. "I've come to—"

He paused; everyone waited.

"I've come to let you know there are no hard feelings—on our part—and under a few conditions we're willing to let you rejoin the church family."

Silence.

He waited.

"Well, we're sort of watching this game," said Arnold.

The man closed his eyes and took a breath. "I don't mean *right now*."

The room echoed with silence—above the almost subliminal presence of the TV.

The man huffed a dry laugh. "O-kay," he said.

The people in the room looked at Arnold and one other; no one knew what to say.

"All right," the man said more briskly. "I came here—I humbled myself—the rest is up to you." Everyone stared. "I just hope you appreciate the dangers of these end times. My conscience is clear."

Even more silence. He let himself out. When he'd retreated a few yards beyond the door, the buzz of voices resumed within, and despite the stares of the beer drinkers in the driveway, he stopped, turned, and listened.

Some laughter—then a sudden surge of muffled sound, and a voice: "*Well hit—Baker going back—back—back—to the wall . . . Goodbye!*"

† † †

## Author's Commentary

This story grew from nothing more than an amusing picture: that of a modern man in robe and sandals and flowing hair leading a group of followers down a sidewalk. I just wanted to know who he was. I could tell he was a good man, not crazy, and I sought to understand him much as one might try to reach the heart of elvisness in an Elvis impersonator. It is not His Jesusness, but his jesusness, that moves us. He is the Great Enabler—that which fills an exact absence in each of us—which explains why he has always been

fashioned by the needs and hopes of every age. My distaste for
what he has become in modern America—the ultimate something-
for-nothing whose value is merely his promise of perpetuating our
middle-class comforts—nurses my suspicion that the harder path
of Kierkegaard is truer: Jesus didn't do anything for us; he simply
went first. And, in that, makes life livable.

† † †

*A splinter of divinity both mutilates and mends.*

# LIGNUM CRUCIS
## Paul Di Filippo

How many pilgrims had trodden these cobbles over the past eight hundred years? Woody Payne imagined an endless line of supplicants stretching down the centuries: medieval nobility and peasants, popes and monks; Renaissance tradesmen with their families; Victorian excursionists; Me-Decade Jesus freaks; Eastern Europeans freed from Soviet atheism . . . Now he himself stood at the temporary apex of that vast historical cavalcade. What a motley, colorful assortment of worshippers this place had seen, garbed in an array of costumes, speaking scores of languages, with innumerable motives, dreams, and prayers amongst them. Yet all united in one belief, a belief that Woody shared:

That standing in the presence of the largest extant piece of the True Cross would somehow help them.

The line that Woody stood in, snaking through the distant Forgiveness Door, jerked forward, and he roused from his musings to survey again this magical place. The Church of Saint Toribio in Lebanon, despite its name, occupied no parcel of ground in the Middle East. Rather, its roots were sunk in a region of Spain dubbed Liébana, high in the Pyrenees, near a town called Potes and a peak named Viorna.

The church's founders had selected this remote spot in an era when marauding Moors still roamed, and the first primitive buildings reflected a certain bunker mentality. But by the time construction finished on the present structure in 1256, the relatively peaceful climate allowed the luxury of a sprawling, asymmetrical church, modest yet beautiful in its humble lines. Wheaten-colored stone walls and red-tiled roof harmonized with arched doorways and squat towers. Stained glass was absent entirely, although some fanciful representational carvings substituted. The surrounding forest touched one side, the trees, now leafing out, providing a simple curtain in keeping with the church's understated elegance.

The whole affair was set on a sloping cobbled plaza, acreage now as warm with vendors and pilgrims, monks and priest and nuns, racing children and doddering elderly. Balloons and religious icons, hot snacks and holy water changed hands. A string quartet on a decorated stage played Bach's sacred music. The church's bells tolled solemnly at intervals. A clutch of amiable policemen circulated, their presence hardly necessary in this devout, well-regulated crowd.

Meanwhile, the April sun poured down its benison. It was the sixteenth of the month: a Sunday. That conjunction defined Saint Toribio's Jubilee Year, an especially propitious time to visit the Lignum Crucis. Woody had planned his whole European trip around this day. Chartres, Lourdes, Santiago de Compostela—all the other sites he had wanted to visit had been aligned on his itinerary to insure his arrival *now*.

He coveted a moment of grace, an epiphanic instant to redeem and transfigure his life. And this place, he believed, offered the most potent possibilities.

Nothing in Woody's life currently discomfited him. His health was fine. He had a fairly satisfying job, his own home, and access to many of the amusements offered by modern American culture: sports, film, music. He attended church regularly. (St. Jude's, where Father James Tierney presided.) His parents, still alive and hale, exhibited all the signs of continuing so for many years.

But, at age thirty-three, Woody felt a persistent unease. His life struck him as circumscribed and unfulfilled. He had no romantic partner or any immediate prospects. High callings had eluded him; boyhood dreams of glory had faded; life stretched ahead as a long vista of unchanging days till the grave. A voice inside him demanded more, that he do something to tap and channel the limitlessness of God's creation.

Thus, this pilgrimage.

With the help of a pretty travel agent—whom he had failed to ask for a date—he had composed this itinerary culminating at Saint Toribio.

The procession shuffled forward, and Woody, parch-mouthed, wished that he'd bought a bottle of water before joining it. However, the stooped woman in front of him turned and, smiling, offered Woody a swig from *her* bottle. He accepted gratefully, and the line lurched forward.

At length, Woody passed through the Forgiveness Door and stood inside the church. Buttery light melted through the high windows, filling the interior with a welcoming radiance. The unadorned stone pillars running in parallel rows led the eye upward to the cross-ribbed vaults. The air was infused with a sempiternal scent of incense and lost days. Murmurs from hundreds of souls made a muted cacophony that the vaults easily absorbed.

Inside the church the pilgrims had diffused—some to the apse containing the ancient wooden statue of Saint Toribio, others to the side chapel that held the True Cross, where they bunched eagerly outside the entrance.

Woody hesitated before heading toward them. Now that he was nearly in the presence of the True Cross, his hoped-for miracle awaited him. Or did it? What if he offered himself before the relic and received nothing? Where did such an outcome leave him: hopeless, with his life irrefutably barren? Or could he survive this disappointment and resume his old existence with only a mild pang?

Praying fervently, he walked toward the side chapel.

This piece of the True Cross allegedly came from the left branch of the instrument of the Lord's torture. Discovered by Saint Elena, the mother of Emperor Constantine, it had come under the care of Saint Toribio during his sojourn in Jerusalem. Fearing for the relic's safety, he spirited it away to this mountain fastness in Spain, where millions had since venerated it. Nowadays it was plated in gold, but the darkened nail hole remained exposed.

Edging into the massed worshippers, Woody noticed the odor of many anxious, excited bodies, a scent that floated above the churchly musk. The crowd circulated forward slowly, as the people nearest the relic yielded to those behind. As he shuffled ahead, Woody intuited the carved ceiling of the chapel, a large hanging light fixture, and the larger reliquary containing the Lignum Crucis. Now only half the original distance separated him from the object of his veneration. He sought to calm his mind, to open his heart and soul for the descent of some celestial leavening—

Shouting. Improbably, someone was shouting harshly. Shouting strange words: an ancient invocation, anathema to this place.

A swarthy mustached man wearing a bulky jacket had bulled past a rope barrier and onto the raised, off-limits area of the reliquary. For one timeless moment, the man stood alone there, shouting, shouting—

*"Allahu akhbar! Allahu akhbar—"*

Several men rushed the terrorist, and women screamed, stampeding. The woman who had shared water with Woody went down as if under a juggernaut.

His mind blank, Woody stood transfixed.

And the universe exploded.

† † †

Steve Dresser ran the Grafton Center, a school for children suffering from autism and other learning disabilities. He found it hard to hire and retain teachers and aides for the demanding, frustrating, low-paying work. He hurried to land any skilled workers he could and then did all he could to retain them. Still, he had his doubts about bringing this particular teacher back onboard.

Dresser supposed that if the fellow was willing to exert himself to handle the job, he deserved a chance. If he failed, Dresser could dismiss him gently later, and he would still have his permanent disability stipend.

A knock sounded on the office door, and Dresser called, "C'mon in."

Dresser hardly recognized his former employee. He walked with a cane. His face had been hollowed and sharpened with pain—grief—bafflement. One side of his skull, near his temple, bore a slight hairless depression. His gaze, once mild and lackadaisical, now had a piercing intensity.

Dresser stood and shook his hand. "Woody, have a seat. How're you doing?"

Woody Payne sat down, his cane across his lap. A small St. Jude medal pinned to his sweater vest caught Dresser's eye.

Woody fixed his old boss with a forthright look. "Just fine, Steve. I had my last scheduled surgery six months ago. Nothing but physical therapy from here on out. The doctors say I might be able to shuck the cane, eventually. I'm down to four meds, and I gave up my afternoon naps last week. I'm almost ready for a triathlon."

Dresser smiled. "Hey, no Iron Man just yet. Take things slow, right?"

Woody's own smile contained complex depths. "That's just what I can't do. If this experience has taught me anything, it's that life's too short to procrastinate. I need to make the most of the time given to me."

"And this job's what you want, even in light of your brush with death? I mean, it's important, but it's hardly saving the world."

Woody leaned forward. "Saving the world isn't in the cards for me. I realize that now. I couldn't save anyone at Saint Toribio—not even myself. It was only chance or divine intervention that spared us survivors. I know some people change radically after undergoing something like that. But I just want to pick up the pieces of my old life, go back to what I was good at—but more intensely. I can't just sit around the house. I need to get back to my kids."

"Okay—I guess. You can have your old class back on Monday. There are a few new faces, but you'll recognize most. They remember you. The higher-functioning ones have been asking for Mister Payne for months."

With the aid of his cane Woody rose. "I really appreciate this, Steve. I won't let you down."

Dresser accompanied Woody to the door. "One last thing, Woody—"

Woody fingered the depression in his skull. "No need to be embarrassed. You're wondering about my mental abilities, right? Never fear. I've got some shrapnel up here. The docs didn't want to operate to remove it—too tricky. Said it was fine where it was. All the tests agreed: nothing but a splinter. You know those clumsy carpenters who shoot themselves in the head with a nail gun and survive? That's me! Still the same old Woody."

Dresser touched his shoulder. "Okay, then. Welcome back."

† † †

The classroom smelled of chalk, paste, and pencil shavings, as well as of vomit and urine. The children, ranging in age from five to twelve, often had accidents. Most were boys. Many could perform none of the traditional classroom activities. Others could do some. A few could do more. Being with these children, tending to their needs, pushing them to fulfill their potential, required a special kind of person.

As soon as he limped through the door, Woody felt at home.

A blond boy with a large, lopsided head tore himself from a young aide named Holly Cupp and dashed over to clutch Woody's leg.

"Missa Payne! Missa Payne!"

Woody patted his head. "That's my name, Cole—don't wear it out."

Cole cackled at the familiar joke. Woody gently disengaged and went over to Holly Cupp.

Holly favored patterned clothes: stripes, dots, paisleys, checks, pineapples and cows. Woody had rarely seen her wear a mono-chrome garment. She dressed her brown hair into a floppy fountain perpetually geysering atop her crown. Her glasses resembled those worn by Woody's octogenarian Aunt Helen.

Holly beamed. "Good to have you back, Woody."

"It's good—no, it's great—to be back. How's everything?"

"Well, Florence finally managed to master Legos. You should see some of the wild things she's built. Burt's on a helpful new med. Cole here is drawing up a storm. We've got four new kids—I'll tell you all about them in a minute. And oh yeah, Pawpaw had a new litter."

Woody looked over at the terrarium sheltering the class's guinea-pig colony. He scented the animals. "Getting kinda crowded in there, isn't it?"

"I'm working on finding foster homes for the new ones. But the kids really love seeing the babies."

Woody sighed. "If you say so. Introduce me to the new guys." The morning passed in a blur of activity. Woody had little time to think, which suited him fine. He had already thought more than enough about what had happened to him.

In the hospital, after regaining consciousness, Woody had weighed his Spanish disaster. Having gone openhearted to a new land, a holy place, following his faith and expecting a miracle, he had instead met hatred, violence, and destruction.

At first he was fiercely angry, cursing both mankind and God. After many tears and imprecations, he entered a period of feeling utterly drained and colorless. A dawning realization, however, succeeded this emotional slough.

After all, he had gotten his miracle. It just hadn't taken the form he had assumed it would: much more cataclysmic, with daunting collateral damage and wasted lives, but a miracle nonetheless. Here the old adage, "God works in mysterious ways," supplied the only possible comfort.

Woody meditated on the bombing's lessons and eventually, with Father Tierney's help, reached an accommodation with his personal history. The feelings he had divulged to Steve Dresser came to dominate his outlook. He even experienced transitory twinges of forgiveness for the bomber. Nothing had happened as he had expected. This, in itself, offered immense room for growth.

By early afternoon of his first day, the children all fed and down for naps, Woody was exhausted. He ate lunch alone, distractedly mulling the morning's activities, things he planned for later, adjustments in his approaches based on what he had encountered. When

the day resumed with some mild gym activity, Woody felt sufficiently refreshed to imagine surviving to quitting time.

But as he tossed a big lightweight ball among a trio of children,
Holly dispelled his calm: "Woody, quick! Josh is seizing!" He
rushed over to a mat where she cradled a thrashing skinny dark-
haired boy in shorts and tee shirt.

"Get the nurse!" Woody's cane clattered away as he dropped to
his knees and took the boy's galvanic body in his arms.

Instantly the boy's spasms ceased. His egg-white eyes rolled
back to normal register and focused on Woody's face. "Mister
Payne—what's wrong?"

"Josh—you're okay?"

Josh broke free and jumped up. He threw his arms ceilingward
like a triumphant athlete, grinning broadly. "Okay? I feel great!"

Holly returned from her aborted errand.

Woody extended a hand and said, "Help me up?"

Eyes wide, Holly reached down slowly, as if fearful of his touch.

† † †

Father James Tierney loved to read. Tottering piles of books filled
every flat surface in his study. Woody had to clear off a chair in
order to sit.

The white-haired priest brought Woody a beer. His hand exhibited a small palsy. "Here, son. You probably need this."

Although Woody was not supposed to mix alcohol with his meds,
he slugged the beer anyway.

Father Tierney sat. "Let's consider this matter calmly. You seem
more rational than when you called me earlier." He tented his fingers. "You still think you performed a miracle today upon this boy?
Such a claim is no small matter."

"I don't know. All I can say is, he's never come out of a seizure
like that before."

"We're not doctors, Woodrow. We don't know what's possible. Isn't it plausible that some seizures could be shorter and milder than others? You may have intervened as he was about to snap out of it anyway."

"He didn't *look* ready to snap out of it."

The father shrugged. "How clearly do we see during stressful moments?"

"I—I don't know. It's just that—" Woody fingered the depression in his skull.

"I thought we'd worked through that idle speculation, Woodrow. There's no way to positively identify that splinter in your brain. Out of all the flying debris that horrible day, to assume you received such a special piece—no, it's too unlikely. And even if we could be sure that a fragment of the True Cross had lodged in your brain, what of it? The Lignum Crucis is the holiest of relics, but no more than that. It's blasphemous to imagine you could receive mystical powers from mere proximity to the holy rood. The legacy of Jesus doesn't inhere in mere common matter."

Woody frowned: *proximity* was an awfully bland word for the intimacy of the contact between his brain and the unknown splinter.

† † †

The week after Josh's seizure, Cole had a birthday party. Everyone, even the most severely impaired children, sensed the day's excitement. Cake and juice awaited them after naptime.

Cole could not stop exclaiming, "Cake'n hoose, cake'n hoose!"

Woody had provided all this fare himself. Such out-of-pocket expenses marked the teacher's life.

Holly tied on bibs. She shuffled paper plates and sippy cups as Woody sliced and poured. After some confusion, they had all the children served and enjoying their treats. Holly dabbed spills and cleaned faces. Woody turned back to the desk where the cake rested, to clear away the leftovers.

The cake remained whole, uncut. The plastic juice jug showed full.

Woody pushed everything off the desk and into the trash. He shoved the cake box atop the mess to hide it.

Would the cake reform beneath the box? Would it, in fact, remain whole in the landfill, ready to be excavated a thousand years hence?

Holly approached Woody. "Got a slice for me?"

"Sorry—nothing left."

Holly stood dumbfounded. "But I thought—"

Something in Woody's expression stayed her tongue.

††† 

On this weekday, only Woody occupied the interior of St. Jude's church. Father Tierney had let him in and, at his request, departed.

Woody knelt in a pew and prayed. There was a cross on the wall, of course, but a stylish modern one. The atmosphere carried no scent of antiquity.

He prayed for many hours, the light growing dim, darkness flooding in, then light returning, until at last he knew.

††† 

"Holly, would you run this form to the front office?"

"Sure."

Once Holly had gone, Woody gathered the children on the floor around him. In the knot of warm bodies, some contorted, he spread his arms as if to embrace them all. The children sat unmoving during this strange new ritual.

"Dear Lord," he prayed aloud, "please drive the demons out of these children."

From the guinea pig cage arose a commotion. Furry bodies

thumped against the glass. One wall of the terrarium shattered, sending glass to the floor. The agitated guinea pigs, young and old, ran en masse down the countertop toward the open window, crashed through the screen, and plummeted three stories.

Woody looked back at the stunned children, their eyes bright and focused, their crazed limbs, if any, now whole.

"Mister Payne," said Cole. "The guinea pigs all jumped. Shouldn't we go see about them? They could be hurt."

"No, Cole," Woody said. "I'm not quite done yet."

† † †

## Author's Commentary

Some time ago, I read a horrifying thing. Survivors of terrorist explosions often end up with small organic bits of the blown-up terrorist embedded in their bodies: flesh and bone shrapnel. These fragments frequently cause small-scale immune system reactions, just as if you tried transplanting an organ without using immune-suppression drugs.

Naturally, having a science fiction writer's mind, I began to speculate on what weird things could happen from having such a foreign object lodged in your body. Somehow, my thoughts eventually turned to the notion of a piece of Christ's corpse being grafted onto someone. But practically speaking, there are no relics of Christ's body. (Lots of saintly fingers and such, sure, but not the Savior's.) Maybe blood cells from the Shroud of Turin . . ? But then I began thinking about the True Cross and the properties it might possess—and confer.

I've never been to Saint Toribio's in Lebanon, but I do have vivid memories of the Spanish countryside from my lone trip there in 1979. Luckily, not too long before I wrote this story, I happened to watch again Federico Fellini's great *Nights of Cabiria*, with its wonderful scene of Giulietta Masina's Cabiria visiting a shrine.

That's the feeling I tried to capture.

† † †

# TOURING JESUSWORLD

## Gregory Frost

D r. Hani found me standing at the entrance to his theme park. Piled in front of me, carved from mammoth stones that would have pleased C.B. DeMille, was the fifty-foot park sign, proclaiming for all to see: JESUSWORLD. A crane was at work moving the blocks, although I couldn't see why. They seemed just right to me.

All around the twenty-foot-high walls lay desert hills, outcroppings of rock—a landscape as forbidding as you could want.

Hani was a small, wiry man dressed in an ivory linen suit. Such clothing always looks as if the wearer has slept in it—in Hani's case, for days. He extended his hand in welcome. "Please, drop the 'Doctor,' it's just plain old Hani the Circle Drawer here."

"Circle Drawer?"

He had heavy-lidded eyes, which he now closed as at some tired jest. "It's an ancient joke a staff member hung on me. Hani was a messiah—a *nabi*, a wise man—who predated Yeshu."

To get here, I'd made a twenty-hour drive from Cleveland in a car I probably couldn't make the next payment on, and already we had our signals crossed. To his credit, Hani recognized as much.

"Why don't you come around back of the sign and let me take you on a behind-the-scenes tour. That way I can fill in details for you. Most people, you know, have so little knowledge of the subject on which they place so much hope and dependence."

"Right." I took out my pen and wrote that down. I also switched on my buttonhole recorder, which I should have done right away. Hey, twenty hours—I was cooked.

Hani held open an emergency exit door in the "D" of JESUS-WORLD and then came up beside me. "Okay, let me get you started, my boy. Even though the park is called 'JesusWorld,' that's mostly to get the public in through the door. If we'd called it the more accurate 'YeshuWorld,' who would make the turn off I-15?" He grinned at the obviousness of that question.

"I see."

"The fact is, his contemporary name was Yeshu, which has come down to us, romanized, as Jesus. It was a very common name of the day. There was a Jesus son of Sec, a Jesus son of Gamaliel, and so on. The name is a shortened form of Yehoshua—the Joshua of the Old Testament. Appropriately, it means, 'God Save.'" He stuck his index finger in the air. "Always, you'll note, a Jesus, son of somebody. That's important. Be careful to step over these cables here. Most of them are underground to maintain the air of authenticity."

"Right. So, who is our Jesus the son of?"

"Delighted you asked. This is a point of great speculation. There's a faction that holds he was Yeshu ben Pantera, *ben* meaning 'son of,' *Pantera* being the name of a Roman Centurion. For a long time, this was thought to be a total fabrication—until the tombstone of just such a soldier was discovered in Germany. So it's just possible he was a bastard son of a Roman. That's actually supported by another faction who say he was called Yeshu ben Miriam—Jesus, son of Mary. You see, sons were always called after their fathers, and if our Yeshu was called ben Miriam, it again suggests illegitimacy."

We had been walking for some time behind the various park building facades. Most were empty shells, intended to be seen from one side only. I could distinguish the shapes of ziggurats here and there, but most features from the back were unidentifiable. We descended a rocky slope until Hani raised his hand and glanced back at me. "Now, this is our first stop. This is where the little passenger train comes out and the tour guides meet everyone. We've actually taken a shorter route."

Hani led me around an enormous outcropping of rock that became an overhang beneath which huddled what looked like three cave entrances. Within the nearest one, a small fire burned. Hay was strewn across the floor and there were some blankets, woven mats that might have been for sleeping. "Mind you, we don't really hold with this story, which I'll explain in a moment, but this is your manger tale."

"But it's a cave."

"Very incisive of you. It *is* a cave. The so-called manger of that derived tale would have been like this. We copied these from real caves that probably were used in this manner."

"But you don't hold with them?" I prodded.

"Not really. The 'poor carpenter and family tossed out on their ear' story is unlikely. In the first place, 'carpenter' was their equivalent of our 'builder.' Do you know any starving builders?"

"Well, no. My brother—"

"Precisely. Most likely, he was a well-to-do kid. Not at all impoverished. Carpentry and rural images run through all his teachings, you know, which indicates he knew how to plant and feed. Only when he got to Jerusalem would people have regarded him as a second-class citizen."

"Why?"

"Well, it was the voice, the accent. He sounded like a hick come to the big town. Jon Voight in *Midnight Cowboy*, that sort of thing."

We walked past the last of the caves and up the hill on the far side while I chewed on that notion—the idea of Jesus the Geek being made fun of by the local toughs. It wasn't too hard to imagine.

Next we descended even farther, to the edge of a broad stream. It hooked around a hogback hillside and out of sight, all apparently natural but of course serving Hani's goal of surprise, for when we rounded the bend, the stream broadened into a river. On our side a sandbar hooked out, forming a huge pool. In the pool's center, about twenty naked people stood up to their bellies in the water, their faces turned from us. They were watching a bearded figure standing with his eyes closed, his hands on the head and one shoulder of a dull-looking youth. The bearded man was muttering something, the people hardly moved. Then all at once the baptist shoved the lad underneath the water.

"John the Baptist."

"Jesus' mentor. Many of Jesus' sayings derived from those of John. He was quite popular—something like five thousand followers, whom Jesus inherited when John was executed."

"Salome?"

"More likely Herod Antipas, who didn't care much for criticism."

I was watching the event in the center of the pool. "He's keeping that kid under for an awfully long time."

Hani's brow furrowed. He watched for a few more seconds, then took out a folding cellular phone and tapped out a code. "Ernie," he said, "get someone to reset John the Baptist's timer, would you? . . . Yes, he's just drowned Jesus." Hani folded up the phone and slipped it into his pocket.

"They're not real, then."

"Heavens, no. Animatronics. Real actors would be sneezing with pneumonia by day's end. However, the crowd is invited to wade in and participate, so getting the timer set is crucial. Let me add, the tour guide can stop the performance at any point, so there's no danger."

He turned away while I continued to watch. There were no bubbles coming up. John was still bent to his work. He could keep that kid down for a week. Maybe they had shut him off in order to repair him. I imagined unseen engineers in subterranean vaults beneath the artificial stream. It reminded me too awfully of another park in Florida.

When I looked up, Hani was ascending the hillside behind us by some mystical force. He beamed at the look of amazement on my face; no doubt it was the effect he'd hoped for. I strode up below him and saw the real means of his rising. There was an escalator built into the hillside. That made sense—you couldn't ask the public to *climb* heights such as these. On a really hot day, no one was going to want to walk very far. I said as much.

"Of course," Hani agreed. "And no one will. The temperature here gets to 110 degrees, but the humidity's so low you hardly notice. Nevertheless, had we been part of the regular tour, we'd have had the option of returning through doors inside the caves, traveling on carts through cool subterranean corridors. There's a refreshment stand and restrooms, tables to sit at. This journey is for the more adventurous." I had to admit, he seemed to have covered the comfort of his flock. Still, I could see one of his problems right off. He needed to install rides. Where was the sense of fun? Where was the laughing Jesus?

At the top we emerged onto a broad plateau in front of what I can describe only as a true spectacle. A hundred meters away, huge stone walls stood before us, buttressed randomly, seemingly

erected straight up out of the hillside. A few domes and rooftops
rose above the heights, indicating a real city within. It seemed to
be the front entrance to an ancient desert city. "Jerusalem?" I
guessed.

He nodded vigorously before leaning in, smelling heavily of
Obsession. He said, "It's really a reproduction of the town of Mar
Saba, not far from present-day Jerusalem, but don't put that in your
article. Jerusalem is what it's meant to be, as it might have looked
in A.D. 15."

"I still have a question about the Baptist."

"We'll get him working," he promised.

"No, my question is: Why did you devise young Jesus to look so
totally vapid?"

"Ah, again, a matter of interpretation. It would seem that John
and other *nabi'im* of the time relied heavily on basic hypnotism to
transport their followers to ecstatic experiences. The practice was
well known even then; there exists written corroboration by the
more ancient Egyptians, who apparently practiced it themselves.
It's likely one of the aspects of the art that John would have taught
his apprentice, who in turn taught it to his disciples in order to
send them out across the countryside, performing their own cures.
I see from your look that you doubt me."

"Not doubt," I replied. "I'm just trying to take all this in. It's not
exactly the interpretation of events the church mentions."

"Well, they wouldn't, would they?" He became somber.
"Churches are the modern equivalent of the temple that Jesus
railed against, and that ultimately crucified him. They have power
and political influence. They're full of iconography, never mind
that it's Christian in representation—the real Jesus would have
loathed it."

We passed through a small doorway in the wall. Within was a

vast complex of buildings and streets. Large flagstones the size of human torsos lay beneath our feet—Roman flagstones, according to Hani. We arrived before a pillared building with a vast doorway, surrounded on three sides by crenellated walls, and on the fourth by a large arch, where we stood.

"This is the Temple of Herod as it would have looked then. Here, he really got into trouble—all his following, behind a man who entered the city on a donkey during the big feast. That was a real slap in the face at the Sadducean aristocrats who ran the temple. You were supposed to enter on foot, you see. To show up on a *donkey*—well, in the first place it fulfilled an Old Testament prophecy, and that couldn't have sat well. In the second, he was laughing at them. He might as well have dressed a monkey in priest's clothing. To his view, they were defilers of all they believed in—rich priests and their families. Oh, they were the kings of nepotism. Were he alive today, he'd no doubt enter Vatican City the same way, and with the same attitude. He'd throw out the Pope, I'm quite sure."

"Forgive me, but you seem to have something against the Catholic Church."

Hani shrugged. "Merely its own history of lies, greed, licentiousness, bastardy, defilement, murder, intrigue and rapine, to name a few items on a still larger list. Where is the truth of their beliefs?"

I stared up past rows of marble benches, to the temple, where animatronic moneylenders sat ready to do business. Were they designed to interact with the public? *I* could have used a car loan. I didn't know my Bible half so well as I should have for this assignment. Mostly I covered the local events calendar—antique shows and circuses and trucks with big tires. "What about Mary?" I tried. "The Virgin?"

"Ha! First of all, the word's misleading. Originally, it was the word *'almah*, which meant nothing more than 'young woman.' It's through mistranslations that she evolves into an icon of partheno-genesis. For most of what today is held as valid in the way of faith on this subject, we can blame the emperor Constantine. It was through his political meddling and siding with various factions in the nascent church that certain unfounded beliefs gained in power over the truth. Mary became the Mother of God in A.D. 431. By a *vote* taken by these same greedy priests. How is one to embrace such nonsense? There is *nothing* to it!" He was breathing heavily.

I must have looked bewildered. He held up his hand and added, "I'm sorry. I am trying only to educate people. Belief is well and good, but belief in obvious falsehoods is madness, futile. I want to change the belief of the world."

I looked into the temple. Except for the moneylenders, who were like sidewalk vendors in their booths, there was no one around. In fact there wasn't a soul in the place except for us. "I've noticed that you don't seem to be attracting much of a crowd."

His bright expression dimmed. He lowered his head. Finally, he admitted, "No."

"You've been open, what, six months?"

"Go ahead, skewer me the way everyone else has. I've had arti-cles written about JesusWorld in every magazine. Most have mocked me for what I'm doing. They don't understand my purpose."

"Or maybe they do," I proposed. After all, I'd read most of those articles on the way here. I hardly felt he had been misrepresented, except by the more fundamentalist reporters. "It seems to me, Hani, that it's you who've made the error. You assumed that people would want the truth about Jesus. The fact is that faith is irrational and thus not interested in the facts. If someone's got a drug problem, say, they might embrace Jesus as a way out. Now, that person's not going to want to hear about what the real Jesus had to say. He's won't care that you can point out the Sheep Pool or

Golgotha or Pilate's house. He's got a personal Jesus, see. It hasn't got a damned thing to do with the real story, the true events. The only people who're going to care about your little world are people who've already blown off the whole story, and who just *aren't* going to travel to a place offering answers such as yours."

To my surprise, he was nodding and smiling again. "Yes! Exactly. The very conclusion I came to, my boy. And that's why we're now adding our newest exhibit, which you *must* write about. The latest, best, and a sure draw." He ushered me excitedly out of the holy city. We exited through a different door, into a short tunnel to the underground rail line he'd had installed. About a dozen small cars waited to whisk us to the next remarkable location.

I climbed in after him. "Now where?"

He put the car in motion and we whisked along the rail. Recessed lights flashed by overhead. He had his back to me as he watched the rail ahead, but his words whipped over his shoulder, and he gestured broadly as always. "I'm looking to the future now, exactly as you suggest. People personalize Jesus, just so. They mix him up in colors of their own choosing, stretch him and redesign him. So I said to myself, how will they next redefine him? What will his next devolution be? And the answer came to me—you won't believe where from."

"Divine intervention?" I hazarded.

"Supermarket tabloids!"

The car shook and slowed. He craned his neck to look at me. "It's really the new folk religion, isn't it? People without a smattering of education embracing all these ridiculous stories about UFOs and past lives and film stars and diets—that's precisely how we've ended up with the absurdities embraced by the church itself. The future as I thus perceive it will be the source of the next phase in the growth of our park."

The car halted. We stepped onto a concrete runway. "You must understand, it's not finished yet. I have the backing, though. The money is there."

"Naturally."

"You'll be the first journalist to see it."

We rode up another escalator. At the top of this one was a pink light as bright as anything I'd ever seen—like looking into the sun. Squinting, I edged along after him. The light seemed to track me; but it soon dimmed, and there before me was a sight that riveted me to the spot: a cyclorama of a great curving hillside full of crosses, undoubtedly hundreds of them. And in the center, right up front, was one made of gold. On it, dressed in tight black pants and a red jacket, hung Elvis Presley. His face, tilted skyward, wore the same soulful look of a million third-rate portraits of Jesus. Hani had captured him perfectly.

He was watching my face, but this time I knew better than to let my reaction show. Give me some credit as a reporter, for Christ's sake. I said, as noncommittally as possible, "This is different."

"Isn't it? And what a draw it will be. They're changing the sign out front right now—you saw the crane as you came in. From now on, no more JesusWorld. No. From now on, it's *KingsWorld*."

"KingsWorld."

"I predict, a hundred years from now, the majority of America, if not the world, will firmly believe that Elvis was the second coming. That he, too, returned from the dead. He appeared on refrigerators like little children's finger paintings. He sang from cash registers. The myriad stories will all tangle and a single entity will emerge. We will be there first. Leading the way. If I can do that, I can perhaps lead them all back onto a more reasonable path. Don't you think?"

I didn't, but I didn't dare say so. He didn't want to hear it. Like everyone else he disdained, he, too, had personalized his Jesus.

Jesus was not Yeshu ben Miriam. Jesus was not the Christ. Jesus was certainly not Elvis Aaron Presley. Nope. Jesus was Silly Putty.

"Don't you agree that by adding Elvis we'll bring the audience we want? People misled for centuries by absurdities and their own confusion?"

"I've no doubt whatsoever." I looked for an exit.

Hani rubbed his hands together. "Wait till you see how I've combined them. We're going to sell a book combining the real teachings of Yeshu with some of the more pithy comments of Presley. We're calling it *Wise Men Say*. Recycled paper, naturally. This crucifixion scene, I realize, is wholly unrealistic, but won't it get them in the door, though? You've got to get them through the door."

"Won't it?" I spotted an exit sign next to the Men's Room and eased toward it. "Hani, will you excuse me a minute?"

"But of course." He gestured in that direction as though I weren't heading for the restroom already. "I'll be here when you've finished. We'll have some lunch."

"Sure we will."

I made a beeline for the bathroom and only deviated at the last moment, without a look back. He must not have been watching, because he didn't come screaming after me. I found myself in another hallway. Another sign pointed the way out. I passed a room under construction, the only time I saw other living beings in the whole damned park. Workmen were replacing the robot head of Lazarus with the head of Elvis. I could imagine all too horribly the musical number that might follow his sitting up, and fled before the performance could start.

Finally, I burst through a set of double doors in the outer wall of the park and out into the deserted parking lot. The roar of machinery surrounded me. Off to the left, the immense diesel crane swung a giant "J" out over the tarmac to where other letters were piled up. I jumped into my car and looked at the display that remained. "USWORLD" it proclaimed.

"Who's the leader of the club?" I asked it as I backed the car out of its space. The front axle shivered violently. It didn't like going backwards.

Twenty hours back to Cleveland. Maybe, I thought, I should detour south and stop off at Graceland before heading home. I didn't want to waste the trip, and it might prove educational. Jesus knew.

*—for Damon Knight*

††† 

## Author's Commentary

This story exists only because the late Damon Knight invited me to submit to an issue of *Pulphouse* magazine he was editing in which all the stories were to have something to do with Jesus. When I finally sat down to consider it, I realized that I knew almost nothing about the historical side of Jesus. Most of the texts in my own library, such as Northrop Frye's *The Great Code*, had more to do with how the Bible came to be assembled—interesting, but not what I needed. So I spent a few days at my local libraries, where I found dozens of books on the history of the time, place, and individual. Some featured solid historical fact—for instance, that mangers would have been caves. Some contained speculation based upon what we know about the culture. At that point I had no idea for a story, but only the hope that my reading would *suggest* one—which is exactly what happened.

Research: It's what's for breakfast.

†††

*The things we carry, the things we overcome . . .*

# CROSS CARRIERS
## Bruce Holland Rogers

### *i. my share of sacrifices*

There are many hungry families in our county, and those of us who care about helping them, we give up a lot. As the director of the Food Bank, I make my share of sacrifices, and not just the obvious ones.

A month ago, during the summer food-basket drive, I said to our receptionist, "Alice, we'll need some extra hands here this weekend. How do you feel about coming in?"

"On the clock?" she said. "Will I be paid?"

I asked her, "Do you know what kind of salary I could earn managing a private business?"

She said, "I don't work for free."

"But you volunteer at the library."

"That's not the same."

Every dollar we spend on staff is a dollar that isn't feeding the hungry. I told her, "I haven't had a vacation in six years!"

"I'm sorry," she said.

We delivered food baskets without her help. Everything got done, but that isn't the point.

The sacrifices I make for this charity . . . I'm telling you, it costs me.

I don't like delivering bad news to anyone, and getting the phones answered without a paid receptionist, well, it's been a strain on me and on the whole remaining staff.

† † †


## ii. *first lady*

Halfway across the country, your husband's opponent has given his concession speech. Now you stand on a floodlit stage with the new President-elect, at his side, half a step back. Red, white, and blue confetti falls. A band plays. Supporters wave signs and chant his name, which is your name, too. When you married him, you kept your own name at first, but his advisors cautioned that such a wife would confuse voters. Really? You are always introduced as "the wife of," or Mrs. His Name, anyway.

Surrendering your name was a small sacrifice. A bigger one: pretending to be his subordinate helper. "What do you argue about?" one reporter asked, digging for a story. You lied. "We don't."

From the House to the Senate, every victory has left him with less time for you. Now, even together in private, you're alone. And alone, who are you? You died and were reborn as a campaign asset.

Now you, the smiling campaign asset, hold his hand and study the already deepening lines in his face. The Presidency ages men. He'll be less and less himself, more and more the office. He will be consumed. Sacrificed. It's only fair. It's his turn.

† † †

### *iii. bartow county, september 1864*

The boy being ushered into the colonel's office looked to be about sixteen, not too young to wear a rebel uniform, though he was dressed in dirty homespun. His feet were bare. The colonel wondered if, perhaps, this boy was the murderer. It would save a lot of grief if he were coming to confess. The lieutenant introduced him. "Mr. Coates."

The colonel, keeping his seat, continued to look the boy over. Fit. Unwashed. A Georgia dirt farmer's son. "What's this about, Coates?"

"Sir," the boy said. He kneaded his hands together, as if to calm himself. "Sir, I've come to see you about Mr. Matthew Barron, sir. He's a neighbor of mine. One of the condemned."

The colonel looked at his aide. "I told you I would hear no pleas for clemency."

"Begging the colonel's pardon," said the lieutenant, "you should hear him out."

"Colonel, sir," said the boy, "Mr. Barron is the sole support of his wife and children. Two girls and an infant son."

"I am not pleased to hear that," said the colonel. "Not at all. But someone shot a federal officer dead in the street. If the citizens of Allatoona will not produce the assassin, then there must be consequences. The condemned men were taken without preference. If I were to release one because of his circumstance, wouldn't I have to consider the circumstances of the rest? I don't say any of these men deserves shooting. But who does?"

"No one," said the boy. "I'm here to give myself up, just the same."

"To turn yourself in?" The colonel stood. "You shot my captain?"

"Oh, no, sir! We're Quakers!" He shook his head. "I mean to ask you to shoot me instead, in order to deliver Mr. Barron."

The colonel did not know what to say. He opened, then closed his mouth. At last he leaned over his desk. "You say he is your neighbor. Surely there is more to it. Is he a member of your congregation?"

"Mr. Barron is a Baptist." The boy looked the colonel in the eye and said, "Will you take me, sir?"

"You put me in a difficult situation, son." The colonel sat down. He rubbed his face with his hand. He stopped. "You might have confessed to the murder and spared them all."

The boy stood a little taller. "Yes, sir. But that would have been a lie."

†††

### iv. first responders

Alfonso Espinoza, flirting with a girl he had just met on the quad, told her that she should stop bothering him and let him go to the library so his excellent grades wouldn't suffer. "Me," said the girl, "bothering you? It's the other way around. And, anyway, I bet I need good grades more than you do. I'm going to be a doctor. My grades are a matter of life and death." He told her that his grades were life and death, too. He was studying fire science. "What's that?" she said. She squinted, suspecting a joke. "Fire science! You made that up!"

Years later, at the Academy, it was clear to everyone that Espinoza was the oldest cadet. He talked about his time in the Army, but not his college years. Some cadets might have thought it was arrogant or foolish, getting the command degree first before even trying out for the Academy.

Other cadets had secrets, too. Don Blackman was broad-shouldered, powerful. He had an easy laugh and took jokes well: "Name?" Blackman. "No kidding!" Or, "Cadet Jones, you think you've mastered that carry? Let me see you carry Blackman!" Only Blackman's wife knew that he sometimes bolted upright in bed from nightmares of drowning.

Stuart Sill was Blackman's opposite. White, wiry, small. He struggled at the edge of physical requirements, but he had heart. He kept his secret to himself until, two weeks before graduation, the examination board asked him, "Do you have problems, Cadet Sills, with any group of people?" He didn't answer. Honesty might sink all his hard work. "Puerto Ricans?" prompted another examiner. "Muslims?" And Sills risked telling them that he didn't like fags, or rather, homos, couldn't abide what they did. "But would that interfere with your ability to do your job?" Oh, no, sirs, he said too fast, telling them what they wanted to hear.

After graduation, Espinoza's wife, the medical student, mentioned at dinner with the Blackmans and Stuart Sills that to a fireman the risk of cancer was as great as the risk of death by fire. "We know, Sweetheart," her husband said. "We don't need reminding."

Posted to separate stationhouses, the three men had their trials. Espinoza watched younger men testing for the job he couldn't even put in for yet. Blackman panicked awake in his station bunk to have another fireman say in the dark, "You okay?" Sills blew his top over a male pin-up on his locker door, then endured the endless jokes now that his station-mates had touched a nerve.

Over the years, they had their choices: Sills on the night when the fire call was to a gay bar. Blackman when his chief asked if he was a good swimmer. Espinoza when the promotions board chairman said, "You do realize, don't you, that Battalion Chief is the rank with the highest casualty rate?"

Espinoza asked his wife, the doctor, the mother of his children, to forgive him in advance for the hazard he might not see until too late.

Blackman stood at the edge of a pond, fitting his dive mask in place for all the good it would do him in such muddy water. A car had been on the bottom for almost ten minutes, and if people inside were still alive and conscious, they were even more scared than he was.

"Two still. Inside," said the bartender as soon as Sills carried him out of the bar. "Trying the. Back door. It's chained shut." And Sills, calling for a hose to follow, walked through fire to save two men.

† † †

### *v. the flying boy*

Oscar said, "I know hating Dad is your religion. But you're running out of chances to say goodbye. Just fly down there."

"Easy for you to say," Will said, and hung up. His half-brother Oscar had been hardly more than a baby when Dad abandoned the family. Will remembered his father lying on his back in the grass. With his stocking feet he raised a laughing Oscar up into the air. "Look at him!" Dad said. "He's flying! He's the flying boy!" His father must have played that game with Will, too. Will couldn't remember.

The last time Will had seen his father, at Oscar's wedding, Will had cornered him. "She was only my step-mother, for chrissake! How could you leave me with her?"

"It was more than twenty years ago. What do you want me to say?"

Will knew exactly what he had wanted him to say. And if the old man wasn't already too senile, maybe he could still say it, just once.

In a room where photos of airplanes covered the walls, Will's father looked up from his chair. "No, no," he said. "I didn't ask for that."

Will's hands were empty. "Ask for what, Dad?"

His father squinted at him. "Are you the gardener?"

"It's me, Dad. It's Will."

His father struggled out of the chair and offered his hand. "Pleased to meet you."

Will stared at the trembling hand, then at the familiar blue eyes that registered no hint of recognition. He had abandoned Will again. There would be no apology. Will kept his hands by his side.

"Why am I here?" he said.

"Right," his father said, as if this meeting had been his idea. He looked down at the rug, frowning. Then his gaze wandered to the walls, the photographs.

Will studied the familiar profile. His father. An old man with trembling hands, who had once, a long time ago, abandoned his sons.

Will let out a breath that he hadn't known he was holding.

"Tell me," Will said, "about flying."

"Oh," his father said. "Airplanes!"

"No, not airplanes." Will rested his hand on his father's arm. "Flying. When you were a little boy, couldn't you fly?"

"Of course not!" He looked angry, insulted.

Will persisted. "Weren't you the flying boy?"

His father looked confused. He opened, then closed his mouth. "Wait!" He smiled. "You're right! I was the flying boy!"

††† 

### vi. from black water

He is dead. The brother who taught you the right way to throw a ball is dead. You want to draw the shades, take the phone from its cradle, crawl to the darkest corner of the basement, alone.

He is dead, the brother who pushed you backwards out of the tree house, the brother who knew your childhood secrets and only told a few. He knew bigger secrets later and kept them all. And you, you were the first to know he was married, had been arrested, had been fired, was going to be a father, was sick. Very sick. You want to brick up the windows, nail shut the doors, and yank the phone wire out of the wall. He is dead, and you want to follow him into the ground. No, even deeper. Even more alone.

Instead, you shower. You dress yourself. You step into open air. You endure his wife, his children, all the people who loved him, people you love. They might understand if you explained. Yours is the grief that seeks caves of black water. But you don't explain. You come out, blind albino fish emerging into the light that burns. It is your gift.

† † †

### vii. next in line, please

I used to love roller coasters: wheels rattling on iron rails, girls screaming, wind in my hair. At the end of the ride, I always wished I could keep my seat and not yield to the next kid in line.

Now I hold court in my living room for visitors coming to say goodbye. My throne is a recliner covered with pillows and towels duct-taped into place, my Rube Goldberg machine for easing pain.

An old chum visits with his grandson. The kid hides behind his grandpa's chair. I say, "Look at these arms! Thin as chicken bones!" I pull at my skin, then let go to show how slowly it resumes its shape. When my friend goes off to the bathroom, I summon the boy closer. I hoist the cuffs of my pants to show how puffy the edema has made my ankles. "You can touch it."

He doesn't. But he asks, "Does it hurt?"

"Some," I say. "I don't mind. My turn is over."

He looks toward the hallway, hoping his grandfather will reappear and rescue him. Well, maybe this memory will make sense when he's older. "Kid," I say, "Have yourself one heck of a ride!"

† † †

## Author's Commentary

I grew up in a family of religious liberals for whom the Gospels were one set of inspiring stories among many such stories from many different traditions. For me, Jesus has always been a heroic figure among many heroes from myth, scripture, and history, so when I consider the importance of the cross, I'm likely to think in broad terms of self-sacrifice. What interests me more than The Cross are all the little crosses that we choose to take up, or pretend to take up, or fail to take up.

I'm also the kind of person who dislikes giving only one answer to a question, and that may be why I ended up writing a story form called the symmetrina, of which "Cross Carriers" is an example. The rather elaborate rules for a symmetrina involve writing several stories around a single theme, with each section written to a strict word count. The form offers me an excuse to respond to the theme of self-sacrifice without having to settle on just one story.

† † †

*"The long and bloody path to the new Golgotha . . ."*

# A Cross of Centuries

## Henry Kuttner

They called him Christ. But he was not the Man Who had toiled up the long road to Golgotha five thousand years before. They called him Buddha and Mohammed; they called him the Lamb, and the Blessed of God. They called him the Prince of Peace and the Immortal One.

His name was Tyrell.

He had come up another road now, the steep path that led to the monastery on the mountain, and he stood for a moment blinking against the bright sunlight. His white robe was stained with the ritual black.

The girl beside him touched his arm and urged him gently forward. He stepped into the shadow of the gateway.

Then he hesitated and looked back. The road had led up to a level mountain meadow where the monastery stood, and the meadow was dazzling green with early spring. Faintly, far away, he felt a wrenching sorrow at the thought of leaving all this brightness, but he sensed that things would be better very soon. And the brightness was far away. It was not quite real any more. The girl touched his arm again and he nodded obediently and moved forward, feeling the troubling touch of approaching loss that his tired mind could not understand now.

*I am very old,* he thought.

In the courtyard the priests bowed before him. Mons, the leader, was standing at the other end of a broad pool that sent back the bottomless blue of the sky. Now and again the water was ruffled by a cool, soft breeze.

Old habits sent their messages along his nerves. Tyrell raised his hand and blessed them all.

His voice spoke the remembered phrases quietly.

"Let there be peace. On all the troubled earth, on all the worlds and in God's blessed sky between, let there be peace. The powers of—of—" his hand wavered; then he remembered—"the powers of darkness have no strength against God's love and understanding. I bring you God's word. It is love; it is understanding; it is peace."

They waited till he had finished. It was the wrong time and the wrong ritual. But that did not matter, since he was the Messiah.

Mons, at the other end of the pool, signaled. The girl beside Tyrell put her hands gently on the shoulders of his robe.

Mons cried, "Immortal, will you cast off your stained garment and with it the sins of time?"

Tyrell looked vaguely across the pool.

"Will you bless the worlds with another century of your holy presence?"

Tyrell remembered some words.

"I leave in peace; I return in peace," he said.

The girl gently pulled off the white robe, knelt, and removed Tyrell's sandals. Naked, he stood at the pool's edge.

He looked like a boy of twenty. He was two thousand years old.

Some deep trouble touched him. Mons had lifted his arm, summoning, but Tyrell looked around confusedly and met the girl's gray eyes.

"Nerina?" he murmured.

"Go in the pool," she whispered. "Swim across it."

He put out his hand and touched hers. She felt that wonderful current of gentleness that was his indomitable strength. She pressed his hand tightly, trying to reach through the clouds in his mind, to make him know that it would be all right again, that she would be waiting—as she had waited for his resurrection three times already now, in the last three hundred years.

She was much younger than Tyrell, but she was immortal too.

For an instant the mists cleared from his blue eyes.

"Wait for me, Nerina," he said. Then, with a return of his old skill, he went into the pool with a clean dive.

She watched him swim across, surely and steadily. There was nothing wrong with his body; there never was, no matter how old he grew. It was only his mind that stiffened, grooved deeper into the iron ruts of time, lost its friction with the present, so that his memory would fragment away little by little. But the oldest memories went last, and the automatic memories last of all.

She was conscious of her own body, young and strong and beautiful, as it would always be. Her mind . . . there was an answer to that too. She was watching the answer.

*I am greatly blessed*, she thought. *Of all women on all the worlds, I am the Bride of Tyrell, and the only other immortal ever born.*

Lovingly and with reverence she watched him swim. At her feet his discarded robe lay, stained with the memories of a hundred years.

It did not seem so long ago. She could remember it very clearly, the last time she had watched Tyrell swim across the pool. And there had been one time before that—and that had been the first. For her; not for Tyrell.

He came dripping out of the water and hesitated. She felt a strong pang at the change in him from strong sureness to bewildered questioning. But Mons was ready. He reached out and took

Tyrell's hand. He led the Messiah toward a door in the high monastery wall and through it. She thought that Tyrell looked back at her, with the tenderness that was always there in his deep, wonderful calm.

A priest picked up the stained robe from her feet and carried it away. It would be washed clean now and placed on the altar, the spherical tabernacle shaped like the mother world. Dazzling white again, its folds would hang softly about the earth.

It would be washed clean, as Tyrell's mind would be washed clean too, rinsed of the clogging deposit of a century's memories.

The priests were filing away. She glanced back, beyond the open gateway, to the sharply beautiful green of the mountain meadow, spring grass sensuously reaching to the sun after the winter's snow. *Immortal*, she thought, lifting her arms high, feeling the eternal blood, ichor of gods, singing in deep rhythm through her body. *Tyrell was the one who suffered. I have no price to pay for this— wonder.*

Twenty centuries.

And the first century must have been utter horror.

Her mind turned from the hidden mists of history that was legend now, seeing only a glimpse of the calm White Christ moving through that chaos of roaring evil when the earth was blackened, when it ran scarlet with hate and anguish. Ragnarok, Armageddon, Hour of the Antichrist—two thousand years ago!

Scourged, steadfast, preaching his word of love and peace, the White Messiah had walked like light through earth's descent into hell.

And he had lived, and the forces of evil had destroyed themselves, and the worlds had found peace now—had found peace so long ago that the Hour of the Antichrist was lost to memory; it was legend.

Lost, even to Tyrell's memory. She was glad of that. It would have been terrible to remember. She turned chill at the thought of what martyrdom he must have endured.

But it was the Day of the Messiah now, and Nerina, the only other immortal ever born, looked with reverence and love at the empty doorway through which Tyrell had gone. She glanced down at the blue pool. A cool wind ruffled its surface; a cloud moved lightly past the sun, shadowing all the bright day.

It would be seventy years before she would swim the pool again. And when she did, when she woke, she would find Tyrell's blue eyes watching her, his hand closing lightly over hers, raising her to join him in the youth that was the springtime where they lived forever.

† † †

Her gray eyes watched him; her hand touched his as he lay on the couch. But still he did not awaken.

She glanced up anxiously at Mons.

He nodded reassuringly.

She felt the slightest movement against her hand.

His eyelids trembled. Slowly they lifted. The calm, deep certainty was still there in the blue eyes that had seen so much, in the mind that had forgotten so much. Tyrell looked at her for a moment. Then he smiled.

Nerina said shakily, "Each time I'm afraid that you'll forget me."

Mons said, "We always give him back his memories of you, Blessed of God. We always will." He leaned over Tyrell. "Immortal, have you truly wakened?"

"Yes," Tyrell said, and thrust himself upright, swinging his legs over the edge of the couch, rising to his feet in a swift, sure motion. He glanced around, saw the new robe ready, pure white, and drew it on. Both Nerina and Mons saw that there was no more hesitancy in his actions. Beyond the eternal body, the mind was young and sure and unclouded again.

Both Mons and Nerina knelt. The priest said softly, "We thank God that a new incarnation is permitted. May peace reign in this cycle, and in all the cycles beyond."

Tyrell lifted Nerina to her feet. He reached down and drew Mons upright too.

"Mons, Mons," he said, almost chidingly. "Every century I'm treated less like a man and more like a god. If you'd been alive a few hundred years ago—well, they still prayed when I woke, but they didn't kneel. I'm a man, Mons. Don't forget that."

Mons said, "You brought peace to the worlds."

"Then may I have something to eat, in return?"

Mons bowed and went out. Tyrell turned quickly to Nerina. The strong gentleness of his arms drew her close.

"If I never woke, sometime—" he said. "You'd be the hardest thing of all to give up. I didn't know how lonely I was till I found another immortal."

"We have a week here in the monastery," she said. "A week's retreat, before we go home. I like being here with you best of all."

"Wait a while," he said. "A few more centuries and you'll lose that attitude of reverence. I wish you would. Love's better—and who else can I love this way?"

She thought of the centuries of loneliness he had had, and her whole body ached with love and compassion.

After the kiss, she drew back and looked at him thoughtfully.

"You've changed again," she said. "It's still you, but—"

"But what?"

"You're gentler, somehow."

Tyrell laughed.

"Each time, they wash out my mind and give me a new set of memories. Oh, most of the old ones, but the total's a little different. It always is. Things are more peaceful now than they were a century ago. So my mind is tailored to fit the times. Otherwise I'd gradually become an anachronism." He frowned slightly. "Who's that?"

She glanced at the door.

"Mons? No. It's no one."

"Oh? Well . . . yes, we'll have a week's retreat. Time to think and integrate my retailored personality. And the past—" He hesitated again.

She said, "I wish I'd been born earlier. I could have been with you—"

"No," he said quickly. "At least—not too far back."

"Was it so bad?"

He shrugged.

"I don't know how true my memories are any more. I'm glad I don't remember more than I do. But I remember enough. The legends are right." His face shadowed with sorrow. "The big wars . . . hell was loosed. Hell was omnipotent! The Antichrist walked in the noonday sun, and men feared that which is high . . . " His gaze lifted to the pale low ceiling of the room, seeing beyond it. "Men had turned into beasts. Into devils. I spoke of peace to them, and they tried to kill me. I bore it. I was immortal, by God's grace. Yet they could have killed me. I am vulnerable to weapons." He drew a deep, long breath. "Immortality was not enough. God's will preserved me, so that I could go on preaching peace until, little by little, the maimed beasts remembered their souls and reached up out of hell. . . ."

She had never heard him talk like this.

Gently she touched his hand.

He came back to her.

"It's over," he said. "The past is dead. We have today."

From the distance the priests chanted a paean of joy and gratitude.

† † †

The next afternoon she saw him at the end of a corridor leaning over something huddled and dark. She ran forward. He was bent down beside the body of a priest, and when Nerina called out, he shivered and stood up, his face white and appalled.

She looked down and her face, too, went white.

The priest was dead. There were blue marks on his throat, and his neck was broken, his head twisted monstrously.

Tyrell moved to shield the body from her gaze.

"G-get Mons," he said, unsure as though he had reached the end of the hundred years. "Quick. This . . . *get him.*"

Mons came, looked at the body, and stood aghast. He met Tyrell's blue gaze.

"How many centuries, Messiah?" he asked, in a shaken voice.

Tyrell said, "Since there was violence? Eight centuries or more. Mons, no one—no one is capable of this."

Mons said, "Yes. There is no more violence. It has been bred out of the race." He dropped suddenly to his knees. "Messiah, bring peace again! The dragon has risen from the past!"

Tyrell straightened, a figure of strong humility in his white robe. He lifted his eyes and prayed.

Nerina knelt, her horror slowly washed away in the burning power of Tyrell's prayer.

The whisper breathed through the monastery and shuddered back from the blue, clear air beyond. None knew who had closed deadly hands about the priest's throat. No one, no human, was capable any longer of killing; as Mons had said, the ability to hate, to destroy, had been bred out of the race.

The whisper did not go beyond the monastery. Here the battle must be fought in secret, no hint of it escaping to trouble the long peace of the worlds.

No human.

But another whisper grew: *The Antichrist is born again.*

They turned to Tyrell, to Messiah, for comfort.

*Peace,* he said, *peace—meet evil with humility, bow your heads in prayer, remember the love that saved man when hell was loosed on the worlds two thousand years ago.*

At night, beside Nerina, he moaned in his sleep and struck out at an invisible enemy. "Devil!" he cried—and woke shuddering.

She held him, with proud humility, till he slept again.

† † †

She came with Mons one day to Tyrell's room, to tell him of the new horror. A priest had been found dead, savagely hacked by a sharp knife. They pushed open the door and saw Tyrell sitting facing them at a low table. He was praying while he watched, in sick fascination, the bloody knife that lay on the table before him.

"Tyrell—" she said, and suddenly Mons drew in a quick shuddering breath and swung around sharply. He pushed her back across the threshold.

"Wait!" he said, with violent urgency. "Wait for me here!" Before she could speak he was beyond the closing door, and she heard it lock.

She stood there, not thinking, for a long time.

Then Mons came out and closed the door softly behind him. He looked at her.

"It's all right," he said. "But . . . you must listen to me now." Then he was silent.

He tried again.

"Blessed of God—" Again he drew that difficult breath. "Nerina, I—" He laughed oddly. "That's strange. I can't talk unless I call you Nerina."

"What is it? Let me go to Tyrell."

"No—no. He'll be all right. Nerina, he's—sick."

She shut her eyes, trying to concentrate. She heard this voice, unsure but growing stronger.

"Those killings. Tyrell did them."

"Now you lie," she said. "That is a lie!"

Mons said almost sharply, "Open your eyes. Listen to me. Tyrell is—a man. A very great man, a very good man, but no god. He is immortal. Unless he is struck down, he will live forever—as you will. He has already lived more than twenty centuries."

"Why tell me this? I know it!"

Mons said, "You must help, you must understand. Immortality is an accident of the genes. A mutation. Once in a thousand years, perhaps, or ten thousand, a human is born immortal. His body renews itself; he does not age. Neither does his brain. But his mind ages—"

She said desperately, "Tyrell swam the pool of rebirth only three days ago. Not for another century will his mind age again. Is he— *he's not dying?*"

"No—no. Nerina, the pool of rebirth is only a symbol. You know that."

"Yes. The real rebirth comes afterward, when you put us in that machine. I remember."

Mons said, "The machine. If it were not used each century, you and Tyrell would have become senile and helpless a long time ago. The mind is not immortal, Nerina. After a while it cannot carry the weight of knowledge, learning, habits. It loses flexibility, it clouds with stiff old age. The machine clears the mind, Nerina, as we can clear a computer of its units of memory. Then we replace some memories, not all, we put the necessary memories in a fresh, clear mind, so it can grow and learn for another hundred years."

"But I know all that—"

"Those new memories form a new personality, Nerina."

"A new—? But Tyrell is still the same."

"Not quite. Each century he changes a little, as life grows better, as the worlds grow happier. Each century the new mind, the fresh personality of Tyrell is different—more in tune with the new century than the one just past. You have been reborn in mind three times, Nerina. You are not the same as you were the first time. But you cannot remember that. You do not have all the old memories you once had."

"But—but what—"

Mons said, "I do not know. I have talked to Tyrell. I think this is what has happened. Each century when the mind of Tyrell was cleansed—erased—it left a blank mind, and we built a new Tyrell on that. Not much changed. Only a little, each time. But more than twenty times? His mind must have been very different twenty centuries ago. And—"

"How different?"

"I don't know. We've assumed that when the mind was erased, the pattern of personality—vanished. I think now that it didn't vanish. It was buried. Suppressed, driven so deeply into the mind that it could not emerge. It became unconscious. Century after century this has happened. And now more than twenty personalities of Tyrell are buried in his mind, a multiple personality that can no longer stay in balance. From the graves in his mind, there has been a resurrection."

"The White Christ was never a killer!"

"No. In reality, even his first personality, twenty-odd centuries ago, must have been very great and good to bring peace to the

.hat time of Antichrist. But sometimes, in the burial of
a change may happen. Those buried personalities, some
, may have changed to—to something less good

rina turned to the door.

.Ions said, "We must be very sure. But we can save the Messiah.
e can clear his brain, probe deep, deep, root out the evil spirit. . . .
We can save him and make him whole again. We must start at once.
Nerina—pray for him."

He gave her a long, troubled look, turned, and went swiftly along
the corridor. Nerina waited, not even thinking. After a while she
heard a slight sound. At one end of the corridor were two priests
standing motionless; at the other end, two others.

She opened the door and went in to Tyrell.

† † †

The first thing she saw was the bloodstained knife on the table.
Then she saw the dark silhouette at the window, against the aching
intensity of blue sky.

"Tyrell," she said hesitantly.

He turned.

"Nerina. Oh, Nerina!"

His voice was still gentle with that deep power of calm.

She went swiftly into his arms.

"I was praying," he said, bending his head to rest on her
shoulder. "Mons told me. . . . I was praying. What have I done?"

"You are the Messiah," she said steadily. "You saved the world
from evil and the Antichrist. You've done that."

"But the rest! The devil in my mind! This seed that has grown
there, hidden from God's sunlight—what has it grown into? They
say I *killed!*"

After a long pause she whispered, "Did you?"

"No," he said, with absolute certainty. "How could I? I, who have lived by love—more than two thousand years—I could not harm a living thing."

"I knew that," she said. "You are the White Christ."

"The White Christ," he said softly. "I wanted no such name. I am only a man, Nerina. I was never more than that. But . . . something saved me, something kept me alive through the Hour of the Antichrist. It was God. It was His hand. God—*help me now!*"

She held him tightly and looked past him through the window, bright sky, green meadow, tall mountains with the clouds rimming their peaks. God was here, as he was out beyond the blue, on all the worlds and in the gulfs between them, and God meant peace and love.

"He will help you," she said steadily. "He walked with you two thousand years ago. He hasn't gone away."

"Yes," Tyrell whispered. "Mons must be wrong. The way it was . . . I remember. Men like beasts. The sky was burning fire. There was blood . . . there was blood. More than a hundred years of blood that ran from the beast-men as they fought."

She felt the sudden stillness in him, a trembling rigor, a new sharp straining.

He lifted his head and looked into her eyes.

She thought of ice and fire, blue ice, blue fire.

"The big wars," he said, his voice stiff, rusty.

Then he put his hand over his eyes.

"*Christ!*" The word burst from his tight throat. "*God, God—*"

"Tyrell!" She screamed his name.

"Back!" he croaked, and she stumbled away, but he was not talking to her. "Back, devil!" He clawed at his head, grinding it between his palms, bowing till he was half crouched before her.

"Tyrell!" she cried. "Messiah! You are the White Christ—"

The bowed body snapped erect. She looked at the new face and felt an abysmal horror and loathing.

Tyrell stood looking at her. Then, appallingly, he gave her a strutting, derisive bow.

She felt the edge of the table behind her. She groped back and touched the heavy thickness of dried blood on the knife-blade. It was part of the nightmare. She moved her hand to the haft, knowing she could die by steel, letting her thought move ahead of the glittering steel's point into her breast.

The voice she heard was touched with laughter.

"Is it sharp?" he asked. "It is still sharp, my love? Or did I dull it on the priest? Will you use it on me? Will you try? Other women have tried!" Thick laughter choked in his throat.

"Messiah," she whispered.

"Messiah!" he mocked. "A White Christ! Prince of Peace! Bringing the word of love, walking unharmed through the bloodiest wars that ever wrecked a world . . . oh, yes, a legend, my love, twenty centuries and more. And a lie. They've forgotten. They've all forgotten what it was really like then!"

All she could do was shake her head in helpless denial.

"Oh yes," he said. "You weren't alive then. No one was. Except me, Tyrell. Butchery! I survived. But not by preaching peace. Do you know what happened to the men who preached love? They died—but I didn't die. I survived, not by preaching."

He pranced, laughing.

"Tyrell the Butcher!" he cried. "I was the bloodiest of them all. All they could understand was fear. And they weren't easily frightened then—not the men like beasts. But they were afraid of *me!*"

He lifted his clawed hands, his muscles straining in the ecstasy of ghastly memory.

"The Red Christ," he said. "They might have called me that. But they didn't. Not after I'd proved what I had to prove. They had a name for me then. They knew my name. And now—" He grinned at her. "Now that the worlds are at peace, now I'm worshiped as the Messiah. What can Tyrell the Butcher do today?"

His laughter came slow, horrible and complacent.

He took three steps and swept his arms around her. Her flesh shrank from the grip of that evil.

And then, suddenly, strangely, she felt the evil leave him. The hard arms shuddered, drew away, and then tightened again, with frantic tenderness, while he bent his head and she felt the sudden hotness of tears.

Somehow she was sitting on a couch and he was kneeling before her, his face buried in her lap.

She could not make out many of his choking words.

"Remember . . . I remember . . . the old memories . . . I can't stand it, I can't look back . . . or ahead . . . they—they had a name for me. I remember now . . ."

She laid one cold hand on his head. His hair was cold and damp.

*"They called me Antichrist!"*

He lifted his face and looked at her.

"Help me!" he cried in anguish. "Help me, help me!"

Then his head bowed again and he pressed his fists against his temples, whispering wordlessly.

She remembered what was in her right hand, and she lifted the knife and drove it down as hard as she could, to give him the help he needed.

† † †

She stood at the window, her back to the room and the dead immortal.

She waited for the priest Mons to return. He would know what to do next. Probably the secret would have to be kept, somehow.

They would not harm her, she knew that. The reverence that had surrounded Tyrell enfolded her too. She would live on, the only immortal now, born in a time of peace, living forever and alone in the worlds of peace. Some day, some time, another immortal might be born, but she did not want to think of that now. She could think only of Tyrell and her loneliness.

She looked through the window at the bright blue and green, the pure day of God, washed clean now of the last red stain of man's bloody past. She knew that Tyrell would be glad if he could see this cleanness, this purity that could go on forever.

She would see it go on. She was part of it, as Tyrell had not been. And even in the loneliness she already felt, there was a feeling of compensation, somehow. She was dedicated to the centuries of man that were to come.

She reached beyond her sorrow and love. From far away she could hear the solemn chanting of the priests. It was part of the rightness that had come to the worlds now, at last, after the long and bloody path to the new Golgotha. But it was the last Golgotha, and she would go on now as she must, dedicated and sure.

Immortal.

She lifted her head and looked steadily at the blue. She would look forward into the future. The past was forgotten. And the past, to her, meant no bloody heritage, no deep corruption that would work unseen in the black hell of the mind's abyss until the monstrous seed reached up to destroy God's peace and love.

Quite suddenly she remembered that she had committed murder. Her arm thrilled again with the violence of the blow; her hand tingled with the splash of shed blood.

Very quickly she closed her thoughts against the memory. She looked up at the sky, holding hard against the closed gateway of her mind as though the assault battered already against the fragile bars.

† † †

## Commentary by Frederik Pohl

Henry Kuttner was a dear man and a wonderful writer. I discovered the second fact with his very first published story, a horror yarn in the old *Weird Tales* called "The Graveyard Rats," which so impressed me that I wrote a fan letter in verse to praise it. (It appeared in the letter column a few issues later, under one of my many teen-aged pennames, but I don't really think it is worth anybody's while to look it up. Hey, I was sixteen years old.) Hank was good then, got even better when he began to turn his talents to science fiction, and got best of all when he had the good sense and good luck to marry Catherine Moore, who, as "C. L. Moore," was a first-rate writer herself and a wonderful asset to Hank. Every now and then, he told me, he'd put in a hard session of writing and take a nap . . . to discover when he woke that Catherine had written the next half a dozen or so pages of his story while he slept.

I don't know if she wrote part of "A Cross of Centuries" for him, because the story had not been written the last time I saw Hank, at a science-fiction event at the Brooklyn Public Library in the early 1950s. But I loved the story when his agent offered it to me, and was delighted to publish it in one of my *Star Science Fiction* anthologies of original stories . . . and am willing to bet that, all these years later, you will have enjoyed it, too.

## Editor's Commentary

This story by Henry Kuttner, which I first read as a thirteen-year-old in a Ballantine paperback belonging to my stepfather, stirred my soul just as did life-sized crucifixes or pictorial images of statues or paintings of Christ. Or maybe I should say it stirred my *imagination* and shaped my taste for lyricism in the service of theological speculation in straight-ahead storytelling. (I think, too, of Bradbury's "The Fire Balloons," Walter M. Miller Jr.'s *A Canticle for Leibowitz*, and Brian Aldiss's "Judas Danced," which contains the line "Science . . . is a system for taking away with one hand while giving with the other.")

In any case, "A Cross of Centuries" haunted as well as inspired me, and, some twenty years on, when I read Dozois and Dann's "Slow Dancing with Jesus," I knew that one day I'd compile a volume of Christ fictions, and that these two stories, along with Bradbury's "The Man," would surely anchor it. That day hung fire for another twenty years, or more, but nothing like the millennia that Tyrell must endure, and now he seems both a hopeful and a tragic figure, a man lifted to a state near that of bodhisattva or a god bereft of divinity. So invested, he reflects us all.

† † †

*Here, for coda and coup de grâce, a heartfelt fairy tale:*

# THE SELFISH GIANT
## Oscar Wilde

Every afternoon, as they were coming from school, the children used to go and play in the Giant's garden.

It was a large lovely garden, with soft green grass. Here and there over the grass stood beautiful flowers like stars, and there were twelve peach-trees that in the spring-time broke out into delicate blossoms of pink and pearl, and in the autumn bore rich fruit. The birds sat on the trees and sang so sweetly that the children used to stop their games in order to listen to them. "How happy we are here!" they cried to each other.

One day the Giant came back. He had been to visit his friend the Cornish ogre, and had stayed with him for seven years. After the seven years were over he had said all that he had to say, for his conversation was limited, and he determined to return to his own castle. When he arrived he saw the children playing in the garden.

"What are you doing here?" he cried in a very gruff voice, and the children ran away.

"My own garden is my own garden," said the Giant; "any one can understand that, and I will allow nobody to play in it but myself." So he built a high wall all round it, and put up a notice-board.

## TRESPASSERS WILL BE PROSECUTED

He was a very selfish Giant.

The poor children had now nowhere to play. They tried to play on the road, but the road was very dusty and full of hard stones, and they did not like it. They used to wander round the high wall when their lessons were over, and talk about the beautiful garden inside. "How happy we were there," they said to each other.

Then the Spring came, and all over the country there were little blossoms and little birds. Only in the garden of the Selfish Giant it was still winter. The birds did not care to sing in it as there were no children, and the trees forgot to blossom. Once a beautiful flower put its head out from the grass, but when it saw the notice-board it was so sorry for the children that it slipped back into the ground again, and went off to sleep. The only people who were pleased were the Snow and the Frost. "Spring has forgotten this garden," they cried, "so we will live here all the year round." The Snow covered up the grass with her great white cloak, and the Frost painted all the trees silver. Then they invited the North Wind to stay with them, and he came. He was wrapped in furs, and he roared all day about the garden, and blew the chimney-pots down. "This is a delightful spot," he said, "we must ask the Hail on a visit." So the Hail came. Every day for three hours he rattled on the roof of the castle till he broke most of the slates, and then he ran round and round the garden as fast as he could go. He was dressed in grey, and his breath was like ice.

"I cannot understand why the Spring is so late in coming," said the Selfish Giant, as he sat at the window and looked out at his cold white garden; "I hope there will be a change in the weather."

But the Spring never came, nor the Summer. The Autumn gave golden fruit to every garden, but to the Giant's garden she gave none. "He is too selfish," she said. So it was always Winter there, and the North Wind, and the Hail, and the Frost, and the Snow danced about through the trees.

One morning the Giant was lying awake in bed when he heard some lovely music. It sounded so sweet to his ears that he thought it must be the King's musicians passing by. It was really only a little linnet singing outside his window, but it was so long since he had heard a bird sing in his garden that it seemed to him to be the most beautiful music in the world. Then the Hail stopped dancing over his head, and the North Wind ceased roaring, and a delicious perfume came to him through the open casement. "I believe the Spring has come at last," said the Giant; and he jumped out of bed and looked out.

What did he see?

He saw a most wonderful sight. Through a little hole in the wall the children had crept in, and they were sitting in the branches of the trees. In every tree that he could see there was a little child. And the trees were so glad to have the children back again that they had covered themselves with blossoms, and were waving their arms gently above the children's heads. The birds were flying about and twittering with delight, and the flowers were looking up through the green grass and laughing. It was a lovely scene, only in one corner it was still winter. It was the farthest corner of the garden, and in it was standing a little boy. He was so small that he could not reach up to the branches of the tree, and he was wandering all round it, crying bitterly. The poor tree was still quite covered with frost and snow, and the North Wind was blowing and roaring above it. "Climb up! little boy," said the Tree, and it bent its branches down as low as it could; but the boy was too tiny.

And the Giant's heart melted as he looked out. "How selfish I have been!" he said; "now I know why the Spring would not come here. I will put that poor little boy on the top of the tree, and then

I will knock down the wall, and my garden shall be the children's playground for ever and ever." He was really very sorry for what he had done.

So he crept downstairs and opened the front door quite softly, and went out into the garden. But when the children saw him they were so frightened that they all ran away, and the garden became winter again. Only the little boy did not run, for his eyes were so full of tears that he did not see the Giant coming. And the Giant stole up behind him and took him gently in his hand, and put him up into the tree. And the tree broke at once into blossom, and the birds came and sang on it, and the little boy stretched out his two arms and flung them round the Giant's neck, and kissed him. And the other children, when they saw that the Giant was not wicked any longer, came running back, and with them came the Spring. "It is your garden now, little children," said the Giant, and he took a great axe and knocked down the wall. And when the people were going to market at twelve o'clock they found the Giant playing with the children in the most beautiful garden they had ever seen.

All day long they played, and in the evening they came to the Giant to bid him good-bye.

"But where is your little companion?" he said: "the boy I put into the tree." The Giant loved him the best because he had kissed him.

"We don't know," answered the children; "he has gone away."

"You must tell him to be sure and come here to-morrow," said the Giant. But the children said that they did not know where he lived, and had never seen him before; and the Giant felt very sad.

Every afternoon, when school was over, the children came and played with the Giant. But the little boy whom the Giant loved was never seen again. The Giant was very kind to all the children, yet he longed for his first little friend, and often spoke of him. "How I would like to see him!" he used to say.

Years went over, and the Giant grew very old and feeble. He could not play about any more, so he sat in a huge armchair, and watched the children at their games, and admired his garden. "I have many beautiful flowers," he said; "but the children are the most beautiful flowers of all."

One winter morning he looked out of his window as he was dressing. He did not hate the Winter now, for he knew that it was merely the Spring asleep, and that the flowers were resting.

Suddenly he rubbed his eyes in wonder, and looked and looked. It certainly was a marvellous sight. In the farthest corner of the garden was a tree quite covered with lovely white blossoms. Its branches were all golden, and silver fruit hung down from them, and underneath it stood the little boy he had loved.

Downstairs ran the Giant in great joy, and out into the garden. He hastened across the grass, and came near to the child. And when he came quite close his face grew red with anger, and he said, "Who hath dared to wound thee?" For on the palms of the child's hands were the prints of two nails, and the prints of two nails were on the little feet.

"Who hath dared to wound thee?" cried the Giant; "tell me, that I may take my big sword and slay him."

"Nay!" answered the child; "but these are the wounds of Love."

"Who art thou?" said the Giant, and a strange awe fell on him, and he knelt before the little child.

And the child smiled on the Giant, and said to him, "You let me play once in your garden, to-day you shall come with me to my garden, which is Paradise."

And when the children ran in that afternoon, they found the Giant lying dead under the tree, all covered with white blossoms.

† † †

# CONTRIBUTORS

**ISAAC BABEL** ("The Sin of Jesus") was born in 1894 near Odessa on the Black Sea. His family soon moved to Nikolayev some ninety miles away. In 1905 the Babels escaped pogroms targeting Jews, and in 1911 Isaac entered a business institute in Kiev. His first story, "Old Shloyme," came out in 1913. In 1916 he published several stories in Maxim Gorky's journal *Letopsis* to good notices. His story cycle *Red Calvary* (1926) made him famous throughout Russia—but, always under suspicion by the Soviets, he was arrested in May 1939. His final plea was "Let me finish my work," but he fell before a firing squad in Lubyanka prison on January 27, 1940. His salvaged life's work includes reportage, a pair of stage plays, several screenplays, and nearly a hundred distinctive short stories. In 1938, Borges noted that Isaac Babel's story "Salt" "enjoys a glory seemingly reserved for poems, and rarely attained by prose; many people know it by heart."

**MICHAEL BISHOP** ("Sequel on Skorpiós") edited several other books before undertaking *A Cross of Centuries*, including *Changes: Stories of Metamorphosis*, with Ian Watson (Ace, 1983); *Light Years and Dark* (Berkley, 1984), an omnibus featuring work by science fiction and fantasy writers who came to full prominence only after 1960, winner of the Locus Award for Best Anthology; and *Nebula*

*Awards 23*, *Nebula Awards 24*, and *Nebula Awards 25* (all Harcourt Brace Jovanovich, 1989, 1990, and 1991). Bishop has won a Nebula Award, for "The Quickening" (1981) and another for the novel *No Enemy But Time* (Timescape, 1982), as well as a Mythopoeic Award for *Unicorn Mountain* (Morrow, 1987) and two Southeastern Science Fiction Awards, for his stories "The Door Gunner" (2003) and "Bears Discover Smut" (2005). He has been writer-in-residence at LaGrange College in LaGrange, Georgia, since 1996.

**JORGE LUIS BORGES** ("The Gospel According to Mark"), an Argentinean with cross-cultural literary tastes and erudition, may be the most accomplished and revolutionary twentieth-century writer denied the Nobel Prize for Literature—after Leo Tolstoy. He invented a unique style of short fiction combining cagey narrative with the speculative and expository elements common to the informal essay, an approach congenial to the Spanish *ultraisme* movement of which he was an antirealist advocate. His work encompasses fiction, criticism, and poetry, and his collections include *A Universal History of Infamy* (1935), *Fictions* (1944), *The Aleph* (1949), *The Book of Sand* (1975), and *Shakespeare's Memory* (1983). "The Gospel According to Mark," whose main character's surname *Espinosa* means "thorny," appears in the collection *Brodie's Report* (1970). Borges died in 1986, one year older than the century.

**RAY BRADBURY** ("The Man") personifies lyrical science fiction for readers who first discovered his work in the 1940s, 1950s, and 1960s in particular. His influence is far-reaching and salutary. His stories, novels, and fix-ups ("novels" consisting of interlinked stories) rendered pulp subject matter colorful, morally and spiritually complex, and thus respectable. Justly famous works include *The*

*Martian Chronicles* (1950), *The Golden Apples of the Sun* (1953), *Fahrenheit 451* (1953), *Dandelion Wine* (1957), *A Medicine for Melancholy* (1959), and *Something Wicked This Way Comes* (1962). He has also written noteworthy plays, mystery novels, juveniles, poetry, and film scripts, including that for *Moby Dick* (1956). His most recent novel, *Farewell Summer* (Morrow, 2006), is set two years after *Dandelion Wine* and again features Doug Spaulding as a proxy for the young Bradbury growing up in small-town Illinois in the early 1930s.

**JACK DANN** ("Slow Dancing with Jesus") is a multiple-award winning author who has written or edited over seventy books, including the international bestseller *The Memory Cathedral* (Bantam, 1995); *The Man Who Melted* (Bluejay, 1984); *The Silent* (Bantam, 1998), a novel of the Civil War; *The Rebel: An Imagined Life of James Dean* (Morrow, 2004); and a number of short story collections: *Timetipping* (Doubleday, 1980), *Jubilee* (Tor, 2003), *Visitations* (Five Star, 2003), *The Fiction Factory* (Golden Gryphon, 2005), and the forthcoming *Promised Land* (PS Publishing in England), a companion volume to *The Rebel*. Almost thirty years ago, he published a volume of poetry titled *Christs and Other Poems* (Bellevue, 1978). Dann lives in Australia on a farm overlooking the sea and "commutes" back and forth to Los Angeles and New York. His Web site can be found at www.jackdann.com.

**PAUL Di FILIPPO** ("Lignum Crucis") says that his career began either in 1977, when his first story appeared in *Unearth* magazine; or in 1982, when he quit his job as a COBOL programmer to devote himself full time to writing; or in 1985, when his second and third stories appeared in the *Magazine of Fantasy & Science Fiction* and the *Twilight Zone Magazine*; or in 1995, when his first book, *The*

*Steampunk Trilogy* (Four Walls Eight Windows), debuted. Whichever date one selects, 2006 saw the publication of his twenty-fifth book, *Top 10: Beyond the Farthest Precinct* (America's Best Comics), a graphic novel with art by Jerry Ordway and a milestone he is proud of. He intends to retire now in stages over the next forty years. Meanwhile, look for the novels *Ciphers* (Cambrian, 1997) and *Time's Black Lagoon* (DH, 2006), as well as several astonishing collections, including *Ribofunk* (1996), *Lost Pages* (1998), and *Little Doors* (2002), all from Four Walls Eight Windows, *Strange Trades* (Golden Gryphon, 2001), and *Shuteye for the Timebroker* (Thunder's Mouth, 2006).

**FYODOR DOSTOYEVSKY** ("The Inquisitor General") was born October 30, 1821, in the Mariinksy Hospital for the Poor on the outskirts of Moscow. After several years in the army, in 1844 he resigned his commission to write. Much like compatriot Babel in the following century, he was arrested by the authorities (for socialist connections) and sent before a firing squad. Unlike Babel, he benefited, famously, from a reprieve in the execution yard and instead served ten years at hard Siberian labor. Finally back in St. Petersburg, he founded a periodical, *Time*, that soon suffered suppression in spite of its patriotic editorial tone. A novelist of overwhelming scope and penetrating psychological insight, he wrote several masterpieces: *Crime and Punishment* (1866), *The Idiot* (1868), *The Possessed* (1871–72), and, of course, *The Brothers Karamazov* (1879–80), a thorough examination of the philosophical and spiritual ramifications of human suffering. A year after its publication, Dostoyevsky died.

**GARDNER DOZOIS** ("Slow Dancing with Jesus") edited *Asimov's Science Fiction* for many years and continues to edit *The*

*Year's Best Science Fiction* to this day. Stories such as "A Special Kind of Morning," "The Last Day of July," and others in his first collection *The Visible Man* (Berkley, 1977) heralded a writer who strove to evoke "the sense of wonder without insulting the rational intellect." In his first solo novel, *Strangers* (Berkley, 1978), he created a lyrical tragedy about star-crossed lovers in homage to Philip José Farmer. In 1983 and '84 he won back-to-back Nebula Awards for his stories "The Peacemaker" and "Morning Child." A volume of collaborations, *Slow Dancing Through Time* (Ursus, 1990), features his and Jack Dann's contribution to this book, while *Strange Days* (NESFA, 2001) gathers nearly two dozen of his best solo and collaborative efforts. Dozois lives in Philadelphia with his wife, the writer Susan Casper.

**JEFFREY FORD** ("On the Road to New Egypt") is the author of a trilogy of novels, all from Avon Eos: *The Physiognomy* (1997), *Memoranda* (1999), and *The Beyond* (2000). His novel *The Portrait of Mrs. Charbuque* (HarperCollins) appeared in June 2002, as did his first short story collection, *The Fantasy Writer's Assistant & Other Stories* (Golden Gryphon). The summer of 2005 saw the publication of his sixth novel, *The Girl in the Glass* (HarperCollins), and a stand-alone novella, *The Cosmology of the Wider World* (PS Publishing in England). His second collection of stories, *The Empire of Ice Cream* (Golden Gryphon), appeared in April 2006. Ford is a professor of writing and literature at Brookdale Community College in New Jersey. His work has won many notable literary awards, of which Ford says little or nothing.

**KAREN JOY FOWLER** ("Shimabara") decided to become a writer at thirty. Her inaugural collection, containing thirteen stories, was *Artificial Things* (Bantam, 1986; reprinted 1992), followed in

1988 by an NEA Grant in Prose and in 1991 by the exquisite *Sarah Canary* (Henry Holt), a novel that earned favorable notices across the literary spectrum, including the Commonwealth Award for Best First Novel. Fowler's subsequent novels fared equally well critically: *The Sweetheart Season* (Holt, 1996); *Sister Noon* (Putnam, 2001), a Pen/Faulkner Award nominee; and *The Jane Austin Book Club* (Putnam, 2004), Fowler's best-selling title to date. To the surprise of few, her second collection, *Black Glass* (Holt, 1998), won a World Fantasy Award, and in April 2004 her short story "What I Didn't See" garnered a Nebula trophy. Along with Pat Murphy, Fowler is a "founding mother" of the James Tiptree, Jr. Award. She often teaches at the Clarion Workshop, and she turns up most summers at the Imagination Workshop at Cleveland State University.

**GREGORY FROST** ("Touring JesusWorld") is, most recently, the author of the dark fantasy novel *Fitcher's Brides* (Tor, 2002) and the short fiction collection *Attack of the Jazz Giants & Other Stories* (Golden Gryphon, 2005). Over the years he has been a finalist for nearly every award in the science fiction and fantasy genres. Also a well-regarded writing teacher, he collaboratively directs the fiction-writing workshop at Swarthmore College and is the lead instructor of the 2007 Clarion Science Fiction & Fantasy Writers' Workshop in its new home of San Diego. His dark and sinister past lives include researcher for nonfiction television (*Science Frontiers*), and actor in "very *very* B" horror films (*The Laughing Dead*). He lives outside Philadelphia with a lovely wife and a cat that grins. His fantasy duology, *Shadowbridge*, will appear from Del Rey in 2008.

**HENRY KUTTNER** ("A Cross of Centuries") foresaw his fatal heart attack ten years later and cried out, *"'Enry 'Uttner!"* On the evening of February 3, 1958, he allegedly had another such vision—of his death the next day. This lore acknowledges that at age forty-two Kuttner died far too young, with much exceptional work yet ahead. A correspondent of H. P. Lovecraft's, he published his first story, "The Graveyard Rats," in *Weird Tales* in 1936. In 1940, he married C. L. Moore, a lifelong collaborator, and at a convention that year received this accolade: "Best Science Fiction Writer in the World." His novels and fix-ups include *Dr. Cyclops* (1940), *Fury* (1947), *The Well of the Worlds* (1952), *Mutant* (1953), and *Robots Have No Tails* (1953). His paperback collections from Ballantine include *A Gnome There Was* (1950), *Ahead of Time* (1953), and *Bypass to Otherness* (1961). *The Best of Henry Kuttner* (Ballantine, 1975) features an introduction by Ray Bradbury, "A Neglected Master," testifying to the respect in which his colleagues held him, the volatility of fame, and his lasting influence. *Two-Handed Engine: The Selected Stories of Henry Kuttner and C. L. Moore* (Centipede, 2006) offers anyone unfamiliar with these authors' fiction a heady smorgasbord. Indeed, before shuffling off this mortal coil, everyone should read—to name a paltry three— "The Twonky," "Mimsey Were the Borogroves," and "Vintage Season."

**ROMULUS LINNEY** ("Early Marvels") is the author of three novels, *Heathen Valley* (Atheneum, 1962; reprinted Shoemaker & Hoard, 2004), *Slowly, By Thy Hand Unfurled* (Harcourt, Brace, & World, 1965; reprinted Shoemaker & Hoard, 2004), and *Jesus Tales* (North Point, 1980, reprinted 1987); two dozen short stories; two operas and forty plays, among them *The Sorrows of Frederick*, *Childe Byron*, *Tennessee*, *Sand Mountain*, *F.M.*, *Gint*, and *A Lesson Before Dying*, a powerful adaptation of the Ernest L. Gaines novel. His plays have been produced in New York, Chicago, Los Angeles, and elsewhere in the United States, at the Young Vic in London, the Burgtheater in Vienna, the National Theater of Norway, and other theaters abroad. His works explore European history, Appalachian life, and modern relationships in New York City, among many other matters. He belongs to both the American Academy of Arts and Letters and the American Academy of Arts and Sciences.

**BARRY MALZBERG** ("Understanding Entropy") reports that *Breakfast in the Ruins: Science Fiction in the Last Century* will appear from Baen Books in spring 2007. A collection of essays, this volume deals with topics on or near science fiction from 1975 through 2000. Malzberg has written many novels, including *Beyond Apollo* (Random House, 1972) and *The Remaking of Sigmund Freud* (Del Rey, 1985), and approximately 450 short stories, "of which," he tells us, "I'd admit, surprisingly, to over four hundred." "Understanding Entropy," a finalist in 1996 for both the Hugo and the Nebula Awards, appears in his collection *In the Stone House* (Arkham House, 2000), along with nine or ten others that rank among his very best. As an afterthought, Malzberg notes that he won Honorable Mention in the Rho Delta Phi–sponsored annual short story contest at Syracuse University in 1960. First Prize: Joyce Carol Oates, "A Confession," $15. Second Prize: Michael David Herr: "Bereavement," $10. Despite its honorable mention, his story, "The Death of Charlie the Nut" garnered Malzberg "not a dime."

**JACK McDEVITT** ("Friends in High Places") is the author of thirteen novels, of which the latest are *Seeker* (Ace, 2005) and *Odyssey* (Ace, 2006). Also recently available is *Outbound* (ISFiC, 2006), a collection of short stories and nonfiction. *Omega* (Ace,

2003) won the John W. Campbell Award in 2004 for best Science Fiction novel. McDevitt's work has been on the final Nebula ballot in ten of the past eleven years, but still not having won this award and lacking any hope for world peace ("barring divine intervention"), he now has a special fondness for lunch. However, the late Charles Sheffield called McDevitt's "The Jersey Rifle," collected in *Standard Candles* (Tachyon, 1996), "the best chess story ever written," an assessment he regards as "better than any prize." A Philadelphia Eagles fan, a member of the U.S. Chess Federation, a bridge player and the father of three, he lives in Brunswick, Georgia, with his wife Maureen.

**MICHAEL MOORCOCK** ("Behold the Man") was born at the outbreak of World War II and raised in a secular environment. He had no ax to grind with organized religion when he wrote "Behold the Man" as, among other things, a study in demagoguery. As well as winning a Nebula Award, this novella prompted ecstatic reviews in the *Catholic Herald* and the *Jewish Chronicle*, fan letters from nuns and priests, and death threats from Texas, where he now lives. *Prospect* magazine noted that Moorcock may be its only contributor to have received a platinum record, for his work with the band Hawkwind, and a short-listing for the Whitbread Prize, for his novel *Mother London* (Crown, 1989), while also earning a British Science Fiction Association award for his editorial work on *New Worlds* magazine. He recently completed his quartet about the holocaust with the publication of *The Vengeance of Rome* (Vintage, 2006). Its predecessor volumes include *Byzantium Endures* (1981), *The Laughter of Carthage* (1985), and *Jerusalem Commands* (1992), but he is probably best known in the United States for his Elric fantasy series.

**MIKE RESNICK** ("The Pale, Thin God") is the author of more than fifty science-fiction novels, 175 stories, twelve collections, and two screenplays, and has edited forty-four anthologies. He has won five Hugo Awards, a Nebula Award, and other major awards in the United States, France, Poland, Spain, Croatia, and Japan, and currently, according to the science fiction newsletter *Locus*, stands first on the all-time sf short-fiction award list. His work has been translated into twenty-two languages. His controversial novel *The Branch* (Signet, 1984) treats of a future messiah. *Santiago: A Myth of the Far Future* (Tor, 1986) remains in print after twenty-one years, and *Kiranyaga* (Del Rey, 1998) features the title story and a sequel, "The Manamouki," both Hugo Award winners. Resnick's collections include *Will the Last Person to Leave the Planet Shut Off the Sun?* (Tor, 1992) and *New Dreams for Old* (Pyr, 2006). He is now writing a series for Pyr under the general rubric Starship; published and projected titles are *Mutiny* (2005), *Pirate* (2006), *Mercenary* (2007), *Rebel* (2008), and *Flagship* (2009).

**BRUCE HOLLAND ROGERS** ("Cross Carriers") reports that his short stories have been translated into over a dozen languages, including, most improbably, Klingon. His latest collections are *Thirteen Ways to Water* (Wheatland/Panisphere, 2004) and *The Keyhole Opera* (Wheatland, 2005). His short fiction has earned Rogers—in addition to two Nebula Awards, the World Fantasy Award, the Bram Stoker Award, and a Pushcart Prize—several distinct coteries of admirers, for he refuses to limit himself to any single mode or category. His stories are as likely to turn up in *The Sun* as in *Realms of Fantasy*, in a literary review as in an original genre anthology. He has published an unusual guide for writers called *Word Work* (Invisible Cities, 2002), and he is currently writing a novel "that sets out to demonstrate that steam locomotives, bipolar disorder, and the futures market are all the same thing." He lives in London, England, with his wife, Holly Arrow. His Web site is www.shortshortshort.com.

**JACK SLAY JR.** ("Murmur's Laws") was raised a Catholic, he is married to a Southern Baptist, and he is employed by a Methodist-affiliated liberal arts college. He has coauthored, with Dale Bailey, a hardboiled suspense novel, *Sleeping Policemen* (Golden Gryphon, 2006), which has already raised a few eyebrows locally. "All by hisownself," he wrote the critical study *Ian McEwan* (Twayne, 1996), and he has published stories in such venues as *Realms of Fantasy*, *Cemetery Dance*, *The Thackery T. Lambshead Pocket Guide to Eccentric and Discredited Diseases*, and *Scouting*. For twelve years he taught English at LaGrange College in Georgia, but two years ago stepped across the terminator and now serves as the college's Dean of Students. Slay is married to Lori; together they have three sons: Kirk, Justin, and Reed.

**NŌNI TYENT** ("Miriam") is the pseudonym of a writer who wishes to make no other personal statement.

**WALTER WANGERIN JR.** ("Ragman"), writer-in-residence at Valparaiso University in Valparaiso, Indiana, teaches both literature and creative writing and holds the Jochum Chair as professor of English and theology. His first book, a fable called *The Book of the Dun Cow* (Harper & Row, 1978), won the National Book Award and spawned a sequel, *The Book of Sorrows* (Harper & Row, 1985; reprinted Zondervan, 1996). An ordained Lutheran minister, Wangerin writes on many subjects; thus, his work includes pastoral guidance on relationships, grief, and meditation as well as fiction, fables, and allegory. Recent historical novels include *Paul: A Novel*

(Zondervan, 2000); *Saint Julian* (HarperSanFrancisco, 2003), and *Jesus: A Novel* (Zondervan, 2005), which presents the life of Jesus as an imaginative literary text.

**BUD WEBSTER** ("Christus Destitutus") is an award-winning epic poet, fantasist, and amateur science fiction/fantasy historian, who provided crucial bibliographic help on *this* project. He is a contributing editor to the *SFWA Bulletin*, writing regular columns on classic science fiction books there and in the online quarterly *Helix SF*. He has written the definitive bio-bibliography of anthologist Groff Conklin, *41 Above the Rest* (Wildside, 2004), as well as *The Joy of Booking* (SRM, 2004), a guide for hobbyist booksellers. Some of his stories are available online at FictionWise.Com. The author lives in Richmond, Virginia, "with a patient and understanding Significant Other and three damn cats."

**OSCAR WILDE** ("The Selfish Giant") is probably best known today as the author of the novel *The Picture of Dorian Gray* (1891) and as the witty, epigrammatic playwright who gave us *Lady Windermere's Fan* (1892), *A Woman of No Importance* (1893), *An Ideal Husband* (1895), and *The Importance of Being Ernest* (1895). Some are thus surprised to encounter his poignant, psychologically sound fairy tales (including "The Selfish Giant"), which he gathered in his first book, *The Happy Prince and Other Tales* (1888). Married to Constance Lloyd and the father of two sons, in 1891 Wilde began a relationship with young Lord Alfred "Bosie" Douglas and eventually served a two-year prison term for homosexuality, then a crime in England. Afterward, he wrote his best-known poem *The Ballard of Reading Gaol* (1898). In November 1900, Wilde died of meningitis in Paris, at age forty-six. As Karl Beckson writes in an *Encyclopedia Britannica* article, "In his semiconscious final moments, he was received into the Roman Catholic Church, which he had long admired."

**JOHN M. WILLIAMS** ("Passion") has published one rock 'n' roll novel, *Lake Moon* (Mercer University, 2002), for which he was named Georgia Author of the Year for First Novel in 2003. He has published a smattering of stories and reviews in *Alabama Literary Review, Zone 3, Sideshow, First Draft*, and other venues; he was the 1988 recipient of the Hackney Fiction Award and a finalist for the 2003–2004 Townsend Fiction Award. An English professor by day, he has written, with composer partner Ken Clark, several stage musicals so far off Broadway they're in Georgia; two of these were staged regionally in the 1990s: *The Kelly's Truck Stop Bop* and *Get It Off Me*. Williams notes that "the Box has a growing number of wallflower manuscripts no one has yet asked to dance; the most recent, just completed and a real looker, *Man Walking Backward in the Wind*, is a family saga of towering achievement."

**GENE WOLFE** ("The Detective of Dreams") has written thirty-eight books. His most recent novel is *Soldier of Sidon* (Tor, 2006), laid in Ancient Egypt and points south. His most recent collection is *Starwater Strains* (Tor, 2005). He has twice won the Nebula Award—for his novella *The Death of Doctor Island* and for the novel *The Claw of the Conciliator* (Timescape, 1981); and he has also won two World Fantasy Awards—for the novel *The Shadow of the Torturer* (Timescape, 1981) and for the collection *Stories from the Old Hotel* (Kerosina, 1989), plus a well-deserved third for Lifetime Achievement. He is generally acknowledged as possessing, in addition to a beautifully flexible style, one of the most intricately creative minds in the science fiction and fantasy fields. Wolfe lives in Barrington, Illinois, with his wife Rosemary; they attend church regularly.

**GEORGE ZEBROWSKI** ("The Coming of Christ the Joker") has written or edited forty books, including the Golden Gryphon story collections *Swift Thoughts* (2002) and *Black Pockets* (2006), both of which received starred *Publishers Weekly* reviews. *Macrolife* (Harper & Row, 1979), his classic novel, has just been reissued by Pyr Books. *Stranger Suns* (Bantam, 1991) was a *New York Times* notable book. *Brute Orbits* (HarperPrism, 1998), a novel about the future of the penal system, copped the John W. Campbell Prize. *Black Pockets*, incidentally, contains both the relentlessly witty "The Coming of Christ the Joker" and a crucifixion story, "Interpose," in the afterword to which the author recommends Winwood Reade's *The Martyrdom of Man* (1872), a book suggesting "why the story of Christ's death moves even nonbelievers." Zebrowski, by the way, contributed much more than a story to this project, namely, some helpful advice, a fine copy of Henry Kuttner and C. L. Moore's *Two-Handed Engine* (Centipede, 2006), and all but a dollar of his own allotted payment toward the purchase of stories by other writers. (May God or the enigmatic cosmos bless you, George.)

†††

# Recommended Reading

This list of novels and short fiction by no means exhausts those works presenting an imaginative portrait of the figure of Jesus Christ or of a figure patterned on him. The listings for novels show, at a minimum, original U.S. publisher and year of publication. For short fiction, I usually list either the place and date of original publication or the first authorial collection in which the story appeared, if not both. For more information, go to an online search engine or to a library and use the resources available.

**Aldiss,** Brian
"Judas Danced" in *No Time Like Tomorrow* (Signet, 1959)
**Asch,** Sholem
*The Nazarene* (trans. Maurice Samuel; Putnam, 1935; Carroll & Graf, 1984)
**Bailey,** Dale
"Epiphany" in *Pulphouse* #18 (ed. Damon Knight; Pulphouse, 2003)
**Barth,** John
*Giles Goat Boy* or, *The Revised New Syllabus* (Doubleday, 1966)
**Bishop,** Michael
"Beginnings" in *At the City Limits of Fate* (Edgewood, 1996)
"The Gospel According to Gamaliel Crucis" in *Close Encounters with the Deity* (Peachtree, 1986)
"I, Iscariot" in *CRANK!* #5 (ed. Bryan Cholfin; Summer 1995) and in *At the City Limits of Fate* (Edgewood, 1996)

**Bradbury,** Ray
> "Christos Apollo" in *I Sing the Body Electric!* (Knopf, 1969)

**Bulgakov,** Mikhail
> *The Master and Margarita* (trans. Michael Glenny; Harper & Row, 1967)

**Burgess,** Anthony
> *Man of Nazareth* (McGraw-Hill, 1979)

**Caldwell,** Taylor
> *Great Lion of God* (Doubleday, 1970) *I, Judas* (Atheneum, 1977)

**Carse,** James
> *The Gospel of the Beloved Disciple* (HarperSanFrancisco, 1997)

**Conway,** Simon & Peter **Crowther**
> "Sitting Pretty" in *Meantime* (ed. Jerry Sykes; United Kingdom: DoNot Press, 1998)

**Cook,** Thomas H.
> "Fatherhood" in *Best American Mystery Stories 1999* (series ed. Otto Penzler, ed. Ed McBain; Houghton Mifflin, 1999)

**Crace,** Jim
> *Quarantine* (Farrar, Straus, Giroux, 1997)

**Dann,** Jack
> *Christs and Other Poems* (Bellevue, 1978)

**de Wohl,** Louis
> *The Spear* (Lippincott, 1955)

**del Rey,** Lester
> "Evensong" in *Dangerous Visions* (ed. Harlan Ellison; Doubleday, 1967)

**Di Filippo,** Paul
> "Personal Jesus" in *The Solaris Book of New Science Fiction* (Solaris, 2007)

**Dostoyevsky,** Fyodor
> *The Brothers Karamazov* (trans. Constance Garnett; Macmillan, 1912)
> *The Idiot* (trans. David Magarshack; Penguin, 1955)

**Douglas,** Lloyd C.
> *The Robe* (Houghton Mifflin, 1942) *The Big Fisherman* (Houghton Mifflin, 1948)

**Farmer,** Philip José
> *Jesus on Mars* (Pinnacle Books, 1979) "Riverworld" in *Worlds of Tomorrow* (January 1966) or *The Best of Philip José Farmer* (Subterranean, 2006)

**Faulkner,** William
> *A Fable* (Random House, 1954)

**Friesner,** Esther
  "Jesus at the Bat" in *Death and the Librarian* (Five Star, 2002)
**George,** Margaret *Mary,*
  *Called Magdalene* (Viking, 2002)
**Grass,** Gunter
  *Cat and Mouse* (trans. Ralph Manheim; Harcourt Brace & World, 1963)
**Graves,** Robert
  *King Jesus* (Minerva Press, n.d. [1946?]; Farrar, Straus, Giroux, 1981)
**Grimes,** Nikki
  *Portrait of Mary* (Harcourt Brace, 1994)
**Grimsley,** Jim
  *The Lizard of Tarsus in Mr. Universe & Other Plays* (Algonquin, 1998)
**Hemingway,** Ernest
  *The Old Man and the Sea* (Scribner, 1952)
  "Today Is Friday" in *The Complete Short Stories* (Scribner, 1987)
**Holmes,** Marjorie
  *The Messiah* (Harper & Row, 1987)
**Kazantzakis,** Nikos
  *The Last Temptation of Christ* (trans. Peter A. Bien; Simon & Schuster, 1960)
**Kessel,** John
  "Uncle John and the Saviour" in *Fantasy & Science Fiction* (December 1980)
**Kilworth,** Garry
  "Let's Go to Golgotha" in *The Songbirds of Pain* (United Kingdom: Gollancz, 1984)
**Klavan,** Andrew
  *Son of Man* (Permanent, 1988)
**Knight,** Damon
  *The Man in the Tree* (Berkley, 1984)
**Kornbluth,** C. M.
  "The Advent on Channel 12" in *The Best of C. M. Kornbluth* (Ballantine, 1976)
**Lagerkvist,**
  Par *Barabbas* (trans. Alan Blair; Random House/Modern Library, 1951)
**Landorf,** Joyce
  *I Came to Love You Late* (Revell, 1977)
**Langguth,** A. J.
  *Jesus Christs* (Harper & Row, 1968; Figueroa, 2003)

**Lawrence,** D. H.
    *The Man Who Died* in *Four Short Novels* (Viking, 1923)
**Levertov,** Denise
    "Ikon: The Harrowing of Hell" in *A Door in the Hive* (New Directions, 1989)
**Lewis,** C. S.
    *The Lion, the Witch, and the Wardrobe* (United Kingdom: Bles, 1950; United States: Macmillan, 1950)
**Linney,** Romulus
    *Jesus Tales* (North Point, 1980; reprinted 1987)
**Mailer,** Norman
    *The Gospel According to the Son* (Random House, 1997)
**Malzberg,** Barry
    "Cop-Out" in *Escapade* (July 1968)
    *The Cross of Fire* (Ace, 1982)
**Mann,** Thomas
    *The Magic Mountain* (trans. Helen T. Lowe-Porter; Modern Library, 1955)
**Marquis,** Don
    *The Dark Hours: Five Scenes in a History* (Doubleday Page, 1924)
**Matheson,** Richard
    "The Traveler" in *Born of Man and Woman* (Chamberlain, 1954)
**Means,** David
    "A Visit from Jesus" in *The Secret Goldfish: Stories* (HarperCollins, 2004)
**Melville,** Herman
    *Melville's Billy Budd* (ed. F. Barron Freeman; Harvard University, 1948)
**Meyer,** Gabriel
    *Gospel of Joseph: A Father's Story* (Crossroad, 1994)
**Mills,** James
    *Memoirs of Pontius Pilate* (Revell, 2000)
**Moorcock,** Michael
    *Behold the Man* (Avon, 1978; Overlook, 2007)
**Moore,** Christopher
    *Lamb: The Gospel According to Biff, Christ's Childhood Pal* (Morrow, 2002)
**Moore,** George (Augustus)
    *The Brook Kerith: A Syrian Story* (Macmillan, 1916).
**Morrow,** James
    "Moon Over Gethsemane" in *Reflections and Refractions* (Dimension House/ Delirium, 2004), supplement to limited edition *Godhead Trilogy* (2003)
    *Only Begotten Daughter* (Morrow, 1990)

**Park,** Paul

> *The Gospel of Corax* (Soho, 1996) *Three Marys* (Cosmos/Wildside, 2002)

**Price,** Reynolds

> "Jesus and a Desolate Woman" in *A Serious Way of Wondering*
> (Scribner, 2003)
> "Jesus and a Homosexual Man" (ibid.)
> "Jesus and a Suicide" (ibid.)

**Rash,** Ron

> Title story in *The Night the New Jesus Fell to Earth* (The Bench Press,
> 1994)

**Resnick,** Mike

> *The Branch* (Signet, 1984) "How I Wrote the New Testament," etc., in *Will
> the Last Person to Leave the Planet Please Shut Off the Sun* (Tor, 1992)

**Ricci,** Nino

> *Testament* (Houghton Mifflin, 2002)

**Rice,** Anne

> *Christ the Lord: Out of Egypt* (Knopf, 2005)

**Ripley,** Alexandra

> *A Love Divine* (Warner, 1996)

**Sailor,** Charles

> *The Second Son* (Avon, 1979)

**Sallis,** James

> "The Genre Kid" in *Fantasy & Science Fiction* (February 2003)

**Saramago,** José

> *The Gospel According to Jesus Christ* (trans. Giovanni Pontiero; Har-
> court, 1994)

**Silverberg,** Robert

> *Son of Man* (Ballantine, 1971)
> *Up the Line* (Ballantine, 1969; reprinted ibooks, 2005)

**Sinclair,** Upton

> *They Call Me Carpenter* (Boni & Liverwright, 1922)

**Theissen,** Gerd

> *The Shadow of the Galilean* (trans. John Bowden; Fortress, 1987)

**Toman,** Michael D.

> "Shards of Divinity" in *SF Emphasis* #1 (ed. David Gerrold; Ballantine,
> 1974)

**Vidal,** Gore

> *Live from Golgotha* (Random House, 1992)
> *Messiah* (E. P. Dutton, 1954; revised Little Brown, 1965) ·

**Wallace,** Lew
      *Ben-Hur: A Tale of the Christ* (Harper, 1880)
**Wangerin,** Walter Jr.
      *Jesus: A Novel* (Zondervan, 2005)
**Watson,** Ian
      *The Great Escape* (Golden Gryphon, 2002)
      "When Jesus Comes Down the Chimney" in *Salvage Rites* (United
      Kingdom: Gollancz, 1989)
**Wibberley,** Leonard
      *The Centurion* (Morrow, 1966)
**Zebrowski,** George
      "Interpose" in *Black Pockets* (Golden Gryphon, 2006)
**Ziolkowski,** Theodore
      *Fictional Transfigurations of Jesus* (Princeton University, 1972)

This last title, incidentally, is not a novel, but a seminal study of works that make use of a "fictional transfiguration" of Jesus, a term that Ziolkowski defines as "a fictional narrative in which the characters and the action, irrespective of meaning or theme, are prefigured to a noticeable extent by figures and events popularly associated with the life of Jesus as it is known from the Gospels" (6). Ziolkowski's chapters include "The De-Christianizing of Jesus," "The Christian Socialist Jesus," "The Christomaniacs," "The Mythic Jesus," "Comrade Jesus," "The Fifth Gospels," and "Rounding the Hermeneutic Circle." His study also features a helpful selected bibliography that I don't attempt to duplicate here; I do cite a few titles that Ziolkowski also cites and gratefully acknowledge that *Fictional Transfigurations of Jesus* is a fine book with a provocative thesis, whose title I seriously considered using as this anthology's subtitle.

† † †

# Permissions Acknowledgments

"Understanding Entropy" by Barry Malzberg © 1994 by *Science Fiction Age*; reprinted by permission of author.

"Murmur's Laws" © 2001 by Jack Slay Jr.; first ████ ████ hed in *Talebones 23* (Winter 2001); reprinted by permiss ████ ████ uthor.

"The Coming of Christ the Joker" © 2003 by George Zebrowski; first published in *Envisioning the Future*, edited by Marleen Barr, Wesleyan University Press; reprinted by permission of the author.

"Passion" © 2007 by John M. Williams, a story original to this anthology and used here by the permission of the author.

"Lignum Crucis" © 2007 by Paul DiFilippo, a story original to this anthology and used here by permission of the author.

"Touring JesusWorld" © 2003 by Gregory Frost; first published in *Pulphouse 18* and reprinted in *Attack of the Jazz Giants and Other Stories* by Gregory Frost, Golden Gryphon Press, 2005; reprinted here by permission of the author.

"Cross Carriers" © 2007 by Bruce Holland Rogers, an original story used here by permission of the author.

"A Cross of Centuries," reprinted by permission of Don Congdon Associates, Inc. Copyright © 1971 by Mayo Mohs, renewed 1999 by Thomas Reggie.